THE LORD TRAP

JUDITH LYNNE

BOOKS BY JUDITH LYNNE

<u>Lords and Undefeated Ladies</u>

Not Like a Lady

The Countess Invention

What a Duchess Does

Crown of Hearts

He Stole the Lady

No Titled Lady—Series prequel

<u>Maids Done Waiting</u>

The Lord Trap

The Lady Escape (Forthcoming)

<u>Cloaks and Countesses</u>

The Caped Countess

The Clandestine Countess

The Castaway Countess (Forthcoming)

<u>Ladies' Own Bakery</u>

The Regency romance comedy serial

DISCLAIMER AND GENTLE WARNINGS

Like all Lords and Undefeated Ladies books, this one is primarily a happy story, and features a character with a disability. Our heroine Lady Viola suffers from depression. The book includes brief mentions of parental neglect, death of near family, suicide, alcohol abuse, firearms, and PTSD. Life isn't always easy, especially in 1814, but this book believes love is always possible, even fun. It is a work of fiction and does not represent any real characters or situations. If you or a loved one feel suicidal, emotional distress, you can call, text, or chat at phone number 988 in the United States, or 988lifeline.org.

PREFACE

My very dear readers;

Young ladies who wish to choose their own fates are often scolded for having that wish, instead of the more pertinent thing, which is how well they choose. See what you think of Lady Viola's choice.

Your most obedient servant,

Judith Lynne

CHAPTER 1

The society surrounding Lady Viola was quiet, as befitted an earl's daughter and companion of a duchess. The role meant sweet ices, parties, always too many invitations, and friends of every kind but the real sort.

Viola was ready to burn it all down.

She could not direct all of London; she could not even direct the samples of its society scattered before her now, men warm in wool coats, women shivering in gauzy gowns.

She could only direct herself. And, given how the letter in her pocket weighed on her like a cannonball, she was about to do just that.

"Lady Viola. Practical as always."

Lord Callendar's appearance at her elbow always startled her, so studiously did she avoid following him with her eyes. She had plans for him, detailed plans, and they did not include making a cake of herself over him in public.

She turned and gave him a smile. She'd practiced that smile. It was pleasant, but reserved. The sort of smile any lady might give a gentleman in a music room like this one, without hinting anything unseemly. "I hope so, but do you mean something specific?"

"The muff." He tilted his chin toward the vast white shaggy muff that Viola wore over her hands. "It's cold as a dungeon in here and twice as crowded."

It was so hard to appear indifferent to him when he insisted on being charming. Of course, every other woman in the room likely had the same problem.

Though the unmarried ones were afraid to show it, afraid they would seem unfeminine if they approached him. The married ones laughed but then moved on, and that was their mistake.

"I doubt many dungeons featured mermaid songs." Viola let her amusement show. "A rather daring topic for Lady Lattishmore's music room, diving for pearly treasures."

He laughed aloud, and Viola felt the rush of accomplishment, both in making him laugh and being the target of other women's envy for a moment.

"Quite," he said, "I'd have thought Lady Lattishmore more fond of Beethoven, given how drastic her corsets are and how thunderous his music is. I hear he has a new symphony. Perhaps now that Napoleon is gone, the music will travel more quickly from Vienna."

"Why does everything good begin in Vienna?" Viola had no knowledge of Vienna; she just wanted him to keep talking. His Roman-emperor profile showed particularly well when he laughed.

And he smiled down at her. "Not everything, Lady Viola." Then with a bow, he moved on.

Behind Viola, two fools in virginal white had chosen to keep their distance, but couldn't stay silent.

"He may come back this way." Titter, titter. Viola didn't turn to look. She'd seen them before. Both mawkish young ladies were dressed as magazine virgins, with yards of silk ribbon draping to the floor, displaying determination to prove their worth to society or their families by making a good match.

Both had their eyes fixed on Lord Callendar, who'd started a conversation on horse-racing among a flock of stiff-backed men in black coats.

He was not coming back this way.

Over her year in the Duchess' company, Viola had come to know Lord Callendar. He was not only handsome, he was kind, and his charm was effortless. Even as she covertly watched, the stiff vultures around him dissolved into good-natured jibes and backslaps.

He was also betrothed.

In fact, there went Lady Cecilia now, as close to him in public as any lady would dare be, not to join in the jokes but to convey ownership.

Like a flag, thought Viola, imagining not the flapping rags of a farmer who strung them up to scare away crows, but rather the battlefield bearer of the standard of a nation.

Even more spectacularly virginal than the tittering girls behind her, Lady Cecilia treated Lord Callendar not as a Roman emperor, but as a great fish of the ocean deep. She had fished for him as hard as she could all winter, and she'd caught him.

Viola didn't know if he'd been lured by her icy demeanor, her elegant figure, or her grandfather's Parliament vote. Whatever it was, it didn't matter.

What mattered was that Jonas looked at her with pride and some satisfied ownership...

...but not passion.

Viola could work with that.

Viola was hardened to the disappointments of reality long before she'd arrived in London. Her mother had sent her north rather than make any effort to introduce her to society. Her brothers had been confused by her because she was not like them. Her father had died.

She still chased hope, clinging to evidence of its presence somewhere; things like the warmth of men's hands when they danced, the number of flirtations happening all around her, and remarks that implied she was one of the good things who had not begun in Vienna.

After a year at the right hand of Her Grace, Viola's position had changed, and so had she.

It had been a year of luxury. Viola had been showered with invitations to dance, exciting entertainments, dinners of delicacies, and every kind of company. It was the opposite of the barren northern house where she'd lived for so long, and it might have dazzled her.

Instead, she emerged with a conviction.

A woman's happiness depended on taking what she wanted, and enjoying what she could get.

The girl behind her preferred romantic dreams. "Lord Callendar spoke to me in St. Anne's garden last Tuesday. Did you see?"

"I did see," her friend assured her, "so dashing."

They didn't know Lord Callendar at all. They knew his looks and his social standing, which had never been in any real danger from the gossip about his *tendresse* for the Duchess of Talbourne.

Viola knew more.

Lord Callendar was a beautiful man starving for passion. He was locking himself into marriage, for power or money, but not because he desired his wife.

And that suited Viola perfectly. Because she wanted his desire for herself.

Still a virgin, Viola wanted change. Drastic change. And since she had no great talent for lying, that would require drastic measures.

Carefully Viola surveyed the rest of the gathering. Her campaign to capture Lord Callendar's person called for subtlety. Side movements, like the Duchess' clever chess game. It required a spectacular feint, capturing one man by first capturing another.

And there he was.

Mr. Waite, true to his name, stood in a corner, surveying the brides within reach of his untitled, undistinguished purse.

His legs and arms were all too long. He was simply too tall. His golden-brown hair fell into his angular face when he tipped his hat because it should have been tamed with more pomade, but he didn't bother.

These were all marks against him, but Viola had picked him because of his eyes.

They were a beautiful forget-me-not blue, large for a gentleman, with a touch of sadness Viola didn't want to admit she found attractive. It was the way they were a little sleepy at the corners, she told herself, willfully ignoring her own impression that he had seen a great deal and survived it.

It made sense for his lean body to stand at attention; he had served in the war with her brother.

It didn't make sense that he wasn't yet married.

He'd spent the season surveying possible wives; that was obvious. By rights he shouldn't have been in Lady Lattishmore's drawing room at all. Viola knew him as a friend of her brother Oliver's, another of the penniless officers winding their way back into society. Gentlemen by war, not blood.

He'd somehow contrived to be invited everywhere, but didn't appear to have money. Young ladies seeking husbands, like the white-ribboned pair behind her, were expert in sniffing out fortunes; they left him alone.

Viola had not discussed his goals with him; they only

nodded to one another in passing. She couldn't recall that they'd ever even been formally introduced. But everyone knew that after twenty years of war, Britain had a significant shortage of marriageable men, and no shortage of marriageable ladies. He should be married by now.

Still here he was, drifting through the season and scrutinizing every young lady for some list of qualities Viola didn't know.

She was about to solve his problem for him.

* * *

LEE WAS in the wrong place. He'd have been better off shopping for a wife at a vegetable market.

These girls were too tender for the life he had planned. Moreover, none would understand his failings. He was old enough to name them and know they would not change.

One was the way his most miserable thoughts lurked in the bottom of liquor bottles. One snuck up his spine now, itching at the back of his neck. The idea that he should never have returned from war. He pushed it away.

He'd once escaped such thoughts by leaving London.

He should have stayed in the country and found a simple country wife. He didn't need anything dainty; he didn't *need* a wife at all.

But it was the accepted way to grow children, and those he wanted desperately.

Lord Callendar's lecture on the year's approaching horse races was interrupted by his betrothed, swathed in a gown as white as snow and twice as chilly. Lady Cecily didn't appeal to Lee at all. He wondered if she appealed to anyone. Perhaps Lord Callendar had simply been gracious enough to accept what must have been the lady's proposal.

Not that Lee cared. He only counted himself lucky to

have escaped the city and found places in the world where people neither shot at each other nor sniped.

Still, he was only human, and it irked him a little that Lord Callendar had a wife pick *him* while Lee still had to look.

A rustle of blue caught his eye. Lady Viola was the only woman in the room looking his way.

Just his luck.

Lady Viola was delicate, with silver beads trembling in the dark hair somehow magically coiled around her head. The mere idea of finding out how to unwind it alarmed him. She had a fragile air, like cold weather might snap her in two.

And she had the same kind of eyes as her brother, the kind that said *come find out.*

He didn't think she realized it. He'd seen her during this interminable winter, at the rare events where desperate society had gathered for warmth and distraction from the everlasting fog and snow.

She was different this spring. Before the winter, she'd seemed pretty and shrewd and a bit suspicious of it all, watching man after man ask her to dance because she had the ear of a powerful Duchess.

But now her look was frankly and openly assessing, a woman on the verge of making a decision only a woman could make. It was similar to a look he'd seen on her brother many a time, and it was a look no one ignored once it turned on them.

Then in a second, he saw the look vanish.

She looked years younger, all in an instant. Not lost, but hopeful. Like a little girl looking for lucky Cupid flowers.

A cluster of footmen placed a supper-table by the fire, something full of toothsome morsels for a group of people so seldom exercised they had no real need to eat.

As he watched, Viola drifted over to the table and,

without looking around to draw attention to her own movements, stole a piece of seed cake from the platter where it had just been cut.

Lee felt himself smile.

She could have had the cake in a moment if she had just waited for it to be served; he wondered why she was in such a hurry.

One hand bare, clutching her glove and massive white muff in the other, she devoured her stolen cake, all while drifting closer and closer to the door.

Then, slippery as an eel, she disappeared through it.

His smile sank into a frown.

It was late, nearly midnight. April had come, as it always would, but the air was still cold. The Duchess herself was not in attendance, as it was no longer possible to politely ignore her increasing condition, and her confinement was no doubt near. Her other companion, Miss Dìaz, stood in the center of a bouquet of laughing men and women, no doubt telling some story in a witty fashion that Lee could never match.

His conversation did not sparkle, nor did he aspire for it to do so.

Viola should have been with Miss Díaz.

Viola had absolutely no reason to slip away that wouldn't be dangerous to her, the Duchess, or both.

This presented Lee with a problem.

She wasn't his charge; she had nothing to do with him. They'd spoken briefly and seldom.

But she was Oliver's little sister, and he owed Oliver his life. More than that, he *liked* Oliver. They had shared a man-to-man silence over Viola's place in public; Oliver, who shunned London social life, silently expected Lee to watch over his sister.

And not for the way her delicate tongue swept her lips when she ate cake.

Lee waited for her to come back through the door; she didn't. More minutes passed; she still didn't. Perhaps he'd been wrong about what he saw. Lady Viola couldn't leave; where would she go? *How?* And why?

The Duchess had worked hard to earn, and keep, an unimpeachable reputation, despite the damage done to it by Lord Callendar over there, the one opining on the merits of Arabian horses.

The three of them together shared that unimpeachable reputation. Now that Her Grace could not visit in public, it was stretched thin, but maintained, by Miss Díaz and Lady Viola traveling everywhere together.

Lady Viola wouldn't risk her friend's reputation by escaping this affair in plain sight of everyone. She wouldn't risk her *own.*

Outside the glistening window passed a carriage—no, a hackney cab. Some peer had discarded it decades ago, by the look of it.

It passed in full view of the music room windows. Worn as it was, its horses were perky.

It made no sense for a working horse to be so alive this time of evening when Waite himself could barely keep his eyes open.

Lee knew it was a failing that he liked things to make sense. They often didn't, especially things about ladies. Oliver proved that constantly; the man defied explanation, sleeping all over the *ton* and catching himself a most charming, beautiful wife. Lee couldn't believe that kind of luck, never having had any like it.

But his own confusion required him to make sense of this. Luck aside, if he wanted to keep Oliver as a friend, he'd have to find out what had happened to his breakable, beddable sister.

* * *

HE FOUND Lady Viola in the wood-paneled corridor, tugging on her gloves. Beside her on a marble table lay her big fur muff, a small beaded purse, a hat that was mostly decorative and a light shawl entirely unsuitable for the weather. The footman who'd brought the things clearly was leaving, as was Lady Viola. But the footman was going in, while Lady Viola was going out.

Lee knew her brother. He was far older than she. He ought to have said something authoritative, distinctive.

All that came to mind was, "Surely there's someone you still wish to meet inside?"

Her eyes flew up, locked on his. The most extraordinary expression crossed her face. Amusement? Astonishment? Was it triumph? Not quite a smile, it was devilishly hard to read.

"Not inside, no," was all she said.

She couldn't have meant to hint that she wanted to see him. They'd barely spoken all season. Lee couldn't even recall if they'd been properly introduced.

He stepped closer.

His arrival had stopped the footman's departure; the young fellow stood properly against the wall. He wasn't the reason for the lady's indiscretion.

Lee tried again. "Miss Dìaz is missing you."

"I doubt it. That story about the Russian ambassador takes a good quarter of an hour, and she's only a third of the way through."

"You don't mean to abandon her."

"I suppose I don't." Still, she'd put on her shawl.

"I mean, you won't abandon her."

"That must not be what I'm doing," said Viola, all agreeable, and without any further courtesy, turned for the door.

"*Are* you?"

She stopped. "Mr. Waite, you can't expect any answer; you haven't asked many questions. You merely made assertions, and in the interest of keeping peace with you, I agreed."

She was not a tiny woman, but the closer he drew to her, the smaller she looked. Perhaps his height was why he'd not found a wife all season.

She still had that funny expression on her face, the one where he couldn't tell what she was thinking, but it must be a great deal. She didn't meet his eyes again, but studied the fingers of her gloves intently as she snugged them into the space between her fingers. "If you have a question, you *may* ask."

"Where are you going?"

"Out of doors." She gestured with one gloved hand.

"You can't mean that." He was near to her now, and bent his head to watch that expression, see if it changed. She tilted her own head back to see him.

"That's not a question," she said, and there was color in her cheeks as if she'd been running. A new expression mingled with the previous one: doubt. "Please don't tell me you haven't any sense. That would quite spoil my plans, and it's too late to change them."

What plans? *Where* plans? The young lady was confusing him more than most did, he'd admit that.

"Don't leave," was what he said.

"Is that a question or an order?"

"Clearly you have no idea what orders sound like." Orders were things shouted over battlefields through clouds of smoke and screams.

"I rather do," she said with the careless air of a woman who had already dismissed him from her thoughts, and, purse swinging from her wrist, moved toward the door, putting distance between the two of them again.

"Are you trying to be confusing?"

"Confusing?" Her face fell as she looked back over her shoulder. He saw a flash of the little girl who'd devoured the cake. "I was trying to be mysterious. Am I not?"

If anything happened to Lady Viola, his good friend Oliver, now the Earl of Rawleigh, would have his balls in a guillotine.

Not to mention what the Duchess of Talbourne would do.

As Lee thought all this, Viola sighed, and swept down the corridor toward the front door.

He had a terrible feeling that she was heading for that cab with the perky horse.

He said to the footman, loudly and a bit abruptly, "I'll have my things." The footman hunched a little, nodded and disappeared.

Lady Viola turned. "You can't happen to be leaving just as I am."

"No," he said, "I'm leaving because you are. You can't possibly go into the street at night alone. We're only a few yards from the Thames. What if you fall in?" He closed the distance between them. Outside, the horse whickered. "You're not going to ride in that hackney?"

"Hackneys are no more dangerous than stairs, surely. And I've used those to get many places." Showing him her back again, Lady Viola reached out and opened the door for herself.

A cold wind enveloped Lee.

Outside, the freezing winter had given way to a freezing spring. Puddles lay everywhere, many capped with crackling ice. The swirling fog looked like it had come straight from the sea.

The footman returned; Waite shoved on his great coat then grabbed his hat, which held his gloves. With a solid fist he swept his cane up in the other hand and followed her with long strides.

"You're taking a foolish risk," he told her when he caught up with her on the stoop outside.

She looked up at him and he thought that in the torch-light, he could see a glint of a small smile.

"I know," she said and walked down the stairs.

CHAPTER 2

As predicted, the lanky gentleman followed her.

Try something simpler. Viola had thought it so many times, so many days before she'd come here, to this night, her heart pounding as she walked across the cobble-stones. *Why all the complication? Make things easier on yourself.*

It would be easiest to escape the burdensome letter in her pocket by simply staying in the ducal palace forever, whiling away her life. How things could be any easier than that, Viola didn't know. She'd be something of a pet: admired, but never loved.

It would be better than her past, but far short of what she wanted for her future.

The hackney was shabby. It had not been fine even when it had served nobility. Someone had discarded it into a lower sort of life. As she approached it, she felt the freezing paving stones through the soles of her slippers.

Had she stayed inside, she would have walked out on a servant-laid carpet, but despite the pain in her toes, her determination stayed firm. A lower sort of life surely had its own kind of freedom.

She was prepared to give up such little comforts; prepared, in fact, to give up every ounce of privilege remaining to her name.

Give them up? She'd throw them away with both hands.

The windows in Lady Lattishmore's curiously public music room faced the drive. Those inside must have seen the cab and its horses. Must be watching now as Viola gathered her skirts, preparing to climb inside. Without chaperone and without Miss Díaz.

Must have seen the man who followed and took her arm.

"You can't do this." He still didn't ask questions.

Viola ruthlessly crushed her disappointment. Should he prove to be a boor, he could make her life hellish. She'd still carry out her plan. He might develop amiability.

She didn't want a boor; she doubted he really was one. He was her brother's friend, that was all; he wanted to protect Oliver's interest in that peculiar possession, a sister.

And she had purposefully put him in an untenable position.

If she wanted him to understand her own feelings, she had best give latitude to his.

He had yet to grasp the negotiating value of questions. "You don't want to do this." Clearly he grasped the situation as well as she did. How compromised she was about to look. It wouldn't be good for his reputation either, and he barely had one.

That, on top of being too tall. Certainly too tall for appropriate dancing.

Part of her couldn't scrape together the hubris to think that she was doing him any favors. Another part of her, however, thought that she likely was. She was not the worst marriage prospect in London, and he hadn't found one on his own.

"I'm leaving," Viola simply said, and climbed into the waiting carriage.

Mr. Waite stood with the door open, cold night mists swirling around him, long arms spanning the whole space of the door—the whole carriage, it seemed.

"What do you expect me to do?" He didn't whisper, nor did he yell. He was exactly what he seemed to be. A man mingling with those above his station, and she was pushing him to ruin her or haul her out of a carriage in full view of the people who would not be inviting him back.

Viola had lived with the Duchess of Talbourne long enough to understand the value of games, but she wasn't good at them. This was her best, her last, her biggest effort.

She didn't answer, only settled back in the seat and looked straight ahead.

Without so much as a noise of frustration, he committed to the thing.

Swung himself up into the cab, which took off.

It's done, she thought as he folded his long limbs into the crowded space and closed the door.

* * *

"Why did you do that?"

Lee had never been this close to Lady Viola before. He had no way of knowing if she always had that unreadable look in her eye. She looked frightened, and determined; he'd seen other people look that way, before a battle.

But underneath all that, she seemed pleased.

Public misbehavior didn't suit her. She was too fine for that sort of thing, the kind of woman whose bones showed under her porcelain skin and drew a map to all her vulnerable places.

"I don't wish to return to Talbourne House." She spoke not to him, but to the window.

Was she on her way to meet someone?

Who on earth would be worth breaking ties with a duchess? Because that's what Lady Viola was doing, haring off into the middle of the night like this.

Also breaking ties with a duke, but knowing their reputations, Lee was twice as alarmed by the Duchess as he was by the Duke. The Duke would slit your throat if you crossed him, but the Duchess would win your boots and leave you to march home before all London without them.

"You must be residing at Their Grace's townhouse. Grosvenor Square," he called out to the driver, leaning out the window on his side, one long arm balancing himself easily as he did. The little carriage tilted wildly.

"I'm not going to Grosvenor Square," she told him and with a burst of strength he did not suspect, she leaned out the opposite door just as he did. The carriage did not tilt in her direction. "Leicester Square," she called, "just as I said."

Hearing her voice issue faintly from the opposite side of the vehicle, Lee slid back inside. Her body hung out the window while the cab rolled over the cobblestones at speed.

Horrified, Lee hauled her inside.

She didn't *feel* fragile. There was more to her than first appeared. The soft solidity of her body made this all real. He was in a cab, driving away from Lady Lattishmore's house in full view of London society.

He'd just been received at his last social affair of the *ton*.

The cold made her cheeks pink. She straightened her hat, which had fallen askew. The shawl she wore was not up to the task of turning away this rotten everlasting winter, especially if she insisted on hanging out carriage windows. Her gown, even her skin had a chill that he felt through his gloves. Fortunately, she retrieved her fur muff from where she'd dropped it, slid in both forearms and settled into it. It fell well down her lap.

"What the hell was that?" He waved a long hand toward the door even as he reached over her to close the inadequate shade. "Hanging out the door like that? Are you trying to crack your head open?"

"I just did what you did."

"Well you can't do that!"

* * *

STAY CALM, she told herself. He wasn't as amiable as she'd hoped. All those months of him lurking in the background of dances and musicales; she'd expected someone more biddable. "Is this why you're having trouble finding a wife, Mr. Waite? This tendency you have to make pronouncements?"

"What the—" Leaning back from her, he tried to put space between them. There wasn't any. "You're a funny type of girl, aren't you?"

"I'm very droll," she agreed, turning again to the window. Since he'd drawn the blind, that meant staring at the blind.

The carriage rocked, and instantly Mr. Waite braced one long arm against the far wall next to Viola, protecting her from knocking against it.

It was a small gesture, but it made hope bloom inside Viola again.

All she needed was for him to be a little kind. Just a little understanding. The opposite of her family.

Perhaps he was, but he also wasn't stupid. "You might as well tell me why you did that," he said again, and Viola's feelings sank, knowing she would have to confess.

She'd expected this, as she simply could not dissemble for long; oddly, now that the moment was here, she felt more awkward than she'd thought she would. And more barbs of shame.

But shame didn't peel any apples. It was done, and she'd see it through.

"To compromise you, of course," she told him clearly.

She half thought he might jump away. At least remove his bracing arm, which was as hard as an oak branch behind her, but warm.

He did neither. Only stared, puzzlement written all over his face. She was close enough now to notice the deep softness of his lower lip. She'd never seen that before.

It wasn't why she'd picked him, but she found it oddly encouraging.

This close, his voice had a softness to it too. "To compromise *me.*"

"Yes." Her confidence was rising. He hadn't done anything horrible; perhaps he wouldn't. "Though I admit it was in order to compromise myself."

"You *wanted* to compromise yourself."

"Yes, and I'm afraid it requires two people." She drew in a deep breath. They were *too* close for her to keep meeting his eyes; they were just the shade of forget-me-not blue they'd seemed to be, and a little too gentle. She looked at the window blind instead. "So I chose you."

The silence told her he was thinking that over.

She rushed ahead before he got entirely the wrong idea. "I'm in love with Lord Callendar, you see. So I'd like to marry you."

* * *

She was surprising the way an incoming cannonball was surprising.

"Lady Viola, I don't believe we know each other well

enough for this conversation." He hesitated. "I don't believe I know anyone well enough to have this conversation."

"I am pressed for time."

That only confused Bradley Waite more. Lady Viola was still young, and obviously lovely. She had no reason to feel pressed for time.

And she was telling him that she'd kidnapped him, and hadn't apologized.

Oliver would kill him.

He decided on a delaying tactic. "Why me?"

Lady Viola then demonstrated how she had become the *confidante* of such a clever and powerful duchess: through the brutal accuracy of her assessments. "You are not desirable. London society ignores you. You're free of bothersome mothers. I would not be depriving anyone by taking you."

"Thank you."

Her assessment was beyond lowering. It was a punch in the gut.

No, it hit lower than that.

Here Lee had thought he'd stayed out of sight all winter, combing through society for a woman who would suit his few future plans.

Lady Viola had seen him, and worse, had read him correctly.

Had he approached the wife business differently, he could have avoided this. Had Oliver not been such a rake in his own way, sleeping with more than his share of society wives, he might have introduced Lee to a better class of people.

No, that was the wrong thinking. Lee didn't want to meet a better class of people. Hadn't he just realized tonight he ought to look for a country wife in the country?

"I should've gone north," he mused, turning to see out his own window as the carriage rattled along. He should have gone back to Glasgow; he'd loved it there. If he'd had to try wife-hunting in a city, it should probably have been a Scottish city.

He'd just been tired of being alone. At least in London he had Oliver and a few other friends with a certain understanding of the kinds of things men went through in war. Oliver, who had tied him to life when those ties had been very thin.

Lady Viola asked, "How far north?"

He turned to look her way. She was finally meeting his eyes. "I should have sailed north from the Scottish isles and kept walking on the ice around the tip of the world," he told her frankly.

"Marrying me won't be that bad."

She really intended to marry him. Because she was in love with someone else. "This is the life you *want?*"

All her poise crumbled in an instant and she was that cake-stealing little girl again. "It sounds awful, I know. Even worse when you say it out loud. I'm very sorry it takes two people to ruin someone."

He wanted to jump out of the carriage and reassure her at the same time. There were no rules for this conversation, not that he was good at them anyway; he threw propriety out the window. "Have you considered just asking someone to ruin you?

"Yes." Her nod was serious. "I don't wish to be *banned* from social affairs, like Oliver. I won't mind giving up parties. I might want to call on my friends again one day, even if I must sneak in the servants' entrance."

"Oliver isn't *banned.*"

The knowing look was back in her dark eyes, and Lee decided not to discuss her brother. The matter at hand, anyway, was himself.

"You'll forgive me, but marrying only to be cuckolded doesn't sound *good.*"

He expected her to deny the word, but she only shrugged those delicate shoulders. "I don't think you're easily shamed, and I will make it as easy on you as I can."

She was less alarming than cannon fire, but only just. "How will you make it *easy?*"

"Whatever it is you want a wife for, I'll provide it. You should get something from the bargain, after all."

She was a child. "I want a wife to bed," he said bluntly. It wasn't the whole truth, but it was enough to shake her out of this mad fantasy, surely.

It didn't.

"Fine," was all she said. "You look pleasant enough, and it can't be that difficult. I've seen plenty of society girls married off as second and third wives, to far older and uglier men. I hope they didn't all expect their wives to be wholly faithful. How depressing," she said almost to herself, looking out the window again.

Well, that look he'd seen in her eyes hadn't lied; she wasn't shy. She was ready for a lot of things. He hadn't expected them to involve him.

"Viola." He wanted to shake her, but that was more violent than he was feeling. Mostly he felt... confused, certainly. And oddly disappointed.

Not because she didn't love him; due to his own peculiar failings, that was the best possible reason for them to marry. She needn't live a loveless life; she'd aimed those hopes elsewhere.

No, disappointed because she wouldn't suit the sort of life in the country he had planned.

Well, that fault was hers; she hadn't asked about it. Hadn't even done him the courtesy of asking him to marry her. Even Lord Callendar's icy betrothed had surely given him that.

She'd turned his way with a quizzical look at the sound of

her name. The silver beads trembling in her hair looked expectant.

"I hope you're less fragile than you look," he said without a trace of humor, leaning across her again to look out the window on her side.

* * *

HE WAS SO LARGE, and *warm,* and the side of his arm where it pressed carelessly across her collarbone was unyielding, yet protective. It shook her thoughts from their path. She pulled them together again.

"I'm not fragile," she informed him coolly.

"Good," he said, "because this driver's going east, not north, and unless I'm wrong we're about to meet some unpleasant characters in an alley by the wharfs."

That distracted Viola from contemplating how small the carriage was.

"Not really," she gasped, noticing that indeed, the rolling of the carriage had slowed.

"Yes really," he said much more grimly. "Once I deal with this I'm going back to Lady Lattishmore's and give that footman a boxing lesson. Did he arrange the carriage?"

"I think he found one passing on the street." Viola now looked all around them. They had indeed turned into an alley that was growing dingier, smellier, and the buildings marched closer together, closing around them.

"Perfect," muttered Mr. Waite.

"Do you box, then?"

"No," he said, tensing himself, "but I know how to hit things."

Viola expected time to ask what he planned to do. Time to critique, perhaps. Revise their strategy before the enemy came closer to bear.

As it turned out, what unfolded moved far more quickly than ladies choosing battle sides in a drawing room.

As soon as the carriage slowed to a walk, Mr. Waite sprang out, his walking stick in one hand. He reached up to grab a big handful of the coat of the driver, and simply yanked him out of his seat.

Once the whiskered man sprawled on the ground, his coat grinding into the rutted dirt, Mr. Waite shoved the knob of his walking stick against the man's chest. The fellow squeaked and stopped moving.

After a few more steps, so did the carriage horses.

It all happened so fast Viola had no time to think, much decide how to feel.

"Where were you taking us?" said Mr. Waite in a voice exactly like the one in which he'd asked her what she expected him to do. There was nothing about him that said he had a man squirming in the road at the end of his cane, yet there it was.

"G—Grosvenor Square," gasped the man.

"Mmm." It was both a denial and a warning. No more menacing than before, but made so by apparent pressure against his cane on the man's chest, over his heart.

"Just to the wharf," the man confessed, now using both hands to try to shove the cane up and away from him. It didn't move. "Nothing would have happened to you—urk!"

The increased pressure had been inspired by the appearance of two much younger fellows in stiff fustian coats and greasy caps.

They strolled out of the shadows, and their kind of calm was menacing.

They looked over the scene with a sense of ownership—the fallen driver, Mr. Waite standing over him with his cane, Viola in fluttering silks framed in the carriage window, unable to look away—and they swaggered over to Mr. Waite with the male assurance of peacocks with tails fully spread. "Now then, governor," said one, with a nasal sort of voice.

Again, curiously, Mr. Waite did not ask any questions. No discussion at all, in fact.

Instead, he put one foot on the chest of the driver to hold him down, and with both hands at the tip of his cane, swung its head in a smooth arc from one side to the other, catching one man across the ribs. With a startled cry, he tumbled over.

While his companion tried to decide what to do, Mr. Waite's cane swung around again and caught that one in the arm, knocking him to the ground. Viola thought she heard something crunch.

"I'm taking your carriage," he told all three of the ruffians with the same demeanor he'd used in Lady Lattishmore's hallway, decisive and simple, "and I'm driving the lady home. If I were you I wouldn't expect the carriage back; but if you want it, it will be at Lord Justice Carter's house on Tanfield Court. I'm thinking none of you will go get it, but if you do, you'll find your horses fed." While the older man groveled in the dirt and the two younger ones grasped their respective wounded parts, he yanked open the door. "Come out," he said to Viola.

She froze. He wanted her out of the carriage? She'd have to step over the men's bodies to do it.

"Come on," he said, pulling his fingertips toward him in a gesture that would have been more appropriate to a horse. Indeed, one carriage horse turned to look. "Out."

"I can't." Her plan had nothing in it of any of this. Suddenly a little frightened of him, the thin paneled wall of the little carriage seemed like at least a little protection, or at least better than none.

"You're a funny girl." With that, he reached a long arm into the carriage and hauled her out bodily, setting her on her feet, showing just how he could have done it at any time.

"Now climb up," he said as if to a toddling child, pulling her forward by the hand to show her where to climb up to the driver's seat of the carriage.

"I can't drive!"

"Neither can I if I'm worried the whole way you've fallen out the back. Step up."

"We can't both fit up here!"

"We have to," said Mr. Waite with the same simple insistence, and, fetching the muff that she'd dropped again, tossed it to her before her feet were even set against the footboard, then climbed on the step himself.

Quickly Viola tucked her skirts around her and wrapped her shawl tight. The muff would not cover enough of her for comfort.

Mr. Waite swept off the greatcoat he'd just donned in Lady Lattishmore's entryway and tossed it over her without ceremony.

Unable to think of a good reason to protest, she moved it from a blanket-like position to something closer to a cape, around her shoulders.

It was warm, and smelled disconcertingly good, like a spiced milk dessert.

Mr. Waite captured her muff again before it slid off the front of the carriage. Dropped it on her lap with no sign of impatience that again, she'd let go of it.

His body settling next to hers made the carriage tilt, but it righted itself well enough as he drove them away, looking over his shoulder from time to time to make sure none of the ruffians followed them.

Viola didn't look back.

"Hold this," he said, giving her his walking stick so he could use both hands on the reins.

She almost dropped it. The knob at the end was unexpectedly heavy, like lead. No wonder it had been such a serviceable weapon.

This wasn't in her plan. But she had wanted chaos, the normal order of things crushed. It was crushed now. "You might have let me know what you were about to do."

He looked down at her as the horses just managed to fit themselves around the narrow corner. "Lady Viola, the word running through my head is *irony*."

"I didn't want to argue about my plan."

"Same."

This was logic impossible to refute, and it annoyed Viola that she had no good answer for it. She ought to feel grateful; she was, overwhelmingly so, because however much she had wanted to escape her gilded cage, she would not have wanted to be at the mercy of those men.

It wasn't at all the same as Mr. Waite being at hers.

"So explain how you think this would work." He continued their conversation as if it had not been interrupted, right in the open air. "You marry me, then run to Lord Callendar to tell him so?"

"No! That would be coarse." More coarse, the way he said it.

"Did you have a schedule for this? See, I'm trying to ask questions."

"I assumed you and I might reach a suitable arrangement." She hadn't expected him to be so capable of precipitous action. She'd just taken all the precipitous action she was prepared to take. There was still a long way to go to effect her plan; indeed, to finish the night.

"You're not giving me much detail. Should I ask more questions, or should I just silently deliver you to the Talbourne townhouse and pretend none of this ever happened?" Mr. Waite handled the reins with the same easy simplicity he'd used to beat back their attackers.

"I'm not going to the Talbourne townhouse. I will *not* return, not to any house where I've ever lived." Reaction set in and Viola found herself trembling. It had all happened so fast, and been so shockingly violent. She'd never been close to anything violent in her life. At least, not physically violent.

At least, not while it was happening. She'd only seen the aftermath.

"You're frightened. Of a Talbourne house? Why?" He looked briefly down where she huddled next to him on the too-small seat. "Someone threatened you there?"

She hadn't expected him to have eyes of his own, or questions. Why had she simply assumed he would go along with her plan because he would get out of it whatever he wanted?

She wasn't the Duchess of Talbourne; she was only a maid in waiting trying to be clever.

Then she thought of the letter folded in her pocket. She'd put it there when she'd dressed this evening because she'd known she'd need fortification. It was there, and she remembered now why she'd put all of this in motion in the first place, and carried it out tonight.

"No one in Their Graces' homes," she said, wondering why she sounded so breathless, if it was because of the shaking she couldn't stop. "But I can't go back there, or anyone in my family. I'm done with all of it. My only hope is you."

CHAPTER 3

*L*ee had never been a swearing man. It was the type of habit people discouraged in a child, and he'd had plenty of people to discourage him.

Still, he wondered if it was too late to adopt the habit, and if it would afford his frustration any relief.

He took it seriously, being anyone's last hope.

"Why Leicester Square?" he pressed her even as he guided the horses down a side street that would take them north after all. "Does Lord Callendar have apartments there? Planning to keep you?"

"No." Her head shook the *no* vehemently, making the silver beads in her dark hair dance. "He doesn't know anything about my plans."

"Does he know you're in love with him?"

"I think he knows."

This kept getting better and better.

He was beginning to realize that getting answers from Lady Viola, however fragile she looked, required persistence. "So why Leicester Square?"

"There's a hotel there, where I intend to stop."

"Why that one?"

"There's a bakery nearby and I like the cake," Viola said quietly.

She still didn't sound ashamed. He admired that. She would carry out her battle plans to the last letter, even if surrounded on all sides.

It was admirable, but stupid.

"Lady Viola. You've put me in an untenable situation—as you intended. If I deliver you to Talbourne House now, I will somehow be feeding you to the dogs. If I deliver you to your brother in the middle of the night, he'll kill me. I've just stolen a carriage, however logical it seemed at the time—"

"Utterly justified," Viola said, and her rock-solid certainty was somehow soothing.

"Fine, but we can hardly take it to Scotland. For one thing, you'll freeze to death." He could feel the night air biting at his limbs too, but he'd slept on the ground during many a French campaign; Viola, even wearing his greatcoat, was shivering. "Another reason to want a sturdy wife," he added under his breath.

"Leicester Square," she said, still certain though her teeth were chattering. "Turn here."

He looked down at her; her dark eyes turned up to meet his.

"I memorized all the paths to it," she admitted, "in case I needed to walk."

So she was determined enough to see this through that she'd have *walked* to Leicester Square tonight. In a thin silk shawl, when it was so cold out he could see their breath.

Brave or stupid, she clearly meant what she said.

"Damn all this," Lee muttered to himself. It didn't make anything better.

* * *

MR. WAITE WAS BEING RELATIVELY GENTLEMANLY about his kidnapping, Viola thought, especially given he couldn't even wear his own coat.

She would have liked to wait a little longer. Certainly at least until the weather improved. But the winter had been the longest and coldest she could ever remember, and she'd feared it might never end. Certainly the letter in her pocket read like the end of sunshine.

I expect you at Morland to care for me, it said in the sort of perfect penmanship that she herself had once been required to learn.

A simple sentence, yet as horrifying as a sea monster reaching its tentacled arms out of the deep and threatening to draw her under.

Mr. Waite wouldn't understand. Viola didn't intend to explain. She couldn't, not completely, not even to herself.

She only knew that if she returned to her family home and stayed for any length of time, it would quite literally be the end of her.

His soft curse told her that he wasn't sure what to do next; since she was, she again offered her solution.

"We ought to simply go to Jacquier's Hotel," she explained. "It will be a comfortable place to spend the night."

"And tomorrow? Do you really expect me to marry you, just like that?"

"I don't see why not. You've never been in London society till this past winter, and you've spent the whole season examining everything London society has to offer in the way of a wife. You clearly want to marry; I know you offered for Lady Charlotte's companion."

"Do you now." He handled the reins gently, as if trusting the horses to do whatever they would. Viola found that reassuring.

"If you wanted someone from the gentry for your wife, you'd have offered for Lady Charlotte."

"Have you *met* Lady Charlotte?"

Viola had; she was a tall and elegant lady, but had a brusque, biting temper, and she'd never compromised in her life. His point was made. "Nonetheless, if you offered for Miss Farsworth, you can't be desperate for a title *or* a purse."

"I'm not."

Feeling a little foolish, Viola asked, "So what did you like about her? She is shorter than I am."

Mr. Waite let out a grunting little *huff* that said he didn't like being questioned when he couldn't leave the room. Viola had met enough men in society to be familiar with the male aversion to being pressed for information. She just let him answer in his own time.

"She's congenial," was all he finally said, guiding the horses around a turn of the street.

Viola straightened in the seat. "I can be congenial!"

He glanced over. "You haven't yet."

"Still. I can be pleasant. And I do want to marry you, unlike Miss Farsworth. I don't believe she wants to marry *anyone.*"

"She does in her own way," was all he said, as their path connected to the southern edge of Leicester Square.

In the frosty night, the dark foliage crowding behind the park fence in the center of the square seemed thick and unyielding. Viola didn't think herself naturally timid, but she wondered if it held more brigands waiting to leap out at her.

Mr. Waite apparently had other fears.

"If I stop at the hotel's door, anyone could see you alight," he muttered, clearly unhappy with the idea.

Viola couldn't judge. She'd never kidnapped a man before. Was he growing more accustomed to the idea of their marrying, or not?

Either way, he turned right, passing a grand house with a brightly lit lamp at its door on the left and following the stone pavement till, halfway along the street, they reached the hotel's door.

It featured a lit lamp shedding a pool of colorless light on the paving stones.

No footmen were about.

"Now I have to decide whether to leave you to freeze with the carriage, or take you into a hotel," he muttered.

He didn't sound like he was warming to the marriage idea.

"I'll stay here," she offered. "You stole the carriage once; you don't want it walking away."

* * *

SHE WASN'T A COWARD; he had to give her that. It wasn't just cold, it was pitch dark beyond the lamp's circle, with moonlight barely escaping the drifting blanket of clouds above.

He'd engage her a room; then, once she was safely locked inside, he'd go to Oliver. Oliver didn't have much of a temper; hopefully he'd hold his questions and his bullets till Lee could deliver news of his sister and be out of this mess.

Viola had compromised herself, but that wasn't Lee's affair. She wanted to destroy her place in society; so be it. Whatever she expected Lord Callendar to do, Lee was pretty sure he wouldn't do it.

Unless Lee delivered the carriage along with his own version of what had happened tonight to the Lord Justice, a fellow he'd met in the service, the ruffians could swear out a complaint against *him,* and some thief-taker desperate for the money would detain him and have him in gaol before he could sort out anything to do with Lady Viola.

He just had to ignore for the moment the ways her calculations did add up.

"Stay there for just a minute," he told her before swinging down and disappearing through the narrow hotel door.

* * *

VIOLA INSTANTLY MISSED HIS WARMTH.

But she had a job to do now, holding the horses here, and she would do it. They weren't any more inclined to leave the little pool of light over the pavement than she was; still, she wouldn't drop the reins.

Somehow she hadn't expected *other people* to cause problems for her plan. She had accounted for the players she knew. The Duchess would be worried once she heard; Virginia would be in genuine difficulty, left alone in Lady Lattishmore's music room. However, Lord Callendar was well known to be a friend to Talbourne House and he would ensure Virginia made it home, perhaps even with his icy Lady Cecily and her mother as chaperones.

It delighted Viola to inconvenience Lady Cecily.

She tried not to be petty, she really did. Truthfully, she didn't blame Lord Callendar for arranging a marriage. How could she? He was a grown man in his prime, very beautiful, and did what he must for his place in society, for the causes he supported. He could not give up his place for mere love; therefore, she must.

But she did blame Lady Cecily for catching him, just a little. Because she didn't think Cecily loved Lord Callendar either.

Truthfully, this would all have been so much easier if the weather had improved, and if Cecily had simply waited for summer.

A long, low whistle drew her attention back to the door.

An usher was there, or perhaps he was simply a footman. He wore a dark damask coat, suitable for service, but it was dark and in the night she couldn't tell the color.

He lifted his stovepipe hat and whistled again before settling the hat back down.

He approached the carriage; the horses stepped a little, forcing Viola to grip harder on the reins. She had no idea how to drive a pair of horses; if they took it into their heads to move, she wasn't sure how to stop them.

"*Chérie*," the man greeted her, followed with a string of French words she didn't understand. Viola had studied with tutors, but she assumed his were not words schoolgirls usually learned.

The man wore a wide grin, close enough now she could see the unkindness in it. "*Eh, mon petit chou*," he spoke to her again, followed by more words she didn't understand. He leaned toward the seat, close enough to put his arms around her legs and drag her off. She wondered wildly if that was what he would do. She wondered if she should kick him first.

Once, in a low moment, she'd felt Lord Callendar's arms lift her and carry her away. It had been the only time she could remember a man making things better for her. Her father never had, nor her brothers either; not even Oscar before he died, and Oscar had always been the kindest.

They'd left her to her mother's mercies, knowing perfectly well the woman had none.

Lord Callendar had carried her once, his strong arms taking care of everything for a few precious, surrounding moments, and while she'd recovered—for she had been very ill—Viola kept returning to the moment again and again, thinking the same thing over and over: *I want that.*

Now she'd set things in motion to *get* that, but there were so many more obstacles along the way than she had imagined, most immediately, that this fellow here seemed about to drag her down from the driver's seat to do... something, she didn't want to know what.

Just before his face touched her skirts, it flew backward.

It was Mr. Waite, big hands gathering up the coat of the usher and shaking him like a dog shook a rat.

From this vantage, Mr. Waite didn't look calm at all. There was a wild light in his eyes Viola hadn't seen while he was dealing with the brigands before, but perhaps she simply hadn't been close enough or high enough to see.

"What do you think you're doing?" and his voice, too, was roughened by some emotion. "Never mind, get out of here."

"*Monsieur,* I work here," the man stammered out through rattling teeth.

"Not any more. You're discharged." He shoved the usher towards the dark.

Disappearing down the pavement, unwilling to argue, the man faded away into the night.

"Are you well?" Mr. Waite asked her, calm again, coming as close as the usher had been a moment before.

"Perfectly well," said Viola, and burst into tears.

* * *

THE PANIC that seized Lee down to the center of his bones was more than a natural worry at a woman's tears.

She was hurt. He hadn't been here, and she was hurt.

Instantly he swept her down off the seat, his hands splayed under her arms in his heavy coat, moving her as quickly as a child could move a doll.

"I'm fine, truly," she said through hiccupping tears.

Feeling through the coat, he couldn't detect any breaks. A broken bone could mean death, he knew that well enough, especially when it forced its way through the skin. She didn't seem to be bleeding.

"I'm fine, I am," she kept repeating, and he realized she was ineffectually trying to hit him with her dangling beaded purse.

He jumped back, hands wide. Here he'd taken massive liberties in public.

But she didn't mention it. Only stood there in his great-coat, silken skirts pooling on the pavement over her slippers, face wet with tears.

"It was just so startling. Everything tonight has happened so fast," was all she said.

Feeling in his pocket for a handkerchief, Lee handed it to her. She was cold, and likely in shock. She was a lady, and unused to violence, and now tonight she'd been in the thick of two bouts of it.

He didn't box, but he could hear a judge calling round two for Lady Viola.

"You need to get inside."

* * *

HE LED her through the foyer of the hotel, past the manager of the house from whom he'd already obtained a key, who cleared his throat and murmured, "And *monsieur's* baggage?"

"*Monsieur* has just sent your door-man packing, because he attacked my wife." Lee fought back an urge to roar in the man's face. Dispatching coach-thieves hadn't rattled him, but someone accosting Viola at the very door to the hotel was a bit much. "As I explained, her exhaustion came of visiting the theater and a party in one night. You only need to stable my carriage. And send us clean water, and something to eat."

"Of course, sir," said the manager, a pompously tall man of whom people apparently often demanded water and food in the middle of the night.

"Leave it at the door, we won't answer."

Without another word, Lee marched Viola up a comfortable staircase to a wide room overlooking the park.

It was a sitting room, sumptuously appointed in velvets and gold tassel, reminding one of the past excesses of French aristocracy while remaining tasteful. It held upholstered couches and chairs, and through an inner door, one could glimpse the drapes of a wide bed.

Viola fluttered about the room examining its details like a captured animal examining its new cage without realizing that it couldn't get out.

Uneasy, he locked the door and slipped the key in his pocket.

Viola sank to the velvet settee. "I'm fine, truly I am. A broken nerve, perhaps."

If she had nerves, they didn't break.

In the time it had taken to fetch her, someone had laid live coals in the little grate. Lee checked to make sure they would catch others, and that the hob was full. He didn't intend to see one more person while in Lady Viola's company, not till he could slip out and fetch Oliver.

Her breathing was slowing; she dried her eyes with his handkerchief. "A kind fiction, to call me your wife. Dare I hope you are warming to my plan?"

"Calling you my wife cost me more than you know." Blunt by nature, the words left him before he could keep them back. They were true; it had. "There's a bed in there; take it and sleep."

"I'm so sorry, Mr. Waite." Viola's voice was soft, as if she hadn't just been sobbing herself. "You've been married before?"

Lee had limits. He knew that about himself. The realization had saved his life. He'd found those limits at the bottom of bottles, and backed away.

"Go to sleep," he bit out, tossing his own gloves and hat on a gilt side table.

Unable to just ignore her comfort, he stalked to the inner room and checked the grate. It had no fire.

He turned and found Viola just behind him.

She looked at the bed sorrowfully. For a fleeting moment he thought she would be missish and shy about sleeping in a room beside him, despite everything she'd said over the course of the evening.

But she only said, "I don't think I can sleep."

"You'll sleep." In the morning, he'd extract from her whatever sent her on this crazy path. Till then she should sleep, and so would he. He'd already been tired at Lady Lattishmore's party, and since then the evening had gotten much more strenuous.

"I may sleep, but I won't go back. The compromising is done, sir. If you plan to abandon me in the morning, a few more hours can't matter. It is *so* cold, and I find myself a bit worn. I'll be right enough by morning, but till then... are you sure you wouldn't prefer to at least share the bed?"

Her speech tightened the muscles in his belly. She had a steely backbone, but she was still slender and her outsides were soft; maybe her heart, too, despite the ruthlessness of her actions. She didn't know what a man would think when she said that.

"I know how that sounds," she quietly contradicted his silent thoughts as if she'd heard them, and wrapped her arms around herself, still wearing his coat. "And I didn't mean all that, not yet. But wouldn't you be warmer?"

Lee had limits, and she was toying with them.

Her affairs weren't his. He'd been looking for a wife who wouldn't feel too deeply, and perhaps he'd found a prospect, but *this* prospect wouldn't do.

My wife felt like a cut-off limb temporarily returned to

him, a ghostly appendage of a former life. Words he'd long done without. Soldiers often felt aches in the parts they lost; was this just the echo of his heart?

"Take the bed," he found himself saying hoarsely. "I'll build a fire in the grate. Go."

CHAPTER 4

*V*iola was convinced she couldn't fall asleep between the chilly coverlets, not after all that. She'd just close her eyes.

She didn't want sleep; Mr. Waite's lean silhouette moved about the room, moving coal in the grate, closing the drapes, and she found watching him reassuring. The racing of her heart slowed, and as her feet warmed, the lids of her eyes grew heavier and heavier till she could no longer force them open.

She woke in the middle of the night. The coal and covers had warmed the room, and she *had* slept, despite lying fully dressed in the bed with stays digging into her side. Pure exhaustion, she supposed.

Yet her nerves were too tightly stretched to stay asleep. She hadn't expected escape to be so dramatic.

The night was still dark, and presumably would be forever. The familiar sensation of hopeless dread frightened her. She didn't have time to succumb to it right now.

For a moment she imagined Lord Callendar lying next to her in this canopied bed. *Jonas,* as she liked to think of him in her head. He wouldn't shy away from her; he would wrap himself around her, giving her acres of warm linen to lie against, perhaps even warm skin. And he would smile.

Viola couldn't get enough of his smiles.

Most smiles of the *ton* had a kind of brittleness to them. As if ready to break. Lord Callendar's smile was sturdy. Real.

Like the wife Mr. Waite said he wanted. Sturdy, and *congenial*.

That sounded to Viola like he wanted a dog more than a wife, but she had to try. She had put him in this situation without asking; she owed him a great deal of trying.

Slipping out from under the covers, the dim glow of the coal fire falling across her stockinged legs, she re-tied her garters before tiptoeing to the sitting room.

The same dim glow warmed the room, but instead of lying on a chaise—which would all be too short for his long frame anyway—Mr. Waite was pacing the room.

His head snapped up as she entered.

She stared at him a long moment, at his hair loose and wild, his soft eyes wild too. He looked like someone to fear, but she didn't.

"You can't sleep?" He might not ask questions, but she would.

"I want a drink." Bluntly.

She looked around; there was a platter of bread and cheese, and goblets of water, but no wine. "You haven't taken any?"

"I cannot. All my bleakest thoughts come out of a bottle."

* * *

LEE EXPECTED that to be the end of it. This conversation, and perhaps this whole farce. He'd admitted a weakness, and women didn't like weakness.

But Lady Viola just walked right in and sat.

Her blue gown looked a little rumpled. It was not designed for sleeping. The silk gathered snugly over her chest, making her slight curves look softer, and little laces reminiscent of a shepherdess drew the front closed between a ribbon edging the wide neck and one trimming the high waist. From there, folds of blue silk fell unbroken to the floor.

Some locks of hair had fallen from the arrangement atop her head, too.

She seemed heedless that she looked, as she was, straight from bed.

"Then you're wise not to start," was all she said, with the same conviction she had pronounced fair his theft of a carriage. As if it were in her power to banish any doubts he might entertain about his own course of action.

She might be right.

She looked about the room. "What would calm your nerves?"

She wanted to calm *his* nerves.

This time appropriately, she reminded him of her brother. As a physician Oliver had always decided his treatment based on his own observation of what his patients needed rather than any theory of humors found in books. Perhaps the trait ran in his family, like red hair did in others.

Yet Oliver had watched Lee drink himself nearly to the grave without once asking what would calm his nerves.

The answer to Viola's question came to him in a rush. "Undressing your hair."

She blinked, but didn't startle.

"You can't sleep easily with it all tied up like that." He waved a hand at her head.

It was the opposite of ridding himself of her and her

problems. It would only entangle him more, quite literally. The lady had quantities of dark hair, all of it horribly awry.

But she'd asked what would calm him, and it would. It looked uncomfortable, and that made *him* uncomfortable. He'd rather put it to rights.

"If you wish to help, I won't refuse." Her sigh sounded more relieved than resigned. "It is pulling at my scalp, but I wanted to see how you fared before I attacked it. It must be a mess."

No one, including Oliver, had ever put Lee's needs before their own.

The situation was bizarre, but he knew doing something with his hands, his body, helped when he felt restless. Once he'd stopped squashing that restlessness with drink, it had driven him out of London, then farther and farther into the country until he reached its edge.

Had it not been for the wars then still raging on the Continent, and battling ships in the seas, he might have sailed on.

He sat beside her on the settee. His legs, so much longer than hers, folded more sharply; he couldn't help pressing one against hers as he turned close enough to begin untangling the swathes of hair.

But Viola didn't jump, or lean away.

Why did he keep expecting her to be shy? She'd *kidnapped* him.

Gently he plucked at the silver beads. They were wound now in silky strands of hair so dark they were hard to see. Tugging on the hair, though, released everything easily. Viola's hair was so smooth it didn't catch on itself; it was just so long that it wound around everything within its grasp.

Lee pulled a strand of hair to one side. Keeping it out of the mess while he untangled more, he realized, would be the key task.

"We need a comb."

Why had he said that? In the dark, the *we* felt suspenseful, meaningful.

He realized he hadn't said *we* to anyone but a soldier in a long, long time.

Viola didn't seem to feel the weight of the word as he did. She only turned her head a little. "I haven't one. Not a comb or a stocking. I did bring some money. I should have perhaps packed better for an elopement. But I didn't want anyone to sense it coming."

"Not even Miss Díaz?"

"Especially not. If the Duchess is angry, I did not want Miss Díaz to deserve it."

"Or were you worried she might dissuade you from your plan?"

Viola turned to look at him over her shoulder. "I would not be dissuaded."

Well, she was firm in her convictions. That was something she had in common with her brother. In fact, she might be firmer.

He lifted a strand of the dark hair that, once freed, hung well below her shoulder. Seeing it, she turned back, resuming her former position so he could work.

He'd vaguely thought it might be like grooming a horse. Horses had in the end proved too tame for him, but they'd been the start of his recovery from London, as he liked to think of it. An animal so large it couldn't be forced to do anything it didn't wish to do. He understood why some people feared them.

And rightly so. That first winter at Faircombe, learning how they raised horses for the gentry, Lee saw a man kicked by an angry horse. The blow stove in a rib or two. The man lived, but only just. He'd still been abed when spring had come and Lee decided to keep traveling north.

Untangling Viola's hair felt just as dangerous as haltering an angry horse, but he wasn't sure why. She wasn't angry.

Indeed, she weathered the small inevitable tugs and pulls stoically, making no noise.

That bothered him.

"So I must ask, Lady Viola. If you wouldn't ask Lord Callendar to ruin you, why not ask him to marry you? I'd bet a guinea Lady Cecily did just that."

She shrugged. "He's not a romantic, you know. Marriage is practical business. I have no political value, and he needs that."

"You're the sister of an earl."

"An earl who cannot be seen in society because he's slept with half the wives of the *ton*."

She kept surprising him. He kept on with his work. "You're not supposed to know that."

"Why not? I'm his *sister*." Her version of the word dripped with venom.

Lee had marched with Oliver through Napoleon's war for years, and drunk with him for many a month when they'd both returned; he well knew Oliver's opinion of his parents and it wouldn't surprise him if Viola shared it. But Viola's venom towards Oliver did surprise him. He'd never heard Oliver say anything chilly about Viola.

In fact, he'd never heard Oliver mention Viola at all.

He tried to pick his next words as carefully as he picked strands of hair from the chain of silver beads. A black silk string, he discovered, had been used to tie twists of hair in place; he picked at that too. "Losing your eldest brother hit him hard, I assure you."

She was peculiarly cool about it. "I'm sure it did. Oscar's existence meant Oliver could do as he pleased. Oliver never wanted to be the heir. Still doesn't, I suspect, though he has the title now. But I'm afraid it didn't affect me the same way."

"Oscar's existence, or his loss?"

"Either. Oscar felt about me just as Oliver and Victor still do. We were told sisters aren't supposed to tumble about in the nursery with boys, or explore the world out of doors. I am a sister, and therefore a stranger."

That didn't sound like Oliver. He'd slept with any and every woman he cared to. He wasn't frightened of women.

Then Lee remembered how out of his depth Oliver had been when he'd fallen in love with his wife and taken leave of his mistress, and how bitter the mistress had been... to Oliver's shock. Oliver might not be frightened of women, but neither did he understand them.

Well, who did?

"You're a lady, of age, and part of a Duchess' court," Lee reminded her unnecessarily. A braid that had been tucked behind the string fell loose and unraveled in his fingers.

"I was my mother's property, and will be again if she gets her way," Viola said, and these words weren't venomous, they shook.

He fought the impulse to take her in his arms and steady her.

If he were to escape this mess at all, he ought not even to touch her.

Though he already was, her hair's silken strands slipping through his fingers and against his skin as softly as any kiss.

And she needed a hug.

He hadn't done it when they were atop the carriage; he hadn't done it when he'd rushed her into the hotel. She'd taken some blows, even if only to the mind, and they'd shaken her, and he hadn't steadied her. It had nothing to do with fragility; a person needed steadying when they took a blow.

But it would only draw him deeper into her dangerous plan if he pulled her into his arms.

Slowly, as if to a dangerous horse, Lee put his hands on her shoulders, and squeezed a little.

Her response was explosive. She shuddered and surged backward into him, practically thumping against his chest. Relaxed all over, as if the heat of his body had melted her spine.

And sighed as she rested her still-tangled head back against his chest.

It was like holding a wild bird that had all in an instant decided to trust him.

She had no way of knowing how he loved, *craved* that sensation. She couldn't possibly know how, as he had worked his way north, he'd found a wounded wild hawk.

He'd spent a month that winter living in an abandoned cottage in the Pennines, letting his clothes grow ragged and losing a stone in weight as he nursed that kite hawk back to health. It had been in some fight, with no official there to record whether it had won or lost, and it had been slashed across its chest by some claw, almost to the heart.

In the battlefields of Europe, he'd seen men fall in every direction, their bodies mangled every way. There was nothing he could do for them. Oliver, who traveled with their regiment as surgeon, could barely do more.

Lee hadn't been able to save most of them, or the wife he'd left behind.

But he saved that hawk.

Its wildness had not changed. He'd barely kept it alive in the shed, barely touched it; when it healed it took wing, without hesitation, and flew away. He only had the comfort of knowing he had fed it as well as he could, giving it sections of hares he perhaps should have eaten himself. He'd ridden on, telling himself that he'd made that hawk as whole as he could before it took the leap back into its own life.

He'd had that sensation many times since.

He had it now.

"Viola." He couldn't *lady* her, not when she pressed against him like this, so soft, her hair smelling of candlelight and night clouds. "You are no one's property. Oliver wouldn't let your mother *take* you against your will."

"He's done it before, and he would again if it saved him any trouble. She's very unpleasant when she doesn't get her way."

That matched Oliver's reports of their mother. Both parents had raked Oliver over the coals when he'd proposed to marry Cass, even knowing she was the love of his life.

"Your father's gone, and Oliver is the Earl. Surely that makes a difference."

"Mr. Waite," said Viola, a little incongruously as she still leaned full against his chest. "Oliver thinks first and foremost of Oliver. Our father left my raising to my mother, and Oliver will follow in his footsteps to keep the peace with her."

"Has he said so?"

"I won't give him the chance. I must be safely married, and it can't be to Lord Callendar. He has one thing in common with Oliver: he is most interested by a married woman."

Lee was beginning to glimpse how Viola's peculiar viewpoint had given her a slightly twisted impression of relations between men and women. "I won't deny Lord Callendar has entered into a marriage bargain without being moved by passion. It would be hard to imagine anyone passionate about Lady Cecily." In his arms, unbelievably, Viola snorted. Lee refused to let that delight him. "Nor can I claim Oliver has stayed away from married ladies." Stay away from them? He used to collect them like silver spoons. "But that isn't the nature of marriage in general."

"I think you're wrong. I had a year, you know, to watch

every marriage in London. Marriages are very light ties within which alliances come and go."

"Some married people are in love, surely." Whatever was broken in him couldn't be broken in everyone.

"Love doesn't last. How long will the Duke and Duchess feel so passionately for one another? Who does, after a decade or two of marriage? Lord and Lady Ayles are the closest pair I know, and that is because their shared passion is politics. Other than Their Graces, I know of no love affairs within marriages. The Prince is furious with his past lover because he had to give her up—hardly fair—and loathes his wife. The Duchess of Oakland surely knows her husband sired children by someone else. If my parents ever loved each other, I never saw it. Love and marriage are two distinctly different endeavors. I want a taste of passion before it's too late."

He'd thought her feelings childish, but hers was as cool and clear-eyed an assessment as he'd ever heard.

Nor did he have an argument for her. He'd seen few marriages in his life, but he'd spent long months at Fair-combe Hall, and its marquess was a horror, as had been his marriage.

Seen her way, her actions made more sense, though he still didn't understand why she felt so pressed for time.

"So you intend to marry me and find love where you can."

"I suppose we both will," she said with the sort of wistful-ness little children used when their paper boats sailed out of sight.

What an odd collection of ideas she was.

"I don't think you mean that." Purposefully, he closed his arms around her. The soft swells of her shape fit far too easily against his body, into his arms made around her shoul-ders, around her waist. Faced with the reality of a man's embrace, he expected her to struggle.

She didn't.

No, if anything, she only wriggled closer to him, stealing his warmth, apparently.

He took it farther, leaning forward to brush his lips against the shell of her ear, pale in the moonlight.

"I don't think you mean to lie in your husband's arms, and then march off to a lover," he whispered against her smooth skin.

"No, that sounds quite uncouth." She sounded a little breathless now, but she wasn't cold. "But why not after a companionable period of time? All the lovers in London are constantly changing partners, as if in a dance. Why shouldn't any woman plan to do the same?"

"Because men imagine women share the soft feelings we hide even from ourselves." Lee didn't know where the words came from; the thoughts felt even more strange. Viola pulled those words out of him, from somewhere he hadn't known they lay in wait. "Like falcons who mate for life, building a nest together, hunting together, sharing whatever they have for as long as they have."

"Oh, dear." Viola twisted in his arms, her dark eyes only inches away looking into his. "Is that how you felt about your wife?"

* * *

OF COURSE she would make a hash of this. She'd found the one sentimental man in Britain to entrap.

She could make herself brave by simply doing brave things. Speaking to him in the dark. Sitting by him.

Shoving herself against him when she felt lonely and cold.

None of those were part of her plan except that she must not be shy of him. She couldn't trap a man into marrying her and then hold him at arm's length.

But this had gone so far in the opposite direction of shy that there were no words for how forward she was being.

Still she felt encouraged, because his arms around her were the refutation of his own argument.

Because Viola loved Lord Callendar, knew that with every inch of her, had loved him for months. Yet Mr. Waite's arms warmed her twice: once with their own heat, emanating from him like a fire in the coal grate, and once from the way they made her heart pound and forced her blood to race through her veins faster than it ever had before.

She couldn't love one man and feel this way in the arms of another unless this was purely a physical response. A natural, animal response.

Oliver had done little to protect her during their childhood or after, but when he'd returned from his medical studies in Scotland he'd pulled her aside and explained exactly how babies occurred.

When she'd asked him why, he'd said grimly that he'd seen too many women have miserable lives—and deaths—because they didn't understand what was happening till it was too late.

Truthfully, Viola had thought she could put aside questions of children till much later. But now, so much closer to Mr. Waite than she had expected to be, those thoughts surged in on her. She wanted to talk about them. Now.

But not till he answered her question about his wife.

CHAPTER 5

$\mathcal{M}$r. Waite sighed a little, and Viola had to tamp down a visceral response even to the sound. She wanted to experience everything there was to passion, wanted to indulge in Lord Callendar the way one indulged in a box of candies. She'd assumed her wifely duties with Mr. Waite wouldn't be unpleasant, and left it at that.

But his breath against her ear had set peculiar pricklings racing up and down her skin, chasing each other like a lightning storm around every part of her body in ways she hadn't imagined when she'd touched herself and imagined being in Jonas' arms.

Far from cold, she now felt hot, and far too conscious of the rough linen of her shift against her breasts. She also felt hungry, and confused, and most of all wanted him to do that again.

Given all this contradicting information, she supposed they should settle the question of children sooner rather than later.

Yet even more, she wanted to know about his past wife.

"My wife—" He seemed lost as to how to continue.

The pain he clearly felt over her loss was almost all Viola had to know. He must have loved her. He still grieved her. No wonder he had approached the process of finding a new wife so gingerly.

But he surprised her.

"My marriage might be a support for your argument," he admitted to her, and raised his hand close to her face. Viola almost leaned into his palm before she realized he was only reaching to untangle strands of hair there.

Viola's maid was practically-minded except for her mania for intricate hairstyles. At Viola's request, she refrained from cutting Viola's hair for the Grecian styles of the day, no doubt recognizing the fruitlessness of trying to curl it. Instead, she managed to get the whole mass to form fantastic shapes using tortoise shell hair pins and silk string, and usually took half an hour to get the whole thing down again when an evening was over.

Why hadn't Viola even planned for her own hair before taking this leap?

She hadn't had a choice. She might not have had another evening like this one, with Lord Callendar and Mr. Waite in the same place. She'd wanted to abscond with Mr. Waite, but foolishly, she had wanted Jonas to see it.

Wanted him to think of her as a desirable woman, even if it had to be reflected in another man's eyes.

For the first time Viola realized that she had assumed that was Jonas' quirk. That he had desired the Duchess of Talbourne because her husband had wanted her first. She understood that; she'd seen enough to find a man attractive when he smiled at his wife. It only made sense.

Now she thought, for the first time, that she might have made a mistake.

"Your wife was faithful to you."

"Yes." He didn't add *of course* but Viola could hear it.

"She loved you."

"Yes, she did."

"And you loved—"

"I believed in her, harder than I've ever believed in anyone."

Viola thought that was an odd way to put it, but Mr. Waite did not give her time for questions.

He went on, "I should have stayed with her, but I wanted to save Britain from Napoleon, so I marched away and left her there." He looked angry, his brows drawing together, but Viola knew it wasn't with her.

"Oh, no." Viola could see other people's interests well enough to help the Duchess; why hadn't she guessed better at Mr. Waite's? "And she died? Oh, no. It wasn't because of a child?"

"No, far worse. She had a child, and lived."

He clearly had no intention of saying more, even to someone only inches away. Viola didn't ask. But she knew the difficulty of needing things one could not say. She put her hand on his where it lay against her hip.

Apparently that was all it took.

"She had a perfectly healthy little girl, and the two of them were just fine, and I congratulated myself on the arrangement of my life. I'd defeat Napoleon on the battlefield and go marching home to them. I was *happy* about it." He swallowed, and even in the near dark she saw a number of wild emotions chase each other across his face—revulsion, horror, despair. "When they both caught fever the following spring I thought nothing of it. Winter was the danger, not spring. Just a fever. Just a... I didn't get another letter from her; the housekeeper wrote that she died. They died."

"Oh, no."

"It was my fault for leaving her." He wasn't looking at her, or anything around them; only deep into the past, perhaps.

"Battles are a hellscape, they didn't need me there. I should have deserted my post and gone home."

"You would have been hanged as a traitor. Or shot." Viola didn't know which, but she knew what happened to traitors.

"My point is…" He blinked, and he was back in the room with her. Viola had the feeling he could have said much more, about a great many things. All he said was, "It was no great romance."

There was nothing else to say. Viola couldn't even weave his story into what she knew about men and women in general. There was nothing general about this. It was *him. His* life, and she hadn't known anything about it.

He wasn't meeting her eyes now; just looking down at their hands overlapping.

"I came home too late, and drank myself into a stupor. Oliver might be a poor brother, but he is an excellent drinking companion. He always arrived at the club with a story to tell. It took him months to suggest that if I drank much more, I might never get out of that chair."

"He said that?" So callous.

"Not in so many words. He invited me to a country party. Support, you know. For his, well, for Cass to meet your parents."

"That was for his benefit, not yours." The wave of fury Viola felt shocked her. It was one thing for Oliver to ignore her; that felt normal, if chilly. It was another for him to ignore the suffering of the comrade-in-arms right in front of him.

"Likely so." Mr. Waite's lean face twisted in a little half-smile. "It still saved my life."

Well, that was Oliver. He did save lives. Just not hers.

One thing was clear from Mr. Waite's story. "You wanted the little girl you never got to meet."

His blue eyes in the moonlight were suddenly on her, wide, too bright, and wild. "Desperately."

"You'd welcome more children, then."

"Lady Viola." He pulled back from her, putting more space between them and taking his hand away from hers; she felt cold again. "You've been admirably frank, so I won't lie. I'd welcome your children, *any* children, more than anything else in the world. That was the main reason I sought another wife. And honestly, I'd prefer a wife who didn't care about me too deeply, as that sort of passion isn't in me. But it won't be you."

"Because I'm not sturdy. But I can be!" He'd just complimented her frankness, and Viola gave him a lie in return. She wasn't physically fragile, but she would fall ill again one day, she knew she would, with the mysterious heavy blank emptiness that settled over her from time to time.

She didn't want to tell Mr. Waite about her illness. She hadn't been ill all year, not since her bout at Talbourne House last spring. Perhaps she would not again. Perhaps she'd finally outgrown it.

He might have revealed an illness of his own by telling her about the effects on him of liquor, but clearly that was his only infirmity, and she did not feel brave enough to do the same in return.

"Lady Viola, you... are surprisingly sturdy in ways I would not have guessed." He moved farther away, a foot, then two, the space between them growing. His eyes had lost that wild look that had been nearly frightening in the dark. "But I live deep in the country, and you plan a life in London. That won't suit me. I'm sure the children you bear will be fine ones, but my children won't grow up in London either. They'll run wild through the trees till the soles of their feet grow callused, they will learn not to be frightened of spiders or snakes, and they will never once wonder why they've been left to struggle through life alone..."

"...because their mother loves a man somewhere else," she finished his sentence for him.

Seen his way, it was impossible to refute. Such a childhood sounded glorious to Viola; not the spiders and snakes, but never being alone. She couldn't deny children should have that; nor could she promise to provide it, since her true purpose was to remain near Lord Callendar.

She had gambled and lost.

But if Viola had learned anything from playing endless games of cards at Talbourne House with all sorts of players, it was how to lose gracefully.

She had miscalculated. So be it. The deed was still done; she was still compromised. She had cut herself off from so-called good society; she still had the rest of the world to discover.

If she starved to death in an alleyway, it would still be better than being at Morland with her mother, and she still might have a chance at her dream of being Lord Callendar's *paramour*. As long as her mother didn't have her imprisoned, she could wait. A little.

None of those things were Mr. Waite's problem.

"I've inconvenienced you far too much," she said formally to him, as if they sat in a candlelit parlor. "And I apologize, Mr. Waite. For luring you into the carriage; for all of it. You've done me only good service in return, rescuing me twice, and I thank you."

He didn't acknowledge that her speech sounded like a leave-taking; that much was obvious.

She thought for a moment that he hadn't heard her; he reached across the space between them, and she hoped for a wild second that he would take her in his arms again. *She* wanted not to struggle through life alone, not anymore. She hadn't known how much she'd wanted that till tonight. That was another favor he'd done for her.

But he didn't hold her again; only reached past her with one of his long arms to take up the knife on the plate of cheese. With a swift, sure motion, he used it to cut the silk thread still tangled in her hair.

He released its heavy curtain. The locks fell all around her face, those still in twists or braids unraveling.

Viola felt bare, seen. She picked up the nearly invisible silk thread, and stood. "Sleep well, sir. I won't trouble you again."

And slipped away into the room with the bed without looking back.

* * *

LEE HAD no right to fall asleep.

Trouble seemed to follow Lady Viola wherever she went. Like a wounded hawk, she needed a little help, and tonight, for better or worse, that was him.

Sliding his key into the door's lock, he put his hand on the knob. He could go out. It would be dawn in a few hours.

But what for? Where would he go? To do what?

The lady had distracted him from that nagging thirst that never entirely left him, not for liquor, but for numbness.

And absent that driving thirst, there was nothing out there he needed. That was rather the point of the conversation they'd just had.

He went back and leaned into the settee, one leg sprawling off the thing, and knowing that Viola was safe abed, he fell asleep.

* * *

VIOLA ONLY SLEPT another hour or two. When she woke, it was still dark out. But the air felt warmer, and she imagined it was not only from the fire in the little grate.

She ought to have felt hopeless, looking out of her window over the hulking great mass of overgrown greenery in the park.

She didn't. Right at this moment, she could still choose how to feel. She decided she felt *marvelous.*

It was the first adventure she'd ever chosen for herself, and it was going well, thanks to Mr. Waite.

Yes, she'd lost, but she'd learned how to do that. She'd also learned how to exchange coins for bank-notes, which were light enough to carry. The Duchess' little gifts of pocket money would go far, if she were wise with them.

She lacked both a husband and a comb; but she had bank-notes in her purse, and the day ahead was *hers.* She could do whatever she liked with it. She had no one to please, not even Virginia or Her Grace.

Swiftly her fingers wove the heavy weight of her hair into a messy plait. It was all she could do.

The cut silk thread lay on the marble-topped table beside the bed.

Viola picked it up, rolled it in her fingers before winding it around the end of her hair. That thread felt portentous. Mr. Waite had set her free, in more ways than one. She knew so much more now than she had the night before. As a potential husband, he was a poor choice; but she'd never regret it.

She'd been a little afraid that the reality of a man's body would be less alluring than she'd imagined. It wasn't. Mr. Waite had been quite alluring, so much so that her veins still hummed with the memory of his warmth.

Women of the *ton* gossiped, and for almost a year gossip had been her whole occupation. Selene, the Duchess of

Talbourne, needed gossip for what she did, and Viola had gathered it assiduously. Plenty of London women despised the marital bed. But plenty did not. Viola had suspected herself one of the latter sort, and she'd been right.

It felt more than reassuring. She felt whole, and for the first time, like she fit the right pattern of a woman.

Naturally, she'd felt sheltered by Lord Callendar's arms as he'd carried her out of Talbourne House on that fateful night. Naturally, she'd loved to look at him, imagining him ever closer as she touched herself and discovered the sensations of pure pleasure of which she was capable. She was not a creature of defects, not altogether; she was a perfectly average mortal being.

Perhaps she'd finally learned how not to hear her mother's sermons. She'd certainly mastered ignoring the ones from pulpits, as did everyone else in London, as far as she could tell. Morals only interested her as practical methods to avoid hurting others, and that was Viola's true compass; she had a horror of hurting others.

She'd hurt Mr. Waite by forcing him to recall memories of the little girl and wife he'd lost. She didn't need to dig deeper to clarify whether he'd loved them too much, or not enough. No one should be in so much pain. She knew that first-hand.

She could make that better by freeing him of the burden of her.

Silently she opened the door between their two chambers. The man sprawled on the settee, finally asleep. He looked younger asleep, even with such long arms and legs tossed any-which-way across the sofa. She noticed again the sunny golden tinge to his hair. It had faded, after a winter within doors; but it was there.

The only sentimental man in Britain. He'd had a first love; he'd have another. It was all right that it wouldn't be her. She had taken him for a heavier clod of a creature; that was her mistake, and she was sorry for it. He already had to deal with a stolen carriage because of her, and likely would not be invited to any more drawing rooms; she shouldn't inconvenience him further.

Peeking into her purse, Viola realized she had no idea if a pound note was too much or too little to pay for the hotel.

There was so much to discover. She had no comb, and still wore the evening gown from the night before, now sadly rumpled. But she had intentions, and though they weren't exactly going well, she would march on.

If she had one great skill, it was not giving up.

Leaving one of the folded banknotes upon a table near Mr. Waite's head, Viola silently crept to the door. He'd left the key in the lock. Slowly she turned it, grateful it was well-oiled and betrayed its unlocking only with a slight *click*; without waking him, she slipped out and was gone.

* * *

In her movements from her parents' house, to her cousin's house at Northfell, to Talbourne House, Viola had not appreciated the dangers of travel.

The night before had educated her. Like learning to lose, she remembered lessons.

She stayed keenly aware of her surroundings and hoped not to be noticed as she sailed past a maid dusting one of the hotel's sitting rooms.

At the front door, she carefully peered out before venturing forth.

There were charwomen on the pavements already, carrying buckets to do work somewhere, and dustmen with hand-carts full of rattling tools. All kinds of men in rough clothes, even some footmen rushing past in white old-fashioned wigs, and maids tightly wrapped in shawls carrying baskets for shopping.

There was a whole world out there as the sky began to glow with impending sunlight, even through the clouds.

Viola felt awkward in her light gown, bare arms showing above her gloves, but as there was nothing to do about it, she pretended to ignore it, behaving as if her muff covered all of her and she was hiding behind it. She walked quickly down the side of the Square to the grand house on the corner they'd passed the night before.

She'd never been there, but had committed its direction to memory. She knew the lady of the house, distantly, and had some hopes of asking a favor.

It would depend, though. She really must not inconvenience anyone else.

It felt awkward to use the heavy iron door-knocker in the chilly pre-dawn light. It was so cold it hurt her fingers, even through her gloves.

A tall, unfamiliar woman answered the door, one with golden hair plaited down the side of her neck like Viola's and a serviceable poplin dress a few shades darker. Her piercing green eyes gave the impression that she would brook no foolishness; or perhaps it was the set of her shoulders.

"I apologize for the early call," said Viola, a little breathless now that this was really happening. "I've come to call upon Lady Arnold, if she's in."

The woman's green eyes widened in surprise. "She is asleep." She seemed about to shut the door, then she noticed Viola's rumpled gown, too light for daytime, behind the all-encompassing muff. "Perhaps you'd like to come in and wait?"

"Thank you, Mrs...?" Viola intended to be grateful to anyone who helped her on her journey.

"I'm Miss Bickering. A friend of Lady Arnold's. Come in, Lady Viola."

Startled, Viola stepped into the foyer, letting the other woman close the heavy door behind her. "My apologies. I don't recall when we met."

"No reason you should. I'm only a baker. You visited our shop with the Duchess of Talbourne. For my sisters and me, it was the greatest day of our lives." With that astonishing pronouncement, she gestured for Viola to precede her into a sitting room where a cozy fire burned in a fireplace; not coal, but crackling wood.

She followed Viola in, and without asking, opened a tin of little biscuits from the sideboard, setting them beside a heavy leather chair and waving Viola to take both.

Viola immediately considered her the loveliest person in the world, after Lord Callendar and Mr. Waite.

Viola nibbled a lemony little biscuit. "Of course I remember your shop. That's some of why I'm here. There are few pleasures in life greater than cake."

Miss Bickering's shrewd eyes took in every detail of her peculiar appointments. "Today you have no duchess, nor other ladies, and no carriage that I can see. They expect me at the bakery, but Lady Arnold may not rise for some time, and you can't wait. You'd better tell me what's the trouble."

CHAPTER 6

*L*ee woke to watery sunlight breaking over his face, which he scrubbed to full waking with cold fingers. His chin bore rough bristles, reminding him he had no equipment for shaving or anything else.

Only a stolen carriage in the stables and a runaway girl in the bedroom.

For it was clear Viola was just a girl who needed to run away from one of the most luxurious houses in England, for reasons he still didn't fully comprehend, and chose him to help her do it.

He hoped Oliver would see it that way. His friend was a great surgeon, but also too good a shot.

When he swept his arms out in a stretch, unkinking the knots in his back, he brushed something off the table by his head. He rolled to his feet and found it on the carpet.

A bank note.

A pound bank note.

He dashed to the bedroom door. It was open, and Viola was gone. She'd had nothing to take with her, and taken it all. The room held not a trace of her existence.

It was her utter disappearance that sparked something into life under his ribs, some sort of urgency, nearly a panic.

Viola *did* live, she had been here, last night had happened, and now she was gone.

Calm yourself. Of course she'd been here; no one could gainsay that. She'd been here, talked with him in the hours before dawn, and disappeared. Leaving him a pound note. As if he'd performed some service.

Well, a good servant didn't let their master simply wander away.

She couldn't have gotten far. She'd likely waited downstairs to give him privacy, that was all.

Shoving his hair back from his face and stuffing on his hat, Lee prepared to follow her.

* * *

But she wasn't downstairs.

A footman jumped forward. "Does the gentleman wish a carriage?"

Lee looked sharply at him to make sure it wasn't the villain from last night, then waved him off.

It didn't look that warm outside; the sunlight barely penetrated and even in the hotel's corridor the air had a wintry gloom, for all it was April. How far could she have gotten?

And more importantly, *why?*

Lee had rejected her plan the night before. Was it that simple? She'd asked him to marry her, in so many words, and he'd said no. Was that the reason she'd left before he was awake? And left him a pound note? Possible; she did have her convictions.

He couldn't say why the money bothered him so. There was the suggestion of it, that he was so poor he should be paid for his time. That only proved Lady Viola knew nothing about him, which also proved that she'd never discussed him with Oliver.

What bothered him more was the finality of it. That it was a good-bye, with no way to tell how long ago she'd gone.

He thrust the bank note into his pocket.

Letting the footman open the door for him, Lee set out to search the Square. There must be shop windows; he'd look in them. Hawk she might be, but she couldn't fly. He'd find her.

* * *

IT WASN'T AS easy as that.

Lee walked south to where they'd entered the square. There *were* no shops here, he realized as he passed door after door of grand houses built tightly together as London squares tended to be.

Livestock lowed as they were driven along the earthen street of the square, and donkeys pulled carts carrying the last of winter potatoes and cabbages.

On the flat stones of the pavement, nearly all the women seemed to be in service of some sort, mostly tight-buttoned maids, a few ladies in bright, looser skirts walking home after a night of their own kind of work. Gentlemen of all sorts bustled along with the women, or climbed into carriages that waited for them, some of them hackneys, reminding him he had a captured one.

Not that he cared about it, but that too reminded him of Viola.

Traversing the square's southern edge and starting up the western one, Lee wondered how he'd find her if she'd left the square. He hadn't asked enough questions. Why had he assumed she would give up her plan once thwarted?

He'd formed his own plan, to return her some way, any

way, to some house that wasn't his; but now that he thought over last night, he couldn't remember Viola ever agreeing to it.

She wasn't a wounded bird to be nursed back to health. She was a living, breathing woman with plans, who knew how to turn a key.

And had bank notes.

Lee squeezed the one she'd left in his pocket as he started up the west of the square, hurrying now.

"You haven't seen a lady in an evening gown?" he asked one old woman moving slower than the rest.

She stared at him from under her shawl, frowned, and pointed at one of the ladies of the evening.

"No, I mean a nicer one."

"Can't judge their quality by me," the woman said, her shoulders pulling away as if he were about to ask her something even ruder, and stalked away.

He'd try a man. "Excuse me. I've had charge of a young lady here in the square, and I've lost her."

"Bad job then, warden," said the young fellow with a grin, bobbing his head in an attempt to be genial as he hurried on.

The spot of panic under his ribs Lee had shoved down earlier was rising again. It was so much easier finding one particular creature in the wilderness, where no one purposefully disturbed the tracks.

There. That looked like a gentleman pulling on his gloves as he strode toward a smaller street leaving the square. "Sir. If I might trouble you for a moment." Lee should probably explain himself a little better if he wanted better results.

The gentleman paused, dark hair visible under the edge of his stovepipe hat. "I am in a hurry, sir. How may I be of service?"

It struck Lee that his choice of words should be more understandable. "I've lost sight of my wife, sir. She was lightly dressed this morning, and I'm worried for her in the cold."

"You have?" The fellow searched Lee with his eyes as if trying to judge if he were the sort of man who should be directed to a lost wife. "Visiting friends on the Square?"

The gentleman looked discerning; Lee thought he'd better hold off on more lies. "No, but we stopped at the hotel," he tilted his head toward the park and the hotel on the far side of it. "Thus my concern; she wished to shop, but she's not familiar with these streets."

"Not to worry," said the fellow, coming to some sort of decision in Lee's favor, "there's little shopping except at the north end where the prince's house used to be. Unless she's gone to Castle Street, she'd be near those shops. Perhaps at the bakery. I assure you it's warm."

Bakery! That was what Viola had said the night before. She'd picked this spot because she knew it had a hotel and a good bakery nearby.

"Thank you, sir," said Lee, tipping his hat and nearly running down the pavement on the only side of the square he hadn't yet surveyed.

* * *

LADIES' OWN BAKERY said the sign outside. Lee only glanced as he raced in. It was the largest shop on the square, and the moment he opened the door a gentle bell jingled above his head and a waft of warm air, smelling of bread and honey, billowed into his face.

This had to be it. Where else could she be?

He stopped himself from grabbing every woman in the place and turning her around to see her face. None of them were as tall and slender as Viola anyway. There were women of every age, shape and size, from the primmest starched maid to the most *louche* of evening ladies, but nowhere that dark head.

She hadn't even had anyone to dress her hair this morning. What must she look like?

As Lee stood in the center of the shop, eyes sweeping over the baskets of baked bread with loaves small and huge and everyone around him trying not to stare, a small woman in a large apron behind the counter asked, "May we serve you, sir?"

When another woman joined her, suspicion flashing in her eyes and gripping a long knife, Lee realized he was the only man in the shop. Perhaps he looked alarming.

She wasn't here. Where should he go? What could he do? He *had* to find her.

Then an inner door swung open, and there was Viola, laughing.

Laughing. Viola of the deep, dark eyes.

Her hair was simply plaited, and she wore a gray poplin day dress and a thick warm shawl. One hand, encased in a warm mitten, held up her skirts; they were too long.

"You have done an amazing job repairing the bakery, Miss Bickering, had you not convinced me the disaster was real I would have—"

She saw him.

Her eyes widened, and her smile faded a little.

Inwardly Lee cursed himself.

Whatever he wanted from life, whatever else he might be, he'd prefer to be someone who made Lady Viola smile.

"Mr. Waite." Then she did smile again, a broader smile, and Lee breathed with better cheer.

The woman beside her, even taller than her and with a golden plait like Viola's dark one, turned and surveyed Mr. Waite from the bottom of his shoes to the top of his hat. She looked unimpressed. "You know this man?"

Viola just stood there, smiling, and Lee felt himself smile too.

"*Do* you know this man?" he asked softly, heedless of the way all the women in the shop were now openly staring at him.

* * *

Viola hadn't expected Miss Bickering to take such thorough charge of her, showing her to a washroom, loaning her clean linens and a walking dress more suited to the day, even providing her with a shawl and mittens.

"Lady Arnold is not yet stirring," Miss Bickering said, somewhat fondly, "and I must go to the bakery. If you'd like, do come."

Going through the motions of an average morning for people who did not stay up playing cards until dawn, Viola was struck for the first time with how brazen she had been the night before. Had that really been her, letting Mr. Waite undress her hair and leaning in to him that way?

No wonder he hadn't agreed to her plan. What a light-skirt she must have seemed, professing her love for one man and taking such liberties with another. Perhaps she was one! She hadn't intended to be, only wished to make the impossible possible.

Maybe one shouldn't wish for impossible things.

In its own way, all the attention from Miss Bickering was balm for Viola's embarrassment. She was used to being in the background while people fawned over the Duchess, but all Miss Bickering's attention, and offers of cakes, was now on her. It was overwhelming, but reassuring too, reminding Viola that she could garner attention for something other than climbing into carriages with strange men.

She agreed that accompanying her hostess to the bakery

was the best plan. As awkward as she felt, it would only be more awkward to await a surprised Lady Arnold in her drawing room.

The maids and footmen curtsied as she passed, and Viola just bobbed her head in return, feeling very much the guest following along in Miss Bickering's wake.

The memory of their short cold walk was instantly banished by the wave of warmth that greeted her at the bakery. There was not only the delicious smell of browned bread and cakes, but three more Misses Bickering to fuss over her and tell her how glad they were to see her again.

She remembered Lady Arnold's glorious *découpage* vase; it still stood in its niche overseeing all the bakery activity, glowing with bright floral colors against its deep black lacquer. She'd thought it art; Virginia, always more romantic, thought it a sign of someone's love.

After Miss Jane and Miss Rose—who seemed to be Mrs. Russell now—promised to cut her some nice bread to take with her, the tallest Miss Bickering, whom Viola now remembered was called Emery, took her back to see Anna, the oldest, in the bakery proper.

In the bustling hot bakery itself, heat emanated from the largest oven; a smaller one towards the back sat a bit crooked on its pedestal. Across the ceiling stabbed pointed black streaks of soot; they gave the clean bakery a dangerous look. Viola thought they only made it seem more exciting.

There was so much life happening outside her prescribed rounds of evening affairs and social calls. She'd traveled more than many women, from Morland in the country to Northfell and then to London, and she'd still seen nothing, nothing of life. This bakery was teeming with life.

She'd set in her mind that she'd be a practical wife in poor apartments somewhere, or, as it seemed likely now, a mistress in even poorer apartments, before she would give up entirely on enjoying Lord Callendar's company. She'd thought those were the only lives to lead, cool-headed wife or starving mistress. Every woman here had a different life, and Viola could only guess at the details of any of them.

Anna Bickering, round and sweet as one of her cakes, dried her hands on her apron and rushed forward. "Lady Viola! Another surprise visit! We had no idea. Yes, the ceiling has marks from a fire we've suffered, but all is well now."

"Lady Viola came to call on Lady Arnold, and I brought her with me rather than leaving her to the mercies of the house."

"If you are awake, madam, we love to have you!" Anna curtsied with floury hands gripping her skirts and apron. "But we have nowhere fine enough for you to sit and be entertained! And I'm afraid that's nothing to do with the fire. We just don't have guests. Emery, take her ladyship upstairs—"

Viola couldn't bear disturbing one more person. "Please don't! You have so much work to do; don't let me distract you from it. Unless I can help you?"

Anna and Emery looked at each other past Viola. "*Can* you make bread, Lady Viola?" businesslike Emery asked.

"I could learn!"

"We would love to have another apprentice," Anna said most politely, "but... don't you live at Talbourne House?" Then she clapped her floury hands, dusting herself with white. "Or have you married? You live nearby?"

"No. Must I be married? I thought—"

"No no, not to *work!* Not in *our* bakery," Anna rushed to reassure. "We only thought, well, your life is very grand! You're a *lady.* It's not the kind of life one exchanges for being a baker." She looked toward her sister. "It's quite hard work."

Awkwardly, Viola wondered how to explain her situation. She was no longer from *any* fine house, nor would any be open to her henceforth. She must find her way in the world somehow, and the banknotes in her purse would only go so far.

She'd made her bed and must lie in it.

"My life is not so grand anymore." Her words were quiet.

In the noise of the bakery—for several men, a large boy, and another woman were all engaged in various tasks at the tables—the sisters seemed to grasp that all was not quite well with Lady Viola. "You had better plan on a long visit with Lady Arnold," Emery said with the same air of propriety with which she'd opened that grand house door. "She'll like that. And of course you're welcome to visit here. Ladies' Own Bakery is for all women, even when they're a bit lost. You aren't, are you?"

"I believe I am, and delighted to be so," Viola admitted, even as she let Emery gesture her back toward the door. She was still determined to take what she wanted, if it were at all possible without hurting anyone, and to enjoy what she got.

That included the delightful, and very different, company of ladies like these.

"Well. Everything will be all right. Let Lady Arnold feed you for a little while, and if you decide to try it, you'll be sturdy enough to bake bread," Anna assured her as Viola followed Emery toward the door. The big boy behind them thumped a massive tub of bread dough out onto the table as if to emphasize the point, and began kneading with shoulders as wide and gnarled as a tree trunk.

Viola just laughed. "I'll eat anything she suggests if it makes me look sturdier."

Her gaze swept over all the women waiting in the bakery shop as she stepped into it. Many wore evidence of their trade: chandlers with wax streaks on their skirts, one a collier bearing coal dust, a dressmaker with long pins thrust through the front of her gown. There were no signs of the fire here. "You have done an amazing job repairing the bakery, Miss Bickering, had you not convinced me the disaster was real I would have—"

Mr. Waite stood in the center of the shop, shocking Viola into silence, so tall it seemed his head would brush the ceiling, and looking only at her. Viola felt herself say his name.

Her stomach fell. She'd already put him to so much trouble. If there was one thing she'd known since the nursery, it was that she caused everyone way too much trouble. When she was lively she was never satisfied, and when she was ill she was useless.

Then Viola pushed away the words that had crowded into her head. Those were her mother's words. Lord Callendar had never said anything like them; neither had Mr. Waite.

And Mr. Waite was *here*.

"You know this man?" Miss Emery looked a bit distrustful of large men appearing in her shop.

Viola realized that at this moment, she could do anything. If she denounced Mr. Waite, she had a feeling he would be put out by all the women around her instantly. He was quite at her mercy.

And had placed himself there again after all the unfortunate adventures of the night before.

"*Do* you know this man?" he asked her, his hat in his hand and his soft eyes on her, as if only the two of them were in the room.

"A little," she said, feeling her smile chasing around to show itself again.

"Then perhaps you'd let me escort you somewhere we might talk?"

Viola's smile faltered. He wanted to persuade her to go to Oliver's house. Or Talbourne House. Either way, she'd be out of his pocket.

But once again he seemed to hear what she was thinking.

"Wherever we go from here," Mr. Waite said, leaning toward her as if only she could hear when every woman in the place was watching him raptly, "I feel we ought to agree. Our fates, you might say, have become intertwined."

"Oh, I do like that," said one of the women, poking her neighbor with her shopping basket. "Intertwined fates. That's good, hey?"

"Mrs. Coxson, do you want a tuppence loaf?" the dark-haired Miss Bickering at the counter asked a little sharply.

"I must let you go on about your business." Viola felt a little breathless again at the thought of walking out with Mr. Waite. She had put him behind her, and ventured on, and discovered many new things already. If she wanted to see what else life had to offer, she ought to go on without him; but it surprised her, how happy she was that he was here.

"We've packed you some food," said little Mrs. Russell, patting a napkin bundle beside her nearly as high as she was. "Nothing fancy, only what we have. You must take it with you."

Mr. Waite leaned over the counter, making it look small, and gave the sisters a nod. "Thank you kindly."

Mrs. Russell, who was blind, didn't respond, but the dark-haired sister gave him the tiniest nod in return.

Then he offered his arm to Viola.

She hesitated, just the barest second. He noticed.

"Only if you're willing," he said, with that intensity that made Viola feel as if she were the only woman in the room.

She took his arm and walked with him to the door, letting him open it for her.

Walking into the raw, cold air outside felt like traveling from one world into another.

It was wonderful.

They walked through the crowd towards Jacquier's Hotel, only halfway down the square. He leaned down to speak with her, keeping their conversation between only them. "Shall we return to the hotel?"

Viola eyed the packed napkin swinging from his fingers. "I'm so hungry."

That wasn't an answer to his question, but Viola wasn't sure what to say. What kind of woman did he consider her to be, after a night like last night? She wasn't ashamed of taking action; action had to be taken. But she wasn't inclined to sing from the rooftops about the way she'd fallen into his arms, either.

She'd taken too much already, and the only thing she had a right to enjoy would be the bread.

Mr. Waite sensed her hesitation. "If we return to the hotel room, you can devour your entire napkin of treats undisturbed while we decide what to do next."

That made Viola feel even warmer than the loan of Miss Bickering's poplin gown. "We?" she said, glancing up at him.

"Yes." He didn't hesitate.

All her life Viola had wanted to be a *we*. Her brothers had been a *we* of their own, and in a different way so had her parents. The Duchess and Virginia had been her *we*, but this *we* felt intimate.

Important.

"But you must be hungry too!" she exclaimed. "We ought to—"

Viola's words stopped dead. So did her feet.

Mr. Waite stopped with her.

There, standing in front of them on the pavement, was the Earl of Rawleigh, previously known as Dr. Burke.

Oliver. Viola's brother.

CHAPTER 7

"What are you doing?" No greeting, just the blurted question.

Given the circumstances, Oliver couldn't be expected to say much else. Viola just wasn't sure which one of them he was addressing.

His turquoise-blue eyes—Viola had always been jealous of those eyes—flicked back and forth between Viola and Mr. Waite, taking in every detail of her borrowed, too-long dress, the napkin bundle in Mr. Waite's hand, and Viola's hand on his arm.

"What are *you* doing?" he said again, and Viola was sure this one was aimed at her. "And why are you doing it *here?*"

Viola felt suddenly ten years old again, trying to follow Oliver and Victor up a tree. They'd nailed planks to the wide trunks and climbed so high they'd disappeared in the green leaves. Viola had insisted she could climb as high as they, and Oliver's blue eyes had looked down out of the leaves at her and said, "No girls."

He gave her the same feeling now. She was in the wrong

place, at the wrong time, and not wanted. She had no idea what to say.

Fortunately, Mr. Waite did. "A morning walk, obviously."

"A morning walk. At this hour. In Leicester Square." Oliver gestured around to the mix of high and low society that was the bustling Square.

"Indeed."

Oliver wouldn't be dissuaded. "Viola, what have you done?"

"Odd," Mr. Waite went on, unperturbed, "most men at a moment like this would accuse me."

"I know you." Oliver dismissed Mr. Waite's whole existence with a brusque wave of his gloved hand.

"Do you, though?"

Mr. Waite's mild words just made Oliver stare at him. Viola watched both of them, wondering what would happen next, and noticing how much taller Mr. Waite was than her brother.

Not that she was truly afraid of Oliver, just... "I'm not going back."

"What *did* you do?" Oliver sounded as perturbed as he used to be with the little girl Viola had been.

But Viola wasn't a little girl. She was of age and then some, not that far from a quarter century, and she'd been maid in waiting to a fashionable duchess. She knew people all over society; she had been able to make her own choices, and she'd made them.

She only wished Oliver hadn't caught her at it.

It was all going too fast. She'd practically kidnapped Mr. Waite, then abandoned him this morning, only to have him trace her footsteps. She wasn't sure *what* she was doing any more. Only that she wanted to discuss it with Mr. Waite, not Oliver.

Which the gentleman beside her seemed to sense.

"We're otherwise engaged, Oliver," Mr. Waite said, just as calmly as last night while dispatching brigands in the street. "We'll call on you later."

"You'll call on me *now*."

"Aren't *you* otherwise engaged? You must have a reason to be here. I know it wasn't to visit your sister."

Oliver's eyes narrowed. With his long dark hair tied back in a queue, he looked old-fashioned and, for a distressing moment, too much like their late father. "A colleague is treating a patient using vital air. The man was in a fire; we've exchanged letters regarding his lungs. I wished to see the patient."

"Oh! Was it the bakery fire?" Those ladies were friends of hers. Nearly friends. Viola could speak about them.

Why did she feel she needed permission to speak?

"How do you know about the bakery fire?" Oliver wasn't a tempery man, but he looked like confusion would soon get the best of him.

Mr. Waite wasn't rattled at all. "And you've seen your patient?"

"Yes." Oliver wouldn't be distracted. "Viola, you should be at Talbourne House."

Mr. Waite's arm under hers, and his matter-of-fact treatment of her brother, gave Viola the strength to respond in the same spirit. "I'm not going back." She'd said the words once and Oliver had brushed them away. Like he always brushed away what she said. Today that would end. "As you can see, I've left, and I'm not going back."

"Where the devil are you going, then?"

"I'll thank you not to use language of that sort in front of the lady," Mr. Waite said just as mildly as he said everything else.

A large man, Viola saw, could be more menacing that way.

Though Mr. Waite wasn't large. He was slender through the body, though his shoulders were much wider than his narrow hips. He was lean and tall, that was all.

And Oliver wasn't cowed by him. But he appeared to be struck dumb.

Mr. Waite went on. "If your business is done, let us engage a hackney. Lady Viola and I would be happy to call upon you at home and explain all our decisions." He patted her hand on his arm, looking down into her eyes. "Wouldn't we?"

"We have a carriage, did you forget?" Viola reminded him. She didn't want to ride anywhere with Oliver; she didn't want to *talk* to Oliver.

But if she had to, apparently Mr. Waite would be with her.

"You have a *carriage?*" Oliver's voice was rising in pitch. As if he'd never imagined anything like his sister riding in a carriage with a gentleman. Certainly not just after dawn in Leicester Square where neither the gentleman nor Viola lived.

"I did forget." Mr. Waite's was a soft, gentle smile, one that said much with little movement, but made his large, fine eyes glow. Viola became lost in the smile. "We've an errand to run before we'll be free. It won't be for an hour. Maybe two."

"Then fetch your d—get your carriage," Oliver stopped himself from swearing, "and I'll see you at my home. You know my direction, I believe."

"Indeed," was all Mr. Waite said, tipping his hat to Oliver before walking on, Viola on his arm.

* * *

Lee hoped that if he didn't turn around, Viola wouldn't either.

He didn't, and she didn't.

Good. He didn't know what this business was with her family, but he intended to find out before this went any further. Before *anything* went any further.

"We'll have to leave the carriage with the Lord Justice then on to Oliver's. Can you drive a carriage, son?" he asked a passing youth with ears so wide they stuck out on both sides of his cap.

The young man stopped short at the question of work. "Sure can, sir!"

"Good man. Drive carefully and there's an extra shilling in it for you. Run ahead to Jacquier's and have them ready Mr. Waite's carriage."

"But Mr. Waite!" whispered Viola as the youth dashed off. "You told Oliver nothing about why we are here!"

"You'd rather I told him we were engaged in a nefarious plot to capture Lord Callendar's affections?"

The lady had no answer for that.

Feeling unaccountably pleased that he knew her secrets when her brother didn't, upon arriving at Jacquier's, Lee opened the door for her himself. Inside, he led her to a sitting room that faced the square, and closed the door.

She kept watching nervously about, as if expecting Oliver to leap out at her from behind the door.

Handing her down into a sofa and sitting beside her, Lee unknotted the napkin, spreading it on his knee.

There were indeed bread and butter sandwiches at the top of the packet, the finest white bread with its crust removed. He handed her one.

Absently Viola slid off her glove and took it. "But what if he..." She took a bite before she finished the sentence.

Then her eyes rolled heavenwards, eyelashes fluttering, and she made a tiny, obviously repressed moan.

Lee's attention was utterly captured.

She thought he was looking at her so intently for an explanation. She chewed and swallowed, daintily covering her mouth with one hand as she hurried to explain, "There's honey in them. You *must* try one."

He didn't want to try one. He wanted *hers.* If he kissed her now, he'd be able to taste it.

It was a visceral and all-absorbing reaction, the way he wanted to watch her bite into the soft, luscious bread, suppressing her sounds of pleasure and savoring the rich, sweet concoction with utter absorption.

That wasn't quite accurate. He would have preferred she not suppress her sounds.

"I happen to know," Lee told her, tearing his gaze away from her lips, "that your brother lives his own life. I doubt he's ever consulted you on his home, his profession, or his choice of wife."

"But you know ladies are expected to... you know, be guided by the men of their family."

"Lady Viola, you should know right now that I have no idea what ladies are expected to do with their family. I haven't one of my own."

"I'm so sorry about your wife and child."

"Thank you." The softness in her eyes was still soothing; Lee didn't mind her speaking about them, when he doubted it would be bearable from anyone else. "But I didn't mean them. I was orphaned quite young. I really don't know what families expect from one another. So you must tell me how yours distresses you."

"I'm terribly sorry to hear it, Mr. Waite."

He wished he hadn't said anything. She had so been enjoying herself, and now she'd stopped. "Don't stop eating."

"But who raised you?"

"People," he said shortly. "Please, Viola. Your brother?"

Viola swept a buttery crumb from her lip onto her

tongue, looking at him with wide eyes. "It's not Oliver's fault—"

"I'll be the judge of that."

"—It's just the way my family behaved. My father raised his sons, and they left me to my mother."

"Horrid, is she?"

"Well..." As if the honey and butter gave Viola strength, she straightened. "Yes, she is horrid. She wants her own way, in everything, and I always disappointed her. Always."

"And what does that matter now? You're of age, and you've left her home."

"I left her home several years ago. She sent me north to live with a cousin."

"Well then! What could possibly concern her now about anything you decide to do?"

"My father died last spring, and my mother says it's time I came home to care for her."

Lee didn't like how the glow in her faded when she spoke about her mother. There was more to the story than an overbearing woman, he was sure of that; but when he handled a wild animal, he didn't coax them to do more than they were willing to do.

Indeed, he'd far rather she eat the rest of her sandwiches.

Watching that was so engrossing that he could see himself doing it for a long while.

"Come," he told her as he saw their stolen carriage roll by on the pavement, "let us go for a drive."

* * *

Viola expected Mr. Waite to leave her in the entranceway, or even the carriage, while he dashed inside to conduct his business.

But no, he helped her down from the carriage and had

her on his arm all the way into the Lord Justice's marble-floored office.

How had he known she was curious to see inside the house of a Lord Justice?

"Waite." The gentleman came around his vast walnut desk, gesturing for Mr. Waite to take a chair, but only got a shake of the head in refusal. "To what do I owe the pleasant surprise?"

Mr. Waite explained in brief, precise words how they'd been attacked and the carriage came into their possession. "Sort it, won't you?"

"Of course," said the Lord Justice, and Viola had the impression that, like Oliver, this was an old friend of Mr. Waite's, the kind with whom conversation always began as if it had ended only yesterday. "You'll swear out your own complaint?"

"They got what they had coming. I'm done with it." Mr. Waite shrugged.

"Your habit of taking and leaving everything as you find it will turn back on you one day," their host said as he shook his formally-wigged head in disapproval. "Don't you think so, Mrs. Waite?"

Viola expected him to correct the gentleman; instead he only said, "Don't recruit my wife to your causes, Carter. She has quite enough to do already."

"Surely she already presides over the cause of *you*," the man said in a jovial way, giving Viola a little bow when they hadn't even yet been formally introduced.

Half of London would soon think Viola and Mr. Waite already married, and the other half would think them betrothed.

What else had Viola expected when she'd lured Mr. Waite into that carriage? Wasn't this what she had planned for all along?

She'd caused it without realizing how incredibly awkward it would feel. If she didn't marry him now, he'd have so many explanations to make, not just to people in the *ton* who would consider him the worst sort of rake, but also to his friends.

She hadn't expected him to have friends.

Which had been stupid. Of course he had friends; one of them was her brother.

"I do think Mr. Waite should take a bit more care with himself, yes," she told the gentleman, truthfully.

"Comes of no one taking care of him before."

Viola wanted to ask a great deal more, but Mr. Waite just turned to the door, her hand still on his arm. "All right, Carter. Give us the loan of your carriage today, and I'll put a roof over your head when next you visit."

"As if I'll ever travel as far as that wilderness you call home. My carriage happens to be waiting; I'll walk. Lovely to meet you, madam, and be well."

With that, Mr. Waite whisked her out as quickly as they had come in. Viola never even removed her bonnet.

"You didn't want me to talk to him, did you?" Viola wasn't ready to simply let go of the first insight into Mr. Waite that didn't come from his short words or her own observation.

"He's very long-winded."

True to the justice's word, his carriage was soon at the door. Mr. Waite handed her up into its spacious seats, far more comfortably upholstered than the shabby scene of the brigand's attack.

Viola rather missed that shabby carriage. "What does he know of you that you didn't wish me to learn?"

"Viola." As he settled back into the seat and the carriage began to roll, Viola realized that he seldom referred to her by title. It was unforgivably familiar, and yet an appropriate emblem of how deeply they'd become enmeshed in each other's affairs, so quickly. "I want to discuss something much more important."

"Which is?" Viola couldn't help but lean into him a bit eagerly.

"Something else is wrapped up at the bottom of this packet." He opened their napkin, which still held several sandwiches, and drew an oilcloth parcel from the bottom.

Unwrapping it revealed four generous slices of the Ladies' Own Bakery summery *gâteau Breton.* A luscious golden cake.

The heavenly aromas of butter, apricot, and honey filled the carriage.

"It's impossible to grasp that yesterday, I thought I could catch your attention by being a mysterious woman, when what you like is a woman who behaves like a piglet." Viola couldn't take her eyes off the diamond-striped cake.

"After a year in society you should know better." He broke off the tip of one of the cake slices, and before Viola knew what he was about, popped it into her open, waiting mouth. "Cake, mysterious women, they're all just pleasures of different sorts."

Some part of her thought he was trying to distract her from questions about their supposed marriage, or betrothal, or whatever it was they were doing; or about his past.

It worked.

* * *

BY THE TIME he reached Oliver's townhouse, two pieces of cake had vanished. Lee had a few bites, but most of them went to Lady Viola.

More accurately, *into* Lady Viola, and Lee was beginning to wonder if she looked so fragile because she'd never been fed.

One overbearing mother didn't seem enough reason for Viola's horror of her family. On the other hand, there were London ladies who'd married to escape less.

He had no intention of leaving Viola's side until he knew that she would be well without him; and he was beginning to think she might never be well without him.

Wild animals had no language to ask for help, but when desperate, sometimes threw themselves in a man's path. Viola seemed to have done the same.

The Lord Justice's carriage stopped at the end of a half-circle road full of respectable townhouses staring into one another from behind their iron fences and looking complacent.

Oliver opened his door himself. "What took you so long?"

"We had an errand." Again Lee handed Viola in first, but followed her immediately, putting her hand back on his arm. He preferred it that way, that was all. "Where shall we send the carriage?" The mews was too tiny for a carriage like this.

"Leave it in the road. You'd better come in." Oliver gestured to the parlor across from his wife's library.

Lee had visited this house many times before. He well knew the butler, who hovered over Oliver's shoulder. "Mr. Adams."

The fellow bowed, then waited for Oliver to let him do his job and take the guests' things.

Oliver didn't. The butler shrugged and went out, no doubt to arrange comfort for the carriage driver.

"I mean *you* come in here," Oliver said directly to Lee, with a purposeful jut of his jaw.

"I know." Lee didn't budge. He didn't just keep his temper from long practice with unpredictable adults.

In all the time he'd spent being tossed from one house to another, he'd developed a habit of being ready for anything, a habit that had stood him in good stead in battle. Oliver had been in many of those same battles. He should have expected no different.

It was interesting that Oliver expected something different just because it involved his sister.

Families were confounding.

"Then I'll speak to you first." Oliver turned to Viola.

Lee was afraid she might crumple. Under Oliver's gaze she was anything but the confident temptress of last night. Just being near her brother seemed to hunch her shoulders in the borrowed gown.

But no, she stayed right where she was, following Lee's example. "No, thank you," was all she said.

Lee wanted to cheer for her.

"Damn it, get in here, both of you." Oliver opened the door with one arm, the muscles in it showing clearly under the black wool of his coat.

Usually in Oliver's company, Lee had cause to consider his own lacks. He wasn't ugly; but any time both he and Oliver were around women, it was as though Lee disappeared into the wallpaper. His friend was, unfortunately, an extremely beautiful man, with a sculpted face and lips that could have been made of silk despite his oft-unshaven, dark-bristled chin. Under the gaze of those turquoise eyes, especially if Oliver let loose his dark waving hair, most women melted.

It was cheering to accompany a lady unmoved by Oliver's looks.

Indeed, as Lee pointedly walked in with Lady Viola on his arm, she didn't even look at Oliver, just took the center place on a wide green striped-silk sofa.

He took the place next to her, setting their napkin on the low table in front of him.

Then Viola, astonishingly, removed her gloves, leaned

forward to undo the napkin, and removed one of the bread and butter sandwiches to hand it to him.

She was right; drizzled with honey between its thickly buttered layers, fresh from the oven, it was delicious. Watching her dispense it right under Oliver's disbelieving eyes only made it taste better.

He chewed while Viola straightened and folded her hands on her lap, facing her brother. "I will not return to Morland, or to Talbourne House. In another day or two, once news reaches them, I doubt I'll be received at either." Some of her confidence faded as she hunched her shoulders a little and looked away. "Likely I'm already unwelcome at Talbourne House."

"What did you *do?*"

"I left Lady Lattishmore's house last night in Mr. Waite's company."

"What... alone?"

Viola's eyes flashed again with a little fire as she relished this part. "Quite alone."

"And someone saw you?"

"*Everyone* saw me."

"What the devil, Viola?" At Lee's glare, Oliver just sank, hands limply dangling between his knees, into the chair opposite. "I mean, honestly, what the devil?"

Before Lee could take issue with his language again, a tall lady with striking gray eyes swept in. "Mr. Waite!" She came straight toward him, her somber black linen gown rustling. She took one of his hands in hers. "Have you come for another visit? And Viola! What a delightful surprise."

Viola looked astonished as her sister-in-law bent close to give her a hug.

There were families, then there was this one. Lee couldn't consider any sample a representation of the whole class. Clearly Oliver's wife, at least, liked Viola perfectly well.

"Mrs. Burke," he greeted her. "Or as I said when I saw you last, Lady Rawleigh." Lee rose to give her the appropriate bow.

The lady brushed away the question of names with fluttering hands and addressed her husband. "Oliver, might you fetch me a chair?"

The shocking informality extended throughout this house, because the staff were all close to Cass, as they called her, long before she met her husband. The informality apparently now extended to Lee.

Cass' words landed softly, as though their harder sounds had been squashed, because of her deafness.

Oliver put the chair where she wanted, between him and Viola, likely the quietest speaker in the room. His mind was elsewhere. "This isn't delightful. My sister is compromised. My best friend compromised her. It's a horror."

Cass waited for more explanation, lips parted, hands spread in the air. When no one added anything, she let her hands drop. "From you, I find that sentiment wildly amusing."

Viola's widened eyes shot from her sister-in-law to Lee, who just took another bite of sandwich. Perhaps the family tide was turning in her favor.

Oliver faced his wife with spread hands that looked pleading. "This is my *sister.*"

"Yes. Of whom we've seen too little. How have you fared at Talbourne House, Viola? Are there really card games every night? I know my cousin is kind, Selene is nothing but; still I feel we abandoned you there."

Viola's eyes widened still more. "I didn't expect you to call."

"You had a right to expect it, but at the beginning of her marriage my cousin couldn't afford the possible scandal of my company." Perfectly calmly, Cass leaned forward and examined the open napkin, now only half full of sandwiches. "Do you like ratafia cakes? I'll fetch some. Yes, the scandal of my company due to your brother's actions."

The slow emphasis she placed on the last words reminded Lee of all Cass had been through the year before. Surely Viola knew the story. But no, she looked as if she didn't.

Lee decided this had been exactly the right place to bring her.

Unable to sit still for long, Cass jumped up out of her chair and went to the door. "Mr. Adams! May we have some ratafia cakes, please?" She came back and settled herself in a rustle of black linen. Oliver's wife didn't always talk, but when she did, it came in a rush. "We have bell pulls, but my maid is also deaf. I'd like to create something that glows at the pull of a bell rope. We did go see the gas lamp illumination on Westminster Bridge, at the new year. Did you see it? Very exciting despite the dismal weather. His lordship—" she said this pointedly at Oliver, who glared at her, "—almost gave up the visit, the fog was so bad. It was an effective demonstration. I can imagine a version safe enough to burn in the house, if one didn't mind the smell."

The door opened and Mr. Adams brought in a platter of cakes.

Yes, this had been the right place to come.

Lee took up the packet from the bakery, wrapping it a little tighter now that it was so light and slipping it in one capacious coat pocket. There was another sandwich in there and two more pieces of Breton cake, and Lee didn't intend for anyone but Viola to have them.

"Truly, I couldn't," Viola said when Lee offered her a porcelain plate with one of the cakelets from the tray.

Instantly he set it down before her where if she wanted more cake, she could have more cake.

"So," said the lady of the house, after swallowing a bite of her own cake and putting it down on her own plate, "Another scandal for the Rawleigh name? Well, what's one more?"

Shooting upright in his own chair, Oliver's hands began to make explosive, complex movements in the air.

His wife responded with the same.

Familiar with the language of the deaf from his previous visits, Lee didn't bother to try to follow it. He only kept his eye on Oliver's face.

After a few exchanges, Cass only shrugged. "I don't see the problem," she said aloud, and Lee knew that was for their benefit.

"You of all people should know how difficult it is to weather a scandal!"

"I had two causes for my scandal. An honest desire to work, and you." After this devastating remark, Cass turned serenely to Viola. "I hope Oliver had nothing to do with your scandal. It's true too many ladies of the *ton* would recognize him on sight, but he never appears at society affairs."

The lady's matter-of-fact approach emboldened Viola, who had visibly enlivened after a little time and a little cake. "No, I caused my own."

"Viola!"

Cass ignored her husband's outburst. "How fascinating! Why?"

"Because my mother wrote me to come to Morland. She wants me to take care of her."

"Oh, Christ." Oliver slumped in his chair.

"And I'm not going to go," Viola added, a little triumphantly, "and you cannot make me."

CHAPTER 8

*L*ee wanted to reward her for that with more cake.

She sat there, a tower of delicate bones and determination, and Lee silently applauded her.

Oliver just shook his head in disbelief, still slumped back in his damask chair. "The woman's a cast iron nightmare. Tried to ruin my life. She sends me letters every day whining about everything that doesn't please her. I burn them. I'm not catering to her whims anymore, Viola. Why would you think I would make you?"

Viola did not back down. "You let her treat me however she liked when I was ill. Once after you came back from medical studies. A *physician!*" Her voice trembled, and Lee thought it was from hurt, but also from rage.

"A surgeon, Viola. Little better than a barber, if you'll recall our parents' judgment of it. And your illness was not of the body."

Her eyes flicked toward Lee as if she didn't want Oliver to spill all the details. Still, she did not back down from this chance to confront her brother. "Did you think I needed to be *bled?*"

Lee couldn't help himself; he took her hand. Such a brutal treatment for such a delicate creature.

On her other side, Cass laid a hand on Viola's arm, as if also wanting to give comfort.

But Viola's attention was all on Oliver, who also now leaned toward his sister, some pleading in his eyes. "It works on fever," was all he could say.

"I didn't *have* a fever. It didn't work on me."

"Nothing did!" Oliver's frustration now was mixed with pain, an old pain.

But Viola had suffered pain of her own, which Oliver didn't notice, or had conveniently forgotten.

Lee experienced a new desire to commit violence *on* Oliver rather than in defense of him.

Viola was trembling but had not backed down. "So you left it to our mother to decide."

"She knew you best!"

"And *whose fault was that?*" Now truly angry in a way Lee had never expected Viola to be. "You were older than me, Oliver! You and Victor and Oscar—"

"You can't blame Oscar."

"Why? Because he's dead? I blame all of you! You let her banish me to Northfell because she was tired of dealing with me, even looking at me. She just wanted me out of sight, and you let her..."

Whatever engine had driven Viola to this point locked together and stopped.

She paused her words, even her breathing, and just sat there, trembling. As much as Lee wanted her to sort out her quarrel with her brother, she seemed to have reached the end of her rope.

So had Lee. "Would you give us a moment alone, please?"

"No!" Oliver shot to his feet. "You've already had too many."

Cass rose too. "Oliver, let them—"

"Don't you see, she had a chance at Talbourne House!" Oliver's glare was on Lee now, and it was hot.

"To escape your trail of scandal?"

"To find someone who'd make her happy!"

"Thanks for that." Lee felt it necessary to notice the insult.

"Not you. You *know* it can't be you."

Their eyes locked on one another, Lee and the man who knew too much about him. It came back to Lee in a flood, the late night conversation by a fire in the continental countryside. The confession. All Oliver knew.

"Oliver." Cass faced her husband. They were nearly of a height. Like an unyielding goddess, Cass announced, "If Viola wants a moment alone to speak to Mr. Waite, you can hardly deny her."

"I do," was Viola's faint reply. "Yes, I do," she added, louder, when Cass looked down at her for confirmation of her words.

"Then let us repair to the library. You can tell me all about this newfound sense of moral outrage, your lordship, while I find those newspapers with caricatures of me from last winter."

The door closed behind them.

Lee had spent months—no, years—looking for a wife. There was no way to go back and capture the optimism of his youthful self, but he still had time to build a family. He just hadn't been able to picture the woman he needed.

Now he didn't have to imagine her. She was real. Right here. And she'd picked him.

This was *his* chance. And unless he explained why they would so peculiarly suit one another, Oliver would explain it his way.

He could do this. He could make her see. A woman in

love with someone else was the best possible wife for him, really.

And it had to be Viola.

* * *

Viola did not want to share any of the horrible things swirling around in her head with Mr. Waite.

But she had to. He had fed her bread and cakes and had not left her side for a moment. When she'd left *him,* he found her. She hadn't suspected the depth of his loyalty, and she'd trapped him in this mess, and he deserved to know why she was no great bargain as a wife.

If he stayed by her side every minute once they were married, he'd find out anyway.

"Mr. Waite." She wanted to lean into his warm, strong arms like she had the night before, but this was daylight, in Oliver's parlor, and she didn't feel that brave right now. "It wasn't just that my mother sent me to Northfell. The visit was a true nightmare."

"Please don't upset yourself on my account."

"But I should tell you. Just now I sounded so petulant to myself. So petty. As if I weren't getting *my* way. I want nothing more than to be completely different from my mother."

"Of course." He didn't move away. Only sat beside her, the warmth of him seeping into her even through the shawl and gloves Oliver hadn't let the butler take away.

"I don't like to think about it." Viola closed her eyes. That made it worse. She could see it all again.

"You needn't tell me anything. You said your mother was horrid, Viola, and she is. I've visited Morland. I've never seen a person more wilfully unpleasant. You're not like that, and that's all you need to know."

"I have to tell you."

"Not if it's painful. What is your cousin's name?"

Such a small question, so artlessly asked, nudged open the door in her mind that Viola had shut so hard her mind had nearly cracked.

"A distant cousin. Evelyn. A family name, my father's. She had the same illness I have." There, it was out; the rest came in a rush. "I fall into very dark clouds, Mr. Waite, where I can't climb out. In the past ten years it's happened many times."

Why must her words keep starting and stopping?

But Mr. Waite did not flounder in the silence. "I know nothing of mothers, but I can imagine that yours must have been the least helpful."

Yes. He understood. Viola pushed herself to go on. "None of the physicians' advice helped, and my mother lost patience. She sent me to Northfell to live with Evelyn where we would both be out of sight. But Evelyn's illness was worse than mine, so much worse."

Viola could see it all again: endless repetitive days in the stone house on the constantly wind-blown moor, the room with the white door.

Evelyn's body collapsed in a chair, and her unseeing eyes.

"Something happened to her," Mr. Waite said in his soft voice; Viola saw he'd leaned closer, as if to shield her from the memory. "I'm sorry."

For once his tendency to pronounce rather than ask questions was calming. Viola didn't have to explain; he knew something had happened. She didn't have to say more; at least, he wasn't asking it of her.

But she wanted to tell him everything.

"The physician prescribed us belladonna for sleep. We were supposed to sleep as much as we could; it was supposed to help. One day Evelyn drank all of hers... and died."

She couldn't bear to see it again. Pressing her gloved hands into her eyes didn't help. The image was indelible, forever.

Hands over her eyes, Viola was startled when her body was lifted into the air.

Mr. Waite's arms were around her back and under her knees. He had lifted her entirely to his lap.

Viola hadn't even noticed her own shaking until his strength steadied it.

Her hands dropped and he was right there, his arms holding her tight. His eyes were such a different blue from anyone in her family. They were kind, such a gentle forget-me-not blue.

"Forgive the liberty," he said again, his gentle voice sounding deeper this close. "This seemed necessary."

This was like nothing she'd ever felt before; sheltered, with the world kept out and only his warmth, *their* warmth, kept in. It helped her say the rest.

"I found her body." She'd never said that anywhere, to anyone. It was a relief. But Mr. Waite must have seen dozens of bodies. Hundreds. "It must seem very silly to you who has been in battle—"

"No." His answer was punctuated with a slight squeeze of his arms; Viola wished he would squeeze harder. "Every time, it's an awful shock. And you can't have expected it."

"I should have. I feel I should have. I thought to myself over and over, well, I have no use but to be Evelyn's partner in illness, I should have noticed how ill she was. I should have noticed. I should have thought."

"Have you ever thought of doing anything similar?" So calm, so near, so free of judgment.

"No." That was why she hadn't suspected anything like that could happen.

"Then how could you have imagined it? It's almost unimaginable. Viola. You can't feel you did anything wrong."

She *did* feel that way, but he made it sound foolish. Or rather, feeling guilty felt a little foolish, because he made her reaction seem reasonable. Sad, but understandable.

It felt so good to be understood.

It loosened a little of the knot she'd felt around her neck from the moment she'd found Evelyn, the noose she felt slowly tightening, the inescapable thought that *soon that would be her.*

Still Viola hated herself for every letter she'd sent her mother begging to be allowed to come home. For not making the best of a home at Northfell, with a cousin who wouldn't blame her for being ill because she was ill the same way. For not saving her.

"I failed at *everything* my mother wanted. I failed Evelyn too." She had to face him.

She hadn't realized tears were running down her face until he wiped them away with his thumb.

"It sounds to me as though you came straight from a desperately sad life to help the Duchess of Talbourne secure her place in society. Which you have done for nearly a year with grace and your wits. I could hardly call that failing."

She laid her own hand against his cheek, so lean and strong. "And snared a gentleman with no reason to suspect me into a trap for another man. I am a *horrible* person."

"A little desperate, apparently. Can't think worse of you for that. Truth be told, you seem resourceful. That's what you call it when a person fashions a solution given practically nothing."

Given practically nothing. Viola had never heard it put that way. She was an earl's daughter, maid in waiting at a London court; no one had ever seen how little she had.

Of course, she'd never told her story to anyone; but her family hadn't wanted to know, and Mr. Waite had.

All she could call her own was one night when Lord Callendar had carried her down to the carriage, and the torch he'd ignited in her heart with just that little bit of care. A torch that had burned there ever since.

And Mr. Waite had given her so much more.

It was the height of selfishness to still wonder what Lord Callendar was doing, and gloat over his passionless attachment to Lady Cecily, when this gentleman was so kind.

Why couldn't she feel the same way about him as she did about Lord Callendar? Because it wasn't the same. Mr. Waite was so... *near.* He was sheltering, but also sometimes alarming. The relentless *reality* of him was so different from her dreams of Lord Callendar.

"I was very ungrateful to leave Her Grace and Virginia so abruptly," Viola felt moved to add. "But I didn't want them to suspect. Selene really cannot afford to be touched by scandal, and her work matters."

"Not more than you," said Mr. Waite with the kind of conviction Viola herself often felt deep inside, a conviction about what was right and what was wrong.

That settled things. In Viola's mind, and inside her.

She'd made an excellent choice. It reassured her to know that. He'd make a good, steady husband, not too boorish at all. He was kind and gentle.

It was too bad she'd already inconvenienced him enough.

Perhaps Evelyn's death had been the beginning of Viola's determination to take what she wanted and enjoy it. Certainly when the letter had come inviting her to Talbourne House, she had left Northfell without a second thought for Evelyn's grieving mother.

She'd been of use to Selene, she knew she had. All she had wanted for herself was one little thing. The passion of Lord

Callendar. All the passion he offered Selene that she hadn't wanted.

And now in pursuit of it she'd made a hash of everything, *like she always did,* said the mean little voice inside her that sounded like her mother, and instead of one big favor that wouldn't inconvenience him at all, Mr. Waite had done many favors for her including some that had endangered his life and limbs.

She ought to take his advice; it would be good, and she owed him that.

"So suggest to me where I should go or what I should do." She made her face brighter. "Not here, not Morland, not Talbourne House. If you don't like Leicester Square, where do you suggest I go?"

That brought a little smile to his face. It was *so* odd to see it from this angle, sitting on his lap, her head on his shoulder. "You're making this too easy for me. You'd better let me make my confession before your brother makes it for me. He's a terrible romantic, and he'd rather you marry a man who could love you."

That made all Viola's newfound strength drain out of her. She didn't move, but she felt like she was falling.

They were still discussing marriage?

But... "You couldn't love me?" Why had she said it like that? She didn't want him to.

"I could. I'm sure I will. Perhaps I already do." Certainly the touch he used to smooth the last signs of tears from her cheek felt tender. "The problem is, it won't last."

* * *

SHE DIDN'T UNDERSTAND; Lee could see that in her face. Well, he didn't understand it himself.

"Because you love your wife?"

Trust her to dive into the heart of it.

He had to tell her all of it and let the chips fall where they may. She was the woman he wanted for a wife, he was certain of it; but if she wouldn't accept him, he'd find another.

"I loved having a wife. Beatrix was lovely and I adored caring for her." It was almost impossible to remember those early times, when everything was easy. "But I went away to war without a worry for her, and when she died—"

That was a memory that was all too clear.

He'd read the letter, read the words. *Your wife has died, and before her your little girl.*

He should have run screaming into the woods with grief. He should have torn his clothes and his hair. The loss was as horrific as any Greek tragedy, and those had been Lee's favorites in school. Nothing ever came to any good, yet they put the stories in *books*.

Perhaps reading those had damaged him.

But no, what broke him was reading that letter. He felt something snap inside, yet he never wept.

"Viola," he told her as gently as he could, "when she died, I lost everything; yet I felt nothing at all."

There it was. She didn't understand, and neither did he, so that made them a perfect pair. He needed her to see that.

"You think your brother is puzzled by you? He's spent years trying to puzzle out the failure of *my* brain and heart. I thought I loved my wife, but when she died I felt nothing except anger at *myself*, guilt in *myself*. Only—" He caught himself. "I so wished I'd met my daughter."

Viola was only inches away; she leaned her forehead against his, close without invading his grief.

He was grateful for that. "So don't ask me about love. I don't know anything. I thought I had it, but it disappeared. I feel like even if I lost them, the love should have stayed, but I can't feel anything like that. Perhaps I loved my parents, but I don't remember. So.

"I lost interest in ladies. Of any kind. I slogged through the rest of my term of enlistment with utter detachment from women or anything about them, came home and tried to drink myself into oblivion, as you know. Alcohol numbs everything, if you understand what I mean.

"So you see I have only an intellectual interest in your great passion for Lord Callendar. Or anyone's." Lee felt like he was showing her the stump of a limb amputated in the battlefield. But she deserved to know. If she shied away from such an incapable man, better now than once she was trapped in marriage with him.

"That doesn't sound right. You *did* love your wife." She was like a dog with a bone, not letting it go.

He parted from her, just a little, to give her a smile. "I didn't question *your* story," he told her lightly.

He only meant to tease her, but she gasped and spasmed in his arms. "I'm *so* sorry! You're quite right, how very thoughtless of me—"

"Viola." He felt her settle. He liked that. "It's fine. Everything's fine. If you don't want to go through with your plan, you can probably settle happily in Leicester Square and make your own living. I don't know how." And he wasn't going to let that happen, either, because he couldn't stand the thought of Viola struggling to buy her bread. There were too many men who'd seen her leave with him last night, and if they saw any of her again without him, they'd assume the worst of her.

Why men whose comfort depended on ladies willing to bed them were so cruel to those ladies, Lee didn't understand. Just another thing about human relationships that eluded him.

But he was only telling the truth about abiding by her choice. "There's my faults, as far as I know them; you'll likely find more, if we wed. But I think we should, and after all, it was your plan."

* * *

VIOLA'S HEAD was spinning even as she still sat securely on Mr. Waite's lap.

"Are you *asking* me to marry you?"

"Yes. I'd like that."

He still hadn't asked. That wasn't a question. It was a statement, but even so, it was compelling.

He'd *like* to marry her? No one had ever suggested anything like that in Viola's life.

"Even if I'm in love with Lord Callendar?"

He shrugged. She felt the hardness of his muscles shift under her. "Well. I can hardly squawk about that. You were before you met me."

"I lured you away to get to him."

"And it's succeeding." His eyes had that soft, almost-smiling look. "And here you thought you failed at everything."

"I trapped you into this."

"I don't *feel* trapped." He leaned back, spreading his long arms along the back of the sofa, leaving her balanced on his lap.

Viola could see that there were *some* irritations in a man who was always calm.

This couldn't possibly be true. He couldn't actually *want* this. Want *her,* under these circumstances.

That was when she realized that she'd *expected* her plan to disastrously, spectacularly fail. "I'm not used to success."

"It won't hurt you. Look here, London is holding its breath waiting to find out if you married very romantically, or fell down in the gutter. I don't think you should keep them waiting much longer."

Viola stood. There was something about the way he discussed it all, the way he would discuss carpet, or someone else's coffee. As if it mattered less than the rain. He'd just warned her he was devoid of romantic feeling, at least the steady kind, and it painted a picture of a peculiar reality. The idea of marrying someone who *couldn't* sustain love was a bit unsettling. "We would live as man and wife?"

"Yes, I thought you might be willing to put the frozen garret aside for a year or two. I know you're in a hurry, but look at it this way. Right now your chances of landing Lord Callendar may be slim. In a year or two, he'll be so tired of icy Lady Cecily that I think your chances could be rather good."

She'd asked about *them,* and he'd mentioned Lord Callendar. She wondered if he were trying to disorient her on purpose. "And my children?"

Then his face grew stern. No, it hardened. That was the unreasoning look, almost of mania, she'd seen on him before, now up close. It was a look she'd never thought to see on a man she was willing to be near. "They'd be *my* children, Viola. Every one. No matter how, no matter when. That feeling won't change. And if you never happen to bear any, we're going to find some and raise them and swear on a stack of Bibles that they're our blood. Because anything we have will go to them. Do you swear it?"

He'd just casually suggested lying to the courts of the kingdom, wearing a look that hinted his next suggestion might be overthrowing the King. Viola was bewitched.

"So... no more adventures for me, then?" He was making a more than generous offer, but she had to ask, as she felt sure of some things about him, but very *un*sure of others.

Mr. Waite stood too. She regretted making him stand; he

was so much taller that she had to bend her head back to see his face. "You think marriage won't be an adventure? I can't offer you the opportunity to sleep among icicles in a garret in Leicester Square, but we still have trials to face that might well be insurmountable. I live in the country, and you wish to be in the city to pursue your light of love."

She didn't like the way he said that, either, as if it didn't matter.

But he went on. "We will face years together, Viola, long years, and we don't know what will happen for any of them. Cold years, floods, fire perhaps, lightning storms and hail-stones. But we'll be *together*. I'll never annul this marriage, so if that frightens you, say no. If it appeals to you, you'll have me. Always. And I do want children, Viola. Any way possible. Swear it."

Was it just the certainty of him that appealed to her?

Would *that* last?

She'd been watching him all winter, plotting and making her plans. In the end, trusting her own observations was the most she could do.

"I don't know how to be a good family." He must surely know that.

"Neither do I. We'll manage."

Why was she hesitating when he offered her all she'd hoped for and more? He'd just said he'd never annul this marriage, even as her heart belonged to someone else. He wasn't just the best man for this role; he was the only one.

And so *tall*.

But he wasn't Jonas. Kind, funny, wholeheartedly caring Jonas.

"It might seem like grasping at straws," Viola struggled to steady her voice, "but how do we know that the... you know, the marriage bed will work for us?" She didn't add *when I love another*. There was no reason to dwell on it; he knew.

He took her question seriously, studying her a little. "I think we can test that, if you'll trust me."

Everything inside her trembled. But if she couldn't trust him this far, she shouldn't marry him. "Yes, I do."

The next instant his hands splayed around her waist, pulling her up and close to him, and he bent down and kissed her.

In a second, it was like being in the middle of a storm. Viola grabbed his shoulders and held on so she wouldn't blow away; her eyes shut as she stretched up to meet his lips, meet all of him. She felt taller; she felt like she was *flying*.

Dimly she realized his arms had gone all the way around her and he'd pulled her close, tight. He felt so hard against her, all muscle and heat.

How could a kiss be all this? She wondered that, to the extent that she could think at all, her hands sliding up of their own accord to frame the lean sides of his face, the day-old bristles there, the flesh and bone. Only their mouths joined, but the kiss had taken over all of her, the taste of him reaching all the way down to her toes.

Being in his arms was *heaven*.

The crashing open of the door pulled her back to earth. That and her brother shouting "I'll fucking kill you!" in the parlor that had suddenly become far too small.

Mr. Waite didn't seem rattled, but he never did. He moved between her and Oliver while Viola tried to repair her rumpled gown, her too-warm lips, and a hungry fire inside her unlike anything she'd ever felt before.

"Swear it," he said, low, urgent.

"I swear," and she felt the word go through her, right down to her shoes.

Turning to Oliver, "You might have knocked," was all Mr. Waite said.

"I know what it means when the talking stops!"

"Your wife doesn't seem to like your manners." For Cass was standing right behind Oliver in the hall, pulling on his arm as ineffectually as if he'd turned to stone.

"She can't hear when you've gone silent, she's deaf!"

"That's enough!" Cass might not be able to hear things more than a few feet away, but she definitely could talk. "This is *my* house, and you're being everything I never wanted in it. Stop shouting, stop being overbearing, and stop trying to punish Viola for *your* mistakes!"

Oliver turned to his wife, and Viola couldn't see his face, but she saw his shoulders slump. Whatever his faults, he clearly adored his wife and couldn't bear to be the cause of her upset.

"I'm sorry." When he turned back to his sister, she could see him contemplating violence, but he only leaned forward, bracing himself with his hands on the back of the chair before him. "Viola, I'm so sorry. I've failed so many people in my life. I never wanted one of them to be you. Don't do this. You deserve a chance to fall in love."

"She's *in* love!" said her new betrothed.

Viola wished Mr. Waite wouldn't be so free with the word, but as expected, it took the wind out of Oliver's sails without being a complete lie.

He glared at Mr. Waite. "If you ruin her life I swear I'll end you."

Half-blocking her from her brother's view, Mr. Waite straightened. He had that stance that spoke to her of military service, but perhaps it was just inborn in him. "You may think of me as someone willing to follow your direction, Oliver, so let me explain that I have my own compass. And now it's Viola. So we'll thank you to get out of our way."

"Viola..."

She tried to keep her face blank in response to Oliver's

pleading look. She'd underestimated the benefits of having a sister-in-law, but had yet to see any from Oliver as a brother.

"Where will you go?" he finally asked, when he saw she had nothing left to say to him.

All the bits of her plan fell back into place. "To Talbourne House, of course. We must sneak in unseen," Viola informed him and everyone else.

* * *

CASS ISSUED a cease fire across the battlefield. "Let me take you to the kitchen, Viola; you look parched, I want to give you some tea."

Lee thought it was just as well they'd gone. When he looked at Oliver, he felt something that, had he not known himself so well, he'd have called the distant rumblings of white-hot rage.

Oliver must have seen his disgust. "Waite, I never knew what to do for her."

"The things you picked were *incorrect.*"

"She falls so ill. Like a corpse still breathing. Do you know how unnerving that is for a physician?"

"And what about for Viola? Do you know what happened at Northfell?" He'd bet Oliver didn't know. All this posturing, and Oliver likely didn't know.

Oliver looked suddenly older. "Our cousin died. She was ill in the same manner as Viola, and she died."

"Did Viola tell you that she found her body?"

Both of them knew what that meant, how that felt.

"No. No, no." Oliver sank into a chair, shaking his head as if he could shake the truth away.

"Viola is your *family,* Oliver, and you've taken poor care of her. She's got as much spirit as you have, maybe more. Don't fight us on this. I can take care of her, you know I can.

Better than you. She doesn't need a bone set or a wound bandaged. She needs something different."

"When she just sinks away from the world... And you did the same thing." Oliver's pointed finger was accusing. "You came back to Britain and crawled into a bottle.

"So I know how it feels." He did. He still remembered it, his body so heavy it seemed like getting up out of the chair was too much work; the faint hope that he wouldn't have to get up ever again. Surely made him a better match for Viola. "And I told her that. I told her everything."

Suddenly Lee saw Oliver's constant drinking companionship in a new light.

"Did you drink with me because you knew I suffered as Viola suffered?"

Sighing heavily, looking disgusted with *himself,* Oliver said, "And still hoped to find some treatment."

"Oliver. Once your service to the army was over, you owed me nothing."

"Lee," said Oliver in the same even tone. "Physicians are volunteers. Why do you think I left the army when you did?"

The wave of feeling that surged inside him was unfamiliar. "That's a good friend."

"Accomplishing nothing." Apparently everyone in Oliver's family was hard on themselves.

"You could have drunk with *her.*"

Oliver straightened from the chair he'd been leaning on, looking old. "I would have, if it would have helped. It never helped you."

That was the simple truth.

"Did you tell her about the money?" Oliver's question had sharpened again.

No, he hadn't. He didn't just want this to be easy for Viola; he wanted it to be easy for him. He wanted to believe in it as best he could.

She had introduced him to the idea of being selfish.

"She thinks I'm penniless; let her. She likes me that way."

"Waite, she's delicate." Oliver looked tortured; Lee couldn't feel any pity for him now, though he might one day. "And she's tender. Don't tie her to you, knowing you can't give her what she deserves."

"I'm going to give her what she *wants*."

Within reason. Her supposed passion for Callendar was looming larger in the back of his head, ringing warning bells as if for an impending fire, but he'd deal with that later. Nothing felt as urgently necessary as settling this marriage business. "And I don't know how delicate she is when she's got all of us, and most of London, spinning on a string."

CHAPTER 9

"Do you do this often?" Lee asked as they picked their way through the trees along the grounds of Talbourne House.

Viola, long hems sopping with wet morning dew, gasped and looked over her shoulder at him. Her expression shifted from shock to faint smile. "You are teasing me!"

"Three brothers and you're not used to teasing? You're certainly proving your story."

"I thought you accepted my story without question." There was a slight hint, the slightest, of sarcasm to her voice.

"Ah, finally! A touch of mockery. If you are going to be so earnest all the time, we will never get on."

She looked over again. Lee began to worry that her feet must be icy cold; she still wore evening slippers. "I should like to hear more of your story," she said, holding up her skirts in a vain effort to keep them dry.

"It's dull."

Her face fell; Lee didn't like that. He, at least, was definitely spinning at the end of her string. "Tell me what I must do for you to smile again."

She didn't seem to like that answer either. Well, she'd likely been told to smile all her life. Lee had, though only by Oliver.

She darted forward across the cropped lawns to massive Talbourne House, which stretched like a whole village over the green.

It reminded Lee of a castle assault.

Viola's plan hinged upon staying out of sight. She had insisted that she not cause any more damage to the Talbourne name by appearing on their doorstep and forcing Their Graces to accept or reject her in public view. Thus, sneaking through the trees to the rear of the grand house.

He joined her at the first available back door, keeping watch out of habit. "Do you have the key?"

"In a manner of speaking."

The lock that lay in her slender fingers was a wide brass cylinder divided into wheels, each one stamped with flowers, odd scratching-marks, and faint alphabet letters.

Viola turned each wheel until the faint letters lined up in order: U, X, O, R. Then she easily pulled the lock open.

"This is a fascinating piece. May I look at it? Where is it from?" Lee had never seen anything like it.

"Not now. It came from China; His Grace corresponds." She bustled him through the now-open door, then stood, concerned once she realized that she couldn't lock it again.

Lee was glad it wasn't an assault. Viola had a general's determination, but not the foresight.

She slid the lock back through its hasp and shut the door, making an unhappy noise. "We must hide you. There's a broom closet at the bottom of the stairs."

"I'm not hiding in a closet unless you come with me." He could make her smile in a closet, he was sure he could. He really wanted to try.

That kiss had stirred things in him he'd long thought were dead.

"I shouldn't have let you come at all! What if the Duke has the wrong idea about who kidnapped whom last night? He can be quite alarming."

"So can I." That was when Lee noticed he didn't have his walking-stick. He'd left it at the hotel. Well, he knew how to do damage without it. "I'm not letting you have an audience with an angry duke alone."

She nudged his arm, gingerly, with her hands, as if suddenly afraid to touch him, closer and closer to the broom closet, then inside it. It was barely high enough for him to stand in. "Can't you see I'm used to being alone?"

"Can't you see I don't wish you to be?" That made her draw in her breath. Fast. He used her wide-eyed moment of hesitation to pull her in with him. "So far we've done best by closing ranks."

He pulled the door nearly shut. They were surrounded by the dark quiet, the smell of washing-soap, and the damp wood of a bucket. He still had her hand in his. He squeezed it.

She squeezed back.

She seemed to like the dark and the quiet. She whispered, "When I fall ill, I won't smile. And you won't be able to cure me."

"Very well." He knew the truth of that first-hand. "But I can stay with you. And I will."

"Oh—"

Lee did not swear, and clearly neither did Viola, but she could use some words right now to vent the emotion swelling in her so hard he could feel it. She was restless, trying not to touch his body with hers and holding fiercely to his hand at the same time.

He kissed her knuckles, murmuring, "Are you so ashamed of me? Wasn't this part of your plan?"

* * *

No, Viola had never planned to stand in a broom closet in a very compromising embrace with Mr. Waite, whom she still barely knew.

The details of this supposed marriage had been hazy. She supposed he'd agree to it, then she'd stay in some tiny rooms somewhere while he conducted whatever his business was, leaving her free to spend her hours on attracting Lord Callendar.

She hadn't imagined his arms, or the kisses, or all these awful confrontations.

She definitely hadn't imagined the broom closet.

"I am not *ashamed* of you at all. I only intend to slip upstairs, have a word with Her Grace and Virginia, then come right back down here."

"Excellent. I'll come along. Hadn't you also better change your gown? Your hems are cold and wet."

She leaped backward, finding herself backed against the closet wall. "I've soaked your trouser legs!"

She could hear a frown in his voice. "Yes, but my point was *your* discomfort, not mine."

His constant insistence that she existed, that she *mattered,* was jarring. Viola would have to do something about it. But there wasn't time now. "If you accompany me, you'll let me handle the negotiations?"

"Quite."

He sounded agreeable, but she was beginning to grasp that under his amiable exterior he could be as stubborn as she was. She hadn't expected him to be trouble.

Still, she was glad he was here.

She led him out of the broom closet. No one was about. It was easy to climb the narrow servant's stairs to the hallway above, paneled with oak, studded with marble-topped tables.

Past the vase full of peacock feathers, she turned a corner. A footman stood against the wall.

"Her Grace is receiving family, isn't she?" Viola waved him away without waiting for an answer, carrying Mr. Waite along in her wake as she sailed into the Duchess' private chamber.

"Viola!" Inside, Virginia sprang to her feet.

There was Selene, the Duchess of Talbourne, reclining on the settee; she was due to deliver her child soon, and to Viola she looked vast and tired under her heavy striped robe.

Viola darted forward, but was blocked by the formidable Duke, whom she hadn't noticed, and grizzled and broad Mr. Lyall, his right-hand man, at his shoulder.

When Mr. Waite followed her in, Viola felt the tension in the room stretch tight and nearly break.

Mr. Waite looked about, taking the measure of everyone and everything.

"Let's not alarm any ladies," Mr. Waite said in his calm voice, moving in front of Viola.

"Are you quite well, Lady Viola?" The Duke's voice contrasted with his stony appearance, the rise and fall of it rich and flowing like honey. Disguising, perhaps, his true feelings, for his eyes stayed on Mr. Waite the way a dog tracked its prey.

"Quite." All this tension, because of her.

Viola circled all the men to kneel by Selene's side. "I hope you haven't worried. I'm ashamed of myself."

"Worried! We sent runners all over the city last night—" Virginia in her own brightly-patterned wrapper took one of Viola's hands and knelt beside her, reminding Viola this was still early for the Talbourne house.

"No great effort," said Selene, squeezing Viola's other hand and letting her head fall back into the cushions. Viola knew she was lying.

"The gentleman didn't kidnap you?" Virginia, her curls tied back from her face in a soft black cloud, stared at Mr. Waite with more suspicion than Viola would have thought possible.

"Quite the reverse," Viola assured her.

That made everyone turn to stare at Viola, except the blind Duchess, and Mr. Waite, who'd had his eyes fixed on her already.

Why had she conceived such a ridiculous plan? Why hadn't she imagined how it would look to others?

She patted Selene's hand. "It's a long story, but nothing important."

"I think it's very important," countered Selene. "Mr. Lyall, will you please ask for our breakfast to be delivered here? And do we need more chairs?"

"I couldn't eat anything," Viola assured her, "I've eaten so many breakfasts already."

This too was greeted with a round of silence, and now Viola wondered if she'd ever said anything to surprise them before.

The men began arranging chairs as the Duchess wished, and Selene used the bustle to speak low to Viola. "Of course I worry when one of my friends goes missing!"

"I'm so sorry." She had not thought of Selene as a friend, more someone who needed her effort. Someone she could please.

The way she'd never pleased her mother.

Apparently many things were not quite as she'd imagined them to be.

"I've behaved in an appalling way, but it's no great matter. I'm going to be married and I've just come for my things."

"Married!" Virginia, wholly astonished, sat right down on the floor where she knelt.

"We also need a special license." That speech from Mr. Waite brought the room to another fraught halt.

"Well, we need one," he said with a little shrug, as the Duke's glare bored into him from one side and Virginia's from the other.

"Lady Viola?" The Duke's tone was both questioning and warning.

The strain of all the conflicting feelings swirling in the room had Viola plopping down on the floor as well. "Please don't lecture me! It's just as Mr. Waite says. We are to be married, and I suppose we ought to have a special license after my performance last night."

"I don't simply dispense special licenses," said the Duke, settling himself in a chair near his wife's head. "Explain."

"She needn't." Mr. Waite couldn't seem to say anything pacifying. He was like a stick in the stream—

And he was right, Viola suddenly thought to herself.

She didn't need to explain herself. Not to Oliver, or her mother; not even to a duke.

In fact, if she owed anyone an explanation, it was Mr. Waite. And he already knew her faults.

The realization freed her from the choking need to justify herself. She could breathe easier, as if someone had loosened her stays.

"Sir," said His Grace, as hard and unyielding as it was possible for him to be, "no one knows you here. Perhaps you should withdraw."

"I'm just off to pack my things!" Viola stood.

"I'll help you." Mr. Waite was closer than she'd realized, and smiled down at her. Viola felt that his eyes didn't look that sad at all, not really.

"There's no need," she said to his offer.

"I wouldn't mind it."

The Duke seemed to feel this threat of folding Viola's petticoats required genuine opposition. "Sir—"

"You might not know me, Your Grace," said Mr. Waite, turning to him with a bow that was just deep enough to be appropriate, "but I know a little of you. Not by your reputation, we all know those are worth nothing, but by the lock Lady Viola just used downstairs. Correctly unlocked, it spells U, X, O, R. *Wife* in Latin. Presuming that your wife vouches for your character—"

"I do, in every way," the Duchess said stoutly from the couch.

"—then I assume you sympathize with a man's desire to keep his wife close."

He kept saying things like that. Each time they felt a little more real. Viola didn't know what to say.

But the Duke had plenty of words. He sat down, his rich imported coat immaculately black and making him look more menacing. "You are not married, and won't be unless I procure you a special license."

"Of course we will. Just more slowly," Mr. Waite assured him.

"I presume you know of Lady Viola's dowry?" His Grace swiftly responded.

Mr. Waite turned and looked at Viola. "Do you have one?"

"This is absurd. Your Grace." The Duchess forcibly redirected the conversation. "I am terribly hungry. Assuming you don't regret how quickly *we* were married, would you be willing to call for some breakfast for me, if no one else wishes any?" Half under her breath she added, "Honestly, I would kill for an orange."

It was obvious the lady desired a conversation alone with Viola; reluctantly, her husband stepped to the door. "Sir," he gestured for Mr. Waite to precede him.

Mr. Waite also saw that the gentlemen weren't wanted, and relented. "I'll wait in Lady Viola's chambers. Starting the packing," he said to Viola, with a cheery wave, and both men went out, followed by door-filling Mr. Lyall.

"Viola. Honestly," Selene said as soon as the door closed, "I wish you had told me you were in love!"

Viola felt guilt wash over her, deep enough to drown in. She hadn't confided, and she was not in love. At least not with Mr. Waite.

Her Grace looked near tears. "I had such plans! You and Virginia here with me when the baby came, and what fun it would be for all of us."

"It will be!" Virginia assured her, patting her hand and putting a fresh handkerchief in it.

Selene had been weepy these last few weeks, tears flowing at the sound of a lonely bird or a breeze, and Viola wondered if that had affected her decision to make the leap last night. Viola didn't like to think of herself as fragile, but being around so many tears felt dangerous. As if she might fall into that pit again just from their presence.

Indeed, the creeping conviction that she was doing something terrible to *everyone* with this plan already made her feel like climbing in bed and not emerging until summer.

"I'm so sorry."

"Don't be." Selene dabbed at her eyes and offered Viola a wavering smile. "It's only—I shall worry about you. Even if you are wildly happy. I'm only being selfish, as we must stay here while you embark on this great adventure. I cannot chance any damage to Virginia's reputation while I cannot go out—"

Any more *damage,* Viola thought glumly.

"—and you won't be in company for a long while." *If ever,* Selene didn't add. But it was true. "Is he a gentleman?"

"Retired from the infantry." Viola only knew that because

she knew he'd served with Oliver. He'd never mentioned his rank.

Virginia could have been angry that Viola had deprived her of the rest of her season, but all she said was, "I will miss your clever company, Viola. I shall have to find new ways to entertain myself without your ability to take the measure of a person on sight."

Could she? She didn't feel so, but Selene only agreed. "So true. That's the only thing I find reassuring. If you are determined to marry Mr. Waite, and so quickly, he must be extraordinarily good."

"I don't know." It was true Viola had never doubted Mr. Waite's fundamental character, but he *had* just pulled her into a broom closet.

"Well," said Selene with a wave of her hand, "perhaps he needn't be so amazingly good, but he must at least be extraordinarily good *fit* for you."

* * *

OF COURSE it was just outside the Duchess' private chambers that Viola, wet rumpled hems and all, encountered Lord Callendar himself.

"Lady Viola!" He drew near with the easy familiarity they had always shared, and smiled down at her. "You're well, I see."

A mess, but well. He, of course, looked like perfection, his cheeks slightly reddened from the cold air above his sculpted jaw, that nose that would suit the profile of a king. His lips had a shape only an artist could create, firmly masculine, yet deeply flushed and rich, reminding Viola of the kiss she'd had with Mr. Waite only a little while ago. The memory caused her to flush a little too; she felt the warmth of it.

She only said, "I'm fine, your lordship."

"I'm glad to hear so. Her Grace was terribly worried about you." He glanced over her shoulder toward the closed door. "Is she in? Is she receiving visitors?"

And just that quickly, Viola again became part of the furnishings.

She had disappeared from a party right in front of him only the night before, with a man who was a stranger. Yet he had no questions.

He was easy with her because he barely saw her. How had she not noticed that before?

She had sustained herself through the winter with the idea that Lord Callendar had deeper feelings for her than showed. That he could not have carried her that way if he had no tender care for her person.

A misapprehension born of the life she'd lived.

He had not noticed her disappearance at all.

"Lady Viola. Your maid wishes to know if—" Mr. Waite appeared around the corner, only to cut himself off at the sight of her speaking to Lord Callendar.

Self-conscious, Viola touched her simply plaited hair and thought of her crumpled hems.

He had none of Lord Callendar's fine features. His face was a little too lean, his eyes a little too sad. He was too tall and gangly, and his voice too gentle.

Nor did he make her feel easy; she felt restless just at the sight of him, torn between staring at his lips, the lower one far deeper than Lord Callendar's, and wishing she could brush her hair.

She could not control anything. Not her life, not her feelings, not the trouble she caused for others, nothing.

"Your lordship." Mr. Waite afforded the other gentleman with a brief bow, then all his attention shifted back to Viola. "My lady, your maid wishes to know if you will still need her services."

"Traveling?" Lord Callendar's question was kind, but that was all; he wasn't even interested enough to wait for an answer. He glanced at Mr. Waite. "Have we met?"

"No," Mr Waite said in his soft way which betrayed nothing of his wilder moments, "I'm no one of importance."

Viola started to protest, but Lord Callendar accepted the self-deprecation at its face value and turned back to Viola. "Good day, then. I'll just see that Her Grace is doing well."

Without another word, he left her there.

Viola didn't know what her face looked like, but when she turned to Mr. Waite, his expression had only softened.

"Are you all right?" he asked gently.

Lord Callendar didn't love her. He didn't even *desire* her. And nothing Viola could do would change that.

"Quite," she told him with a fleeting smile. It was false, but she wanted to give him that.

"Your maid wishes to know if you will retain her services. I'm sure Talbourne House would find a place for her if you like."

"Oh!" Another thing Viola had not foreseen. "You and I haven't discussed it. I am sure I can do without her services, Mr. Waite, if you cannot afford to employ her."

* * *

LEE mostly still wanted Viola to change out of that gown. He'd marched through many a wet winter, and the first rule of soldiering was to keep one's feet dry. Viola might get ill; she certainly had to be uncomfortable. Yet here she was, worrying about things she might have asked about before she carried him off in a carriage, if they really concerned her.

Then her next words clarified things a little. "I never even asked if you have a house at your disposal, or only rooms. In Her Grace's service, my main employment, if you will, has been society. I hope you have a little space for entertaining as well."

She'd mentioned no such thing last night or all morning. "I have some," Lee told her, trying not to sound wary.

He didn't want to spoil this arrangement with a discussion of his financial situation.

"Really? And would you mind if I entertain friends? I believe I underestimated how much Virginia and the Duchess will miss me. They might come for a late supper, once the gossip has died down." That smile he knew was fake came and faded again. "Who knows, perhaps even His Grace and... Lord Callendar. Will you mind?"

Yes, he bloody well would mind.

Something inside him howled that she couldn't be serious. How could she say the things she'd said, *be* the things she'd been with him through this last night and day, and still imagine for a second that she could be happier with Lord Callendar?

He knew his own shortcomings, knew she hadn't selected him for looks or, obviously, money. But surely she must see that selecting him to make Lord Callendar jealous would not work. The boy was a popinjay following the Duchess' train.

Then Lee remembered three things.

He'd promised her his own feelings wouldn't last. That had begun to eat at him, but it was only true.

Everyone in this house, including Viola until last night, followed the Duchess' train. Viola had gone from her mother's control to a palace where she was not queen. The idea of being central to anyone's life was still foreign to her.

And third, Viola didn't really believe she could be happier.

Hadn't he himself, somewhere in the last few hours, thought that it was *better* to contract a marriage with a woman who didn't expect to love him for a lifetime?

When had he lost track of that idea?

Thinking fast, he pulled together the best answer he could.

"Hadn't we mentioned a year to ourselves? Before you renewed your campaign?"

"That's right."

Had she forgotten? His stomach sank.

He had to stay calm. All his life, difficult conversations had happened best when he was calm.

To Viola, he knew just what to say. "Best to follow your original plan. I daresay you'll be tired of me once winter comes again." He tried to sound careless.

Far from being reassuring, the idea cut at him. It had not escaped his notice that he still said *we* in all his plans, while Viola said *she* would entertain.

After all, he had no control over whether his feelings, whatever they were, faded before she tired of him, or the other way round. What was important was to enter into this marriage in honest expectation.

"By the end of a year," he added, "we'll both know better what you like."

"How?" She seemed genuinely perplexed. No wonder, if she'd just seen that foolish boy and still thought she had a chance of winning his attention.

"Because you'll tell us both."

With that he took possession of her hand. He liked it on his arm. He liked the company.

As she so often did, she seemed to hear what he didn't say. "We're both expecting to be forsworn, aren't we? If we marry?"

He'd already found it best not to let her dig herself too far into a pit of worry when she started asking questions. "I don't know," he told her, still feigning carelessness, "I've never been to a wedding. What do they swear?"

"I don't know either," said Viola, blinking. "There are vows."

"Well then." He took her hand and placed it on his arm. She was marrying *him,* not Lord Callendar, after all. "We'll fight that enemy once it's met."

CHAPTER 10

"This is your house?"

Lee didn't want to disappoint his soon-to-be wife, nor did he want to lie to her. "The Faircombe family leases it," he said, which was the complete truth. "They've kindly given me use of it for a while."

He helped her down from the Talbourne carriage. Its plush seats were commodious, clean, and soft-riding; on the long drive back from the palace, Viola had fallen asleep.

It had shocked him, how pleasant it was to have her lean on his shoulder and then grow heavy. He'd turned just enough to hold her there for all the rest of the drive. His muscles were a bit sore; he was delighted.

When a footman started down the stone steps, he waved to their carriage. "My wife has valises, Charles, see to them."

"Yes sir!" The footman's face split with a huge grin. "Congratulations, sir!"

"Yes, thank you."

He helped Viola up the stairs and into the house.

"It's so grand!"

It was an entryway lined with pink Grecian marble and

an ivy-patterned wool rug from the north of England. Lee watched her reactions carefully. "What is it you like?"

"Lovely colors, and soft, and the shine," she said artlessly, looking down at her shoes. Fortunately, they were dry.

He'd convinced her to change into her own clothes once they'd reached her chambers, then brought another pair of shoes and stockings for her to change into again once they returned to the end of the Talbourne drive... where the sumptuous carriage had awaited them. Making sure they were not seen at the great house's front door.

He'd had no shame at all about watching his betrothed roll the sheer silk along her legs.

She talked as easily as if he weren't watching her change her stockings, but the color on her cheeks said that she noticed. Then when he lifted her foot into his lap to fasten her shoes for her, she tried to brush him away.

"Oh! You needn't."

"How often have you fastened your own shoes?" he dismissed her concern, enjoying the miraculous curve of her calf as it narrowed into something as tiny as her ankle.

She'd agreed to be his wife, and he would enjoy every second of it while it lasted, and that included seducing her as soon as possible. He intended it to be persuasive.

He felt relieved, wholly relieved of the emptiness with which he'd read the news of his first wife's death. That feeling might well come back; like a thunderstorm in the distance, someday it could be here and the lightning could well set fire again to everything he currently felt.

But right now he *did feel*, and it felt wonderful; and he was determined Viola should feel it too.

As she stepped into the front parlor of the townhouse, he wanted to know if that little gasp she made was a good thing or a bad one.

"This is lovely!"

Intently, he watched her as she studied all the details of the room, unaware that she was the loveliest thing in it.

"What do you like about it?" He wanted to know more of what she thought. He wanted to know everything.

She touched the carved mantelpiece. Lee wouldn't have chosen it; it looked busy, he thought, against the cool blue-gray of the walls, and drew the eye away from the green tile at the fireplace and the damask drapes that matched the wallpaper.

Viola, unwilling to say a bad thing about anything, even a mantlepiece, didn't mention it, only said, "This is such a cool and lovely room." She touched a piece of ivy arranged in a vase to one side. Unlike the Duke's massive Chinese porcelains, this was only a small crystal vase; she didn't seem to mind the size of it.

Good. He wanted to know her tastes in everything.

The housekeeper came in, hands clasped at her waist and a face full of questions.

"Ah, good. Mrs. Winfrey, this is my wife. I'd like her to have something hot for a nuncheon."

"Mr. Waite!" The woman's round cheeks nearly made her eyes disappear under her white linen cap, she smiled so hard. "Always surprising us. Welcome, Mrs. Waite! I'm Mrs. Winfrey, the housekeeper, at your service."

"Thank you, I should have introduced you. Vi—Mrs. Waite, would you like to meet the servants now? Or perhaps later? I know you're tired."

She shot him a look of mixed surprise and warning, as if she didn't expect him to notice her fatigue when she'd slept on him the whole way home and certainly didn't want it mentioned before a servant. Her eyes flicked back and forth to Mrs. Winfrey.

He knew what was worrying her. If all the servants thought they were already married, where would they hold the wedding? If they were lucky, the Duke would relent and they wouldn't have to explain anything awkward to a rector in church.

"The contracts are all signed," he lied immediately to Mrs. Winfrey. "We will likely hold a celebration."

"Marvelous!" He could see Mrs. Winfrey already planning the cake. "*Do* you wish to see the householding, Mrs. Waite?"

"Perhaps later. I'm quite all right." Viola had the world's tiniest scowl.

Lee ignored it. "So very true. A hot nuncheon, Mrs. Winfrey, and I believe I'll have it in my chambers. Our chambers, now."

"Of course, sir."

Viola came closer. Lee quite liked that and wished she'd come closer still. "You can't introduce me as your wife everywhere!"

"Why not? The Duke promised us a special license. We ought to be married in a matter of days. I'm only anticipating it slightly."

"It feels quite odd!"

"Does it?" He slid his hand around her waist. As if to steady her. Yes, that could be his pretext. "Not to me."

It *didn't* feel odd, and that was peculiar. Of course, he'd been married before. Incapable of deeper feelings, perhaps he was simply slipping into the comfortable familiarity of the wedded state.

"We're doing something shocking." She looked torn between being embarrassed and pleased by the idea, and it set off one of those warning bells in the back of Lee's head.

"Yes, terribly shocking. Something that has resulted in the existence of every man, woman, and child in Britain. Is there a wrapper in your small valise?"

"I think so, why?"

"I want you to take off your stays and be able to sleep comfortably once you eat."

She didn't blush at the mention of undressing, and he liked that about her. He wanted to see that look in her eyes, that *come find out* that had drawn him across the room to her —had it only been last night?

It felt like they'd lived a lifetime since then.

She was eager, but not actually for him. "I would desperately love to be free of these stays," she whispered.

Why hadn't he thought of that? She'd slept in the damn things. "I should have loosened them in the carriage." She gasped a little; he pressed his hand to her waist. "What?"

"I hadn't expected you to be so comfortable with a woman's company. But then, I didn't know you were married before."

"I don't dwell on the past." Leading her out of the parlor, Lee accompanied her to the grand staircase. He particularly liked how its stairs were so wide and so shallow; it was easy to climb.

"But I wish to know *so* much more about you! I believe I've entered a deep cave without a candle." She did indeed mount the stairs easily; he stayed by her side in case she misstepped. "For instance, who were the people who raised you?"

He might easily adore everything about her except this ability to cut to the heart of things.

"Strangers."

Her face fell. He hated that.

The master's suite lay directly ahead of the top of the stairs, for the master's convenience. In this case, it would be for Viola's.

There were chambers for the lady of the house, directly to the left; but Lee had no intention of putting Viola in there.

Viola noticed anyway when he led her into the heavy oak-lined chamber reminiscent of Restoration wars. "Isn't there a lady's chamber?"

"You'll be more comfortable here with me." He'd better start telling her things, or she would deduce too much. "Anyway, Lady Charlotte has left things in there we won't disturb."

"Lady Charlotte! I didn't know you were that close with the family." Viola straightened with surprise; Lee gently helped her bend again, to sit on the edge of the bed.

The footman had brought the valises. Her trunks would be there later tonight, her maid tomorrow. Lee wanted some peace and quiet. "Didn't we pack a hairbrush?"

"Lady Charlotte arranged to loan you this townhouse?" Viola's eyes narrowed. "What sort of arrangement do you have with Lady Charlotte? You said she was frightful!"

"I said no such thing." Nor would he, though he thought she was. "When I sold my commission, I returned to London and did absolutely nothing with myself for far too long. Oliver invited me to the country, and it was like remembering that I once existed before the war. I went to stay at Faircombe Hall for the winter and learned a great deal about horses."

No one who had even met Lady Charlotte in passing ever forgot the lady's passion for horses.

Viola was back to narrow-eyed, and Lee liked it. It was cheering, to think she might be a bit jealous of his company. "Lady Charlotte invited you to Faircombe Hall?"

"No, I'm delighted to say I was quite beneath her notice." He didn't bother to hide his grin. "Ah, Mrs. Winfrey. So good of you. Thank you."

He took the tray from the housekeeper at the door, set it on the bed, then returned to shut it.

If Viola was at all alarmed at being alone with him, she didn't show it. That was cheering too. Lee thought that after her lowering encounter with Lord Callendar at Talbourne House, she might have changed her mind about things. Him, this, all of it. But no, she only looked intent as he returned to help her back off the bed.

"So then you—What are you doing?"

"Unlacing your dress."

He'd excused himself while Viola had changed in her rooms at the palace, but now he wished he'd paid attention to however her maid had tied this stuff.

"I, ah... Mr. Waite."

"I've fastened your shoes," he said, moving closer, letting her get used to his presence as he would a restless horse. "And I've undone your hair. Will you let me?"

"It's, uh..." She shivered, and he wanted to hold her, protect her from the chill in the room, from anything that upset her. But he wouldn't touch her if she preferred he not.

She turned, and looked up into his eyes. "You won't abandon me now?"

Everything inside him locked into place, and he felt solid and whole, as if he'd been broken till this moment.

"*Never,*" and he let himself kiss her.

His arms went around her so easily, fit her to him so perfectly, and she matched him touch for touch. He'd known women who went limp in his arms, as if waiting for him to do his worst, and women who liked to play at fighting, who pouted when he instantly let them go, as he found struggle about as arousing as mud.

There was nothing of games about Viola. Her lips parted for him, welcomed the taste of him, giving him soft touches he'd never dreamed of while her hands tangled around his neck, in his hair, her arms pulling him closer.

"I believe you," she whispered when they parted for a moment, and it felt like a gift.

He was so hungry for this, for *her.* She was so soft, so warm, and apparently, so willing.

He had someone to care for again, and it was better than he'd ever hoped.

"You need to stay warm, and eat something while it's still hot." The tray held a bowl of stew, the sort of simple fare every hearth kept hot through the winter; the last of the winter's bounty made it hearty and thick, with beans and potatoes and carrots. He wanted her to eat it.

He wanted her luxuriously comfortable.

Pushing the bed covers back, he quickly untied the last ribbons of her gown, letting her step out of it. Blue, like the night before. She liked blue.

He'd remember that.

"I'm going to climb in the bed and hold you against me," he told her as his fingers made quick work of the ties that held her short stays together, leaving her in a shift so fine he could almost see through it.

"What for?" She wasn't the least put off, only puzzled. Because no one had ever taken careful care of her.

By God, he was going to do it forever or die trying.

"So that you'll be warm."

Oh, her sigh. He'd read her right. She liked leaning against him. She felt comfortable that way.

He liked it too.

He quickly illustrated his intention by doing it. Leaning against the oak panel at the head of the bed, he drew her between his legs and settled her on his lap before sliding back.

Yes, she'd liked that. Like last night. She liked being in his arms. That was the main thing; that was everything. She proved it when she murmured, "Do married people truly get luxuries like this?"

"Only the lucky ones," he told her.

With a long arm he snagged the bowl of stew from her tray and placed it in her hands before him.

"I can't be hungry again!"

"Because you think you shouldn't be, or because you're incapable?" The idea of her telling him that, here, and the memory of her against him the night before, so fired his blood that he felt himself go from half-hard to harder than steel in mere moments. It had been so, so long since he'd felt anything like that.

She must be aware of him, but didn't ask questions. As if they sat politely side-by-side on a settee.

He smiled into her hair. Whatever she wished.

"See if you can eat a little," he urged her, and against her contradiction, she tasted the stew. The little noise of pleasure she made was worth any effort.

"But what will you do while I eat? This must bore you!"

She really had no idea how diverting she was. "I am not bored."

To prove it to her, he leaned forward and nuzzled her ear.

She didn't jump, only melted against him in the most delicious surrender, real and hot.

He had a chance here he hadn't expected, but wasn't that everything about this sudden affair?

Slowly, he swept the last strands of loose dark hair away from her neck. Found, with regret, that he was too tall to kiss her there while they were locked in this position.

But he'd go to hell before he moved.

Instead he had to limit himself to stroking one thumb down the column of her neck. Her skin was very fair, and he couldn't help but contrast it with the sun-given color of his own hand. Like a farmer, or a blacksmith; someone else who worked out of doors.

He needed to marry her before she found out anything about him she didn't like.

He continued to distract her from the rest of his history with the Faircombe family, and she continued to eat her stew, bite after dainty bite.

"*Why* am I hungry again?" she asked in wonder, then shivered a little as his fingers wandered forward to caress her throat the same way.

"You had a very busy night, little sleep, and a very long and busy morning," he told her. It was frustrating, being unable to reach more of her with his lips. He'd like *her* to be the warm thing he had for nuncheon. When she wasn't so tired. When she was all his.

No, he'd like to do that to *make* her his.

"You needn't worry I always eat this much. And I do have a dowry."

He wasn't clever enough to sort through the emotions that surged through him at her little speech. "If you've eaten enough, put down the stew, Viola."

Immediately, she did.

She'd been wavering. The more people they saw, the more people who made her question her choices. He wanted her confident of her choices. Last night she had, without even consulting him, picked him out of a crowd to marry, when that hadn't been Lee's wish at all.

It was now.

When his hands moved lower and stroked the side of one breast, then the other, feeling the shape of their slight softness through her shift, she only sighed, and let her head fall back against his shoulder like it had the night before.

She trusted him. She was here; she was his.

"Shall I stop?" He let both his thumbs brush over the peaks of her nipples through the soft, delicate linen; they both hardened. And Viola shifted.

"*No*," she said with the firm conviction of which he knew she was capable.

The texture of her, hard for him, wanting, when every-where else she was so soft, was fascinating. He was so hard himself that if she moved against him, he might spend.

He'd take the risk.

Pulling her into him and upward a little made it possible for him to reach her ear with his lips. When he nuzzled her there, and tweaked one nipple again, his other arm tightening her against him, she sighed and reached back to hook one hand behind his neck.

She wanted this. She wanted him.

"Do you trust me to touch you?" He heard the quiver in his own voice. What did he have to fear? She was already here.

"Of course." Instant conviction. "You said you wouldn't abandon me."

Nor would he. But the very faith she had in him held him back.

He shouldn't risk a child with her, not till they had the marriage done and recorded. No one knew better than a soldier that no one could guarantee they'd be alive in the morning.

On the other hand, he could not leave this room till he saw his Viola sated.

He pulled the coverlet up over her feet. He should have done that before. She didn't feel cold now though, nowhere he could feel, and he could feel many places. He slid his hand down her delicious thigh, and hooked his fingers around the hem of the shift.

"If you'll spread your thighs," he whispered, eyes closing, nearly spending just by imagining it.

And it was real. She did.

She let him slide his hand along the soft flesh of that leg, belying any fragility, higher and higher till he found the warm soft center of her.

Slick from his attention.

Now Viola jumped. No, she wasn't startled; she was only arching her back.

"Are you trying to make this easier for me?" he asked. Because this was the easiest thing in the world, stroking the softness there with his fingers, parting the lightly-curled lips, stroking within.

"No, just because I want it!" she gasped, and twisted a little in his grasp.

That was everything he wanted to hear.

"Then you'll have it," he soothed her, slipping his fingers between her lips.

As with her breasts, she was hard for him there. Throbbing. Desperate. But unlike him, also soft and yielding, and so slick that his fingers stroked her more easily than over fine silk.

The noise she made then was heavenly to hear, a mix of gasping shock and desperate hunger. *No one ever fed her hunger,* Lee mused to himself.

Now he had the chance, and he reveled in it. He wanted so much more, but on the other hand, this was everything.

"Mr. Waite!"

So proper, and so free. Wild and too tame all at once.

"Soon you'll call me *husband,*" he said as much to himself as her, pressing a little harder at the base of that all-giving nub at the core of her. He wanted her to reach the peak. He wanted to see it. And he wanted her to sleep.

Whether from his whispered words, the caress of one hand on her breast, or the action of the other, she reached it. He felt her arch, muscles straining as her pleasure carried her up and over the peak, and a little cry escaped her.

He wanted more. He wanted her *louder.*

But that was enough for right now.

She sagged against him, gasping for breath.

"Do you think you can sleep now?"

"I cannot avoid it," she said, and indeed her words were a little slurred, as if she were drifting to sleep already.

Carefully, he slid from behind her, threading his leg around her and tucking her under the quilts. For a second he was afraid she didn't want to meet his eyes; but then hers opened, and she gave him a sweet, sleepy smile.

"You're too kind," she told him, and wriggled down into the warm covers.

The sight of her there in the bed they'd just warmed, with the faint smell of her skin and her pleasure tickling his nose, undid him. "No, I'm not."

He swept up her bowl and the tray, moving them out of her way in an instant and out the door.

In the hall, he set the tray on the floor, catching up its napkin.

Freeing himself from his trousers, he gave himself a deep, merciful stroke. It was heavenly relief, but not enough.

Still it would do. Viola needed to sleep.

He pictured her again, sleeping in his bed. Stroked himself again, and a third time.

The final pleasure jolted up from his spine, poured out from him while he bent over himself as if he'd been shot.

And, gasping himself, cleaned himself with the napkin before tucking himself away so no one else in the house would see him.

He couldn't remember how long it had been since he'd even touched himself, much less had a woman in his arms.

It felt like he might finally be home from war.

CHAPTER 11

*V*iola woke in the haze of confusion that came from sleeping during the day.

In fact the day had gone. No light tried to creep in under the heavy drapes over the window.

She blinked over and over again, willing herself to wake.

Mr. Waite sat in a low chair, his legs sprawled before him in the yellow glow of candlelight. Her slight movements caught his waiting eye; he put away his book.

It was all unpleasantly like waking up from being ill, so much so that Viola threw back the coverlets and pushed herself out of bed, standing on the carpet beside it.

The look on Mr. Waite's face as he surveyed her from top to toe made her realize that he could see through her very fine shift.

That reminded her of what had happened before she'd fallen asleep, and she climbed back in the bed, feeling flushed with heat.

Mr. Waite's low laugh did not make it better.

Viola had enjoyed imagining herself as a sophisticated

lady, married to one man while indulging in the pleasures of another.

She had *not* imagined what those pleasures would actually be, and now all her calculations about the world were knocked askew.

"I didn't mean to be any trouble."

"No? It's pretty clear you intended at least some of this."

"I mean the..." Viola slid lower under the covers. Would he notice if she pulled them over her face? Then she saw the twinkle in his eye. "You know what I mean."

"I think I do, but teasing you about it is almost as fun."

Torn between the desire to hide and the desire to know more, Viola pulled the warm coverlet up to her neck and stayed there, fists balled together under her chin. She had many questions. *Many.* So many she didn't know where to start. It seemed like the easiest way to begin was to ask, "*Was that fun?*"

He'd slid down in his chair to watch her too, one leg hooked over the other and his hands folded against his stomach. It was incredible that she knew so much about his body there. "Definitely."

"*Why?*"

Viola wasn't stupid. She had a basic knowledge of how these things were done, and he'd done none of the things she'd expected a man in such a position to do.

And now he just sat there, studying her as if she were the book, his head propped on one arm against the dark leather of his chair. "Why *wouldn't* it be fun?"

This wasn't teasing; he seemed in a good mood, but asking.

Viola felt a moment of serious regret over luring him into that hackney cab.

Nothing had worked as she expected, nothing. Yet she was here, in this gentleman's bed, and as far as she could see, about to be married to the person she'd picked for that very thing.

She was getting her way, except that she could not conceive of sharing the pleasures they'd just shared, and then doing the same thing with someone else.

"You've been terribly good to me in all this."

He wiggled his fingers in her general direction before resuming his contemplative position. "Are we still talking about the nuncheon?"

"Oh—" He was being difficult on purpose. He was enjoying *this*, that was clear.

Shooting upright, Viola reached behind her for one of the pillows and threw it at his head.

"Hey now." He caught the pillow with one hand.

Just the sight of his spread fingers, such a large, masculine hand, clutching the light pillow, brought back all the unbelievable sensations he'd caused and Viola felt warmth pool again, low inside.

"Honestly, Mr. Waite, why are you being so good to me?"

"Now, what interests me is why you think it unlikely."

"Well, it's a... I don't expect..." Oh, she'd just have to say it. "Surely a man wants something for himself at such moments."

"Oh, Viola." Now his eyes were glittering again, and not entirely with humor. "I had a great deal for myself."

She folded her arms across her chest. It felt foolish to hide under the covers again. "Very well, I'm a fool, then. It was nothing I expected."

"I want to hear this. What did you expect?"

"*Mr. Waite.*"

"I found you a hairbrush."

Disoriented, Viola only sat there. She thought her jaw might have fallen open.

He stood and took up an ebony hairbrush from the table, turning it in his fingers as he edged closer.

"Yes, it seems new, though I'm going by the fact that there's no hair in it. Not Lady Charlotte's, if that suits you; I found it in the room Miss Farsworth used last."

"Now how do you know which room Miss Farsworth used last?"

He grinned at the acid in her tone.

"I thought if you didn't mind I'd just—" He gestured with it toward the general vicinity of her head. "Use it."

When Viola didn't say anything, because she couldn't think of anything to say, he took a step toward the bedside. Then another. Slowly.

"I think," he said as he bent to slide the silk thread from the end of her plait, "that your nuncheon interrupted my story about visiting Faircombe Hall."

Warily Viola glared at him even as she slid over in the bed so he could sit.

He *was* rather fun. But also alarming. Like those parlor games where one used an electrical machine to store lightning in one's lips, then challenged a gentleman to try and kiss.

Except he wasn't turned away by a little lightning.

The way his fingers undid the tie of the silk thread rather than just sliding it off in a knot spoke to his forethought. That she would need it again.

Viola had certainly never valued forethought as much as she should.

"So." His fingers undid the braid, though it nearly undid itself, her hair was so slippery. He applied the brush to it, smoothing out the few tangles that remained. "I spent that winter at Faircombe Hall, learning about horses."

Viola leaned away and peered up at him. "Let me guess. You approach them warily, from the side."

His wave of the ebony hairbrush indicated general agreement. "Especially the ticklish ones."

"I'm not ticklish."

"Did anyone call you a horse? How dare they." Slowly he plied his brush, and Viola subsided.

He went on. "When spring came, I needed something besides horses. I just walked north. I don't know why it never occurred to me before. Here I'd marched all over Napoleon's lands and never thought to walk through England."

"Weren't you afraid?"

"No."

Something there made him look serious, made a muscle in his cheek tighten. Viola wanted to ask more, but she also wanted to hear the rest of the story. "You must have seen so much."

"I found England covered in farms." Whatever concerned him loosened a little. "It makes sense, but I hadn't realized it in my bones, you see. If you want to see anything wild, you have to keep going."

"How far did you go?" The repetitive motion of the brush calmed Viola a bit. As it did horses, she suspected.

"Quite a way. The roads are wilder the farther you go. The towns are smaller. The air tastes different."

"Not all the way to Scotland!"

He grinned down at her. "All the way to Scotland and well into it, my lady."

That made Viola smile. He'd never called her that before.

"By the time I came south again winter was calling and it was a cold one. I stopped at Faircombe Hall for a visit, then came on to London. So did Lady Charlotte and Miss Farsworth, as you seem to know."

"Yes, I do." Part of Viola's work had been to keep track of who appeared at social functions; the Duchess depended on others' eyes for that.

"Well, there you are. The rest is private."

Viola put up her hand and ran her fingers through her hair. It was loose, smooth. And her questions weren't answered.

"So you did offer for Miss Farsworth."

"As it happens, I did." He behaved as though he were just recalling it. "Around Christmastime."

"And did you offer for anyone else?" The idea ruffled Viola's feathers. She'd picked him partly because he clearly wasn't having success. But how many ladies had he courted?

And why on earth would any of them turn him down?

In that way they had of seeming to know what the other was thinking, he grinned again, setting the hairbrush on the table near the candle and himself on the edge of the bed with her. "No, turns out I'm selective in my proposals."

"Unless someone kidnaps you."

"No, even then."

He was so near now it seemed only natural for his arm to brace behind her on the bed, giving her a warm, strong place to lean if she wished. Natural for his lips, so close, to brush hers. Natural for him to rub his cheek against her temple, feeling the silkiness he'd created in her hair.

"See now, I'm not so kind. I'm just indulging myself with a little chase," he explained, and the brush of his breath on her skin made her shiver. "Personally I like sneaking a little close to you, sort of unexpected, and then capturing you like this."

His kiss was indeed claiming, and Viola felt herself bending, softening, falling under his spell as she moved into him, leaning against his chest, something that now felt so natural it was inevitable.

When they parted, he stayed close enough that she could look right into the blue depths of his eyes.

"It's like taming something wild," he told her softly.

"You are the wild thing." The words just came. She didn't feel awkward saying them. This was the least awkward place in the world to be. "Sometimes there's a look in your eyes—it makes me think of wolves, or hurricanes, and I've never seen either one."

"Is that so?" He looked a little taken aback, and a little pleased. "I've heard nothing about this. Tell me more."

"Aren't you used to being admired, Mr. Waite?"

"No. And neither are you. But I intend to change that."

* * *

SHE TOOK his words as if they'd been a threat, shying back a bit. In between the little cake-stealing girl and the temptress was someone like a skittish horse.

Someone no one had brushed, or exercised, or petted.

Obeying an impulse, Lee threaded his fingers through her hair, reaching into the dark curtain to find her scalp. Pressed it with his fingers, squeezing a little. Her eyes fluttered shut.

Then she opened them again, firing him an accusing look. "You mean to be very distracting."

"Not at all. You're free to admire me as much as you like." He let his fingernails scrape lightly across her scalp; her eyes fluttered closed with bliss.

He thought she'd stay silent, but not Viola.

"You're so kind. I've inconvenienced you so, and in return you've given me nothing but protection, and loyalty, and support."

He wished she'd end her list with *and nuncheon*. She didn't. Pity.

A quavering sigh left her lips and it called him to draw closer, but she took one of his hands in hers and he let her pull it away from her. She pointed to the bed. "You go there."

Obligingly, he rose and threw himself across the bed where she pointed.

She looked disgruntled by her own success, likely missing his heat. Good.

And then she went *back* to praising him. "You're strong, fair, and honest to a fault. I... I quite like your hands."

He tamped down his smug smile; she was trying to be serious, and he was trying to let her, though open kindness made him want to leave.

As it did her. He'd endure.

"Most of all, Mr. Waite, and I ought to have said this sooner, you have the most beautiful blue eyes."

That shocked him.

"And I can see," she added, "that *you* are not used to anyone being careful of you either, or praising you. So I'd like to know, if you don't mind my original question, why *my* pleasure was such a pleasure for you, if it was."

"Viola, why aren't you running Parliament?" She sat there in her transparent shift, such a fascinating mix of slenderness and curves, dark eyes and serious mouth, and she made him believe there was such a thing as nobility.

"I haven't any interest. Please, sir. Explain what gives you pleasure."

It was such an innocent question, full of deep dark secrets at the same time, secrets she wished to unpack and savor.

Lee had sampled ladies' comforts before marriage, in high marble towers and below taverns, and none of those encounters, not one, had ever hinted that somewhere there was a fragile-looking woman with eyes that looked into souls who could be shy even as she kidnapped a man to coolly arrange her own love affairs.

"This." Leaning on his elbow, he studied every inch of her he could see in the candlelight, taking pleasure in her mere presence.

She put out a hand and smoothed his hair back from his face, much as he'd done to her. When he didn't elaborate, she prompted. "Say more?"

Now that she was running him through the same paces he'd set for her, he found out exactly how awkward they felt.

"Viola, you can't take me as an example for all men. But I like to feel your pleasure and know I caused it. It makes me feel big and strong."

"You are big and strong." Her fingers kept stroking his hair.

"I've seen the tallest men become pathetic. Offered a choice between being gentle and using force, they chose force."

She nodded a little, her face clearly telling him that she didn't understand but would keep trying. "I suppose that makes sense."

There was so much more to it and he was putting it into words so badly.

Taking her touching hand in his own, he pressed a kiss into its palm. He thought she was brave; he'd try to be.

"Viola, you're a dream I never thought I'd dream. You look so breakable, but you have a general's heart and a mind so sharp it could cut me. To tell you the truth, I *wished* some woman would offer for me and save me the trouble."

That earned him a slow smile. "It's rather nice to think I saved you at least a little trouble."

She still didn't understand. How could he say this? How had she just said it?

"You're clever and lovely and you have the kind of hair poetry is written about. No one has taken sufficient care of you, perhaps ever, and I'm honored to have the chance."

She gave him a little nod even as her brows crushed together in thought. "Thank you. So a woman with—"

"Not any woman, Viola. You."

That startled her again; he saw her jaw fall open. She can't have done well at the gaming tables when her face was so easy to read.

She whispered as if it was one of those deep dark secrets, "I really like how you say my name."

Of course she did. She was exactly like him. Adrift. Alone. And starving for any type of indulgence. He wanted to give her every kind.

He laid flat on the bed, his face upside down to hers to make tough things easier to say, and laid her hands against his own cheeks. "To be honest, I'd love to hear you call me something besides Mr. Waite."

"Is that not your name?" Far from alarmed, she stroked the sides of his face, fingertips brushing the bristles there as gentle as a moth's wing. "Are you like Oliver, hating a title no one knows you have?"

"No." He'd meant to make the room comfortable for her; he felt safe in it too, in this room, in her hands, in the dark. "Unlike Oliver, I have too few names. The men in my company call me Waite, and too many other people called me Bradley."

"All those strangers who raised you?" She'd remembered. "How many strangers were there?"

"Ah." He had to count. The solicitor; his wife; their housekeeper, when their own children came and he was put out of the nursery. That distant cousin, *his* wife, then the cousin's grandfather, the one who'd died. Lee missed him. His father's business partner, for a while, and his rough crew of men, no women there; then the governess where he'd spent that one summer in someone's house. He couldn't even remember whose it was. "Ten or eleven, I suppose, all told."

"What?"

"Then I went to school, like boys do."

"Ten or eleven strangers before you even went to school?"

She didn't stop touching his face, only held it in her hands. "What *happened?*"

"My parents died." Such a simple thing with such disastrous consequences.

"Parents do die. Their children aren't buffeted from house to house!"

"I was." House after house where he was the least important thing in it. Even the dogs had a purpose; they could hunt. There was no purpose to a three or six or nine year old boy.

"That's appalling! Had you no guardian?"

"Oh yes, I did. The solicitor where I started out. He arranged many of my places; then my father's business partner felt he was doing a bad job and took me on himself. Bold move, as there were no women in his factory, but I mixed in perfectly fine with the other orphans brought in to apprentice. In fact, now I think of it, that might be why I liked the army. There's a pleasure in being part of a group like that."

"Oh, Mr. Waite."

She didn't look pitying as much as she looked concerned. As if she could go back in time and make sure his socks were darned and his porridge eaten.

"Exactly. All those voices shouting *Bradley* all the time." None of them pleasant. "I don't mind the *Mr. Waite*, but it does seem formal."

"What did your parents call you?"

"I wish I knew."

There it was, the wound at the heart of it. She'd cut to it quicker than her brother could have with a scalpel.

She didn't shy away from it. "Do you remember them at all?"

"No. If I had one wish..." He'd spend it on this, because Viola was his future and his parents were far in the past. But he wasn't ready to tell her that. "I'd like to know something about them. Not the things all those guardians told me, about their birthdays and breeding. It's the little things I'd like to know. What did they like for supper? That sort of thing."

She nodded as if she understood. Certainly she understood distance from parents, though hers was of a different sort.

"What do you call yourself in your mind?" Now she was leaning over him, closer again the way he liked. He hoped she liked it too.

He preferred her blocking out his sight of the rest of the room. Because he'd just realized that his main hope for marriage was just what he missed about the army and apprenticing. To be part of something larger than himself.

"Just Lee," he admitted to the woman who'd taken the place of the rest of the world in such a short time.

"I think Lee sounds lovely," she murmured against his lips, and kissed him.

It focused the world down to one charged instant. Nothing mattered other than her lips on his, tasting, trusting. Her hair fell down around the two of them, a shining curtain of silken strands, putting them in an otherworld of silence.

He'd been so determined to make her feel safe he hadn't noticed himself edging toward danger.

Because this didn't feel like his first marriage at all. That had been comfortable, reasonable, expected.

Nothing about this situation was expected, and nothing about Viola either.

When she released him, he said quietly, "I think I see what you mean about that combination of frightening and alluring. I think the word you want is *thrilling.*"

"This is thrilling?" That clearly delighted her.

"Well, let's check. You'd better try it again."

Laughing, she did.

It was like kissing hope. A million new futures spread out in front of him, and he wanted them all. Anything and everything he could get and have with her.

He didn't know if the Duke would relent about the special license. It would take weeks to announce the banns if they had to visit a parish church, and that once they found a church official who wouldn't squawk about the fact that he'd never darkened their door.

Some things would have to wait; but other things couldn't.

Still laughing—he'd kissed her laughter—Viola broke away and said, "Why didn't anyone call you Lee?"

"Well, I never understood that myself till I met you. I think it was because they never asked."

CHAPTER 12

*V*iola's heart broke for him a little more. His pronouncements didn't carry much detail, but she could imagine the rest. A little boy tossed from home to home where no one even cared enough to ask him his name.

Now a grown man, hungry for so much more than food.

"And Miss Farsworth? Did she call you Lee?" Viola didn't know why that little green cloud of jealousy kept hovering around the edge of her vision. She'd never felt anything like it before. Jealous of Oliver's beautiful eyes and Victor's place in the tree fort, yes. This kind of jealousy, no.

Mr. Waite—Lee—only chuckled. "She most assuredly did *not.*"

"And why didn't you marry her?"

"She didn't want me."

Viola had always noted the nuances of things, long before she'd entered Her Grace's service. She saw and heard the prickle of pain under the careless words, and tried to banish it with some teasing of her own. "Didn't want you? Despite the hands and the eyes?"

With mostly real humor he said lightly, "I didn't question *your* story."

With one finger, she traced the curves of his face. Upside down to her, he looked weird, unearthly. Yet still there was the same jut of his cheek, the same cushiony lower lip, the same blue to his eyes she never saw anywhere else.

"Then it must be a great assurance to you that I personally selected you to ruin my reputation," Viola pronounced with some satisfaction. She had little to offer, but she could offer that.

His hand grabbed her wrist.

The constant startlement of him ran under her skin everywhere, like a hot river. He was right; the word for it was *thrilling.*

And this time the surprise became him kissing the inside of her wrist, then all along her inner arm, his breath hot through her thin linen shift, to the inside of her elbow, where he bit her lightly, turning the river of pleasure into a surging wave.

Gently he drew her further down, over and beside him, till they lay side by side, two curves interlocking on a feather bed that felt to Viola both very big and a little too small.

"Selfishly, I want to pleasure you," he said in his usual voice, the calm declaration of fact, and Viola felt her insides melt and burn at the same time, as if she were made of hot wire. "I don't want to risk burdening you with a child when one never knows what tomorrow will bring, and you may come to your senses in the morning. But I do want to pleasure you, for as long as you'll let me, and it is a very selfish want, Viola, I assure you. Just tell me I am the one you want to marry."

Only a day before Viola had thought that she knew what marriage was. Now she knew she'd had no idea. Not just the marriage bed and everything that happened there, but the ties between two people who needed something from one another, found it in each other when they'd found it nowhere else.

He'd threatened to love her; he very well might.

And Viola was beginning to wonder how she truly felt.

She hadn't felt like this about Lord Callendar. Mr. Waite wasn't *always* kind, nor did the idea of him feel safe even when he wasn't there. He seemed a little dangerous, joked when he should be serious, and never left her side at all. The rest of the considerations that had gone into choosing him had begun to fade.

She didn't know what that meant, but she could give him one definite answer.

"Sir, you are definitely the man I want to marry."

That unleashed him.

Like a tiger he sprang up, stalking over her on hands and knees to kiss and nip her with his teeth—her nose, between her breasts, one rib, the soft flesh of her belly through her shift, a thigh, her knee. When he returned to nibble the soft dip of her waist, she squirmed. "Sir, that tickles!"

"I told you, I know how to handle a ticklish horse."

Before she knew what he was about he'd flipped both of them, and she found herself lying atop his hard body, the heat of him searing through her shift, everywhere under her, while he easily spread her thighs and nestled them on either side of his head.

"*Mr. Waite!*"

"What, does it tickle here?" He bunched her shift upwards over her rear, smoothing the bared skin there with both his enormous hands. "Or here?" He turned his head to one side and, having conveniently placed himself, lightly bit the inside of her thigh.

"I can't..." This was too intimate. Baring. Shocking.

"Can't, or don't want to? You're allowed to enjoy yourself, you know. Let me show you."

That thought shivered up through her from her core outwards, as earth-shaking as any touch.

She could enjoy that.

It was more foreign than any geography, the idea that she could simply enjoy something. Not something; *him.*

Braced on her knees, she lifted; surely she was heavy on him. "I do want to."

"Then stop trying to escape." Gently he pressed down on the small of her back, his hand feeling wider than her waist; she let him take her weight again. If he wanted her here, she'd indulge him.

Then he kissed the inside of her thigh, a little higher than last time, and a liquid heat flooded into Viola that she felt might carry her away.

"Come here."

Far from feeling like a horse, Viola felt more feminine than ever before as she followed his call, sliding against him —higher for him, lower for her—and let his lips brush the outside of hers in a kind of kiss she'd never imagined.

"Well done," he said, and then spoke no more, because he was devouring her.

This was impossible. It passed awkward in the flash of an instant and went straight to bone-meltingly pleasurable. He knew how to do things, things with his lips, things with his *tongue* that far surpassed anything Viola had ever imagined.

She just managed the conscious thought that her tentative touches to herself had been pathetic.

"Lee! Don't—"

The swirling pleasure stopped. "Don't what?"

Even the sound of his voice, muffled by her body and the linen of her shift, seemed unbearably personal. "Don't trouble yourself too much."

"Ask a starving man if a feast is too much trouble." With that enigmatic answer, he busied his mouth again.

It was too much. Viola had no words left. Falling against him, she wrapped her arms around the narrow space above his waist, rubbing her face against the linen of his shirt, for he still wore that and trousers. He still wore his *boots*.

And her, she thought with an inward giggle, realizing that he'd spread her over him like a blanket and she was keeping him warm while he set her ablaze.

Had she always been at this fever pitch, ready to ignite into passion at a single touch? Because it seemed like only seconds since he'd taken such thorough possession of her, yet Viola felt the trembling in her legs that always presaged the peak.

The thought that he must know that, from earlier that day, pushed her over the edge.

She shuddered against him, unable to suppress an animal noise of release that matched the satisfied, wordless growl that answered her.

He knew she had reached the peak, but still he went on.

"You can't—" When had she last been able to speak a whole sentence?

"I can't? Or you can't?" And then, hell-fiend that he was, he tickled her ribs.

Laughing, she collapsed onto him again. She hadn't realized how she'd tensed. "You're awful!"

"I'll survive. Breathe. I'll be gentle. Just breathe."

So she breathed. She breathed in the scent of him, his skin through the warmth of the linen over his belly. She was making it damp with her breath, she realized; then she didn't care.

The slow flat motions of his tongue roused her again, took her higher than she thought possible too fast for her to stop and think. When she circled her hips a little, trying to draw them closer without smothering him, he made another approving noise deep in his throat.

All he wanted from her was this.

It was freeing, it was ferocious, but it also wasn't enough.

Flailing forward she laid her hand over the bulge she could see in his still-buttoned trousers. That made him buck upwards with a deeper grunt.

It encouraged her to know she affected him too. All this pleasure shouldn't just be for her. She'd never even *imagined* the things he was doing to her; he deserved something for himself.

"I know what you're doing, Viola," he stopped to say in a warning voice.

"I am... enjoying myself?" The smallclothes were more snug than she expected; it was difficult to push them down.

And the sizeable portion of him that she freed was more than she'd expected.

It was hard, and when Viola gripped it in one hand, softly smooth as well. He made that noise again.

"You're doing something for me because you can't bear anything that's only for you."

She'd been foolish to imagine this man would never challenge her. He knew far too much about what she was thinking.

But he was wrong, because the second she'd taken hold of him, she felt she had something else that was for her: *him.* The core of him, hot and eager because of her. She sighed, still holding him, and slumped against him again.

"I wanted this," was all she said, and he dove into her again.

The slow, sliding pleasure seemed to go on forever. Occasionally he hit a particular spot that made her shudder all over, and judging by the noise he made, he liked that. She punctuated those surges of pleasure with a squeeze and a stroke of him, his tip starting to drip as wet as she felt herself to be, and she was lost in the circle of giving and taking that seemed to never end.

"We must stop sometime," she panted, writhing against his shirtfront and the hard chest beneath it.

Instead of answering, he shifted, turning his torso a little and raising a shoulder, an arm between her legs, spreading her wider. Tucking her thigh firmly into the pit of his arm and, not coincidentally, thereby holding it still, he slid a long, demanding finger inside of her, making her cry out.

"You have no idea how long I can do this," he muttered, and Viola gasped again at the implication that so could she.

The feeling of him as foreign and invading faded as fast as her doubts. She'd thought she'd gone to the most unimaginable places; she was wrong.

"That's only one finger, of course. Perhaps two is better."

He matched his actions to the words, causing Viola to press her open mouth into his wet shirt, muffling her silent scream.

This was too good. It wasn't possible for something to feel like this over and over.

But apparently it was, as Lee kept inexorably moving in and out of her, slippery and unyielding all at once, and dimly Viola realized that if she could get more of him inside the place he was worshiping with so much devotion, it might be, though it seemed impossible, even better.

And he *wanted* it to be this good for her.

"Come, Viola, you can do it again," he whispered right against the most pleasurable nub at the center of her, and shattering, Viola did.

It was deeper this time, reverberating through her belly, down to her toes, up to her heart, and she melted for him, unable to stop the trembling, jerking motions he caused in her.

"That's perfect." His own voice was deeper now, rougher. "And if you want to see how much I enjoyed that, squeeze me just a little harder."

Lost in the fog of everything she'd just felt, Viola dimly realized that she still had him in her hand, hard, throbbing, even larger now and making her hand look small.

Nothing pleased her more than to do just as he asked.

The feel of his silky skin under her palm, her fingers, *was* what she wanted, and she pulled him toward her a little, her palm skating over the tip of him before stroking down, and again, and again.

With a roar he gripped her hips hard against him, his face buried in her heat, and she saw the explosion begin in him, a shaking stiffening pulse before his hand shot down to cover the tip. A hot liquid gathered there and dripped against his clothes. Even in crisis, he'd thought of her, protected her from his final volley.

Breathing hard, he fell back against the featherbed.

And Viola, who had never gone anywhere or done anything that wasn't sanctioned by her mother, her aunt, or her Duchess, lay in a pool of heat and sweat and dripping pleasure and gave up on thought, propriety, or anything else that would force her to move from her place atop his sprawled, warm, sated body.

* * *

ONCE LEE RECOVERED A LITTLE, he realized it was on him to move; Viola showed no interest in it.

His arms shook, but he managed to roll them so Viola could lay again on the dry sheets. He was soaked; so was she.

"I'll fetch you a dry shift," he whispered when she made an unhappy noise and looked at him with huge, dark, trusting eyes.

She stretched her arms out upon the bed, letting him pull the linen off her. It was the first time he'd seen all of her, every smooth sweet inch. Her curves were delicate swells, every creamy expanse of skin flawless. "I'm so tired," she whispered.

So was he. Sleep pulled at him. "Then sleep. I must attend to some matters this evening, but you rest all you like. I'll order you a bath. There are books here; I'll send you a brighter lamp."

She only blinked, and Lee saw what a trap he had set for himself. She was in his bed, in his room. Those were his books.

But she only said, "As you please."

As he *pleased?*

Not trusting himself to speak, he tucked the coverlets over her, trusting them to keep away the chill. He ought to put another shift on her, but if he did, he'd climb back into that bed with her and the marriage ceremony would be irrelevant.

Blindly he stumbled to the door.

Closing the heavy panel between them felt like crossing an ocean. He was too far from her. His hands splayed against the wood.

Something was happening to him. Every breath was deeper than the last, faster, wracking his body till it felt like sobbing.

He'd had a wife, and that had been his measure of what devotion felt like. It hadn't felt like this.

Holding Viola made him imagine a home and children, yes, but also an endless summer of passion that would never stop. It would bleed into winter and winter would disappear. They would never be cold.

He'd promised her his feelings, once risen, would fade. Now he had to wonder: what if they did?

Losing his family had left him hollow, the world hollow. Every day had been pointless, every night a forever. He had not grieved like a man in love, but he had felt the loss, such desperate loss.

And he felt it echoing in him now, and it terrified him.

Whatever happened tomorrow, or the days after, he'd marry her. She'd said he was the man she chose for that, and he would do it. The need to do it swelled under his ribs, filling up every place inside him between all the refuse that was his lungs, his guts, his heart. This strange new hunger was dangerous, he could feel it. Hunger like this did not simply fade. It had to be fed.

It required that he marry Viola and made sure she didn't regret it.

CHAPTER 13

"*Y*ou slavering beast. The Duke is sending you a vicar."

"Morning, Oliver." Lee pushed aside the toast he'd been pretending to eat. "I take it you're moved to call at such an unholy hour for good reason."

The toast was flavorless. Lee sipped at his coffee. It was bitter and bracing, and he needed that.

He'd had a long night in the vast drawing room down the hall from where Viola slept. He'd told himself that after muddy trenches, a sofa in a heated drawing room could not be called a hardship.

He'd been wrong. He'd been conscious all night of Viola's proximity, nothing between them but one door, a door that wasn't even locked. He could climb right into bed with her and she'd welcome it. He was sure of it.

The vision of her, sated and sleepy and smelling of their shared pleasure in that bed haunted him like the most beautiful nightmare all night.

Oliver threw his gloves on the breakfast table. Apparently in lieu of launching them at Lee's head.

"You've won," Oliver snapped. "He's bringing a special license. He should be here within the hour."

"You can't mean *this* hour."

"His Grace delights in waking the clergy."

Cass bustled in behind her husband, thumping a massive basket onto the table. "Is Viola awake? Also, good morning."

"I don't know. Mr. Darby?" Lee waved toward the butler who had just shown the visitors in. "Inform Lady Viola that she has callers."

"You don't know if she's awake?" Oliver's eyebrows were suspicious, and high.

"No. Have some coffee and shut your mouth."

"I told Oliver that you would be gallant while Lady Viola was perforce in hiding with you," Cass said, seating herself at the little table and helping herself to toast.

"Gallant!" Oliver grumbled under his breath.

Lee knew exactly how foolish it would be to take Oliver for harmless; he kept his eye on his friend. "Not gallant the way you used to do it; the real kind." Then he remembered Oliver's wife. "My apologies, Lady Rawleigh."

Her smile was wan. "We are all friends here." She brushed away the discomforts of marrying a rake with one hand in the air. "Oliver knows that he cannot change the course of true love."

True love. The phrase throbbed in Lee's head, reminding him of the rushing, panicking breaths he'd taken outside Viola's door last night.

Cass sipped at the cup of coffee offered to Oliver, and made a face at its bitterness. "As soon as we got the Duke's note, I insisted on coming to stand with Viola. I might help trim a gown for her wedding."

The rest of Lee's sleep-lagged brain caught up with the conversation. "Wedding. Today, yes? Thank God," he muttered into his own coffee.

Mr. Darby, all bald propriety and thin shoulders, reappeared in the door the way good butlers did. "Lady Viola will be ready to receive forthwith."

"Go and see her, Lady Rawleigh," Lee said, a little loudly to make sure she would hear. "She'll be glad of your company."

Cass nodded and disappeared with her basket.

Oliver just sat, ramrod-straight, in his chair.

It was only a few seconds before Lee lost patience with the man's stare. "What? Planning to challenge me to a duel? If you are, aim your bullet better than you did your gloves."

"No, no. Cass convinced me to see the better sides of this. You'll be true to her, I know that about you. If you can't love her, that's her battle to fight when it comes. God help you if you disappoint her, you know. Viola has quite a hard streak."

"Can't imagine where that came from."

"My mother," Oliver said with a simple shrug, the buttons of his morning coat stretching over his chest as he leaned forward. "She's been a fury since my father died, and I ought to have contained her better. But you must believe, I would never have let her force Viola back under her wing. *Viola* must believe that. Because if she's only marrying you to escape that fate, she needn't."

Lee didn't really want Viola convinced of that this morning. "What ails her? Your mother, I mean."

That made Oliver slump back with a sigh. "Spoiled all her life, I suppose, but also stubborn about it. The older she's got, the worse it gets. The whole world is as she sees it. There is no other option."

It didn't sound that bad, but Viola was no fool. If her mother terrified her into taking such drastic action, she *was* that bad.

"Viola does seem to want to marry me."

"And you had nothing to do with that."

Very little, but Lee wasn't about to admit it. "As you say. She's made her calculations, and I suit." With some misgiving he added, "Except that she thinks I'm penniless. Romantically penniless. Hold your tongue, would you?"

"What the hell has she been drinking?" Oliver tasted his coffee, made a grimace similar to his wife's, and set down the porcelain cup with a forceful *clink*. "Has she been reading Byron's poetry or nonsense like that?"

"*A beauty and a mystery,*" quoted Lee with a shrug.

"Christ, she has, and she's done something to you."

Lee kept his eyes down, determined not to show any thoughts about anything Viola had done to him in a carriage, a hotel, or upstairs. "I'm going to take care of her." Those words felt clean and right. "You've done a pissing poor job of it, and your parents too."

When he looked up, Oliver's oceanic gaze was fixed on him and radiated pity.

"Waite, you're marching right down the same path you took with Beatrix. Taking care might be the start of a marriage, but there has to be more."

That was an unfair blow. Oliver knew too much.

When Lee stood, so did Oliver, clapping his hand on Lee's shoulder. "Waite. She's my sister."

I need her. The words were right there, ready to spill out.

But Lee didn't *need* her. He'd never *needed* anyone. He'd walked the length of Britain on his own two feet, after all.

It couldn't be that the one thing he needed was his best friend's sister.

"Pretend she's not," he grumbled. "Pretend we're friends. You've trusted me with your life; trust me with this, keep quiet, and you can be my groomsman." He looked over Oliver's fashionably severe coat, hoping to distract him with a tweak about his weakness for clothes. "Is that what you're going to wear?"

* * *

THE INSTANT VIOLA opened the door, Cass took over the room with her height, her basket, and her curious eyes.

"His Grace has dispatched a clergyman and a license!" Cass plopped onto the unmade bed, her basket silently landing beside her. "I hope that's good news!"

Viola wanted to hide behind her hands. Or the door, or possibly some large, solid building. She'd been awake and hiding in this room in her morning wrapper for quite some time.

Was it good news? She couldn't think. The haze of pleasure in which she'd fallen asleep lulled her into dreams more unearthly than any drug, and still hung in the air when she woke up.

Last night simply could not have happened. She could not have taken *that* position atop *that* man and done *those* things. It wasn't possible.

Nor was it possible for her sister-in-law to be here so early with such news.

The room held no clock, but Viola felt time ticking away.

Cass pulled a folded gown from the basket, a cloud of lavender lace. Without thinking, Viola shook her head. "My mother put me in so many lavender dresses."

"Because of your name. I understand."

"I prefer blue."

"I am trying to devise something for your wedding day, Viola."

Her tone conveyed that she knew Viola had plenty of evening gowns, but doubted any of them had the right sort of flavor for a bride.

That reminded Viola of all the simpering fools setting their caps for Lord Callendar. White was so virginal, so false. More so on her, after last night.

Though she was vehemently aware that she still had more innocence to lose.

Cass studied her with a gentle but measuring look. "Are you with child?"

"*No!*"

"Heavens, you needn't howl!" Cass rustled again in her basket. "You of all people must know that all of London will assume so, after your disappearance. And a special license on top of that." She pretended to be absorbed in her trimmings, but her voice was kind. "I would understand. So would Oliver."

"I'm sorry to say Oliver does not understand me. He never has."

"Perhaps not, but he does understand how with passion, one can be carried away."

Ugh. Viola did not want to contemplate her brother and passion at the same time. But Cass was close-mouthed, married, and possibly her last chance at the kind of womanly advice her mother would never give.

Viola sank to the edge of the bed.

"I am not carried away with passion. My decision to marry Mr. Waite came of long, careful deliberation."

Cass' face fell. "Oh dear."

That sent Viola back on her feet. "Shouldn't it have?"

Cass' light eyes clouded over, and her expression was one straight from a Grecian statue. One of the goddesses who had seen too much. "Lady Viola—"

"For pity's sake, we are related. Call me Viola." One more careful performance and Viola would scream.

If nothing else, she'd spent a night and a day free of society watching her, *expecting* things of her, and she was not ready to submit to more surveillance.

Cass dropped the lace into her lap, her hands rising as if

to speak with them, then she dropped those too. "I meant nothing by it. You and I are different."

Meaning that *her* marriage had been more about passion than deliberation. More things Viola didn't want to know.

But one thing she did. "How do you stand it? Society, when you know Oliver has—" She stopped herself. This was cruel. "I'm sorry."

"You've tarred yourself with Oliver's same brush, you know." Cass put away the lace, pulled out a thin white shawl. It was silk, embroidered with flowers on the ends. Hearts' ease, perhaps. Viola paid little attention to flowers.

"*I?* Oliver has bedded half the *ton!*" She blurted it out before she could stop herself.

Cass only grimaced. "And it is the *ton*'s unfortunate habit to vilify a man only after he's reached that mark, when a woman may only indulge herself once. You, dear sister, left a party in the middle of the night with a man not your husband, and therefore you, dear sister, are a jezebel."

Viola opened her mouth, then closed it again.

If she protested and fanned her cheeks, she'd be the same sort of fool she'd despised, wearing white in drawing rooms like an advertisement.

"Can I not be something in between pure and soiled?" she muttered.

"You know that answer already. You chose this," Cass said it slowly and carefully, "when you left Her Grace's service *very* unexpectedly. So only you know whether it is worth it." She dropped her too-penetrating gaze, pretending to focus on the shawl she shook out before her then draped on her lap. "If not for passion, it had better be for something valuable. You traded Her Grace's trust for it."

Viola felt herself crumple inside. Her voice lowered to a whisper. "How can you ever be sure what your feelings are worth?"

"As an old married lady, I can tell you this. There are chances to doubt every day. So you'd best be sure of *something*."

For once Viola felt as fragile as she looked. "He is—"

Generous, caring, and yes, passionate. She hadn't known any of those things before. When she'd labeled him perfect for her needs because he was desperate, penniless, and above all else, lacking a title.

Just like *jezebel* and *virgin*, they were only words, and they didn't do him justice. He was so much more than all that.

Viola felt ill. He was the kind of man who deserved someone who loved him with all their heart.

Why shouldn't he deserve that? Why shouldn't everyone?

Because most don't get it, she thought silently and bitterly.

Lord Callendar cared nothing for her. It hurt, but she could survive it. It was as nothing compared to what she was about to do. A passionate affair could pass and leave no repercussions; a passionate marriage was something else.

Mr. Waite hadn't promised to be faithful. She'd told him flatly she didn't plan to be. It was an appalling foundation for a marriage, but more importantly, one she couldn't put right once it began to tip over.

On the verge of getting exactly what she'd planned, she realized it was picking Mr. Waite's pocket. She needed time to understand exactly what had happened with Lord Callendar. Where had she gone wrong? How could she understand? Without those answers, how could she do better when it came to Mr. Waite?

Because she rather wanted to.

"The most important thing," Cass pronounced with the certainty of one's elders, "is that you talk to one another as you go. You cannot do without that."

And wiping clean the butter knife from Viola's breakfast tray, she used it to slice the white shawl cleanly in two.

Viola felt she might cast up her accounts.

Possibly now. Or possibly at the altar.

* * *

THE SERVANTS, convinced that the ceremony was only the church recognition of contracts already signed, went about arranging the house with a quiet efficiency that Viola would have admired had she not felt so ill she could barely walk.

The halves of Cass' silk shawl, pinned to her waistband, lightened the front of Viola's walking suit, her coat edges pinned back to show the white. Her hem's embroidered scallops, three rows deep, made the skirt more festive; her high lace collar surrounded by pointed tippets recalled the petals of a flower.

Complete with the feathered bonnet clutched in Viola's fist, at least it was warm enough that if necessary, Viola was ready to run.

The room's wide window had a high view of the street, and had Viola spotted a waiting carriage, she might have made a mad dash for it.

She should have asked to speak to Mr. Waite before the ceremony. Why hadn't she asked?

"Ah, excellent." In front of her, the man's soft jowls perched atop his cassock. He bent his head and they half-folded, like bread kneading itself. His flat pointed hat remained steady as he sipped the last of the coffee someone had given him. "Lady Viola, I presume."

"Yes." She could ask *him* what he thought of marrying a man she barely knew. But he didn't look like he expected deep questions over his coffee, so she kept her peace.

When Oliver came in and stood next to Cass beside the settee, Viola couldn't meet his eyes.

In her head she'd called him a rake. Heartless. Selfish, for not sharing his tree fort. Stupid, for not seeing her pain.

Now after half an hour alone with his wife Viola had the sneaking suspicion that he was just a man, flawed, at least wise enough to marry a woman who wholeheartedly loved him.

Viola might not deserve that; the way things were going, she was unlikely to get it.

But Mr. Waite deserved it, and she had no idea what to do.

Traps were only traps when they weren't easily escaped. She'd planned a trap for Lord Callendar, and instead she'd trapped a good man who deserved better.

Better than her half-hearted attention and selfish demands.

But then Mr. Waite appeared, and all the churning inside Viola calmed. She breathed easier. She could see again.

And he came right toward her, captured her hand, and tucked it into his arm the way he had so often the day before.

The world tilted back the way it should be.

Viola stopped trying to explain it.

"Shall we?" he asked, pitched for her ears alone.

"You needn't." She could still give him an honorable escape. She could cry off at the last minute. She'd be ruined, but he'd be free.

"Nor do you. Don't fear your mother, Viola. You don't have to do this." His eyes reminded her that she'd started it all. "As for me, it would be my pleasure."

The way he drew out the word painted her skin with fire as all the memories of the night before came rushing back.

It hadn't just been pleasure, if anything about it could be termed *just*. It had been a promise of sorts. Viola felt that now.

And hadn't Her Grace and Virginia praised her for her instincts about people?

She wasn't Cass. She couldn't be sure of forever. She couldn't be sure why something inside her tolled like a bell ringing *this man, this man, this man.*

She only knew that the thought of leaving him here made her want to cry.

And standing beside him felt wonderful.

In fact, she was so calm as the ceremony began and went on, and on, and on some more, that her mind had time to wander and wonder. Why did clergy all have that rise and fall to their voice? Was it the repetition? Or did they practice in school?

She also thought it mad for the sermon to claim that marriage was intended to repair the sin of fornication, when so many people entered into it for exactly that.

Her attention only focused when the words began to sound clear again, like pebbles in a stream.

"Wilt thou love her, comfort her, honor and keep her, in sickness and in health and, forsaking all other, keep thee only unto her, so long as ye both shall live?"

The vows. She'd forgotten them! If society flouted its own rules, so would Viola; but it troubled her to think of being forsworn.

"I will," said Mr. Waite, easily and firmly.

Of course, that was how he said everything. Still, it sounded astonishing. And bracing.

Then the bishop turned to Viola, and she realized with horror that he was about to ask her the same question. The one Mr. Waite thought she didn't want to answer.

"Wilt thou have this man to thy wedded husband, to live together after God's ordinance in the holy estate of matrimony? Wilt thou obey—"

Suddenly seized with violent coughing, Mr. Waite bent at the waist, his tall body alarmingly bent in half.

"I say!" The vicar, jowls trembling with concern, went to fetch his own coffee cup where he'd set it on the mantelpiece, but thanks to the efficient footmen, it was gone. "Can someone fetch us some tea?"

"No need, no need. I'm just—" Mr. Waite doubled over again with another deep cough, his face flaming red.

"Gracious." The fellow cast about for another vessel containing any kind of drink, but there was nothing in the room. "You're almost to the end of the ceremony, you know."

"Am I?" wheezed Mr. Waite, never looking at Viola, who held his arm as if tethering him to this world.

She'd begun to suspect he was fine.

"Yes yes, just the bit about the woman obeying and honoring and forsaking others, all that bit."

"Don't worry, I'll get through it." Mr. Waite made a violent hacking noise, then stood as if recovering, one hand outstretched, the other on his hip. "I'm always delicate in spring."

Viola had to clap her free hand over her own mouth to smother her involuntary snort.

The vicar regarded her with much more suspicion.

"So then, young lady. Wilt thou obey—"

This time Mr. Waite let out a long, low wheeze as if he'd swallowed a pelican. It was the most astonishing noise Viola had ever heard a person make. Hand still over her mouth, she leaned right into him, turning her face into his coat lapel.

If she wasn't careful she was about to laugh very loudly right in the vicar's face.

This time the fellow seemed more concerned at marrying the young lady to a man so near death. "You *are* willingly marrying the gentleman, are you not?"

"Oh yes, I will," Viola assured him instantly.

It contributed to Mr. Waite's miraculous recovery. "There, you see? She will."

"Yes, I will." She squeezed his arm.

"All the—" The gentleman squinted at his book. He hadn't been reading before, only reciting the service from memory.

"Yes," Viola said brightly.

"Well, all right then." Reluctantly, the vicar turned a page or two, but since they bore no relationship to what he'd been reading, he was lost. "Uh, who giveth this woman to be married?"

"I do," Oliver said roughly behind her, and Viola went from smothering laughter to silence. She refused to turn and look.

The vicar tried to take Viola's hand, but frowned to find it was already locked on Mr. Waite's arm.

"All right, repeat after me. I, Bradley, take thee Viola to my wedded wife, to have and to hold from this day forward—"

"I, Bradley—"

A frown at the interruption. "There's another bit coming, son, wait till I get it all out."

"Oh, I doubt it," said Mr. Waite easily. "Who knows if I'll live till we cut the cake?"

Viola decided it was time to come to his aid. "He's had a terrible case of croup."

"I'm worried it's become a pneumonia." Mr. Waite turned and looked over his shoulder at Oliver. "Is that how you say it? Pneumonia?"

"I don't know where you learned that word." Oliver sounded like his jaw was locked shut.

"I think it was from you."

"Anyway, I've got it. I, Bradley, take thee Viola to my wedded wife, to have and to hold from this day forward. Yes, I'm doing that." He lifted her fingers to his lips and kissed them, with that twinkle in his eye that reminded him of the moment he'd tickled her.

She couldn't suppress her smile.

"And I, Viola, take thee, Lee, to my wedded husband, to have and to hold from this day forward. That's right, isn't it?"

"No, that's not right." The vicar turned pages as if the text in the book had changed while he wasn't looking. "You didn't even get the name right."

"Here." Mr. Waite pulled a slender ring from his pocket and laid it on the open pages of the priest's book. Its glint of gold was suspiciously bright; Viola thought perhaps it was a ring and also a seven-shilling piece. "You need to bless this, sir, I'm sure of that part."

"Not exactly, no. It's because I'm marrying you, you shouldn't put any superstitious meaning on the handling of the ring. It symbolizes the contract between—"

"Thank you, Father," said Mr. Waite in solemn interruption. "And what do I say?"

The vicar, who had lost the thread of the affair entirely, gave up and let himself be led. "You say, with this ring I thee wed, with my body I thee worship, and with all my worldly goods I thee endow." He named the trinity and the final *amen*.

Mr. Waite scooped the ring back up off the book and turned to Viola.

His cheeks a little flushed, his eyes bore down into Viola's like twin blue flames. "With this ring I thee wed. With my body I thee worship. And with all my worldly goods I thee endow." And he finished just as the vicar had, emphasizing the last *amen*.

If eyes could speak, his were repeating every word.

Her own breathing coming faster, she turned to the vicar. "Do I say it too?"

"No." A little brusquely. "Kneel and let us pray."

All four of them knelt, Viola and Mr. Waite, Oliver and

Cass, and Viola didn't hear any of the words, only felt his arm as steady as an oak tree under her hand.

He'd married her.

A peaceful breeze wafted through her middle, like cool air on a hot day. She still wasn't sure what any of it meant. But this felt right.

The vicar fumbled with more words about letting no man put them asunder, reaching down to link their hands and finding them still linked from before. Beginning to show real dissatisfaction with the affair at hand, doughy frown lines collected between his brows.

There were quite a few prayers to follow. Viola listened to them all, more as music than words, the priest's rising and falling intonation rocking along with the slower, calmer beating of her heart now.

Mr. Waite knelt and listened too, his head bowed in all seriousness. Only once it jerked upward, when the priest said something about *he that loveth his wife loveth himself.* Then he bowed his head again.

When they finally rose, he helped her up, and Viola found herself standing in a borrowed drawing room, married.

She missed Virginia, and Selene. She wasn't too numb for that. Their absence reminded her that only one person had arranged all this: her.

It felt right to her, but how did it feel to Mr. Waite?

Oliver was gruff. "You have a license for us to sign, do you not?"

"Oh yes."

While he fumbled for it, Cass leaned in and kissed Viola's cheek. "I had to wait *weeks* for my wedding," she whispered. "Yours was much better!"

Her *wedding.*

Viola signed her name. All their names were on that paper. It was real.

"Excellent," said the vicar, waving the paper in one pudgy hand, "I trust you'll inform His Grace that—"

"Don't be ridiculous," came a shrill voice from the stairs outside. "I have every right to see my own daughter, *especially* if she is getting married."

Viola's gaze flew to her brother. Her jaw fell open. His clenched.

"Brace yourselves," Oliver announced to the room in general, "that's my mother."

CHAPTER 14

"First rank," said Oliver, as if they were back in the infantry, standing in rows, preparing to fire muskets. He squared his shoulders and steadied his feet.

"Second rank," muttered Lee from habit, even as he sprawled in a chair with a good view of the door.

The tension in the room would have suited the approach of a dragon.

Instead the gates were breached by a round little woman whose potato shape was only emphasized by the polished bronze silk of her turban and matching coat.

"Oh Oliver!" She raised two pudgy hands, both loaded with sharp jewels, and charged in Oliver's direction. Lee felt his legs clench, preparing to spring if needed to repel an attack. "How dare you leave me all alone in your house, not knowing which way to turn for help!"

"You were in my house? I hope not."

Cass too took a seat, lightly, also ready to spring, on the opposite side of the room. Lee couldn't tell if it was perfectly possible to hear the dowager countess given her volume, or if Cass would rather not hear her at all.

Oliver still glared down at his mother with obvious suspicion. "Why are you in London?"

"I had to find out where you were by reading the notes on your desk. You know perfectly well I've been wintering with Lady Kellery, waiting for you to come to your senses about my money."

"You have exactly what is alloted to you, and a cottage in Buxton."

"You *cannot* expect me to rusticate *that* far from London. How would one get news? Papers? I will not exhaust all my friends by requiring they write me all the necessary letters. You must arrange a townhouse for me." She looked around at the luxurious appointments. "This one would be very nice."

Lee was fascinated. At the mere sight of Oliver, she'd instantly forgotten that she'd rushed in here because of Viola's wedding. It was like seeing one of the sailors who lost a few quid at cards suddenly lose his memory. But stuffed into a feather-trimmed walking gown.

"Someone who isn't you is already using this house. Madam. You force me to remind you that you were not invited, neither to my house nor here." His eyes narrowed. "Wait, you went to my house? Before noon? *Today?* Why?"

"I heard some mad rumor about—see, there's Viola right there, and perfectly well." Still she didn't greet her daughter, only waved one bejeweled hand as if brushing away her cares. "You should stop the rumors floating about town regarding this family. You are head of it now, Rawleigh, you should do it."

"As you know, I don't care for the title. Yet you insist on addressing me so."

The dowager countess made a blowing noise of careless dismissal. "Still the title is yours. You should use it."

"What, to force people to respect this family? I can't think why they should. I'm surprised you're still trying to dictate what others believe. It failed, you recall, when you tried to convince my father that I was a bastard."

Viola's indrawn breath was stopped by the hand covering her mouth.

The change in the dowager countess was drastic. There was nothing careless about her as she took another step toward Oliver, managing to look menacing when she was barely over five feet tall. "You forced me to take action. *You* proposed to marry a morbidly ill commoner."

Lee sat up straight.

Cass just lifted her hand, obviously signaling he should subside. She clearly could hear quite well enough, and had heard it all before.

Lee had known Oliver through years and hardships. He was at his core a gentle man, one who grew sick of the killing and dying long before he came home. Surgeons spent their own money to attend the wounded as best they could given sparse supplies alloted by the Crown. Oliver had stuck to his post long past what was good for him.

Lee had never seen him this hard.

"My lady wife is seated behind you. Be civil or I will have you put into the street. The only mistake I made about my marriage was ever seeking your approval."

"Your determination to destroy this family put your father into an early grave!"

Lee saw the shot hit. It was gentler than a musket ball, but only just. Oliver kept his feet, though his color faded.

Second rank, Lee thought.

"Madam. Hello." Staying seated, he wiggled his fingers at the horrifying woman to take her attention. It was rather like flagging down an angry bull. She had the same piggy little red eyes. "If you'll excuse us. I've just been married and I'd like to enjoy it."

"Yes. To me." As if she'd just found her voice, Viola stepped forward.

"Nonsense." The dowager wiped this news from the air with a slice of her hand. "You'd never do such a thing without my permission."

Lee was beginning to understand Viola's dislike of pronouncements.

"Yes, I have. I've just been married." Viola didn't sound like Oliver sounded. She sounded blank, not hard.

"*Viola.*" Now the dowager rounded on her. "You would never do something so *stupid.*"

"I have." Viola didn't give an inch.

Lee thought Viola didn't grasp the theory of shooting from organized ranks so that one wouldn't be hit by a stray flying shot. Also, he refused to call this interloper Lady Rawleigh while Cass sat right there. "My lady," he said instead. "This is a private affair and I'll have to ask you to leave."

"Absurd." The lady drew herself up, one outraged potato. "This is my family."

"Mine too, as I've just married into it." Lee decided to draw his main weapon. He stood and peered down at the dowager countess from more than a foot above. "You have not been invited to the celebration."

"What effrontery! Viola, surely you haven't been married."

Viola just extended one arm to point at the vicar, who cowered, open-mouthed, against the far wall, hoping not to be noticed.

"I must be going," the man mumbled, "felicitations to you both—His Grace will I hope be pleased with the favor from —but I have to be going, most regretful, I beg your pardon." And in a flurry of excuses the vicar placed the paper in Lee's hand, crumpling it a little, and fled.

"What was that? Let me see that paper!"

Lee had every reason to suspect the vile woman would toss it straight into the fire. He folded it in thirds and slid it into his vest pocket, securely under his coat.

"Viola! The Duke of Talbourne would never countenance this kind of debauchery! What have you done?"

Viola folded her hands in front of her. Lee noticed that her knuckles were white. "It's so funny you should say that, madam. I was just thinking over the sermon, which claims that one marries to avoid fornication. Isn't that funny?"

There was something in the cloth both Oliver and Viola were made of that didn't shy away from carnality. Lee found himself wishing he'd gotten to know their father better on his one visit to Morland.

But then, the man had chosen to let his wife run roughshod over the whole family, so perhaps Lee hadn't missed much.

The dowager countess pressed a hand to her chest as if unable to breathe in the face of such crudity. "This is what comes of allowing you to converse with Oliver! *I* never mixed you in with my sons. I sent you to the oversight of the Duke and Duchess. Surely Their Graces can put right whatever insanity you've set in motion."

At the mention of his name, Oliver straightened. "I've just realized I don't like *any* of my names...when used by you. Madam, you will leave. And take care you aren't using your time with Lady Kellery to spread rumors about anyone in this family."

"Or what? What will you do? I *know* people in London, not just the sorts of villains you consort with."

"Military officers," Oliver said, looking at the ceiling.

"I've wintered in London for *decades,* and who *but* me has the right to speak about my own children?" As if noticing Lee for the first time, she stared up at him. The height had no effect, he thought. "If Viola *were* to do anything so foolish as marry you—and I do not know your name—it would only be to spite me by connecting our family to the sort of nameless, penniless nobody I presume you are."

That volley hit.

He looked over at Viola, and her pleading eyes, and the glancing blow turned into a gutting one. Because he saw it was true. Viola *had* wanted a penniless nobody to strike back at her mother while setting a trap for Lord Callendar's passions.

No wonder she'd been so adamant that he was poor.

"All right." He'd had the wind knocked out of him; that's why he couldn't speak any louder. As entertainment, the woman had worn out all her value. "Our wedding breakfast awaits, and sadly, there will not be enough for you. Out you go."

"How *dare* you put your hands on me!"

"Hadn't thought of it, but it's a fine plan. Out."

"Someone tell me the name of this shockingly rude man!"

"It's Bradley Waite, madam, and I can't say it's been a pleasure to make your acquaintance. Again." With one hand he gestured to the door; if she stood there another second, he'd use the other hand to shove her out of it.

"Waite? *Waite?* What are you, a *shopkeeper?* I've known some by that name." Again she turned toward her daughter, ignoring Lee's gesture completely. "Viola, what *have* you done?"

But Lee didn't shove. He was immobilized by the landing of an explosive cannonball. Had she known his parents? Actually seen them? His next words were involuntary, rasping and raw. "What were they like?"

* * *

VIOLA COULDN'T STAND any more.

Her mother was at her worst when said things that were true. She flung her accusations like knives in all directions, trusting some of them to hit, and her last two had.

Viola *had* chosen Mr. Waite partly to upset her mother. Her mother, puffed up with pride since Viola had been invited to join the house of a duchess. Her mother, devoted to appearances.

So devoted that she had taken issue with Cass' deafness and completely ignored that Cass and Oliver were in love.

Cass herself had reached some sort of limit. "Just to refresh your memory, *Lady Rawleigh,* you had nothing to do with Viola serving the Duchess of Talbourne. That was me. You have not been invited; you are not welcome."

"How dare you speak to me!"

Cass raised her arms and dropped them dramatically. "Somehow, I dare."

But Viola couldn't let her mother go now. Not after a pronouncement like her last one. "Madam, you think you knew Mr. Waite's parents?"

"Of course I did! Impudent frauds who tried to climb their few invitations into a better echelon of society!"

"What were they like?" From wanting to keep her distance, Viola now swept in close to her mother, pinning her in the space beside Mr. Waite. "What did they speak about? Did they drink port or sherry? Was she tall too? Was he?"

Unfortunately, Viola never remembered her mother's ability to smell when something was wanted of her, and do the opposite.

The dowager countess sniffed, eyes darting from Viola to Cass, also standing now, and pointedly ignoring the gentlemen.

"Viola, you know you don't want to strain your mother's heart this way. Come home to Morland and I'm sure Oliver will sort out whatever mess you've just made. A paper is only a paper. Broken things can be mended."

"I've broken only what I wanted to break." Viola's mistake was obvious; she blamed herself for it. It had been a trying wedding, for all it had been hers. "You must tell us something."

That *us*, so pleasant to say, seemed to burn her mother's ears. "Us? What us? You can't honestly expect to live with—"

"Oliver. Make her talk."

Oliver looked ready to heat up the fire irons and practice illegal things, but Cass interrupted. "Can we all agree that these conversations do no one any good, and this one has gone on too long already?"

Over the dowager's blustering, Oliver met his wife's eyes, and nodded. "As always, I accept your conclusions in all things."

Viola was about to protest again when Mr. Waite took her hand and tucked it into the accustomed place on his arm. "Let her go," he said quietly, clearly enough for all to hear but just as clearly intended only for her.

"But she—"

"It's fine."

It wasn't fine. Viola had always feared her mother; in this moment, she hated her.

But the other three were in agreement, and Oliver marched his mother to the door with both hands firmly on her shoulders. "If you breathe a word of your poison to anyone, anyone in London at all, I will cut you off without a penny."

"My house!" protested the dowager, forgetting Viola and her marriage as soon as something she deemed more important was waved past her nose. "My widow's portion!"

"I will bankrupt you and see you starving in the gutter before we have this conversation again. I mean it. You know my resolve. You're the one who claims it killed my father. Take Lady Rawleigh out, please," he waved to the largest footman he could find. "And I mean make sure she is outside this house and lock the door."

Viola looked up at Mr. Waite. He'd been nothing but kind, more than kind, and this was how her family repaid him. This was how *she* repaid him.

How had she ever convinced herself her scheme was harmless?

"I'm so sorry."

"Don't be." He patted her hand. "Who knows but that she will have a change of heart at Christmastime and write me a long thoughtful letter?"

The idea of her mother writing a long thoughtful letter to Mr. Waite almost had Viola smiling. Almost.

"I absolutely agree with your decision not to live with that dragon, by the way," Mr. Waite said, sounding a little more like himself with every word. "Though it must be easy to brew a good pot of coffee at her sweet little cottage by the gates of *hell.*"

Cass snorted, and patted Mr. Waite's arm herself. Oliver returned looking as tired and worn as they all did, making Viola wonder if this was how it felt after firing stopped on the battlefield.

"Christ," was all Oliver said. "Christ."

Mr. Waite didn't reprimand him, presumably because it could well have been a prayer.

"Well, I think we need a very *strong* wedding breakfast now, don't you all?" Oliver moved to a sideboard and lifted a decanter of golden sherry next to a crystal glass.

Worn as he looked, Mr. Waite moved fast, extending a long arm to cover the glass.

"Coming home from war to that? Understandable. But you don't need it any more."

Oliver just met his eyes, and Viola didn't understand everything that passed between the two men without words.

Oliver stoppered the bottle.

Thank you, Cass mouthed to Mr. Waite, then slid her arm through the loop of her husband's. "Let us investigate the breakfast table, my dear Dr. Burke."

And the two of them went out.

"What was all that?"

Mr. Waite gave her a long look with those gentle eyes of his, and seemed to decide Viola didn't need to be protected from the truth, either because she'd survived her mother's treatment or because they were married now.

"It's my opinion Oliver just likes to forget. The war, the men he couldn't save, your mother, even the women he's bedded. He just likes to forget."

"The sister he couldn't heal."

Mr. Waite's brows went up, and he nodded. "Well spotted, Lady Viola. No wonder in Her Grace's court, you were the clever one."

"*Her Grace* is the clever one! And I believe I've just discovered Oliver's distaste for the family titles. I'd much prefer to be simply styled Mrs. Waite."

He looked neither pleased nor surprised, and Viola wanted to put a curse on every hair on her mother's head. Of course now he thought she just wanted to irk her mother with marriage to a commoner...which had once been, to an uncomfortable extent, true.

Trust her mother to find that thorn, sharpen it into a knife, and twist it into the side of a man she'd just met.

A man Viola had only really known one day. Two now. That didn't feel true; it felt like they must have known each other longer, much longer. It felt as though they had walked a long way together and arrived at the expected place.

That place was marriage, and she wanted to celebrate

with him. But how could she do it now without sounding false?

"I'll wager now you're glad I don't intend to visit my mother," she said, feeling awkward for once even with his arm under hers.

"There's no pleasure in it," he admitted.

Viola wanted to run after her mother and pull her hair till she told what she knew. Even forced out of the room, she'd taken all the possibility for joy with her. She was so good at that.

Viola was terribly afraid she was too.

Oliver thrust his head back into the parlor. "I forgot to tell you. I couldn't get them here in time, but I did send a note to Victor and Ginnie, and hopefully they'll call this afternoon. And the Duke's note said Miss Díaz would also pay a visit."

Viola just walked beside her new husband, noting how he shortened his stride to match hers. It would be nice to see her brother and sister-in-law, but they'd never been close, any more than she had been with Oliver; and Virginia was just one more person inconvenienced by her plans.

She could not imagine forcing food down into the maelstrom of feelings inside her.

Nor could she grasp why Mr. Waite did not throw the marriage license into the fireplace.

CHAPTER 15

"This is a very careful campaign to rescue your reputation."

Virginia had come, a traveling bubble of spring in her sunbeam dress bejeweled with her own wide smile. Viola could never decide if her friend's smile seemed brighter because of its contrast with the rich brown of her skin, or because she so clearly meant it.

They'd withdrawn to the vast room where Viola had been married, the rest of her family gathering below in the dining room, where the wedding breakfast had turned into nuncheon that threatened to extend throughout the day.

Viola half-wished to be down there, not with Oliver or Victor and their wives, but for her own new family. Her husband.

The wishing made it hard to concentrate. "Why rescue my reputation?"

Her question arrested Virginia mid-sip of tea.

Virginia's social life would not be too badly curtailed. They'd planned to spend the last few weeks of the Duchess' confinement at Talbourne House in any event. Now here she was, bursting with plans Viola had never expected.

"Parliament will stay in session however long it takes to receive the treaty from France and finish the war. That's to our advantage! Every hostess in London will be struggling to devise new entertainments, and the general feeling of good-will once the treaty is signed could bode a flood of new invitations for you. I am utterly serious. If Lord Castlereagh can return to government after fighting a duel, you can certainly return to society after an impulsive marriage."

"Lord Castlereagh is a genius of diplomacy, and he won that duel." The tea tasted like ashes to Viola; she set her own cup down. "And he has a title."

"I think it's more to the point that Mr. Canning was terribly unpopular. Viola, you must stay in London long enough to be seen *not* with child."

That thought made Viola's stomach turn too. She had never liked being the object of society's attention; in her role at the Duchess' side, she was not. The eyes were always on the Duchess, or if not there, on Virginia. "I suppose you have a careful schedule of appearances at which my waistline can be publicly measured?"

Virginia stayed firm, one slender dark hand balancing the porcelain of her cup. "Is it really your wish to be separated forever from me and Selene? Are you so angry with her?"

"I'm not angry with anybody!" Well, Oliver. And her mother. Those hurts were fading now, as if scarred over by the interview today. Her mother was even more unpopular in her family than Mr. Canning was in Parliament. That was soothing.

It would have been more soothing, but Viola felt her mother's barbs planted deep under her skin, barbs full of poison. And the poison was spreading.

"You know the risks of a damaged reputation; you helped

repair Selene's. She would have been thrilled to host your wedding. I can't imagine why you chose to do it this way."

"Any cornered snake will bite," Viola muttered. Her mind spun back and forth between two poles. *My mother hung over my neck like an axe,* and *It was my only chance with Jonas.*

Silly, silly Viola.

Those thoughts were coming faster and faster, and Viola could not ignore them, or how much she wanted to sleep.

Virginia asked simply, "Who cornered you?"

And when Viola didn't answer, she added, "I would have thought you would tell me. I thought we were friends."

Virginia was truly a ray of sunshine wherever she went. She'd never understand what had driven Viola to sacrifice Mr. Waite's bachelorhood, how Viola had crumpled under the weight of threats from her mother and dreams of a man who could care for her.

She didn't understand how Viola took things from everyone she met.

"Lord Callendar hasn't asked about me, has he?"

"No, why would he?" Virginia just blinked.

"I hoped he—" She stopped. Hoped he *what?* Was it the sickness inside her that kept repeating that if she just did something differently, it would all come right? She didn't want anything different from what she had.

But Virginia was no fool. "Hoped he what? Viola. Did he say something or do something that pushed you into this marriage?"

"No." The word was dry in Viola's mouth.

"I'm glad to hear it. He ought to behave himself, after he caused that disaster with Her Grace last year. I'm glad you never set your cap for him; he'd have snapped you up, then you'd be married to *him* now."

"I doubt that."

* * *

Lee hadn't been standing at the door long. Just long enough.

He stayed there, one hand flattening against the painted wood, so forgetting the tray of butter and honey sandwiches in his other hand that there was danger of them dropping.

Two nights ago he'd thought it would be simple to rescue a girl and rid himself of her. A time measured in hours. When had he forgotten the *ridding* part?

He should go in. It was only that hearing her ask after Lord Callendar had caught him unawares. He'd had to close his eyes.

He couldn't blame her for wanting to escape her mother's reach. He could blame Oliver for his lack of protection, but clearly Oliver had just learned how to stand up for himself, and his own wife.

Funny how a man who was a dead shot with a pistol could be brought low by words.

Lee certainly felt the dowager's poisonous effects, and he hadn't been raised by her. Hadn't been raised by anyone, really. For which he was now thankful. No one in the world could cut him with words the way the dowager did her family.

There were benefits to his childhood.

"Lady Viola," he said, pushing the door open. "You should eat." *I am in no way interrupting your thoughts of Lord Callendar with sandwiches,* he thought grimly.

"Thank you." She acknowledged his placement of the plate at her side with a tilt of her dark head, but that was all.

He sat beside her because he could not leave her there like that.

"Miss Díaz wishes you to spend the rest of the season in London?"

"Yes!" That lady, gloves in her lap, had already taken possession of a sandwich. With her other hand, she raised an emphatic finger. "Even Lady Fawcett has pledged to help. People find delicate women more plausible."

"Do they?" He nudged the sandwiches closer to Viola. "Is that why you are so determined to stay frail?"

She was his *wife.* He ought to carry her away to where he could feed her. Brush her hair. He wanted to bathe her. He wanted to lose himself in her, kissing every drop of water from her skin with his own mouth.

She'd captured him. He'd surrendered. The marriage license in his pocket was the treaty.

As with most contracts, the reality of it would prove out afterwards.

"Likely you should listen to Miss Díaz. I know nothing of the machinations of society, myself."

Viola's dark eyes finally came up to meet his. "Should I?"

The presence of the other lady squashed Lee's freedom to say everything he wanted to say. Viola would know what he meant. "Don't you want to carry out your own plans?"

"I doubt they will work." Viola's gaze dropped again.

That wasn't the answer he wanted. He wanted *No.* One good *no* to her previous plan, and he could launch his own.

"What plan?" Virginia looked back and forth between the two of them, sandwich forgotten in her fingers. "Because Selene thinks with this plan, we..." She set down the sandwich and dug a tiny notebook from the reticule beside her on the sofa. Consulted a page inside. "...should have you back in society within four months. More ministers' houses, perhaps, and less lords." She closed the notebook, adding regretfully, "Likely not Almack's."

"I don't want ministers."

It concerned Lee that Viola seemed to have fewer and

fewer words. Virginia hadn't noticed that she was providing plenty for both of them.

So Lee asked Viola the pertinent question. "What *do* you want?"

Viola only shook her head, not even lifting it enough to meet his gaze. It might be that she was fascinated by the grain of the marble in that table-top, or it might be she was drifting away.

Her body was still here but her mind had gone somewhere else. Not a daydream; just not here. He'd seen it in animals. He'd felt it in himself.

Yet a day ago she'd been lively enough to venture out into Leicester Square in an evening gown and find herself friends and a bakery.

Lee wasn't a gambling man. If he had to put money on the cause of her decline, he couldn't have chosen between their marriage, her mother, or lack of sandwiches.

He could only hope that it wasn't their marriage, keep her away from her mother, and provide as many sandwiches as possible.

Putting aside that she'd never answered, he spoke again. "Your brother Victor would like to see you downstairs before he goes, if that suits you."

Viola stood as if ordered, and drifted out.

Virginia stood too, but then put up a warning hand when Lee moved to follow his wife.

"I have a message for you from His Grace." She didn't look so sunny now, her girlish jaw set.

"So?"

"You've moved too quickly for His Grace to find out more about your background and your intent. But he assures you that if he ever hears the least inkling that this marriage is not to Lady Viola's liking, he will have it annulled, even if it is *years* from now."

"That's quite a feat." Lee understood the message. "Even if there are children?"

"Multiple children?" Virginia could look quite suspicious.

"You're talking years, Miss Díaz. Who knows how many there could be by then? Not usually a case for annulments."

"Henry the Eighth managed to annul many marriages." Her glare was as though a hopping little rabbit had threatened to cut off his head.

Lee took it seriously; rabbits were vicious. "Henry was a king."

"And our government is now ruled by a shaky Regent. You'll find a duke is quite close enough."

"Well. Duly noted." He lifted the plate of sandwiches for her. "One more?"

She shifted her suspicious gaze to the sandwiches, then back to him, then to the sandwiches again. "Yes," she said in the same distrustful tone, taking another.

"Warning delivered, may I ask you a question?"

She only glared and chewed.

He risked it. "Is Lady Viola falling ill? Does it happen quickly like this?"

All at once her suspicion faded and she forgot about the sandwich.

"She doesn't seem well." She looked at the door where Viola had gone. "She declined slowly last year, spent weeks in bed. It was just after she came. I didn't know to look for the signs."

He pounced on the word. "What signs?"

"Oh... sleeping so much. Unwilling to rise, unwilling to eat."

"And if you see the signs?"

"I haven't, not since then. Oh, she'll be subdued for a day or two, but not so ill."

"Perhaps having a friend noticing helps."

"Perhaps. But when she was ill, she was truly ill. I could not rouse her from the bed for anything. It was more than worrying, it was frightening. Nothing interested her." She looked up at Lee with a different expression, less threatening, more pleading. "You seem to interest her, so if you think you can keep her from falling into such a stupor, keep on."

"I know little of ladies, but something of such illness. It may befall anyone, from a field marshal to a field mouse. A bout would not be your fault, nor mine, or anyone's. Don't blame yourself."

He'd put his finger on an open wound. Virginia looked grateful for the reassurance, as if she had worried about exactly that. "I don't know. Don't people fall quicker when they're pushed?"

Thinking of Viola's mother, Lee admitted, "You've won that point."

* * *

THE GUESTS DID NOT LEAVE till well after supper.

Lee couldn't decide if it was because there was no wedding trip planned, if the sudden wedding had destroyed all their propriety, if they were reluctant to leave Viola alone with him, or, given her listless conversation, if they were reluctant to leave Viola at all.

It was a relief to him when they were all finally gone and he could coax Viola to the chamber he now thought of as hers. Set her into the low chair there, the one where he'd sat just the night before and pretended to keep his distance. He knelt to untie the ribbons that held her slippers on her feet.

It would take hours to prepare, but he asked anyway. "Should we order a bath?"

"I bathed this morning."

He sat at her feet. Would it help or hurt to touch her? He

knew what it was like to march long miles, and Viola had been through the equivalent today.

Her foot felt small in his hands, and fragile. Yesterday he'd thought the fragility a lie; today he knew it was. Strong men foundered when buffeted by hope and despair in too-quick succession; there was nothing weak about Viola.

Squeezing the top of her arched foot, he moved the pressure in gentle circles, hoping to find a spot that could release her into sleep.

The doctor at Northfell might have had a good idea in the middle of his misbegotten drugging. Sleep might help; but there were all kinds of sleep.

"The physician at Northfell wasn't the one who bled you, was he?"

"No." Viola showed no interest in the question, or in his hands on her feet. Yesterday's Viola would have asked why he cared.

Through those weeks of nursing that hawk, Lee had learned when he was seeing a healthy hawk and when he was not. It reacted as it must, not according to the rules of society or even a shared understanding of words. If it pecked him when he approached, it might not be angry; it could also be frightened, or hungry. He had to judge its progress by the set of its eyes, the tone of its muscle, and its willingness to eat.

Viola didn't look any less well than yesterday, but she was unwilling to eat, and that mattered.

"We never discussed a wedding trip." He let his hands shape around her heel, then pull forward, along the arch. Nothing like a hawk's talon, supple and soft and strong all at once. "Would you like a trip?"

"Mr. Waite, I don't want to cause you any more trouble."

"You haven't caused me any trouble." That was a lie; he wanted to see if she rose to the bait.

She didn't, not really. Tears filled her eyes. "If it weren't for me, you'd be a free man today, and we could be doing something that mattered to you. Finding out more about your parents. If my mother knew them, someone else her age might. You never told me your parents were in society."

"Because they weren't. Others might well have thought of them in the same flattering terms as the dowager countess."

"But they were here."

His fingers slowed. "If it really was them, I'm glad. I've been unable to imagine them for so long, sometimes I wonder if they existed at all."

"Somewhere they did, for here you are."

"No one's ever questioned that." For their own selfish reasons, but that he didn't say. "It must have cut Oliver to the bone, his father threatening to disown him as a bastard."

"I wasn't there for any of that. But you changed the subject. I spoke of your parents, not Oliver's."

Lee considered any argument a good sign. He tried to fan the flames of it. "And you said I should be free to do something that mattered. Doesn't this?"

"You needn't. I'm quite ready enough for the wedding night, whenever you say."

So many types of horror flooded through Lee at once that he stopped moving. "What?"

"If you still wished to..." Uncertainty flickered across her face, just visible in the candlelight. "I thought, after last night... did you not?"

"Viola." He put down one foot and took up the other, keeping his face down. Whatever was on his face, this was no time to show it. "I would happily indulge with you in all the things the law now sanctions between us. Even more. But on a night you feel well." He thought about it. "Or a day, I wouldn't mind. Morning. Afternoon. Your choice."

"Have you stopped already?"

"Stopped what?" He was still rubbing her foot.

"You said yesterday you might love me, but after everything I did, everything my mother said... I quite understand if you've stopped."

"My dear lady wife." He was careful to rub each toe. "If you and I prove one thing together, it's that emotions are impossible to understand, charging in and out of one's soul following rules too silent for us to hear. If we were soldiers on the battlefield, we'd avoid enemy fire by staying at our posts and exchanging only very clear signals. Perhaps it would lessen the danger among all these mysterious enemies if we did the same. Honesty has worked well for us so far."

Which was true. Viola had neglected to say how attached she was to his lack of social status, both for lowering her own and for striking at her mother. But he must perforce overlook that; friendly fire on the battlefield was always possible.

As she had done before, Viola gave voice to his thoughts. "That would include things we do *not* say."

A dangerous bargain, for Lee didn't intend to swear, even to his newly-minted wife, to say everything he was thinking. And hiding.

"Within reason. If you buy a hideous hat, I'm not fool enough to say so."

"Why not? I shouldn't wear a hat you find hideous."

"Viola." This was harder than the hawk, for so many reasons. There was a part of him urging him to sweep her into his arms and into that bed and worship her until the pleasure melted away her ill feeling. He knew it wouldn't work that way, but parts of him hoped it would.

But it was more important for her to be able to say what she wanted. He didn't know how he knew that, any more than he'd known that hawk was weak from lack of blood. It seemed logical to him, and so he must act.

"Wear a dozen ugly hats if you like. Forget your mother,

forget all of Britain. You need to understand what *you* want. Forget pleasing anyone else."

"But I would like to please you!"

That made the animal part of him harden; inwardly, he cursed it. Marriage wasn't for a few minutes; it was for a lifetime, and he, at least, had sworn never to break it. "One thing at a time."

He stood, and she caught his hand before he could leave her side. "So you'll tell me, then. When you stop loving me."

Oh, God.

Lee couldn't explain why her sad little speech clawed so at his insides. He shouldn't have told her about Beatrix; he shouldn't have told her about his own shortcomings. Let her find out in her own time.

That was exactly the reason not to promise complete honesty, but it was also closing the gate after the horses had escaped.

"All right." He drew her up to stand. She wore a blue walking-suit, and hadn't walked anywhere today. He unbuttoned its pointy collar and the spencer jacket beneath.

Viola raised her hand and laid it over his. He found it encouraging that she wanted to touch him. "You needn't. My maid is here."

"I'd like to." He would. Soon lost in a sea of tapes and buttons, it felt reassuring to him. He'd been afraid to touch his hawk too much, afraid it wouldn't go back to hunting on its own; with Viola he had no such worry. He could brush her hair as much as he liked.

And he did. It was wound in a simpler design today, tucked into its own knot and secured with silver combs. He slid the combs free and the whole mass unwound itself, like something alive.

"Do you have a fresh night-rail? You shouldn't sleep your shift."

About to rummage through her clothes-press, he caught sight of her eyes, still glittering wet in the candlelight.

"What?"

"You will tell me, won't you? When you stop loving me."

"I'll draw you charts, Viola. Like rising and falling stores of corn. You'll know everything. Do you have a night-rail?"

"I'll get it myself."

Only fair; it was not his most noble part that wanted to see her without those last coverings. "Then sleep. And tomorrow—*would* you like a trip out of London?" Because to Lee, London was the source of all bad feelings. "It would complete your original plan, wouldn't it? To ruin your reputation?"

She had the tiniest, the very tiniest frown. "Don't imagine I had some great step-by-step campaign in mind like Virginia has in her notebook. I wasn't even sure you'd marry me. Certainly I never expected it so quickly."

"Right. Of course. You expected to be ruined and take up begging for bread in Leicester Square. I think you could have made it work. You've got a talent for making things work. You even picked a bakery that could have given you cake as well as bread."

"It's the most delicious cake."

That sounded encouraging. "If there's cake at the end of it, would you take a wedding trip?"

"It certainly seems as if you wish to. Of course I will."

That wasn't saying what *she* wanted, but Lee would settle for it. He was afraid that all she wanted, all she'd *ever* wanted, was Lord Callendar.

And Lee didn't want her to have that.

"Well done." He checked the coverlets; the warming pan had made them toasty. "So hop in bed."

She did, sliding over the sheet without meeting his eyes, and turning on her side, showing him her back.

She'd forgotten the night-rail, or never wanted it.

Resisting the urge to slide in behind her and hold her was one of the hardest things Lee had ever done.

"Sleep well," he whispered as he tucked her in securely and left.

Outside the door, he put his ear against its wood for a moment; but she seemed to stay settled.

Downstairs, the servants were all still busy clearing away from the guests.

"Mrs. Winfrey." He drew the housekeeper away from a gaggle of maids. "We're going north in the morning. Send a footman to buy every seat on the mail carriage north, and send someone ahead on a horse to arrange a private carriage in York. I'll write a letter he must take. Someone reliable. And the most important thing, I need someone to go to a bakery in Leicester Square, I'll give you the direction, and beg, borrow or steal their prescription for cake."

"A prescription for cake, sir? Only that cake will do?" The housekeeper, likely awash with ways of making cake, wobbled in her confusion.

"That specific method of making cake, no matter the price. Can you do all that?"

"Immediately, sir, if not sooner," said the woman stoutly, already summoning a footman with a wave of her hand.

"Sooner would be best."

* * *

THE SOUND of his footsteps faded away outside the door, and Viola didn't know if Lee had gone back downstairs to go on with his evening without her, or withdrawn to another room to sleep.

Maybe Lady Charlotte's room.

She could do nothing right. She should have remembered

that before she'd taken such a rash step. And involved poor Mr. Waite, who didn't deserve any of this. Certainly not to be saddled with *her.*

And her vile, vile mother.

Viola should have found it a little soothing that Oliver had just as much trouble with her mother as she did. It had nothing to do with Viola, and everything to do with her mother.

But all the various humors and feelings mixing inside her added weight to the awful thoughts and blocked the good ones away. From two poles of thought about what she'd done wrong, her mind had now multiplied to having hundreds.

Jonas didn't care

Selene was so disappointed

Mr. Waite could have married Lady Charlotte

Oliver would rather she die

Cass had ruined her shawl

Virginia came all this way

Mrs. Winfrey had to go to all that trouble

Mr. Waite hadn't even wanted to share her bed

Lee hadn't wanted her bed

Lee hadn't wanted her

The list of people she'd disappointed and things she'd done wrong was infinite. They crowded into her head till there seemed no room for any more, and kept crowding. The ache they caused throbbed behind her eyes.

Rolling over in the bed, Viola pulled the pillows over her, buried her face in the featherbed, and cried and cried until she cried herself to sleep.

CHAPTER 16

It seemed another sort of waking nightmare to find herself ensconced in a coach, in the dark before dawn, men shouting outside and tossing bags and boxes onto the roof of the thing making it thump.

Viola would indeed have thought it a dream had not Mr. Waite thrown himself into the carriage before it began to roll off.

"Plenty of rugs? The weather has to warm sometime. There's a hot pot of stew at your feet, so don't kick it." He addressed her as though they met every day in carriages.

Today, of course, they were married. Viola wasn't so distracted that she couldn't remember that.

He treated her exactly as he had before they were married.

The litany of reasons for him to hate her faded a little; it didn't disappear. She tried to ignore it, tried valiantly to take an interest in the battered carriage in which she found herself. It was elegantly painted in red and black, but the floor had been scuffed by many feet, and the seat-cushions crushed by many a passenger.

Mr. Waite sat opposite and waved her attention toward the window as the inn and the yard-wide clock on its wall disappeared into the pre-dawn gloom. "There's a blind, but no glass. Just tell me if you grow too cold."

She ought to be amusing. Provide some sort of conversation. She knew they were going north, but not how far north they would go. "What did you want to talk about?"

"I don't need any talking." Arms folded around his chest, one lock of brown hair escaping his tamped-on stovepipe hat, he looked as if he meant just what he said.

Well, hadn't they agreed last night on honesty? "How will you manage?"

"How will *you* manage?"

She didn't want to tell him that sitting in silence was all she could manage right now.

Without making her answer, Mr. Waite—Lee—*her husband* just shrugged without stirring from his spot. "Army life is long stretches of silence punctuated with cannon fire. You learn to like the silence."

"Where are we going?"

"To where I live."

That was encouraging. Viola knew it was. At least he didn't plan to discard her at Morland. "We're not going to Morland, are we?" It had been years since she'd seen her family house, and the idea of setting foot in it again was horrifying.

Her husband made some sort of strangled grunt. "The only way I'd set foot at Morland would be if I had positive proof your mother was locked up somewhere else far, far away." He considered. "I might also settle for her head on a spike outside."

Viola felt something like a laugh trying to bubble up.

It was an awful jest, but the truth of it was refreshing, like washing her face in cold water.

"Did you tell Miss Díaz your direction?"

"I will if you want me to."

That blue of his eyes, as if he were lit from within, fixed on her, and Viola felt uncomfortable at the attention. How had she walked the streets before dawn a few mornings ago, in an evening gown no less, without expiring of shame?

"I don't see how it matters what I want."

"Yet it does." He looked out the window. Bustling streets full of people walking were everywhere, along with every type of cart. Viola could barely see them. Her head still throbbed.

She put one hand to her head, trying to disguise the welcome pressure on her skull as smoothing down her hair. He'd dressed it for her, she remembered now. The morning was so fuzzy. "Why did you plait my hair?"

"Because your maid quit."

"Oh no! Why did she?" That roused Viola a little.

"Because she didn't wish to go north."

Another person ruined because of Viola's whims. "Whatever will she do?"

"Do? She'll eat Mrs. Winfrey's good food until she finds another position. I sent Cass a note to find her one, or get her a respectable letter of character."

"Oh no!"

Mr. Waite just raised his eyebrows in question.

Viola felt inwardly crushed. "Just one more person whose life I've destroyed."

"Huh."

Whatever Viola had expected him to say, it wasn't that.

With effort, she focused her eyes on him. He looked hale and hearty in his bundled overcoat, one booted ankle carelessly crossed over the other just next to her feet. Well, next to the pot of hot stew under her feet.

"Huh?" she echoed him.

"Just huh." He went on, probably because she looked confused. "I don't think your senses are serving you properly right now. Everything in the world seems to be your fault. That man's cabbages." He pointed out the window where a cart had tipped, rolling several cabbages onto the pavement accidentally; the pedestrians tripping over them shouted and swore at the carter. "Horse dung in the street. Probably the fall of Napoleon's empire. I don't think you have that kind of magical ability, but if you do, I'd personally credit you with Castlereagh's success as much as Napoleon's failure. I've seen your thoughts more steady, and I'm just waiting for them to steady themselves again. I have time. Till then, my job may just be to say, *huh.*"

"Huh?"

"Exactly. I assume you don't want to be contradicted."

Viola shook her head. "No."

"Well then." He settled himself back, tipping his hat forward so his head rocked on the carriage wall. "Not necessary to amuse me. Amuse yourself. Watch out the window."

"Won't you get tired of saying *huh?*" Viola cradled the little spark of curiosity inside her. She wanted it to live.

"I could easily say *huh* all day every day," was all he answered, eyes closed, comfortable in his seat.

So.

With nothing else to do, Viola watched the passing scene out the window.

* * *

AT THE COACHING inn that night, Lee couldn't tell if it was wishing on his part, or if Viola looked a little better since they'd left London.

If anyone was guilty of superstition, it was him. Leaving London had saved his life. That didn't mean it would suit Viola.

But the truth was, he wanted them to have time. Time away from well-meaning friends who wanted to rescue her reputation, time away from *anyone* in her family, and definitely time away from Lord Callendar.

If Lee were lucky, that man would fall in his bathtub and drown while they were out of town.

Also, though it might have been his imagination, as they went north the air seemed to grow warmer. It was a mixed blessing, as its dampness cut into their wool and linen clothes, almost malevolently trying to chill the skin.

The only benefit of Viola's listlessness was that she didn't seem to mind him acting as her ladies' maid.

"Where will you sleep?" That was Viola, not paying the least attention to his unbuttoning of her coat, also ignored the chamber's steaming copper tub by its roaring fire, the hot soup and cheese on the table, and the cloth-swaddled pot of tea.

"Right beside you." There was nowhere else to sleep, not that it was in question. Plus, he had a loaded flintlock pistol atop the open valise by the bed.

He wanted his pistol close at hand if anyone below decided to cause any trouble.

They'd grumbled enough, the other travelers, when Lee had relieved them of all their tickets for the next day's coach; but once he'd paid them triple the price, they'd relented.

He'd worried that Viola would have qualms about sharing the room, but if anything, the prospect of sharing it with him seemed to cheer her. "You won't find it too repulsive?"

He paused for a moment in the unbuttoning of her spencer. "Huh," was all he said.

When he set aside her stays, Viola crossed her arms in front of herself.

"Are you cold?"

"I'm just—I don't want to inconvenience you in any—"

Following the same instinct that helped him judge the mood of wounded animals, Lee took her in his arms, and kissed her.

She was all soft warmth, so sweetly giving in the way she tasted his lip, his breath.

It was the first kiss since they'd been wed, and he wanted it deeper. More. *All* of her. Swelled with heat at the first touch of her mouth, at the smell of her skin so near his, at the warmth of her underneath her thin chemise.

He could wait. He *would* wait. He wasn't an animal.

Even if she brought out those instincts.

When she blinked up at him, her eyes opening after they parted, she looked more confused than aroused. And that wasn't enough. That made it easier to wait.

"I don't understand," was all she said.

"Do you feel quite well? The truth, now."

She dropped her eyes and her plan to say something he wanted to hear.

"Not really." Her voice was just above a whisper.

"There you go, then." *He could wait.* It was his name, curse it all.

He needed that restraint, and all the nobility he could muster, when he slipped off that chemise.

She was a dream of beauty, every inch of her the kind of perfection sculptors rendered in marble then fell in love with, hoping their sirens would come to life and love them in return. Every slender limb spoke of purpose, something easy to snap with force but indomitable in will.

Lee felt a pang as she let him help her into the steaming

water. Her questions stopped, as though he wasn't even there.

He had to believe that she wasn't totally indifferent to him. She hadn't been before; she wouldn't be one day again. And he'd had the right idea removing her from London. Once she regained herself, there'd be him.

Only him, to an extent she didn't yet know.

For now, he had that tender skin to wash.

He'd had Mrs. Winfrey strip the house of nearly everything she might want, sent from Talbourne House or not. The Faircombe family would have to replace their stock of hard-milled soap, their drying linens, their spare buttons.

Fortunately, she had her own hairbrush back.

"Did you intend to wash my hair?" There was Viola, arms clenched around her knees, eyes closed in the blissful heat of the bath, ignoring how the sleek length of her hair threatened to dip into the water.

Lee swallowed.

"No. I don't want it to be wet when you fall asleep."

Carelessly, she nodded, and he had to reach quick to keep her hair dry.

Hoping desperately he was doing the right thing.

* * *

BY THE TIME they were almost to York, their days had a rhythm.

Viola didn't feel it so much as the echo of it. She barely noticed when he put food in front of her, but it did happen several times a day. The rocking of the carriage wheels was repetitive, but the landscape changed.

At one point he leaned out the window and shouted something about stopping.

"You can't stop the mails, gov'nor," the driver grumbled,

even as the horses hung their heads, taking in deep breaths, seemingly grateful for the pause. Viola noticed that. She felt like that.

Mr. Waite tossed him a coin and led her to the verge of the road.

A meadow lay before them, clear and open to the sky. And it was full of bluebells. Thousands of nodding, delicate heads, each one the color of nothing else, a rich violet-blue so vivid that it almost hurt the eyes.

"Just for you." He handed her down the heaped earth that edged the road.

She crouched among the flowers and their rich, clean scent, spicy and green at the same time, surrounded her, filling the air as if winter had never touched this valley.

"Are they too purple, or are they blue enough for you, Mrs. Waite?"

She looked up.

He was a tower of sunshine, the sun glinting gold on the hair that escaped his hat, framing his grin. He turned his face up to the sun as if to bathe in it. Then looked down at her with eyes so many shades lighter than the bluebells, joyfully gathered at the corners as if to say *isn't this grand?*

"You like this." It felt good, remembering that people did like things.

"Nothing better."

"Even with me here."

"Especially with you here."

He helped her up, kept her gloved fingers in his.

"I don't understand." She didn't. There was both too much and too little every day, and she was so tired.

"All you have to understand is that you're ill, but it won't last forever," he told her firmly, tucking her shawl more firmly around her neck.

That seemed like asking a great deal.

Her head hurt, all of her hurt. The blanket of sadness was so heavy on her that she could see the pretty bluebells, but they didn't touch her, not inside where they should. She was wasting them. They were wasted on her, and that made her angry.

"You should leave me here."

"No," was all he said, and before the driver's grumbles could get loud enough to hear, he bent down and picked a few bluebells, tucking their stems in his coat's breast pocket.

Then led her back over the ledge of the road to the carriage, and helped her inside.

As he tucked her feet under the heavy rugs they wore each day, he had a smile playing around the corners of his mouth.

"What on earth is there to make you smile?" Impatience bubbled in Viola, aching to get out. It would be better than this endless numbness. But she worried impatience might anger him.

It didn't. He only settled back in his seat, which, facing backwards, had the last view of the meadow of bluebells as they left them behind. "I'm just glad I got to see them with you."

* * *

THAT NAGGING SENSE of irritation was still with her when they reached York. It was still daylight, though little found its way through the tightly packed buildings to the stoop of the inn.

He seemed highly pleased with himself as he surveyed the high pointed roofs. "Just enough daylight for a stroll. What do you say?"

Viola said nothing, but as always, Mr. Waite seemed to

have nothing to do but accompany her. Viola found herself walking along a wide river past a bustling broken bridge.

The sight was odd enough that Viola stirred to look.

There were people clambering round, some hauling massive stones rolling on poles, some rigging ropes.

"They're rebuilding the bridge," Mr. Waite explained, with that knack he had for knowing what she thought. "It's been years, with years still to go."

"So long to wait!"

She didn't think they were still talking of the bridge when Mr. Waite drew closer, patting her hand once more tucked in the crook of his arm. The air was softer than it had been in London, warmer, even this far north. All the shouts and splashes of the river below were framed by the branches of trees overspreading their walk, and everything smelled green and new.

"Viola, humanity has always demonstrated patience in accomplishment of great things. How long do you think it took us to build the pyramids in Egypt? Or the sphinx?"

"You make it sound noble." She looked up as they walked, watching little birds rocking on the branches above them, scolding them, their feet clutching thin branches between tufts of new green leaves.

"Do I? I don't mean to. That little fellow there is waiting what must feel like an endless time for his family's eggs to hatch. Waiting is a feature of life."

"So many wasted minutes."

Then his face grew hard, and Viola's endless fountain of fear made her think she'd angered him again.

But no, all he said was, "I've lived hours that felt like years. A man's life can't be measured by the clock. I know some people in London, even in this city right now, love to watch hands tick on a clock and insist each passing second make them richer. Likely some of them are shouting at the mail driver now, for being ten minutes past time."

"Oh no." She felt sorry for him, but it was a kind of pleasure, feeling sorry for someone else.

"Never fear, my lady. I paid him well, and he got to see the bluebells too."

* * *

SLOWER CARRIAGES TOOK them north out of York, and Viola wanted to wonder if they would keep going till they drove into the frozen sea. But wondering was too much effort.

It was all she could manage to stay upright for hours on the seats. Mr. Waite took care of everything else. Food, sleeping, bathing, walking—he coaxed her to walk a little farther each day, relieving her muscles from the endless jouncing of the carriage-wheels.

It felt so much warmer now that Mr. Waite even changed her woolen shawl for a cashmere one, lighter and softer.

"Aren't you tired of walking with me?"

"Huh," was all he said, steering her around the corner of the inn. This inn was sleepy, far into the country, with an apple tree hanging over its low door. Its limbs were fat with blossoms, all the flowers leaping out of their buds as if they'd spent the past month impatient for the cold weather to be over, too.

A gang of chickens clucked around the side of the inn, searching for their fare, working hard. That was what the creatures of the earth were supposed to do. Viola had heard that sermon somewhere, that every creature that walked or crawled had its purpose and must do its work.

"I'm not doing any work."

"Well done," said Mr. Waite. "That chicken looks mean.

Don't you think it has a cruel glint in its eye? I bet it pecks the others' eggs."

"Maybe that's what it must do."

"No one told it to do that. It's just bloody-minded, that's what it is."

Shocked, Viola almost tugged her hand away. "Mr. Waite!"

But he just grinned down at her. "Bad language, that's a way to rouse you?"

"It seems so unlike you!"

"True, it is." He seemed to ignore the chickens scratching under the apple tree as they walked on, and sunshine hit both her face and his. "I don't know why I think so little of that chicken. She strikes me as having a bad character."

"What can one do about a chicken with a bad character?" she shrugged, not wanting to move away even if he were to say such things.

The truth was, his arm was more than strong. It was always there to lean on, and even as she remained convinced it would disappear, she relied on it more and more every day.

"Eat it," he said bluntly, "because chickens do not know justice."

And as they walked on grass cropped short by the quiet sheep ranging around the inn, heads down, thoughtfully chewing, Mr. Waite explained what he thought a chicken court should look like, complete with chicken magistrate and chicken bailiffs.

Viola almost smiled.

* * *

SHE DID notice that the last vehicle was more wagon than carriage. She sat huddled against Mr. Waite on the seat. It reminded her of the first time they met.

The air was cool, but when the sun struck her face, it felt nice.

The road had become more of a path, only wheel tracks in the dirt, and as they rounded a curve into the start of a spreading valley, Viola saw that the hills lifted in all directions, before, around them, green mounds reaching up to the sky. They looked deceptively soft, as if she could prop her feet on them, when it would likely take hours to reach their summits if she tried.

Blocking her view was a four-sided tower standing all alone on the hillside, halfway to a line of trees marching down toward her.

The tower was rough-hewn, ancient, and studded with very few windows. At its base two arms of low stone wall extended out then back in, like an embrace. They stopped well short of meeting; the gap held wooden timbers.

Mr. Waite jumped down and opened their gate.

"Go on, Chuck. Willsy. Shove over, Madge," he told the pigs inside before climbing up and driving his wagon right up to the door.

He took Viola straight inside the tower.

There he sat her on a low wooden chair covered with sheepskins, clean and soft.

"Why are there coals?" she managed to ask as he built a small stick fire in the grate over the banked coals there, blowing on them till the thin dry wood caught fire, snapping upward, crackling and spreading.

"Because a man on horseback can travel faster than a carriage," he said, and Viola didn't care enough to ask what he meant.

She just sat quietly in her chair, head leaning on the soft springy wool behind her, watching Mr. Waite unload the trunks and valises with an exhausting amount of energy.

Her head still ached. The bouncing of the wagon had not helped.

"Sleep if you like," he said, and she drifted off as if only awaiting his signal.

* * *

LEE DIDN'T FIND it difficult at all to recover his old rhythms, but now at a faster pace.

Once leery of her questions, now he only wished there were more as she took everything as it came, sleeping long nights, passing short days, uncurious in a place he knew was unlike anywhere she'd ever been before.

He took care of all her needs, glad no one was there to see him learning to nursemaid this particular rare creature, holding on to the pleasure of at least having her care all to himself because there was nothing else right now. It ached, watching her suffering, and it was no comfort that she had warned him. Sometimes he wondered if he'd appeared to Oliver like this, silent and unmoving. Sometimes he wondered if she might stay this ill forever.

But those thoughts he did not let himself think.

The day he brought her the cake, striped and sweetly full of honey, and she barely glanced at it, he knew that there was nothing that could rouse her before the illness ran its course.

"How does it compare?"

The apricots called for in the hastily scrawled instructions existed nowhere in Northumberland that he could reach, so this cake was filled with plums instead.

He tried a portion, and missed the summery tang of the apricots, but there was no way for butter, honey, and plum jam to avoid being delicious.

"Very nice," said Viola after a taste, putting down her plate at the table he'd put conveniently at hand, and not taking it up again.

He had no other medicine to try. There was no medicine for this but time. His patience was his last and only treatment, for her and for him.

* * *

AND SO PASSED the next few weeks.

CHAPTER 17

"Where have you been?"

Greeted with this question, Lee almost dropped the armload of wood he held before he kicked the wooden plank door shut.

"Talking to bees," he said, as if Viola greeted him every day with questions. "They're terrible gossips," he added, stacking the split wood next to the ancient stone hearth.

"Huh," she said in a disbelieving way, huddling deeper into her sheepskins.

Nothing inside had changed; her low chair still stood close by the fire, his bench and the rough-hewn table nearby. More sheepskins hung against the wall, keeping any chill from the thick stone walls at bay. The floor's packed earth was as ancient and hard as cement, and swept clean, while buckets, axes, and other tools stood in their places near the heavy plank door.

Brushing flakes of bark from his clothes, Lee dared to come closer.

He wanted to answer her first question, not wash it away with a flood of his own, though his rushed to his tongue, clamoring to get out. "I thought I was the one who said *huh*," was all he said.

Week after week of tending to everything in and out of Hawkshope Peel, wondering if his new bride would be ill forever, racking his brain for something else to do for her.

He'd been too precipitous with all of it. Agreeing to her scheme, carrying her away to the townhouse, marrying her. None of it made sense to *him* now; how could it make sense to her?

It only felt right to have her here, even if all she did was stare into the fire. "Shall I rub your feet?"

"Why?" She stuck a set of dainty stocking-clad toes out from under the rug, then pulled them back. "I never walk anywhere."

This was different. It felt different. She could have said those words two days ago, or ten, but today they felt different. As though she meant them. As though she was really there.

"Not so." He felt his heart galloping as he knelt beside her and lightly touched her forehead. No fever; no change to anything he could see. Perhaps a change to what he couldn't. "You walked outside with me this morning, remember?"

"Yes. It *was* warm. But the pigs have not made the yard pleasant." She yawned and looked up, up the stone wall where the open window showed a small, crook-sided square of sky. "What's on the other side?"

If Lee hadn't already been on his knees, he would have fallen to them. He covered his face with both hands.

It had been an eternity of waiting. He'd been prepared to wait much longer, but there was no denying the days had crawled past, not because he wasn't busy, but just because he was waiting for Viola to come back to him. She'd been right there, sitting by the fire most days, yet so far away. He scrubbed at his face with both hands, hearing the bristle of his beard against his palms. He must shave more often. "You're feeling better."

She seemed to forget about her question. Lee didn't care. The important thing was that she'd asked it. She'd asked almost nothing during the whole journey here, and spoken few words since. He'd begun to wonder if they should just keep traveling. They could have sailed across the sea to Denmark, even on to Norway. No journey would be too far.

The terror he felt was palpable. What should he do now that she seemed to be improving? Should she walk farther? Less? Did she need more to eat? Less?

He had to calm himself. If he'd helped get her to this point, he'd keep at it.

"Is it stew again tonight?"

She'd noticed the stew? "Of course, unless you want something else." He'd by God walk to Billingham if she wanted so much as a biscuit.

"It's fine." She didn't seem to care much about the answer, but she'd asked the question.

And then she put out her hand and laid it against his bristling cheek. "You look thin," she whispered.

He'd lain abed beside her every night of the past weeks, keeping her warm, keeping her safe. Now she remembered he existed.

Outwardly he fought to stay calm but there was a parade in his heart, with fireworks.

He just had to hope that, once she was fully herself again, she wouldn't be too angry about the things she had yet to learn.

His oak bench sat across from her low lambing-chair, also piled with sheepskins. Lee went and sprawled in it, feet toward the fire, pretending to normalcy he did not feel.

For the first time, he felt like there were two people in the house instead of one.

* * *

VIOLA DID NOT SUDDENLY START SPRINGING about, but it was only a few days later that she did wake and notice his arm around her.

At least, Lee assumed she noticed, because she stiffened.

It was another moment to cherish. He'd rather have a Viola full of doubts than a listless Viola who wasn't Viola at all.

"Ah... are you quite comfortable?" she asked quietly.

The cot was narrow but made by him, for him, strung long with rope so he could stretch out his legs. There was barely enough room for both of them to lay on it side by side. He'd slept every night with Viola tucked between him and the wall. "Extremely so, thank you."

"I mean... it's been quite warm."

So it had been, both because of the April sun and because there had been a fire burning every minute since she'd set foot in the tower.

"Do you need more room? I can leave you this bed." There wasn't another, but the floor would be fine.

"No, I'd prefer you to stay."

Lee's chest couldn't hold all the air that rushed in at her words. The pressure was excruciating. "Don't take this amiss, but I'm rising now."

She turned in his arms and smiled at him. "Not at all, a new husband can't always be cooperative."

Quickly, he kissed the tip of her nose. That soft brush was all he had time for; he had to get outside. Let her think he was desperate for the necessary.

He left the door open, swinging himself over the low stone wall opposite from the pig pen. It was only a few strides into the trees from there.

Laying his hand on the bark of one rough, silent trunk, he

let it be his only witness as he let that explosive pressure out.

The sobs shook him from his shoulders to his knees, taking him over as he gave into them, great gasping breaths turning into tears.

Old soldiers knew how to cry, they just didn't let anyone catch them at it.

The weight of crushing fear rolled off that place in his chest that had been compressed for days, weeks, *forever,* and the relief made him feel so light that he leaned both hands on the tree to keep from flying away.

It had been so long since she'd said she preferred anything at all, he'd been afraid it would never happen.

* * *

BY THE TIME HE RETURNED, Viola had swung her legs down from the cot and sat on its edge, staring intently at her toes on the floor.

This was both another good sign of recovery and a perfectly rational response to having a tiny brown creature covered with shifting spines snuffling her toes.

"Herbert!" He bent to scoop up the creature and evict him. This was Viola's house now, and he didn't want her to think it no better than a pigsty.

Even though just outside the door there was a pigsty.

"No, don't!" She touched her slender hand to his, staying his motion. His hand curled around hers instead. "I don't mean to inconvenience him. Does he live here?"

"Viola, surely you can at least feel free to inconvenience the hedgehog."

"He's a *hedgehog?*"

And in the next instant, she bent double, trying to get close enough to the little creature to see each one of its spines. Her hair spilled to the floor.

"Let's brush that hair."

She looked around. She knew where she was, obviously, but this was the first time she took an evident interest. "There are no maids?"

"No." He spread his arms wide, then linked his hands behind his head, elbows akimbo. "I like my space to myself."

"Then why am I here?"

"You're my wife."

A little smile appeared at the corner of her lips. He wanted to kiss it so badly. "And this is where you keep all your things?"

That ventured a little too near to topics he didn't want to discuss too soon. She *was* his wife, and he wanted her here. He didn't want to disappoint her. At least not yet.

The light place inside that the tears had washed clean whispered: *none of that matters.*

That had to be true. They *were* married, and she was with him, and she wouldn't suddenly take a dislike to him over anything she might learn. She hadn't yet.

Truth be told, he liked it better this way.

Herbert, never a creature of self-doubt, continued to investigate Viola's toes, and Viola to stare at him in return. "So Herbert is a pet?"

"Not exactly." Kneeling at her feet, he did scoop Herbert up so his lady could see him better. "Careful, the spines are sharp."

"I see." She brushed one with her finger.

"Herbert thinks your toes are grubs, so I intend to put Herbert outside."

"Oh no! But Herbert was here first!"

"Nonetheless. I didn't marry Herbert." Lee let the little fellow sniff his finger, then stood, put him down outside the door. "He needs to get on with finding his daily grubs. He's simply used to poking his nose in here."

"He knows the place well."

"He spent time here. I found him with his leg off, gave him a chance to get well again."

"A leg off! I didn't even see!" Viola rushed to Lee's side at the door. Herbert was nowhere in sight. "But shouldn't he stay inside?"

"No, he needs to live a hedgehog life out where there are hedgehogs. If every animal I nursed decided to stay here, the tower wouldn't be fit for me."

"Every animal! How often do you do that sort of thing?"

"Whenever I get the chance." He looked up the slope toward the treeline. High above them, he saw a hawk circling. He pointed it out to Viola. "There's a fellow planning to eat something besides Herbert. Hopefully."

"I should hope so!" Viola peered suspiciously at the hawk.

Lee grinned at her. "It's a goshawk. I think I nursed him too. He's a little shy of tailfeathers, see? But he still has enough to fly."

Her mouth fell open with surprise, and he saw her considering this new wrinkle. "So then are you cheering on Herbert, or the goshawk?"

"I can't worry much about who eats whom once they leave, Viola. It's just how the world works."

* * *

VIOLA REMEMBERED THE JOURNEY, but only dimly, like a dream. A dream interrupted by one vivid image of a field of bluebells.

Had she taken the time to imagine what Mr. Waite's house in the country would be like, she wouldn't have imagined this.

She couldn't have. She'd never seen anything like it. The raw stone piled high overhead was pierced by only one window, and even there the stone was thick. Down where she was, it must be yards thick.

The sheepskins everywhere made the furniture soft and warm, but the floor was bare, which made sense if Herbert or others like him made a habit of strolling in and out.

A vast mantlepiece hewn from pine hung over the fire where Mr. Waite cooked their stews. Similar timbers held up planks high overhead, forming a ceiling solid but for one opening.

Above a ladder.

"So one can go up?"

"One? Yes. You? No. You've been sitting for a long while."

"It's not so high." She smiled at him over her shoulder. It felt easy, not false. "You'll steady the ladder?"

"All you wish. Every day. But Viola—"

It was an extraordinary sensation, feeling the hard floor under her bare feet. Feeling her skin under the loose shift, without stays, without even a gown. Even her hair felt free. "I can imagine why you left London."

She was too restless to sit back down. She didn't exactly feel strong, but her aches were less, her headache gone, and she was tired of sitting and of sleeping.

The ladder looked sturdy, its steps deep. She started up, then stopped, conscious there was a breeze under her linen. "If I climb this, will I lose all pretense of modesty?"

"Only if I'm lucky," he said, standing right behind her and sounding heartfelt.

"You're *awful*." At least her illness had not driven away his sense of humor.

"Every day," he agreed.

Viola decided not to let modesty stop her. Who knew when that heavy blanket of sadness would fall again? Better to use every possible moment.

She did pause halfway up, her knees more shaky than she'd like.

"Viola. Do come back down." He sounded pleading. A little unease raised goose-flesh on her arms.

She trusted him utterly, had from the moment she picked him to lure into a carriage. But she still did not know him well, and if he had secrets, he kept them here.

She looked down. His lean bristled face stared up at her, full of concern.

Perhaps she'd ask first. "Is this where you keep the bodies of all your previous wives?"

"Only the fresh ones. Truly, Viola. There is a conversation we should have before you climb to the top."

"Can we not have it up here?" Climbing on, she poked her head through the heavy planks, now forming a floor. The room was square and bare.

In moments she stood on its empty floor with Mr. Waite beside her. His billowing linen shirt, soft from many washings, hung past the top of his worn trousers.

She had not seen him wash any laundry.

Growing more and more curious, she pointed up. "I assume the skeletons are stored higher?"

"There's no skeletons. Please, Viola."

She could not recall him ever saying *please*.

"I'm sorry." Why had she taken a notion to suddenly be thoughtless? "What did you wish to say, Mr. Waite?"

"Please don't apologize, you've done nothing wrong, and please don't call me Mr. Waite."

She didn't want to explain that she still did not feel bright and cheery, and in her head, *Lee* ought to have someone bright and cheery. After all, neither of them could dictate that the other be cheery. "I don't wish to be disrespectful among company, sir, but of course. When we're alone."

"Say *Lee*."

"Of course. Lee. I'm—Yes. I do. I will."

That wild look came into his eyes, the one that seemed lit by fires close enough to burn. He stepped closer and grasped her by the arms. It ought to be frightening, but she was no more frightened than she had been of the hawk flying up above, or the hedgehog. Only cautious. The moment clearly called for caution.

"Tell me again that I am the man you wished to marry."

"You were and you are, sir. If you like, I'll say so every day."

She hadn't known how wisely she'd picked. She knew now how lucky she was. There was no other man who would ever be as kind to her, as loyal, or as careful of everything she needed. Not even the illustrious Lord Callendar.

Her heart had picked better than her head.

Holding her arms, he asked, "Will you kiss me?"

She wanted to tease him a little about asking an actual question, but really, she didn't.

He was her husband, and they were alone. It was easy to flow up against him, even barely dressed as she was. The warm spring air felt like it helped her float higher as she reached up and wound her hands behind his neck.

He tasted of sunshine, and the tang of pine and sweat. And of the same wildness that was in his eyes, hungry and untameable. His hands spread along her sides, lifting her into his kiss.

The urgency of it cut through the remaining bits of fog in Viola's mind. Something was bothering him. More than bothering.

All she could think of to say was what he'd been saying for the last few weeks. "It's all right," she murmured against his lips, one hand coming forward to stroke the high, raw bone of his cheek. "Everything will be fine."

"And you'll tell me that too, every day?" The teasing was false; the hope was real.

"Every day. Show me the rest of your tower."

He led her to the next ladder, and up to a room that was yet a smaller copy of the one below, even containing another ladder. He had nothing else to say, only held the ladder for her so it wouldn't wobble; it was smaller. A plank covered the opening at its top; she pushed it aside.

First she saw the sky, a deep blue bigger than anything she had ever imagined, extending far beyond the few white clouds she saw in the distance. Green hills in every direction, and no pig pen; on this side of the tower, the hill below her rolled down, joining the valley below.

In the distance crouched a low dwelling of timber and thatch, cattle crowding around it.

Men were everywhere among the cattle, slapping their sides, throwing hay into troughs. Farther away, the animals were so small they were only dots among the fresh green grass.

Both the herd and the dwelling must be huge to be seen at that distance, she realized.

And on her left, the tower grew outward. It was a stone house, attached, built halfway up the tower's side, one with turrets of its own and a plank roof like the one where she stood.

Careless of the breeze, she stepped forward and laid her hand on an iron cage suspended between two spits of ancient stone.

"Whose house is this?" When he didn't answer, she turned to face him, standing behind her. "Whose cattle are those?"

He had his hands clasped, rubbing the knuckles of one hand with the other, the only outward sign that he was genuinely concerned.

"I'm truly sorry, Viola. I'm very rich."

CHAPTER 18

It would feel stupid to say she didn't understand; the words were perfectly clear. They just made no sense.

Viola gave in and said it. "I don't understand."

Then to make herself feel less foolish, she added, "You enlisted in the army. That's seven years, with no way to get rich. How...?"

"The traditional way. Inheritance."

Viola had never been good at assembling dissected puzzles. Now she saw there were many pieces scattered through their conversations that she should have pursued.

As always, he seemed to divine what she was thinking.

"It's not a complicated tale," he told her, still rubbing his knuckles. She took his hands; he stopped. "My father owned many concerns and a great deal of land. He made pots of money selling uniforms to the army. Imagine a great many sheep. All over hillsides like this. All that wool. Spinning factories. It's funny, I'd never even been here until I walked here, looking for a life that could settle the..." He rubbed a fist on his chest, searching for the word. "...the *churning* in me. Once I reached these hills, I knew I had to find the farm where my parents began. I still own it. I like this better."

She could imagine. It wasn't what she would call… "A shopkeeper?"

"The dowager countess has a simple view of things, doesn't she?" Lee's smile twisted a little sideways. "My parents *were* in London for a little while, tried to entertain; of course they were shunned. Not the right lineage. Not the right *accents.*"

"A duke may come from Sussex, or Northumberland…"

"And attend the correct schools, learn the correct way to box and eat and talk. Most importantly, they have *titles.*" He spread his hands wider; she didn't let go. "I eventually had schooling, but no title. And no parents. Their ship sank in the North Sea. I don't remember what they looked like, and I don't know why I wasn't with them."

He must have been such a hurt, frightened little boy.

It was hard to imagine it when he was so tall, his hands calloused from his axe. He'd been cutting all the wood they burned in the fire, Viola realized.

And cooking her food, and bathing her.

For once she felt less ashamed of herself than amazed by him.

"They would be so proud of you." She slipped her arms round his waist and shook her head with sheer disbelief at everything this man was, everything he could do. "As I am."

His arms closed around her in return, one big hand cradling her head. "It was silly, but you were so enamored of the idea of your penniless garret. So determined to ruin yourself. I didn't want to disappoint you."

"And then everything else happened."

"Everything happened."

"But you should have—why agree to my ridiculous plan,

why *marry* me, when you could literally have any woman in Britain?"

"I like the one you picked for me," he said simply. "I told you that."

"But you could have married a lady with a title. A duke's daughter; anyone."

"Viola, I learned many things growing up shunted from house to house. I learned that everyone is willing to put a roof over a rich boy's head. No one is willing to hug him."

He said it calmly, clearly, the way he said nearly everything. Explaining his insistence on giving hugs when he felt they were due. The words were balm to the nagging, brutal thoughts she still had to push away, the *he doesn't want you,* the weighty *you're useless* that dragged her down. What he said, he meant.

His raw emotion had faded; he looked again like he might fit in a drawing room.

Except for his sun-browned face, untamed hair, and callused hands from doing work.

He added, "I tried to warn you about the life I could offer. This is it. I thought it called for a sturdy, uncomplaining woman. Instead I got a marble dryad who's come to life. Look at you, hair blowing in the wind, barely dressed. You're wild. Living art. You should be in a palace, or on a mountaintop. Yet here you are." He pulled her against his side with one arm, the other waving toward the valley, the farm, the hawk overhead, all of it. "There's no village. The sea is far away. The farms are far apart. The Scottish border is long settled, and these watchtowers no longer signal with fires. I doubt you ever imagined this kind of quiet. But will you try it?"

The prospect was truly breathtaking.

She'd been so foolish to think she knew every kind of life one could have in Britain. The windswept moor of Northfell, the rolling green parks of Morland, all the pockets of London; they were nothing like this.

"You tried London; why shouldn't I try this?" She pushed away thoughts of London. He'd made his aversion to it clear. He wanted to stay here, forever. It was a better plan than living in a garret as an outcast mistress.

Her plan now felt childish, while she could barely grasp his.

He didn't miss the hint of hesitation in that *try.*

"This marriage is real, Viola. I never asked you to put me in your heart. I'm asking for this. I want this house full of roaring children who leave frogs in the washtub and stay still in the woods to watch the deer. I still want it. I know I should have explained it before I married you, but you started an avalanche of everything happening and I..." He slipped his hand under her hair; it slid free over his fingers. "I think I was worried that if I didn't hold on, you'd escape."

"I'm so sorry. I set a trap for you, never dreaming anyone in London wanted anything like this."

"The trap wasn't for me." She saw his jaw tighten a little, saw him relax it.

She hadn't just stolen his place in society. She'd stolen his chance at the life he wanted. Needed. He needed a home, somewhere to belong, and a family of his own. A chance to make what he'd never had.

And she'd never imagined anything like that because she'd never had that, not really.

"I must be honest with you, sir—"

"Please do. Every day." This time his hand in her hair was more of a caress.

He spoke so easily of *every day,* he touched her so tenderly. Yet he never mentioned love, neither offered nor asked it. What did he know that she didn't?

She'd never loved Lord Callendar. That was obvious now.

She'd wanted him and set out to get him so she could feel desired. Safe. And most of all, free to enjoy whatever she could.

Lee offered a different kind of freedom. And to be safe, and desired. She knew she could feel those things with him.

Every day.

"To have and to hold you, Mr. Waite. That was *exactly* what I wanted." Even as she said it, she knew it was true. She had. She did.

His arms pulling her into him, tight; those were just what she wanted. She couldn't imagine any other kind. Couldn't imagine kissing anyone who wasn't so tall that he pulled her right off her feet as he was doing right now.

The hunger in this kiss grew into something ravenous, bigger than both of them, making the world so small that it faded away.

Even so he took care for her, remembering where they were. Breathing hard, he pulled back. The blue in his eyes was nearly gone, they were so black. "You're shaking. Warm weather or no, you've been ill. Let's get you back by the fire."

And he moved so decisively to herd her back down the ladder, trying to be both above and below her at the same time to ensure she didn't slip, that Viola wondered if he realized how they might have started on his plan for all those children right then. If he hadn't been in such a rush to be her nursemaid.

No matter; she could wait. Not that it would be easy; she hadn't been shaking from the cold.

* * *

As it turned out, Lee knew many things Viola didn't know. She'd been terribly hungry, even for the stew which was beginning to bore her, and terribly tired. She'd slept a long time, cradled in the warmth of his body on the narrow straw tick bed.

But the next day he was gone when she woke, and she donned a morning dress feeling foolish, and a little daring, leaving off her stockings. She only took a soft pair of slippers.

It felt different now, being in an ancient house all alone.

She couldn't find any servants. Looking back into the fog in which she'd been living, she knew her clothes were always clean, as were his; someone was somewhere, doing the work Lee didn't do. All the nearby evidence, though, was that he had done everything that made their tower comfortable.

She had to leave the tower to find a way into the house, out past the pigs and around. The house proper had a smaller door, and its heavy-timbered floors and ceilings reminded her more of Queen Elizabeth's time rather than ancient raiders.

The house held little furniture, and some dust. In its dining room, there were no linens on the worn plank table, and the window shutters were closed. The house was sleeping, not alive and warm like their tower.

Which wouldn't be warm either, come winter, mused Viola as she wandered through the empty rooms.

Finally she found a kitchen, most of its crocks and washtubs as empty as the rest of the house. Only one hearth on the far wall, a newer one, showed signs of life.

It held burning coals, black coals, under a huge copper kettle, and the flagstone floor tipped its way, leading everything toward the warmth or a narrow iron grate that must be a drain.

He was heating water for the constant baths he gave her. Carrying it into the tower to pour into her tub, while he himself likely washed right here, letting the water run out through the floor.

While this part of the house had clearly been built long after the tower, its windows were still high, and small, as if to repel attacks. One cut through the stone wall only yards from the hot hearth, and Viola stood on tiptoe to look out.

It was the side of the house that faced down the hill toward the farm, what she'd seen from above. She thought she discerned the remains of a kitchen garden.

No greenhouse; no oranges. She smiled, thinking of the Duchess of Talbourne in such a rough place.

"Aye, y're up."

Viola whirled.

A woman stood in the middle of the floor, a sturdily built housewife in a wide white bonnet.

Viola stood frozen as the woman nodded, then tossed a flat, wide loaf of bread out of her basket to the table. "There's yer stottie," she said, every word rolling right after the other with an up-and-down cadence that didn't separate them at all. She did not curtsey.

"Good morning. Madam." Viola curtsied; she wasn't sure why.

The woman's eyebrows flew up. She muttered something Viola couldn't understand at all. Then she nodded at the window where Viola had been looking out. "S'clarty that way; be havin' boots if y're plodgin' out."

None of the words made sense, even the ones Viola thought she could hear. She did get the general idea that she'd have to change her shoes if she went out. "Of course," she tried, as it was an answer that had stood her in good stead in many a drawing room. "I am Lady Viola Waite." She remembered in time to use the correct name. "May I have your name as well?"

The woman's eyebrows couldn't go any higher. "Mrs. Scott." Nothing hard about that.

"Mrs. Scott. Lovely." Viola felt she was getting somewhere. "And where did you come from?"

The woman made a little noise of scoffing disbelief. "Doon d'farm," she said, as if astonished Viola had to ask.

Of course. That *was* the only place from which she could have come. "Thank you. And you've brought Mr. Waite's bread?" Sidling toward the table with small steps, she snuck up on the flat round loaf of bread, then pinched off a bit of its edge. She felt terribly rude, but also hungry, and it smelled so good.

It was nothing like the Ladies' Own Bakery bread in Leicester Square. That crackled on the outside, and was light within. This was dense, and soft, tasting of pure wheat, a little sweet.

Viola's eyes widened. "Mrs. Scott, I wonder, if you could spare any time some day soon, if you might teach me to bake bread?"

The woman's demeanor loosened, and without a word, Viola understood that her standing had changed. It might only be her imagination, but she thought she might have shifted from the useless unseen lady of the house to a woman of some worth.

"Alls'is work d'do," the woman admitted, as if grudgingly allowing Viola to do some of the work would be a gracious favor on her part.

"Thank you. I'll look forward to that." And, not knowing what else to do, she bobbed her head again, an abbreviated copy of a curtsey.

Surprisingly, the woman bobbed her head back, waving before she pointed warningly out the window, then left the way she came.

"It's interesting country," Viola murmured to herself as she pinched off another bite of the bread.

Mr. Waite might be rich, but no woman in London could have known that and expected it meant this sort of life.

Clever of him to keep it under his hat.

Continuing her interrupted examination of the kitchen, she touched the tops of the tables, marked with years of knife-cuts, and a stone slab worn a bit hollow by perhaps centuries of some use she didn't know. Long and short-handled skillets stood stacked to one side of the hearth, some of them with faint signs of rust, and brass kettles on a shelf opposite showed aging as well.

Well, Mrs. Scott had a lot of work already without fussing with the pots, that was clear.

A rounded slab of wood jutted from the wall near the low hearth where she'd found the heating copper pot. Its end featured a smaller lever that looked like it could be pushed. She pushed it.

Instantly she was sluiced with cold water hitting her in the chest, splashing up onto her face, and wetting her down to her shoes. She fumbled to turn the lever back.

"All right," muttered Viola as she dripped on the floor, watching the rivulets drain toward the edge where she suspected they did indeed run out toward the garden and make it *clarty*.

She wasn't going to master this life in one day.

* * *

THE BED CALLED to her once she returned to the tower, offering Viola a refuge that would be quiet, and warm, and dry.

She didn't give in. There was too much to do still, too much to find out.

If she had to keep changing, though, she'd soon run out of

shoes. She might change five times a day in London, but only a few of her shoes were suited to all this.

Dressed anew, she ventured out into the sunshine. The thick stone walls had kept the air cooler inside than out.

She let her hair go free, hoping it would dry. She didn't want to worry Lee, and if she explored, it seemed likely she'd find him.

The thick grass fought its way up toward her knees, waiting, perhaps, for the day the cattle would come up and shear it off. It was still easy to see in all directions. No doubt that was why the tower was here.

But the pines had been allowed to grow lower and lower, spreading dark green down the slope toward the rising tower. Viola wondered if there was a reason.

Her husband, she'd learned, often had reasons for the things he did.

Once among the trees she picked her way through the young branches, wondering if she could deduce some of his reasons.

The wool market had collapsed years ago. That she knew from conversations at Talbourne House. Therefore spinning and weaving trades must now earn less too, and with the end of the wars, there'd be less use for uniforms. If Mr. Waite still made such things.

The farm below hosted cows, not sheep. They were bigger; perhaps they ate more grass. They might well eat a valley's worth, in the time it took to raise them for market.

If Mr. Waite intended to make a profit, he might grow those herds as widely as he could, knowing that they'd eventually encroach up these hillsides. If he *also* wanted room for Herbert and hawks and the kinds of creatures he liked to care for, he might keep the woods broad and low to shelter animals unsuited to short-cropped meadows.

She had no great talent for arithmetic. No doubt *all* the

ladies in Leicester Square knew more than she about profits and ledgers. If she wanted to be of use to her husband, that wouldn't be the way.

Then she rounded a tree trunk and forgot all her troublesome worries about what he ought to have from her, and remembered what she wanted from him.

She spotted him mid-stroke of the axe, both hands raised overhead. In the dappled light, she saw what he meant about living statues. He had the golden shape of a hero out of myth, but too alive to be stone. He glistened with sweat, his hair was soft enough to blow in the wind, and he breathed.

In fact, he sucked air into his powerful chest before each stroke, the muscles gnarled there and along his shoulders and down both arms twisting at each mighty effort, punctuating each strike of the axe with a deep, effortful grunt. He wore no shirt; she could see every stretching, contracting movement.

How had she ever thought him thin? Clothes simply lied about him. He was lean and long, but without his coat to hang over his shape, all that taut flesh was perfectly proportioned.

He looked rugged, uncivilized, dirty, and she wanted him. Now.

Surely she wouldn't have to explain what she was thinking.

Nor did she try, only moving close enough for him to see her and plant his axe in a ragged stump. Then she flew at him, trusting him to catch her, trusting him to understand.

Maybe he did, or maybe it was his nature to catch her against his chest, trying not to flatten her against his dirt and sweat but also trying to reward her visit with fleeting kisses on her temple, on her nose.

She didn't care about her dress. Someone, likely the taciturn Mrs. Scott, washed clothes; they'd have to wash hers as well. Or perhaps she'd just have to live in nature, wearing as much dirt as any other forest creature.

She hoped he understood from the clutch of her hands around his neck and the way she kissed into his lips, taking what he'd taught her to take, giving what she wanted to give, that she wanted her husband to come back with her to the house. Very much.

Perhaps he didn't believe what she was trying to say. "Your dress—"

"Doesn't matter."

"Viola, I'm filthy." Whispered as he kissed his way down her neck; she leaned back to help him.

"Lee, you are *irresistible.*" He was. Surely he knew that.

Slowly it seemed to come to him, because he let her lead him back down the hill toward the house. Its side door, not the tower.

She took him right to the heating hearth, clever enough now not to drench herself. One of the old brass pots made a perfect vessel to scoop water that was hot and gently steaming from the cauldron, then, knowing the trick, she carefully moved the wooden lever, mixing in water that was fresh and cold.

"You'll get soaked." His eyes followed her movements, wondering what she was up to and, she hoped, hoping.

"I believe I've mastered this part. You do keep soap here, don't you?" Because the only way the garden was *clarty*, the kind of wet that needed boots, was if he'd been running water here, bathing himself after working all day for her.

He jerked his chin towards a small shelf, one that bore a bar of the same hard soap she used in the bath.

The unseasonably warm April gave Viola ideas; Lee gave her inspiration.

Slipping out of her wrapping gown and chemise, she

stood before him entirely bare and dipped a tankard in her pot, preparing to drench him from head to toe.

She'd never had the chance to see him like this before, blue eyes turned almost black, the shape of his trousers doing his talking for him.

Though he did say, "You don't have to do anything. I can wait."

"But I can't," was her honest reply, and had no words for the look on his face—gentle and fierce, acceptance, approval, permission all at once.

CHAPTER 19

*H*e pulled off his boots, kicking them to one side before she could offer to touch them. Stripped away all his trousers and smallclothes and stood naked for whatever she willed, his arms spread wide, the rest of him proud and hard.

"Is this what you want?"

Viola would tell him again that he was awful, but he knew that. He wanted her to talk, to ask for what she wanted.

"I—you're so *tall.*"

He sank to his knees, then pulled one back up, planting his bare foot and resting his forearm across his thigh as if he thought he should be ready to spring.

The way he gave himself, readily, completely, yet still left her wondering what would happen next. All that made it harder for her to ask for things, not easier. Still, she couldn't imagine another man making her heart thunder like this.

She'd picked him with no idea of all she would get.

Slowly she tipped water over his head, then as he bent it, along his neck, over his shoulders. She reached down to lift his chin and tilt his head so she could run the water through his hair. Her fingers loosened needles from the trees and bits of bark from his hair, leaving it slick and dark.

"The pot's too heavy for you," he said, his voice rough, shaking his head a little so the drops flew.

"Clearly it isn't."

Exchanging the now-empty pot for the soap, she rubbed it between her hands, then along the places it was easy to touch. His wet shoulders grew slicker under her hands, the bubbles dripping slowly down his chest, down his back.

"Give me your hand." Demanding was easier than asking. She'd have to wonder why later.

Of course he let her have it, and then she could work her way down his outstretched arm, feeling unaccountably more shy as she slid her hand through the hair below, a spot that no one else ever saw.

His arm stayed rock-steady, patient for her, as she soaped down each ridge and groove of muscle, the bone of the elbow, down to the knuckles of his wide, outspread hand.

She was glad he didn't joke as she dug around the little fissures there, making sure each part was clean.

By the time she did the other arm, she felt easier. He hadn't done anything different; it was her, her tension easing, the pleasant repetitive motions of her hands on his skin growing her confidence to match the height of her hunger.

Every bulging muscle of his chest got its own attention. There were scars there, some that showed, pink and white, and some she could only feel with her hands. One ridge on his ribs. So many stories she didn't know yet. She couldn't wait to find out.

Once she'd worked the suds down to his waist he lowered his other knee and spread his arms again, letting her see all of him, all she did to him.

He parted his knees for her, for once looking up, completely in her hands. "This is how you want me?"

"Every day," she murmured, and her slick, hot hands grasped the length of him, shaping it all.

$$* * *$$

HIS DREAMS HAD COME TRUE.

Only in a dream would a wood nymph who looked exactly like his Viola come wandering through his trees, find him in a state of filthy effort no society lord ever undertook, and reward him with kisses and a wordless, sweetly filthy offer to get him clean.

He didn't need dreams any more. He didn't need a house, or a forest, or money at all, as long as Viola wanted this from him. And he could see that she did.

Grateful first, foremost, and forever for her indecent offer in a hackney carriage.

The way her eyes widened was as gratifying as the way her hand closed over him, exploring every inch of his hard length. She deserved to know everything about what she'd married, after all.

Thankfully, she clearly liked the look of him. He wanted her against him, around him, under him, but even from here he could see that her skin had flushed warm and her breathing heavier as she'd tended to him. Claimed him.

She didn't speak. There was nothing to say. Everything they needed to know was conveyed in her fingers sliding over his slick skin, exploring every inch of him she wanted to explore. She crouched close so she could reach her soapy hand down his shaft and around the heavy softness there, not so soft now, and she made a satisfied little sound.

It nearly broke his determination to let her do as she would.

"Do I get to wash you next?"

"I'm not dirty," she told him, her hand sliding slowly up

his length and down again, her fingers brushing everywhere, forcing his eyes closed when he wanted them open. He wanted this picture of her, decisive, taking. He wanted to be the one to give.

For her, he *needed* to be the one to give.

When she stood in a fluid motion, he gave in to the urge to wrap his arms around her thighs, trying not to squeeze too hard, desperate to stroke his face along the soft skin of her belly right in front of him. His head rubbed against her thigh; her fingers tangled in his hair.

"I'm going to rinse the soap away," she whispered, as if it were still important.

* * *

EVERYTHING about the unbearable intimacy of this was easier now that Viola was sure he wanted it too. Wanted her and the things she did for him.

She couldn't *always* take.

She mixed another pot of water and brought it slowly over his head. "Careful of your eyes."

Trustingly he kept them closed, spreading his arms so she could reach. She let the water dribble slowly, rinsing him clean, then said a little playfully, "Now bend forward."

He opened one eye to give her a dubious look, then did as she said.

She dumped the rest of the water over the back of his head.

"There," she said, setting the pot down to shake her fingers through the mop of his hair. "I think there are no more birds nesting in it."

Gasping, he flipped his head back to look at her with one threatening eye, keeping the other shut as he ran his hands over his face and shoved back his hair, pushing the rest of the water to stream over his neck and down his chest.

"If you're trying to torture me, it's working."

"I know. It's torturing me, too."

He wiped the last drops of water from his lips with his thumb as he stood. "Say one word, and I'll relieve all your suffering."

"I don't think I'm ready."

She'd wanted passion; he was made of it. She only had to be brave enough to take him.

She knelt on the flagstones by his feet, loving the noise he made of anticipation and surprise, like a magnificent animal. She enjoyed every instant of running her hands down the bulging muscle of his thighs, the hair on his calves, till she could stroke the arches of his feet. All the textures of him were fascinating. Hair she didn't expect; soft spots she didn't expect. Everywhere hot, hard, crying out to be touched, kissed, loved.

The noise he made then sounded like a different kind of animal, one whose survival depended not on being wild or tame, but on her letting him touch her next.

"Viola. Please."

"Please what?" She might be teasing; he thought she was.

"Let me wash *you*."

He didn't seem to have much patience now; that was fine with her. She was running out of patience herself.

Instead of giving him what he asked for, she took for herself.

It was easy to slide his hard tip into her mouth, tasting him the way he'd tasted her so long ago.

The groan she ripped out of him that way was more than satisfying. It made her want more, the heat pooling where she would ultimately have him, feeling the need for him there growing.

It also tested his strength in ways she hadn't expected. The ropes of muscle in his belly and thighs flexed, as if holding himself back, letting her move him, have him.

She suspected her control of him was an illusion.

Still, she wouldn't give it up. Clearly her mouth pleased him; she wanted more of that, more of him in her mouth. It was a daunting prospect; there were realities regarding the size of him and the comparative size of her. But she loved the idea of trying.

It helped to use her hands to hold him still. She tried using both.

The sounds he made sounded like muffled curses, but that was so unlike him, she couldn't be sure.

"Viola, I can't..." *Stay this way,* he apparently meant, because before she'd well settled in, he'd lifted her up as only he could, his hands below her arms, setting her on her feet.

He didn't look like he was playing a game. He looked deadly serious, using his hands so much bigger than hers to mix her water and, far more efficiently, trickle warm drops all over her skin and lather her with soap. Those hands were tools of precision, pressing into the flesh of her shoulders, her rear, her breasts, down her belly, backing her into him the way she loved so he could slide his fingers down to touch her while his hardness pressed into her soapy back.

"I want to do this for you a million times," he murmured as one hand held her, spreading her open, stroking her, and the other cupped her breast and lathered her nipple with his thumb.

His rapt reverence sounded as though he wished he had more hands to worship her with, and Viola wished that too.

She knew it was too easy for him to push her over the edge like this, knew he would, knew it the moment before it happened.

The shaking intensity of the sensation he caused could

have made her fall, but he kept pulling her up and into his body, determined to adore every inch of her, meshing them together and melting away anything resistant in her, like shame, or bones.

She ground down into his hand to make the pleasure last, knowing he wanted her to reach that peak, wanting to hear the *well done.*

Perhaps she said so, or perhaps, as so often happened, he knew what she was thinking, because he whispered, "*Very well done,*" as she collapsed in his hands, trusting him to hold her up, shaking from the flood of pleasure. Then he added, "Please."

"Anything." She couldn't catch her breath, but there was nothing she wouldn't give him.

"Let me rinse you and take you to bed."

"Anything." It was agreement this time. She raised her arms.

Slowly he washed away the suds, taking care to get them all; excessive care, given that she was nowhere as dirty as he'd been.

She had a hazy feeling he just liked touching her, hazy not because her senses did not work, but because he had over-whelmed them.

Then she was swept up in his arms, never doubting he would get her wherever they needed to be, and found herself in his cot, under his body, her husband poised over her with corded muscled arms that held him steady and asking quietly, "Please?"

This was what she'd been waiting for. This was what men and women did in bed, she was sure of it. "Please," she said back, both agreeing and asking, because she wanted it too.

Slowly he levered his body between her thighs, nudging her, easing her, lowering himself so he could give her the light kisses they both loved, along the edge of her lips, along the curve of her nose. All the while slowly, slowly sliding inside her, the stretch and fill of him as breathtaking as the sight of him half-naked under the pines.

She'd been wrong. She knew nothing at all.

"Stop," she said, and instantly he did, arms trembling with the effort of holding still and trying to hide his concern even as his face shifted from bliss to worry.

"Are you hurt?"

"Only a little. Slower. Please."

"Anything," he told her, kissing her lips, nuzzling his hard cheek against her skin. "Everything," and he sounded like he meant it, proving it with the tiniest, tiniest motion forward of his hips, taking his time, her time, their time. His patience was infinite, and there was nowhere else they would ever have to be.

"That's lovely," she sighed. The pinch eased, and she felt her insides soften for him, as welcoming and wanting as it was possible to be. She didn't know how her body could want something it had never had so badly, but it did. She did.

"Anything you want, Viola. You need only ask. Anything. Forever."

"Then more please." The tension had lessened, and the fit between them was perfect. She couldn't ask for anything better, yet she needed something, and the only way she could describe it was *more.*

Fortunately, he understood.

Slowly, ratcheting higher at the perfect speed, he moved a little faster for her, deeper with every stroke, the whole thing filling and overwhelming and so masterfully *good* that Viola thought she might scream, or cry, and knew he wouldn't mind anything, that she could do anything with him and he would go through it with her, be there with her on the other side.

"Thank you very much," she said on a rising gasp into a

cry into a scream that echoed off the stone, trapped inside with them where no one else could hear.

Lee chuckled a little, holding her as she shook, slowing, feeling her come down from that mountaintop to his arms, the place she'd never left.

"So formal," he teased, slowing yet more but still stroking deeply inside her, once, twice, an excruciating level of sensation coursing through her at each stroke. She felt not just pleasured, but on fire, as if the heat of him made her burn.

"Do you want me to tickle you?" She barely managed to form words.

"No," he smiled into the side of her neck, still stroking, an inexorable glide she could neither bear nor stop.

Viola grabbed his ears in both hands and looked deep into his eyes. "Then you reach the top too. I want it. That's all I want."

Startled, gripped by her softest clutching places, over-whelmed with emotion Viola could see but couldn't name, he did.

* * *

THAT WAS *HIS* VIOLA, asking for *his* pleasure. After all these weeks, Lee had so trained every part of him to hope that she would ask, for anything, anything at all, that she shocked him into the peak, the hot pleasure hitting him deep and rolling up slowly through him over and over as if desperate to make sure she got everything she asked for.

He'd yearned to be here with her, inside her, *with* her; yet it was not like he'd expected. It was so much better.

There was no space between them, no differences to cross, not in body or mind, not now, perhaps not ever. At their wedding he'd loathed the idea of loving his wife as he loved himself; now he saw the possibility of it, because he felt part of the whole, two made one.

He somehow knew that, understood it, right down to his bones. It was all he understood.

"That was everything," sighed Viola, wrapping her arms around his neck. She seemed in no hurry to be free of his weight; careful not to crush her, using his knees and elbows, he was in no hurry to move either.

"Yes, everything." What could he say but to agree with her? It had been. The earth, the stars, the moon and the sun. Worth living for. Worth surviving a war.

The kind of miracle that banished dark thoughts from the bottom of liquor bottles.

He didn't want to tell her that, not now. His dark thoughts poured into glasses; hers seemed to come from the ether, swarming and attacking her according to some plan he might never know. It wouldn't change anything. He'd be there to hold her.

She didn't need to know that his heart had never felt so light, that he'd never felt so young, and so full of purpose.

All he said was, "I hope that was the beginning of our family." Because to him, *family* meant *whole new world*.

He'd surprised her. She blinked. Then the slow, wide grin spread all over her face. "I hope so too," and he knew they were thinking the same thing.

CHAPTER 20

May insisted on being colder than April, and Lee thought that was just spiteful. When was May ever colder than April? The cattle didn't care for it either.

It didn't bother Mrs. Scott, but then nothing did.

"Gerrout," she shouted at someone in her vast kitchen filled with a heaving throng of women making every kind of food. He hoped the shout wasn't directed at him. The women just kept on working, preparing to feed all the men and boys tending his cattle

All but one who tiptoed down the center of the great flag-stone room, separating herself from the rest.

That was his Viola. The Duchess' maid in waiting, jewel of every London drawing room, in her plainest poplin dress, an apron tied over it to make her look more like the rest. The similarity was faint. Her blue-green dress was made of finer stuff, but then so was the woman inside it.

"Look." Viola, hair tied back in a kerchief, snuck up to him as if afraid Mrs. Scott would see, as if they weren't standing in the middle of a thirty-foot kitchen. "See what I did?"

The loaf of bread she held up was lumpier on one side than the other, and so heavily browned it was almost burnt. Lee thought it perfect.

"Well done," he said admiringly, sniffing it. It would make a delicious supper, and he could have his wife for dessert. "I hope you're not concerned that you need to be useful."

She twisted back and forth a little, like a small girl, smiling at the bread in his hands. "No, I'm not. I just enjoyed it." She stopped. "Is that wrong?"

It was hard not to kiss her. "It's exactly right. You don't need to do *anything*, Viola, except be here with me."

She flushed a little as if he'd said everything he'd been thinking. Or maybe it was from the implied *well done.*

No one could have imagined this kind of wild success when he'd gone south to find a wife. Certainly he'd seen her many times but never imagined that she could be all this. Now she fit into this room, the landscape, into his house and life and bed, as if it had all been in ruins needing only her, the crucial piece, to make everything whole and new again.

Covering her flush, Viola grabbed her bread back. *"You'll* have to do something; you'll have to share."

"Always. In fact, that's why I'm here. To share the letters."

"Letters?" Tossing him back the loaf of bread, she started searching his pockets.

"Yes, for you." Every kind of Viola was his favorite kind of Viola, but Lee treasured every moment with this one.

Laughing, she waved her search's prize, a packet-folded letter. "It's for me!"

"Why else would I bring it to you?"

"To share," she teased without paying much attention, turning it over in her fingers.

Sometimes Hawkshope seemed like the farthest end of the world, but the mail service kept running north. It wasn't just London growing by leaps and bounds as men came back from war and took their families to cities to look for work. It was Glasgow too, and Edinburgh. The roads didn't run through these hills, and he couldn't imagine they would, but he wondered if he should be writing to his stewards looking for ways to profit from the shifting populace.

He'd never had a day's interest in growing his inheritance, only wanting it not to be squandered, hoping to pass it along someday to a family of his own. Now he felt an interest. What if Viola gave him *multiple* sons who'd want holdings and families of their own? What if he had to dower *daughters?*

Every one of those prospects delighted him down to his boot-heels, and he sometimes found himself in the woods, forgetting to see what was around him, carried away by plans for lives that didn't even exist.

Viola prodded at the letter's sealing-wax.

He should have brought her a letter-opener. Lacking one, he reached out to carefully pry up the seal with it still in her hands.

Like most letters, the inky writing crazed the cream-colored page in both directions, using every inch of the precious paper to say as much as it could.

"It's from Virginia! Oh, Mr. Waite, the Duchess' baby has arrived."

Everything sounded different to him these days. The world smelled better, the spring was the prettiest the world had ever seen, and he instantly thought the Duke probably considered it *their* baby, not just his wife's. But Lee thought it impolitic to say so.

Certainly the Duchess had done the lion's share of the work so far.

He recalled how he saw her last, draped over that settee with a very large, robe-covered belly.

Then Lee frowned. He didn't like the idea of Viola with a belly like that; not that it wouldn't be beautiful, but it suddenly struck him as onerous. Baking bread was one thing, but that would be far more work.

He'd lost a cow last spring because she was too small for her calf.

"So much news! Lady *Hadleigh* has a suitor, can you imagine? She's forty if she's a day," Viola whispered confidentially without taking her eyes from the paper. "I thought she might have been Lord Callendar's..." She looked around, and lowered her voice, aware that everyone who could hear in the bustle was listening to every word, "...*confidante* at one point. They so often play cards together."

To hell with Lord Callendar and his cards. The silent snarl rose up in him, but he didn't let it out.

It had been absolutely delightful not hearing that name for weeks and weeks. In fact, he'd happily live out the rest of his life never hearing it again, if he had his way.

It didn't appear he *would* have his way. "We are invited to Talbourne House; Virginia says the gaming has stopped as Her Grace recovers, and the family have the run of the house. Oh, shall we go? No one would see us if we kept to the prescribed wing."

"You forget I never cared if anyone saw us before," he reminded her, but his usual calm was slipping.

Calm was his habit, long born of finding himself always somewhere new, not knowing what might come his way from the people around him. Calm fit him like a suit of clothes, one he'd worn for so long it had become almost part of his skin.

Now he felt it peeling back, and it pained him, like surviving a burn.

He didn't want to go to London. He didn't want Viola to decide she preferred her life there. He didn't want to mix with gaggles of titled people who thought they were better than him, and he did not want to see Lord Callendar.

That last want dwarfed all the rest.

But there was his Viola, daubed with flour everywhere—Mrs. Scott must have been an indulgent teacher, as wasting flour was not her usual practice—sparkling with excitement over the letter and the prospects of a visit.

He'd have taken her to Scotland if it would make her feel better. He reminded himself of that. He'd have taken her over the top of the world or around it. He'd have taken her to the antipodes, had that been her want or need.

So all in all, what was one more trip to London?

"Now that you've grasped the meaning of a life with no shops, you'll have more to buy." He managed to shake the words loose, though they didn't want to come.

"*Will* we? Oh, that's lovely! *Thank* you! Should I pack?" She turned, then turned again, as if unsure if she should help finish dinner before dashing back to their tower.

The image flashed into his memory, of her in that blue dress, surreptitiously stealing that cake.

She looked happier now, so much happier. Lee wanted it to be because of him.

It likely wasn't because of the bare stone of their tower chamber, the emptiness of the valley, or the pigs.

Though it might have been because of the bread.

The bread she trusted to his hands as she ran to consult Mrs. Scott in quick whispers, then returned to take his arm again and lead him out.

He tried to see Hawkshope Peel from her eyes, peering at it in the distance. It had everything they needed, but only what they needed. She had come from luxuries. She should have more than a sheepskin bench.

He'd started to imagine how to furnish the rest of the house, but he needed to go faster. Why hadn't he done something with all his carefully-gathered details about furnishings she liked? The marble in the Faircombe house, the color of the paint?

Because when they'd arrived, none of that would have moved her. He had to recover from *her* illness, had to remember how to want more than simply a Viola who would talk.

She was all he needed. But she deserved so much more.

"I must read the entire letter! Virginia may be right that the season will go into summer because of the treaty. Gracious, I don't even know what's happened with the treaty! Do you?"

No, because treaties healed no hedgehogs. But news was clearly something she liked. He'd start taking a paper. "I suppose you'll find out soon enough."

She chattered all the way back to the peel, Lee only half-listening, staring at the old house and compiling a list of all the things it should have for her.

He should have someone rebuild the garden. Did one build a garden? He didn't even know. The house was sound, but so empty. It needed rugs other than sheepskins. Paintings. Plaster.

It needed *servants,* for pity's sake.

For here was Lady Viola, earl's daughter, maid in waiting to a duchess, flying about a raw stone chamber, tossing her own chemises onto the bed to pack while trying not to step on a hedgehog.

Shoving away the twinge he felt, berating himself that he hadn't noticed all along something wasn't right, he remembered why he'd gone to the farmhouse to fetch her. It hadn't just been for that letter, which he now wished he'd thrown in the fire.

"I finished your present," he told her after clearing his throat.

"You did?" That paused Viola's flight.

The present had been a mystery for days, one of which he'd allowed her no peeks. He'd trooped in and out of the house proper, carrying things for days, emerging at the end of each one nicked and sweating.

He flattered himself she rather liked the sweating.

He'd been smug every minute, imagining Viola's pleasure, both over the gift and in use of it. Now it felt like less than enough.

But Viola only tugged him out again, past the pigs. Why hadn't he moved the pigs? In fact, why did he *have* those pigs? The other cattle were all down the valley at the farm.

Then he remembered the days when the pigs had been his only company.

"Where is it?"

"Up there," he jerked his chin to the timbered staircase.

If she didn't like the room he'd picked for it, he was out of luck, because the thing wasn't moving.

Up the stairs and down the hall, Viola put her head into each door, taking quick account of every chamber's bare walls, till she came to the room at the end.

It was over the kitchen; it would be warm in winter. Lee wasn't sure he'd made the right choice, though no other view in the house was as grand.

The window's shutters lay open, letting in the spring, and nothing, not even glass, separated them from the sky and the air and the sweep of the valley.

In the middle of the floor stood a vast bed.

Its posts were heavy and square, holes bored around its rails, the best he could do with an axe and little patience, for he had yet to refill his store of that. He'd strung it with rope and filled it with clean straw ticking, topping the whole with more sheepskins.

Hawkshope had no shortage of sheepskins.

"I thought you'd like a wider bed." He was afraid of crushing her in their narrow cot, as well as wanting more room for them to play.

Her eyes were wide as she ran her fingers over the posts. Lee winced. They were too rough; he'd had nothing to polish with. She'd get splinters.

But she didn't look afraid of splinters.

"I'll keep at the finish," he promised, "it's just for now. You might find a better bed in London."

Then she looked up at him with her dark *come and find out* eyes.

"There is no better bed," she told him with that conviction he loved.

There was no hiding from it; he loved her. And he had no idea what tomorrow would bring.

But *now,* he loved her fiercely. Wholly.

And he didn't need to say it, because she understood exactly what he'd imagined as he'd hewn the heavy pieces and notched them together.

"I'm going to have your children in this bed." She said it with her deep conviction, and Lee had to close his eyes.

"We're going to *make* your children in this bed," she told him more lightly, her voice drawing near. She touched his eyes to open them.

Then took his hand and led him exactly where he wanted to go.

When they lay at peace again, Lee sprawled on a bed made to fit his size, Viola sprawled on *him,* he wondered if that letter had only been a bad dream.

* * *

ONCE HIS PLEASURE EBBED, Lee let sleep pull him under, knowing he had everything he needed in his arms.

He was unaware when Viola slipped away, when his skin took the parting as broken treaty and fired rifle shots into his mind.

Had he been able to promote some inner part to keep order in the ranks of his senses, everything would have been put in its proper place, not allowed to wander his dreams, armed and ready.

His waking mind knew he had everything. Everything. This time, he would not lose it.

It planted that flag in his battlefield of sleep, mustering forces against the murmurs of uprising and making disjointed plans to kill or die.

* * *

VIOLA'S STORE of married knowledge grew every day. Certainly she grasped that once completely satisfied, her husband fell asleep.

She could take as much pleasure as she liked in watching the rise and fall of his chest.

His fingers twitched as she rolled far enough away to sit, pulling in her knees and resting her head on them so she could watch him, her riches, her everything.

She must compliment him often on the solidity of their bed. Like the floors, it made little sound, only a slight rustle giving away when she slipped out to find her shift, mindful of how her skin was cooling.

His trousers lay on the floor where he'd thrown them. That made her smile. He was a careful nurse and a decent housekeeper, but this habit never stopped. His trousers were always on the floor.

She nudged them out of her way with one foot as she took up her shift from the foot of the bed. Something shook loose.

It was another letter, half falling from Lee's pocket. She slid on her shift and picked it up.

Its direction was to *Mister and Mistress Waite.* How delightful. She pried it open.

It was from Oliver, and it was short. He repeated tidbits of news from London society he thought they'd like, and he chose well, only choice gossip mixed with his original observations. There were more soldiers in London every day. The docks were overrun.

I hope Waite hates Northumberland ale.

That was a peculiar sentiment, perhaps some code between soldiers. Viola ignored it.

"Viola?"

Lee had turned, his bare arm searching the bedding for her.

"Every day, sir," she murmured, taking delight in leaning over the bed and kissing that arm.

The arm turned ferocious, catching her close and rolling her over to prevent her escape.

"I'm not escaping," she pointed out into Lee's bleary eyes as he blinked awake. "I'm captured."

"Good." And that was all he said with words for a long time more.

* * *

Viola drew something with her fingers on his stomach that he couldn't perceive, as if making art from the sweat of his pleasurable labors. She liked him sweaty, he was sure of it.

But her words were all anticipation of London. "Will

everything be well here? Can you travel? Who will mind the house?"

Lee scoffed. "This house minds itself. Mrs. Scott will be saved her daily walk to deliver us bread. If there's a storm, she'll sweep out the litter."

The windows didn't even have glass. How had he brought his bride to a house without *glass*?

Viola didn't think far enough ahead to worry about glass. Only everlasting London. "Herbert waits on himself, but who will manage dinner for the pigs? Madge can be so mean, shoving the other two from the trough. Oh! I just understood what people mean by *pig-headed!*"

"Chuck and Willsy should stand up for themselves. The pigs will be fine." Even now, on the far side of the house, he could faintly smell the sty. He should have moved the pigs weeks ago. He had a wife to talk to now; he didn't need the pigs. "I'm taking the only charge I have with me." And he squeezed her closer.

* * *

VIOLA BLINKED.

Was she wrong, or had he just said *she* was his charge? Like a hedgehog with a leg off?

Well, she had been when he'd brought her here, hadn't she?

She'd just never imagined he still thought of her that way. Something about it hurt a little. She didn't want to be a *charge*. Her legs were fine. *She* was fine.

Wasn't she?

She'd felt well for weeks. The nagging thoughts were easy to shove away. If she said something self-effacing and shamed, Lee just said *huh,* and they went past it as though it hadn't happened.

What would happen in winter, though? When it was cold and dark, with almost no daylight? For this far north, the nights must get terribly long.

What would happen when they had children?

This bed was a glorious indulgence. He would give her everything, she knew that. Bankrupt himself to bring her a plum. She remembered now, faintly, that he had indeed procured cake. A week ago? Two? Her favorite cake, the Breton cake, stuffed with plums instead of apricots. She hadn't even thanked him.

He'd give her his boots and walk over glass in bare feet if she wanted. Anything she wanted, right down to harassing a vicar out of making her say vows she didn't want to say.

He could indeed have used a sturdy and congenial wife. He'd taken her. Nagging thoughts aside, all she'd ever wanted was to be happy. Lee would say she managed it fine, with a little more effort than others.

But now she wanted more. She wanted *him* to be happy, and any effort that took fell to her.

She wanted to be more useful than a wounded animal.

It was foolish to go all the way to London, but she *so* wanted to see Virginia, and Selene, and the baby. They ought to make the trip useful. In her head she began a list of things *he* might need.

She should ask about his finances. Wasn't that a thing responsible wives did? She must learn to care about his time, and especially his money. She'd never bothered about it before; she must learn.

People who took care of others had to weigh treats against their pocketbooks, she could see that.

She sighed, watching the faint hairs on his skin shiver. "It's such a long journey. I wish I could at least make it quicker."

His hand slowly stroked along the curve of her spine, a

luscious, drugging sensation. "One can sail out of Newcastle and shorten it a few days," he murmured, as if it had nothing to do with him.

"Well," she said, turning her head and laying her cheek on his belly, "can you afford that?"

CHAPTER 21

*I*t was a great deal more pleasant to travel when she felt well.

Viola wanted to explore every inch of Newcastle-upon-Tyne. Its center bustled, its buildings marched right down to the water, and when her husband walked her down to survey the view and the silvery river, she could see massive poles and ladders supporting the skeletons of growing new ships.

"Just think. But for you, I might have spent a whole life in London, never knowing there was more to the country than unhappy houses."

He seemed lost in his own thoughts as he took in the sights. "You'd never have thought of visiting Newcastle?"

"Never! Its lord is so bitter."

Lee's attention returned to her, laced with confusion.

"Have you not met His Grace? An unpleasant, unyielding man."

"No, my stolen invitations never reached those kinds of heights. Nor have I ever thought to visit a place because I'd met its duke."

She stretched herself taller, trying to see every detail of

the men working on the ships. "Isn't it clever, how they've built a ramp all the way up to the top?"

"I had no idea about any of this business."

It felt jarring to have their thoughts out of sync, as if she were dancing with one slipper. Lee didn't seem to share her pleasure at the sight-seeing, but neither was he out of sorts. He was just... somewhere else. Perhaps his thoughts were weaving in and out among the crowds, or perhaps they were over the sea ahead, thinking of the men he'd left in Europe. In the ground.

"I don't even know if you like travel." The thought came out before she realized she was saying it.

"What? Oh, I like it well enough." He surveyed the ship-building again, then over to the docks where finished sea-going vessels slowly rocked and awaited their cargo.

"Did you want to see more, or were you hoping for dinner?"

"The inn will keep our dinner." Then he seemed to come back to her, looking down with consternation. "Hungry? A town this size must have cake."

Viola couldn't be sure, but the prickle of irritation she felt at his words wasn't because of any illness. "I'm not delicate, you know."

His eyes only ran all over her, taking her measure in some fashion before he subsided. "All right."

The implication that she might be delicate even as he accepted her refusal of cake bothered her too.

She tried to revive their conversation. "Are all those ships going to London?"

"No idea," he said with the carelessness of a man who'd walked the length of the country and had no interest in ships. "I suppose so. Ours is." That he did share, pointing out its low curve against the water.

"So many ships sailing back and forth to London, and they're building more!"

"Digging all the coal and sending it to be burned and forgotten." Now he looked as if he tasted something bad. "It'd be no loss to Newcastle if London burned to the ground."

That seemed excessive, even for Lee's dislike of London. "If the people here couldn't sell coal, what would they do?"

"Something else." The two words rolled off his tongue like cannonballs.

Then he patted her hand, and seemed more like himself.

"If you want to see your friends, we'd better prepare to sail. Dinner first, then luggage to the boat."

* * *

LEE FOUND THE PASSAGE HELL.

Viola loved everything: the rolling ship under her feet, the smell of water, the fresh spray turning salty as they set out to sea.

There were others on the collier ship, cheerfully packed into small cabins the captain seemed to begrudge, apparently because each one took precious space from his cargo of what he called *black diamonds*.

Viola watched the other travelers, the same way she'd watched lords and ladies in drawing rooms, quietly taking note of things till one mother, daughter in tow, asked about her plans for the trip.

Soon the women all gathered around Viola, who did her best to mimic Miss Díaz' way of telling her story about the Russian ambassador. They were transfixed.

She should have more people to talk to, Lee grumbled inwardly as he stared past the deck to the waves, watching for any to come in out-of-bounds high.

That night Viola lay comfortably on their bunk, wrapped in wool blankets, while Lee kept watch.

All night.

He could ignore the ship's pitching during the daytime, but below decks he felt boxed in, at the mercy of the sea, waiting for it to turn on him and take away everything he loved.

It'had before.

When Viola woke, she was sleepily surprised to find him still sitting over her, both arms braced against the walls, his eyes burning red.

"Did you sleep at all?" Twisting beneath him, she pulled an arm loose. It felt like it was stuck to the boards.

"A little," he lied.

"This is awful. Your arm is hard as rope." She rubbed the knotted muscle, much like he'd rubbed her feet, what seemed a long time ago.

"I wish we were at Hawkshope."

"Do you?" She sprang upright, sitting against the wall. "Should we turn back? Can the ship turn back?"

"Nothing so urgent." He should be more careful with his words. Her inclination to treat his wishes as near-commands might have fallen to a reasonable level, but she still gave his words too much weight.

She studied him in the gloom. The darkness was nearly total; he didn't know why it wasn't. The danger of fire dictated he not burn candles all night, and the chamber had no windows.

Perhaps she gave off light.

She made an unhappy noise. "I should have thought a sea voyage would be uncomfortable for you. I'm sorry."

"Why should you?" Why *was* it?

"You mean, other than your parents dying this way?"

Startled, he loosed his other arm. The pain of it bending

again was agony, but it was brief. How many hours had he stayed like that?

"I wasn't there," he reminded his wife, reaching out in the dark to stroke her hair. It was soothing.

"For which I'm glad." Turning so she fit back against him, soft against his body, she wiggled until she was just where she most liked to be, and his arm closed around her. He felt his breathing slow. "But I should have guessed a man who walked across Britain for fun might prefer not to sail."

"It's fine," he assured her, dropping his cheek against the curve of her head.

"Huh," was all she said, and he felt laughter bubbling up inside him.

* * *

STILL, the rest of the day was harsh, cool breezes turning downright cold as they swept in off the water, worrying him all day that Viola would catch some chill.

She didn't look ill; she looked happy as a lark, exploring every nook of the ship and even conversing with the other ladies, who deferred to her if only due to her title.

He didn't think it was only due to her title.

"Lady Viola. You asked about dinner. Yes, there is butter for the bread, and smoked fish in the stew." The ship's mate approached her on deck with similar deference and a deep bow, even if his eyes glittered a little as they took in her shape under her wool cloak.

Thank God he'd thought to buy the thing in Newcastle; she should have had one before this. The weather in the Cheviot hills was seldom of the kind where she should be running about in bare feet. For all he knew, they'd never see a day that warm again.

As Viola passed, deep in conversation with the mate about some detail of the food, another sailor stopped and watched, his eyes roaming every inch of Viola with no restraint at all. He made a long, low whistle, not for Viola's attention, which never shifted, but to call his fellow sailors to take a look. Some did.

The white-hot rage at Oliver's house had been only a distant echo of thunder. This was a hurricane inside him now, unleashed, spinning, and destructive.

He found the man's throat in his hand, his arm pushing the man backward. The sailor wouldn't fall overboard... unless Lee kept doing what he was doing.

Loosening his grip, Lee hissed through his teeth as he'd once done to enemy soldiers. "Stop."

"Sorry, sir. Sorry." The man's words came clearer as Lee let go. They had a rasp in them, from the squeeze. "I didn't know you accompanied the lady."

Lee wanted to squeeze again. "Here's a thought. Just pretend every woman on the ship is traveling with me. Every day. From now until you're dead."

"Yes, sir. Sorry, sir. Truly. You can—you can put your hand away."

The flat way he said *hand,* such a clearly Newcastle intonation, cleared away some of the smoke and fire in Lee's head.

What on earth was he doing?

Nothing bad had happened. They'd be in London soon, yes, but it was only a visit. Viola would come back to Hawkshope with him afterwards.

Whether she should or not.

"Sorry." Lee rubbed both eyes with one hand. He just had to sleep tonight. "I didn't sleep."

"Ah I see!" The sailor, perhaps just from delight at not being strangled, treated this as important news. "It rattles every son of Tyne to get out to open sea. Frank! Where's your whiskey?"

"I'm not from Tyneside." Exhaustion soaked down to his bones with the sea spray. "Don't know where I was born."

"All the more reason for a drink. Go on. If you need sleep, there's your answer."

Lee tried to shove the bottle back at him, but the sailor only pushed it towards his chest.

"Truly, sir, I'll not bother the ladies again."

* * *

THAT NIGHT, bracing Viola in their bunk, Lee breathed the sea air deep, then let it go. It was just a box. Just a ship. Just a few miles out to sea.

He couldn't do this. Not without sleep.

Tomorrow they'd reach the London docks, a carriage ride away from Talbourne House. He'd need to wear his good coat all the time. Viola's grand friends were no doubt ready to entertain her, whether or not his hasty letter had reached them. She'd have dinners of twelve courses, all kinds of nourishment, all cooked for her by someone else.

She wouldn't need him.

He'd propped the whiskey bottle in his open valise when he'd set his loaded pistol there, well after Viola had fallen asleep.

He was married now. He couldn't lose her. Not legally, anyway.

This was different from the war. *He* was different. He only needed a little sleep.

If there was one thing whiskey could do for him, it was to send him into dreams.

Reaching himself the bottle one-handed, unwilling to rise

and risk waking Viola, Lee pulled its cork with his teeth and took a swig of the strong-smelling liquid.

It felt foreign, the way it slid down cold and hot at the same time.

But it warmed his belly, and after a few swallows, he could feel that warmth seeping out into the rest of him. His sore arms, his cold feet, everywhere.

It was easy, easier than he'd even expected, to wrap himself around his wife and fall asleep.

WHEN VIOLA WOKE, she found Lee still slumbering. His arm lay heavy across her waist and she hated to move it, but she had to find the necessary, and in their tiny cabin that was a delicate feat.

There was little she could do to keep from waking him, so she didn't try.

Rolling her weight over him, she kissed his rough cheek as she passed. "Plan to wake soon, sailor?"

"Mrgghph," he said, batting at her with one hand.

"Cogent," she responded, as if he'd made a sound argument, and wriggled her weight off him to the floor.

Against the wall was an open valise, just beside their bunk, and propped among his shirts were a bottle of liquor and a flintlock pistol.

"Huh," she said to herself, taking up the bottle, afraid to touch the pistol.

These were new. At least so far as she knew. She hadn't been married long, but she thought she knew her husband's routines, and she hadn't expected to find these.

Blearily Lee rolled back towards her, blinking in the faint light. She held up the bottle. "Breakfast?"

"Medicinal," was all he said, batting at her again like she

was a cloud of gnats before sinking back into their nest of blankets.

He was never very good at explaining himself.

Well. No matter. They'd soon be at Talbourne House, and he'd sleep better there. If he'd had a drink last night, when he hadn't in all the time she'd known him, he must have found the crossing unpleasant indeed.

He looked bleary. Perhaps from the liquor. She wondered how much he'd had. "Are you ready to face the ravaging hordes?"

"Every day," he said without meeting her eyes, and she knew his heart wasn't in it.

* * *

THE CARRIAGE RIDE to Talbourne House was quiet. Viola had plenty of time to examine her husband, and didn't like what she saw.

Despite the sleep, he looked haggard, his lean cheeks thin under bristles he couldn't shave aboard a pitching ship. His hat was tipped carelessly back on his head. During their weeks together, his hair had grown so long that it brushed his collar. If he didn't cut it soon, it would quickly grow to rival Oliver's.

She wondered if he planned to cut it, wondered why she didn't just ask.

He looked melancholy. London clearly did not agree with him. But then she was prone to imagine such things.

"Did you bring your wife to London?" When his confused expression swung up to meet hers, she realized she should be clearer. "Your first wife. Beatrix."

"Ah, no. Just a farm. In Cambridgeshire." He still looked puzzled. "I told you I never went far north till after the war. No one ever saw Hawkshope till you."

Viola found his answer just as puzzling. "I am only making conversation. I don't want you to think you can't speak about her. Or your little girl." He never had. "What was her name? Your little girl. I don't even know it."

He only looked back out the window.

As a conversationalist, she was failing.

"Anyway," she continued without his answer, "Hawkshope has visitors. Mrs. Scott has seen it, and everyone at the farmhouse. Not to mention Madge and Willsy." She could leave out Chuck. Chuck was oblivious.

He snorted without turning. The last houses of London were giving way to trees as the track wove toward the Duke's palace. "Madge and Willsy," he muttered. "Fine company."

"Didn't they laugh at your stories about the bees?"

"I did not tell them about the bees, because they are pigs."

He might not feel like laughing, but he was still funny. "I feel clever, accidentally finding such a funny husband."

He didn't find it so funny, but his eyes lightened a little. He patted her hand as he used to do, even though he had to lean across the carriage to do it. "You do little by accident, Viola." He sat back and watched her sway with the motion of the carriage. "How long did you plan that whole escapade?"

"Far too long or not long enough, depending how you judge my results," she told him frankly, trying to make him smile.

He didn't. "How do *you* judge your results?"

"Very well so far."

Every smidgen of humor disappeared again. Hers was *not* a welcome answer.

Surely he wasn't still worried about his feelings fading away.

She might not have been married long, but she knew enough to know she'd been wrong. Even if the whole world held only one pair of married lovers, that pair would be her and this man. She knew it.

Somehow he'd known not to ply her with lies when she'd been ill. The last thing she'd needed then was someone telling her the world was right side up when hers was upside down. Still the urge was strong to begin a litany of reassurances. She didn't. Fears, she knew, did not respond to logic.

"How long did it take you to choose Beatrix?" She didn't know why the topic kept coming to her, only that she wanted to keep discovering everything about him. If she had the secrets of time she'd turn back to the moment he'd returned to Britain's shores, if not all the way back to the time he'd been very small and needed the hugs he so freely gave her.

"Not long. She wasn't complicated."

The intensity of his gaze was uncomfortable, but Viola ignored that. He wasn't always comfortable, and that was part of him. She ought to have recognized the lack of heat between her and Lord Callendar once she'd encountered the genuine thing. "I suppose I'm not simple," she said with a light shrug. "Am I easier to nurse back to health than a hawk, or more difficult?"

"More rewarding," and he did almost smile.

"And will you promise to take a holiday from rescuing fragile creatures? Or should we find you a croupy squirrel?"

He only shook his head slowly, looking, if possible, even sadder. But he didn't speak.

* * *

No, Viola, Lee thought to himself, his mind lurching and rolling in unaccustomed tracks, *I never wish to take a holiday from you.*

* * *

TALBOURNE HOUSE WAS *NOT* empty of guests.

To Viola's surprise, as she handed the footman her hat and gloves, she distinctly heard faint voices far away in the grand ballroom.

She gave the footman a questioning eyebrow.

"Her Grace is receiving in her apartments," said he, surely hearing it too. Talbourne servants were always listening.

"And we simply... walk up there?"

"Indeed, madam."

With a look, she asked what her husband thought. Lee just shrugged. If the Duke and Duchess didn't care about their reputation, he certainly didn't.

The walk felt easier than the last time she was here, paradoxically, as it was actually farther from the grand entrance to the family's rooms than it was to sneak up the servant's staircase.

At the door by the peacock feathers, Lee tapped her on the shoulder, making her turn.

"You go in. I'm nothing but filth from the ship; I'll bathe and see the baby later."

"Excellent plan," Viola instantly responded, taking his arm to lead the way to her old chamber.

He just shook his head. "Her Grace will want to see you. Don't wait for me."

"I'm none too fresh either," she told him tartly. "Yours is the better plan."

"Go on in."

Viola felt foolish that she didn't really want to see the baby for the first time without him. Do *anything* without him. But perhaps time to himself was what he needed in a holiday.

Certainly it felt as though they'd spent every moment

together since their fateful hackney ride. Together, and him waiting on her.

"I'll join you in a moment then," she nodded, trying not to sound forlorn and nodding to the footman.

She didn't look after Lee; he left her there as the footman announced her. "Lady Viola Waite."

"Oh, *Viola!*" Selene sailed to the middle of the room, hand outstretched for Viola to take. "I'm so glad you've come! All my little dreams are coming true along with my big one."

She took Viola's arm and led her to the side of the crib, trusting Viola to steer her around any unexpected obstacles.

The crib was a masterpiece of carving, tiny and majestic at the same time, with a solemn angel face presiding over its head and four little pillars braced with crosspieces on the floor. Within its red-and-peacock borders lay the tiniest new branch on the Talbourne family tree.

And the Duke himself sat in a chair by the crib, occasionally reaching out a finger to touch the baby's toes then remembering not to wake her and pulling it back.

Selene pressed her shoulder into Viola's. Whispering. "Allow me to introduce Lady Aurelia Anna Georgina Redbeck Hayden."

"Gracious. And what do you call her?" Viola whispered back.

Selene chuckled under her breath. "Who could decide?"

Her ladyship wiggled under her quilted silk coverlet, and all of them held their breath. Then she subsided back into sleep.

Viola wanted to touch her too, but it felt dangerous. Her ladyship was so terribly tiny.

Plus it looked as though the Duke would bat Viola's hand away if she even tried. "Your Grace." Viola offered him a small curtsey.

"I think he plans to sit by that crib until she is of age," Selene added softly, fondly.

"She must have everything," the Duke simply said, not tearing his eyes away from his new little girl, but catching his wife's hand off his shoulder and kissing it more deeply than Viola had ever seen him do.

"Everything she *needs*," Selene corrected.

The Duke just shook his head. "I did not misspeak."

"May I steal you for a visit?" Viola felt like this was the wrong time to intrude, but Selene dispelled the idea, tugging her towards the inner door.

"Oh my, yes! I'm so tired, and I could use some amusement that isn't tiny toes. Though I'm not really tired of tiny toes. It's very hard to explain."

In Her Grace's chamber, there was a small table set up with a chessboard; Selene gestured Viola to sit.

"Will you mind terribly if I lie down? I am... healing," Selene said delicately, sighing with relief as she sank into the featherbed.

"Naturally! You need not entertain me. I only came to greet you because we've just arrived."

"Perfect. Your husband too? Wonderful news." Her pretty features winced a little as she shifted position.

It made Viola start up out of her chair. "Should I—what can I do to help?"

"It's only time that must pass." Selene's tired laugh said she wouldn't change things if she could, but still felt worn. "I suppose you'll discover that one of these days, if things follow as they often do."

"I hope so." She did. In fact, there was a chance that she was already on her way to finding out. Silently she spread her hand over her belly, wishing as hard as she had ever wished for anything in her life.

"Never say so! Do you have news?"

If she did, Viola would save it for Lee first. That was the most *we* conversation there could be. "I hope so soon," was all she said. "Tell me what's happening. Virginia's letter said Talbourne House was empty."

"Oh, we tried turning the gamesters away after the confinement, but they just come anyway." Now Selene sounded quite tired. "And once there are eligible men, Lady Villeneuve insists on driving here with her interminable marriage-seekers."

"I don't mind her so much. I would have been one but for your generosity." Viola would have been lucky to be one, in fact, as she'd have been more likely to remain at Morland than find her way to Lady Villeneuve's coterie of second-rate virgins.

Indeed, part of her inspiration to capture Lord Callendar had been avoiding just that fate.

What advice could she give Lady Aurelia Anna Georgina Redbeck Hayden twenty years from now that might keep her from taking such a circuitous route to happiness?

What advice might a better mother have given *her?*

Well, she had time to decide.

* * *

OF COURSE, whose path did Lee cross within a dozen steps of the Duchess' door but that of Lord Callendar himself.

Lee felt sticky from the sea, exhausted and sore as if the ship itself had beaten him with sticks. He had no patience left, and if he had, he wouldn't have spent it on this popinjay boy with his puppy-dog eyes.

"Mr. Waite." The fellow greeted him with half a bow, not even asking after Viola. Though that wouldn't have improved the meeting.

"Tell me, Callendar. Do you never tire of being pathetic?"

<h1 style="text-align:center">CHAPTER 22</h1>

"I beg your pardon, sir?" The young man seemed to swell in his tightly buttoned coat.

"Never mind." Callendar was only being polite, pretending not to hear Lee's insult. This was not the way to begin the visit. Likely the stuffed nob would be hanging about every meal, staring at Miss Díaz, the Duchess, or Viola, and making all the women feel sorry for him for absolutely no reason at all.

"Indeed." The gentleman sketched a bow so stiff it was in danger of snapping, and turned on his heel to show himself into the Duchess' chambers.

Where Viola had gone.

Lee stalked to Viola's room, less palatial than the Duchess' but no less sumptuous.

Either their letter had not arrived, or every new guest was greeted with this flurry of servants fluffing the bed, turning the coverlets, spreading fresh linens, and polishing the oak parquet dressing table.

Viola didn't have a dressing table at Hawkshope.

"Sir." One maid curtsied, and Lee was half surprised she'd

even noticed he was there. "We've readied a room for you just down the hall. If you'd like me to show you."

"No, I'll stay here."

The glances between the maids only ripped new invisible cuts across the wounds Lee was already feeling. He knew it wasn't the done thing for finer couples to share the same room. Well, he wasn't fine and he'd be damned if he'd sleep in some other room than his wife's.

"Of course, sir." He could see her calculating the dimensions of the chest of drawers, wondering if his things would unpack into the furniture Viola had available.

He almost told her to take anything that didn't fit and throw it on the floor.

"I'll have a bath," he said instead.

"Very good, sir. And your valet?"

That caused several seconds of wondering why she'd asked after such a nonexistent person. "I'll dress myself."

The staff knew their business, conducting whole conversations silently as they tucked and smoothed and prodded. They couldn't stay if he were to bathe in here. They had to work quickly.

He was seconds from simply walking out the door and trying every room in the palace till he found one where he could be alone.

Indeed, with another moment's contemplation of Viola's fine frilled room, Lee noted one shortcoming the servants could address right now.

He leaned out the door with both hands on the jamb, the way he would have done in his tower.

"John," he called the footman in the hall. The lad's name was almost certainly not John, but Lee didn't know him, and in a mood like his any name would do.

"Sir," said the young fellow, snapping to his side.

"I'm going to have a bath, and I'm going to want something to drink. I don't want any sugary sherry. See if you can find me a decent glass of gin."

* * *

WHEN VIOLA ARRIVED in her room, it held a flurry of activity the like of which she had never seen.

"Madam!" The butler, Mr. Collins, looked shocked and starched all at the same time. He had dark clothes over his arm, either coming or going, while two footmen darted about like he was conducting and they were the orchestra.

By the fire squatted a valet polishing boots and another with a tray. A third man bent over the tub, shaving her husband.

Viola just stood aghast in the middle of the floor. She had never seen anything like it.

"That's all right, she can stay." From the midst of the chaos one familiar long arm just waved away the butler's horror and anyone else's possible contradictions.

"Mr. Waite?"

"Lady Viola." He blinked solemnly; she realized he didn't want to move and disturb the barber. Given the razor, that seemed wise.

"What on earth is happening?"

"I'm dressing."

"I thought I'd seen it before. I suppose not."

"*Madam.*" Mr. Collins, obviously overcome at the idea that she had seen her husband dress before, withdrew.

The man by the fire drew out what Viola now saw was a tray of clay curling-rods, heated in the fire.

"Ah!" She flung up a hand to ward the things off.

"I'm trying it," said her husband. "I didn't set paper curls last night."

Viola tiptoed closer. She feared that the wrong step would trigger some sort of explosion. "You're doing *what?*"

"I curled my hair when I first came to London. Oliver told me to try it. Said ladies appreciated a Brutus cut."

"I cannot think of anything less pertinent to our current situation."

"A gentleman needs a good quantity of hair to get the right appearance," said the fellow with the curling-rods.

"A gentleman needs not to burn off his hair before venturing into company," said Viola firmly. "If you will all excuse us."

Too well-trained to complain, all of them gave Viola looks of consternation or outright disdain till Lee waved them off.

"Gracious," sighed Viola once they'd gone. "Have you spent all this time at Hawkshope longing for a storm of hair-dressing?"

"I don't know much about society, but I know we're in it." Lee's fingers paddled in the water. He was absurdly folded to fit in the tub. "Who knows what kind of kidnapping I'd have attracted if I'd kept up with dressing my hair?"

That hurt.

It hurt so much that Viola's hand pressed to her stomach as she stared at him, wordless.

Finally she could breathe enough for one word. "What?"

"Was that rude? I didn't intend it." Lee shoved himself out of the bath, water raining in all directions, some of it splashing on the fine inlaid furniture. He crushed her to him, heedless of his water and her dress, and for the first time, it didn't feel good.

"No apology needed," she said before she realized he hadn't made one.

He just turned to the bed, drying himself shoddily before tossing the cloth on the floor and shaking out one garment after another as if they held moths. "I suppose I'm dressing for a night of card-playing? Chess? Don't tell me we're to put up with that Callendar idiot all night."

Viola's storm of confusion ranged far beyond her illness. She'd done nothing to cause this, any of this. She was as sure of that as she was of her own name. "Lee. You've caught a fever. You should rest. Do lie down."

Just like that, a change washed over his features, and in three steps he was standing before her. Viola felt her breaths quicken, whether from nerves or other anticipation she didn't know, but he only took her face in his hands and kissed her, his familiar gentle kiss, though it tasted bitter. He smelled of sandalwood and sugar again, and she realized it was the packing for his city coats. At least that was the source of the sandalwood; the sugar might be him.

"Nothing to worry about," he murmured against her lips. "Dinner and smiles, then we'll both sleep. Right here."

"Of course. I'd planned to bathe."

"I'll tell the footman."

Half-dressed, he went out and left the door open.

Viola just looked about the room in helpless confusion. Something was wrong, but it wasn't the linens or the trunks.

Beside her elbow, a silver tray on the dresser held a short crystal tumbler. Viola brought it to her lips, hoping for a sip of water.

But it was empty, and had a strange smell.

It took her a long while to place it. Ladies at London parties drank ratafia punch, or sometimes sherry. The gentlemen's rooms were the ones with the stronger smells, the leather and cigar smoke.

Sometimes gin.

He hadn't become an entirely different person in the last few days. They might not know each other well, but she knew that.

Some change might be working in him, but it wasn't his love disappearing. That she knew. Whatever it was, they'd survive it, the same way they'd survived her own illness. And would again, if it came back.

But now *she* must care for him, and she wasn't sure how. Forget bread and pocketbooks. He needed something different.

Sleep. He needed sleep. She must find Oliver, ask him whether belladonna was better than gin. Just the thought of it sickened her stomach, but this was no time to be missish about medicine that might serve. She didn't trust Oliver with her own illness, but he might be useful to consult about Mr. Waite.

Lee. *Her* Lee.

* * *

THE DINNER WAS WORSE than the crossing.

Lee had seen his share of London houses. Some had a cool tranquility, with their blue rooms and crystal lampshades; some had exuberant blood, with Roman red walls and heaps of gold tassels.

Talbourne House was nothing like any of those. Talbourne House was a palace.

Its wide hallways spoke of kings and their retinues sweeping in to trade treaties, or break them. The privacy of this wing with its ducal apartments, their favorite salons and nurseries and libraries and sitting rooms, was an illusion. The house rambled on, housing in truth the equivalent of a village, mostly servants who kept its every function running smoothly, along with some forever guests who called the place home and the social hopefuls who partook of the neverending Talbourne entertainments. Those hopefuls dressed in their finest every night for a glimpse of or a favor from their august hosts, never guessing that their primary purpose was to funnel news out of London to where it might do some good.

The private dinner, therefore, was unusually enclosed, even though the table was laid in a salon that would have held the entirety of the main floor of Hawkshope and more.

Lee didn't want any of it. It was excruciating to know that he was trapped, for if he left the residence wing he might be seen by one of the guests, and by all rules of propriety, he should not be here.

As if society would rather he'd let Viola climb into that carriage alone.

Some part of him thought the whole London *ton* couldn't be villains, but the larger share of him was convinced they were just that.

Villains with jewel-box houses that suited Viola like a precious setting for a pearl.

The disjointed way his thoughts bumped along bothered him primarily because they felt thorny. Painful. They might not have made sense, but his gut told him they were nonetheless true.

He'd thought Viola perfect in their ancient stone tower, but she looked just as beautiful here. She'd look beautiful anywhere. Here she was comfortable, her feet in soft slippers and cushioned by wool rugs, surrounded by priceless furniture covered in silks and satins that wouldn't chafe her skin, warmed by constant fires and spotless men in livery who jumped to do her bidding before she even called.

At Hawkshope her choice of conversation partners had been limited to him, or pigs. *Even the hedgehog was a kind of pig,* he mused as he watched cut glass decanters circle around the tables.

"Mr. Waite won't have wine," Viola said across from him, directing the footman with one wave of her hand. Without a flicker of surprise, the man disappeared and reappeared with a pitcher of something golden that he poured in Lee's goblet.

Defying the convention that drinks wait for toasts, Lee tasted it. Ginger tea. Expensive medicine for babies.

The ball of loathing in his stomach did not dissipate.

It was a gathering of family and old friends, and Lee was very much the outsider. The tables were closely set, with the Duke and his Duchess at one end and Virginia and Viola beside them. A Lady Redbeck was rolled in by a clearly devoted old Scot. He proceeded to fuss over her safety and her supply of tea. From the conversation, Lee divined this was the Duchess' mother.

By the time Oliver arrived, Lee wanted to retreat.

"Thank God," Lee said, clapping his old friend on the shoulder. Oliver's wife went to kiss the Duchess, reminding Lee they were cousins.

"What the hell happened to you?" Leave Oliver to be blunt.

"The sea crossing was hell. Shorter, and Viola liked it better, but hell."

"It must have been. You look like you drowned a few weeks ago." At Oliver's summoning wave, a footman brought him a cup of tea. Oliver held it cautiously, as if it held frogs, or maybe only parts of frogs. "My lady wife is no physician, but she's prescribed tea instead of wine."

That made Lee feel better, but he didn't mention his own goblet. It felt lowering somehow to have a false cup of wine rather than a blatant cup of tea. "She worries for you."

"So? Does Viola do the same? Or are you fighting some other battles? You disappeared after the wedding so quickly that had it been anyone but you, I would have sent armed battalions north after you."

"Come and try it. Hadrian's Wall has stopped better men than you."

Oliver snorted. "It's a lump of dirt."

Viola laughed at some witty remark; Lee turned to see, hungry for it.

Oliver noticed. "If you're worried about my mother, don't be. I bundled her off to Buxton using every restraint but chains. I'll put on chains too if I must. If she's determined to be miserable, she can do it alone."

"Good news," but Lee hadn't been thinking of Viola's mother at all. He'd practically forgotten what had sent her sinking low in those days right around their wedding. Maybe it hadn't been her mother. Maybe it had been their wedding.

It was hard to stay unnoticed next to Oliver. Oliver peered at him. "You look low."

"Thanks. You're short."

"I'm not starting a fight, you arse, I'm trying to see if you're well. You fly off like Apollo in his chariot of the sun, dragging my sister into a wilderness of trees and more trees, and come back with her laughing while you look like you were scraped off a ship."

"Married life has its ups and downs."

"No, it doesn't." Oliver gave him a sour look over the edge of his teacup. "Not like that. Not unless you make it that way."

"From how many married women did you collect all this sage advice?"

At that, Oliver's hand shot out and seized Lee by his coat lapel.

In just a heartbeat, Oliver's control returned, but he still had tight hold of Lee's coat.

"You're well, Oliver?" That was Cass, calling from her place near Selene. Everyone wanted to be close to the Duchess.

"Fine," said Oliver, his gaze locked with Lee's as he let go of the coat. *"Fine,"* he shouted more loudly over his shoulder, in case his wife hadn't heard.

She just nodded and went back to listening raptly to the latest report, something about baby hair.

God. Everything in this palace made Lee's stomach roil.

And he wasn't sure why. He *wanted* Hawkshope full of her children. *Their* children. He wanted that more than he wanted his next breath.

But how could he keep asking it of her when she so clearly belonged right here?

Just then, a lull in other conversations meant he could hear Viola's voice. "When will Lord Callendar's wedding be?"

Lee just sighed and closed his eyes.

"Are you drinking?'

Oliver's question caught him unawares. The man was close enough to smell Lee's breath. The gin's effects had worn off; how much damage could one glass do? He and Oliver used to put away quarts of the stuff, staring at each other like the miserable sods they were across the corner of a smoky gentleman's club, letting time tick away.

"I've drunk plenty in my day," Lee reminded him. "So have you."

Shoving Lee before him, Oliver forced them both out of the salon, gathering surprised looks from the company, even His Grace. "Soldier's bet," he offered as a pathetic explanation as he closed the door behind them.

Then he jammed Lee against the far wall with another far-from-gentle grip on Lee's coat and a shove that betrayed Oliver's solidity.

"You're a poisonous little pill when you drink and you know it, I don't care how tall you are." Oliver's hissing growl was inescapable. "You told me you gave it up. I haven't heard two words of gossip about you all winter, so I assumed you'd kept hold of your calm."

"I have. I'm always calm."

"Not when you drink you're not." Oliver let go with more disgust than he'd shown the phantom frogs in his teacup. "What is *wrong* with you?"

"Nothing! I had a swallow or two of whiskey on the boat so I could sleep. Had a glassful before my bath."

"That's not whiskey, that's gin. I can smell it."

"I always liked gin better. You know that."

"Don't you *dare* say anything to hurt Viola."

"I would *never*." Even as Lee said it, the image flashed in his mind of Viola standing away from the bath, holding her hurt feelings in with one hand and pain in her eyes. "Oliver. She's the love of my life."

"You poor sod." His friend searched his face. "Do you even know what that means?"

No. Lee didn't. He didn't know how his insides worked. What use were complicated explanations anyway, when everything inside him kept changing all the time?

"How fare the old friends?" Cass appeared at his elbow, her elegant eyebrow raised in acknowledgement of the clear tension between the two men in tight conference against the wall.

"Just like old times," sighed Oliver before giving his wife a faint smile. "In fact, my love, I was about to return. Physicians are always too popular or not popular enough, and Mr. Waite seems tired of my company." Without any further acknowledgement, he went back to the salon.

Curious, Cass' eyes wandered over Lee's face, but when Lee didn't say anything, she just turned to follow her husband.

"Wait."

Cass paused. Lee found he was gripping her elbow rather hard. He let go.

"I wanted to ask—how do you do it?"

"I do a lot of things, Mr. Waite, you'll have to be more specific."

"How do you show your face in public knowing how many women your husband loved?"

Cass' lips tightened.

He thought she wasn't going to answer, and indeed she said, "I can't imagine a question more rude. But for Oliver's sake, and because of the letter you once sent me, I'll tell you. Why *should* I doubt my husband's love? Jealousy? Shame? The scandal inoculated me to shame. Likely it helps that I had work long before I had him. I know who I am, and I know what I can do." She searched his eyes as if trying to understand his question. "As for jealousy, I can't prove how it works, but I imagine it it the result of a great imbalance. Nature abhors a truly empty space, so I imagine all kinds of things rush in to fill a void in one's soul unless it is quite filled with certainty. About one's love, and about oneself."

Then she patted his hand in a way that said she was done talking, and followed her husband back into the salon where her friends and family dined.

He had her answer, and it helped nothing.

How had Cass known? How had she known about the empty, howling space inside him that had been left by Beatrix' death?

And your little girl, said the bitter voice, still there, just waiting for its moment, crawling through the open wounds left by Cass' words and the sight of someone else's tiny little girl.

He'd filled that howling space. Viola was everywhere in him, every*thing*. He was as healed as he could get.

And if it all disappeared again, there'd be nothing left.

Beatrix. Beatrix. She kept asking about Beatrix. As if she sensed somehow everything he couldn't explain, as if she wanted to know why Lee could repair anything but the holes in himself.

He that loveth his wife loveth himself.

He could do anything for her but that.

He knew he couldn't find a better version of himself at the bottom of a bottle. He knew it, and still wanted another glass of gin. To feel numb. Forgetful. He *wanted* to forget.

But Oliver was right. He'd had all the medicine he could handle for tonight. He needed to brace up and go back into that salon. Drink his ginger tea. Tomorrow he could buy something for her, and he'd stay away from the damned gin, and things would go back the way they were. Like nothing had happened. Nothing *had* happened.

And then he caught sight of Lord Callendar, leading Lady Cecily toward the salon.

CHAPTER 23

She was giggling—he was surprised the frost didn't fall off her in chunks when she did that—and batting her eyes like a childish coquette. "Even betrothed, I shouldn't let you lead me into the depths of this house!"

Callendar gave her a tight, falsely indulgent smile. "No one is compromising your virtue, Lady Cecily. This is a gathering of close friends, and as you and I will soon be wed, I want you to meet them."

"Why don't they dine downstairs?"

"Their Graces are... eclectic in their close circles."

The lady clearly didn't know what that meant, and would have asked more questions but for the sight of Lee lurking in the hallway, just beyond the reach of any candles.

"Not him!" She rounded on Callendar with evident ire. "He's nobody, your lordship. And you promised me you wouldn't see any more of that lunatic with the cow eyes who pines for you at every social affair."

The fury that exploded in Lee had no more relationship to anything he had ever felt before than a blacksmith's furnace had to the sun.

It was only a very, very distant thread of control that kept him from snapping the woman in two like the icicle she was.

He found himself far too close to her, in far too easy arm's reach. "Don't speak about my wife."

Shying away, she put a hand on Callendar's arm as if to seek his protection, and only spoke to him. "See, he knows all about it. *Are* you faithful, sir, or not?"

Callendar tried to brush off the question. "She doesn't matter."

Callendar's rushed, careless words set off something in Lee he didn't care to tamp down.

In an instant, he backhanded Callendar across the face as hard as he could.

Lady Cecily gave a little scream and staggered back, raising her arms as if warding off any further attack. Callendar took the blow, feeling his teeth as he slowly straightened. A trickle of blood filled the split in his lip; his glove came away red.

"I decided not to bother removing my gloves," Lee gritted through his teeth. "You will give me satisfaction, sir."

"You quite insult Lady Cecily with your conduct right now," Callendar returned, all ice himself. "This is no way to behave before a lady."

"You can't instruct me on how to behave to a lady. I have every evidence you know nothing about it."

Callendar looked round in time to see Lady Cecily disappear down the hall, no longer concerned about being caught alone in the palace's quieter places.

Lee only muttered, "I'll give you instruction." He didn't care where Lady Cecily went. "Let me fetch my pistol."

"I will not *shoot* you in Their Graces' residence." Now Callendar looked both furious and appalled.

"I'm not so discerning."

Striding down the hall, Lee knew exactly where his flint-lock was and how it was loaded.

And if he could get this man outside, how he would shoot him.

* * *

CALLENDAR DOGGED his steps back to the room. "Do you have any idea what you've done?"

"Broken some deal exchanging votes for a wife. You're a cold-blooded snake. I'd say you deserve her." The valise wasn't on the floor; damn servants. Lee had to search. His powder flask was on the table and went into his pocket. The pistol lay in the Italian chest of drawers, of all places, on one of Viola's petticoats.

He touched the soft linen with his fingertip, pulled out the gun, and slammed closed the drawer.

"You're right that there were a great many contracts depending on my marriage to Lady Cecily. As with most marriages among the gentry."

"Not mine."

"Surely you understand that with a different class of people—"

Lee whirled and shoved his fist into Callendar's chest so hard, crushing him into the wall, that the oil lamp on the nearest table rocked, in danger of toppling.

"Don't say one more word about my wife and classes of people or I swear to God I'll put a bullet in you now."

That might have been a flash of genuine fear in Callendar's eyes. He tried to raise his arms. "You must calm yourself."

Lee's grip slackened, then he grabbed Callendar the collar. "I don't believe I will this time."

* * *

"This isn't how it's done." Hands raised at his sides, trying to look unthreatening, Callendar winced as he was shoved right past the ballroom door below.

Dozens of people inside craned their necks to look, and somewhere it sounded as though Lady Cecily was crying. Lee felt perversely glad of that.

He'd like to go in there and wave a weapon at anyone who had said anything bad about Viola, but right at this moment, he wouldn't take the time.

"John." He thrust his chin at the footman by the door; the lad jerked upright. "His lordship requires a pistol. We'll be out on the lawn." He peered through the door's glass.

The sun had not yet set, but clouds had rolled in, dimming the light, forgetting it was May.

Still plenty of light for anyone to see by, if he happened to kill this fool.

"Probably in the trees," he added to the footman, who helpfully opened the door, allowing Lee to shove Callendar out of doors.

* * *

The people who took the time to drive all the way to Talbourne House for an evening's fun *lived* for nights like this.

That had surely been Mr. Waite ushering Lord Callendar outside, under the *most* distressing circumstances.

Whispered anecdotes about both men rustled through the room like summer rain, soaking in silently, fast, and deep.

So quiet, Mr. Waite, and hadn't he eloped with Lady Viola? The Duchess would never allow her maid in waiting to make a precipitous choice.

No, others said, *the Duchess was in confinement and knew nothing about it. Lady Viola was a lightskirt. She took advantage of Mr. Waite.*

No, others answered, *he wickedly seduced her.*

Whatever the variety of opinions swirling about Lady Viola and Mr. Waite, the consternation was unanimous about Lord Callendar's behavior. Lady Viola was now safely wed; that news had spread. No one was quite sure whether it had been by special license or at Gretna Green. Still, no one questioned that justice had been done.

Lord Callendar, on the other hand, clearly had a corrupting streak that was only getting worse. Just last year he'd caused all that trouble openly visiting the new Duchess of Talbourne at her townhouse, heedlessly allowing rumors to circulate. Now Lady Cecily, who'd left the room in his company, reappeared in tears, only to be immediately escorted out by her mother.

Leaving quiet Mr. Waite to hustle Lord Callendar out the door, calling for pistols.

No, visitors didn't come this far just for the cards.

* * *

"Madame." No mere footman, the butler himself bowed at Viola's right hand, interrupting her conversation with the quietest of words.

Viola was surprised; she thought she'd committed a forever offense by interrupting her husband's *toilette*. "Mr. Collins?"

He stepped back, indicating with his eyes she should follow, which was doubly surprising. Viola couldn't expect anything to happen in this house without Selene knowing about it instantly. The butler should have nothing to tell her in private.

"Madame," he said again once she joined him, still so quietly no one else could hear, "your husband has escorted Lord Callendar from the house, and asked our man to bring them pistols."

"*What?!*"

Everyone turned to look, but Viola's attention locked upon Mr. Collins to the exclusion of all else.

"Where did they go?"

"They were on the lawns, madame, opposite the gazebo."

Dragging Mr. Collins behind her, heedless of the rest the room, Viola clutched her skirts and ran.

Her feet flashed so quickly down the servants' stairs that she felt like she barely touched them. Mr. Collins, who was no longer a callow youth, was breathing hard by the time they reached the bottom of the stairs. He openly leaned on the wall to catch his breath, clearly abashed at losing hold of his dignity by not remaining upright.

She waved for him to undo the lock. Her hands were shaking too much. "Lock, lock, lock!"

The butler wheezed a little. "Madame," he said, trying to gather his composure, "it is on the other side of the door."

* * *

"For me to give you satisfaction, we ought to set a day. Appoint our seconds." Callendar could clearly keep his head, but he surveyed their lonely place in the trees with apprehension. "It is not an act of passion any more than battle."

"You know exactly nothing of battle. You know even less about passion. You'd be wise to keep your peace."

"Sir, you are clearly overwrought."

Lee had managed to open his powder flask one-handed, tipped too much powder into the pan. It spilled over the top of his pistol to his fingers; he dropped the flask in the grass.

Was this what overwrought felt like? High time he knew.

Callendar hadn't given up talking. Likely because he still had no pistol. "Surely you know better than most when killing constitutes a crime."

Lee's hand shook, and some of the gunpowder in the pan drifted silently to the ground. At least this way he could do Viola some good. "See here," he said. "Any paces you like. We'll fire at your mark."

He wasn't overwrought; he was logical. Callendar would surely miss him because he must be a terrible shot. Lee would certainly miss Callendar, because Lee was fairly good. If a stray ball happened to catch Lee, then Viola would have her Callendar after all. Should it catch Callendar instead, well, Lee would have solved his least favorite problem.

There ought to be witnesses, to help ensure neither of them landed in gaol; but he wasn't in the mood to fetch any.

And Callendar hadn't answered his question. "How many paces?"

Callendar exploded. "Why are you *angry* at me because I don't have what you have? You think everyone gets to marry for love?"

* * *

Viola would have preferred a door to the grounds that was *not* directly opposite the ballroom, but not every wish came true.

When she finally rushed out, Mr. Collins long forgotten behind her, the footman near her just pointed in the direction of the trees.

Oh God. There were *acres* of trees. The last duchess had hunted game out here with her falcon. It was a whole forest, but not *Lee's* forest, where she wished with all her heart she had stayed.

The trip had worn on him before it even began, and she'd chosen not to see it.

Between her and the trees lay wide swaths of cropped lawns that Viola had to cross. She ran, skirts still in her hand, uncaring who saw her stockings.

Above her a faint flare of lightning was followed by a distant roll of thunder.

She paid it no attention at all.

* * *

"IF YOU WANTED to marry for love, you'd have married Viola." Callendar's hair plastered across his forehead. The air was thick with moisture and impending summer rain. "I don't know why I'm explaining to a man why I never loved his wife, but I didn't. Should I say I'm sorry? I *like* Lady Viola, and I feel this is all a trick to push me into saying something to get myself shot."

Neither of them wore hats or gloves; in the trees, both dark coats barely showed.

But Lee could see the snowy shirt over the man's heart.

Callendar, working harder with every passing second to find the right thing to say to get Lee to drop his aim, huffed out a heavy breath and shook his fist. "I've no idea why love happens, or how it happens to me. If I were a wiser man, certainly I'd have fallen in love with Viola. But that didn't happen, and I... I'm just getting on with my life."

"Contracts." Callendar was lucid, and the more time passed, the more calm Lee felt, even though he didn't want to. "You sold your marriage bond for very little."

"As I said, sir, we can't all be you."

A suspicion scratched at Lee's mind, the reason Viola had thought from the start that Callendar would prefer a married woman. "You tried to seduce Her Grace. Everyone knows that. Likely why you chose such a chilly wife, hoping to get nearer to the Duchess."

Callendar's face fell, along with his hands, his whole posture conveying that he gave up. "I simply like... to be around Selene. Because... She is the best person I know."

"*Mr. Waite!*"

Viola's voice drifted through the trees.

* * *

She'd been wrong about reassurances. Lee wasn't her. Perhaps he'd needed to hear repeated how much more she loved him than she'd ever dreamed of loving Lord Callendar. How much she wanted to return all his care.

How desperate she was for him to hold her.

"*Mr. Waite!* Are you out here?"

Make it simpler, Viola, but she couldn't, there was so much. All the things she felt for him, all they'd shared, everything from a hackney cab to butter sandwiches to a field full of bluebells and she wanted everything they had yet to enjoy, she wanted *him* more than she had words enough to say.

The trees seemed to crowd around her, all of them conspiring to keep her away from her beloved. Why had she never *called* him that? What if he didn't *know?*

He should know. They'd said it to each other often, just not with the words other people used.

"Mr. *Waite!* It's Viola! *Every day, please! Every day!*"

* * *

"*Every day!*"

Viola's cry rang in his ears like the most desperate bell, demanding his action, a demand he couldn't ignore. That he'd *never* ignore.

304

He'd dropped his aim the second he'd heard her voice. Overwrought he might be, but not enough to fire a pistol in woods that contained Viola. Most of the powder dropped from the pan; the weight of the pistol pulled down against his finger and the firing pin flipped. The scant remainder of the priming powder ignited, flame chasing over the barrel to bite at his hand, and it only took one spark.

The next instant, the ball fired into the ground.

Cursing, he laid the thing down, wishing he'd dropped it earlier, wishing he'd dropped it into the sea. Perhaps when they'd come from Newcastle. Perhaps when he'd come back from war.

Callendar might deserve this kind of display, but Viola didn't.

That gentleman leaned against a tree trunk, catching his breath as if he'd sprinted a mile, while Viola's bright dress came into view between the trees.

"*Lee!*" She screamed his name and ran, clearly seeing no pistol and having heard the thing discharge.

"It's all right. Everything's fine." He caught her up in his arms as she launched herself there, trying to pull her against him, trying to soothe her.

She wasn't having it. Her hands flew everywhere, checking the breadth of his chest, his hair, his arms for the wound from the ball.

"Every day, Lee. Every day."

"I know." He did. "Every day."

She never even looked at Lord Callendar. The man could have bled to death and she'd never know. Only searched under Lee's waistcoat, even pulling out his shirt and running her hands over his sides, down his front, all the way to the bulge of his thighs.

For all she cared, there might only have been one man in those woods.

Callendar, shaking his head and showing the strain of being the target of a pistol for too many minutes, just lurched away, and then there *was* only one man in the woods. And Viola.

"I should have told you I never loved anyone but you." Trembling now, Viola's words started to tumble out. "I should have said those stupid vows. I would have meant them. I still do. Lee, didn't you *know?* What are you *doing?*"

It was the first thing that made him see how far he'd gone in a meaningless direction. "I don't even know," he muttered into her hair, embarrassed that it was the truth.

"And why would you—never mind, it doesn't matter."

Snatching his pistol off the ground by its butt, she clutched his sleeve with her other hand and marched back toward the grand house, dragging him after.

* * *

LEE GRUNTED with surprise when they didn't return to any house doors. Viola simply marched around to the front, keeping hold of his sleeve to make sure he didn't disappear.

There was far too much roiling around inside her, and she had to attend to first things first.

She wouldn't release either pistol or husband. Only marched to the footman waiting by the lamp-lit marble stairs. "I require a carriage. Now."

An elderly lady was just maneuvering herself to the ground with two canes, silvery sausage curls trembling with the effort. A girl in everlasting virgin white stood beside her with the same hair, tinged with gold.

"Immediately, madame," the footman said smartly, "I will remove Lady Dunsby's carriage this instant."

Viola couldn't wait. "I'll just take it."

She faced the elderly lady. She neither knew nor cared what she looked like. "I'll send it back immediately."

"Take it, my dear," was the woman's unexpected answer. "The horses will be well, won't they, Nathaniel?"

"Indeed, ma'am," the driver called back.

"Well, there you are. We'll be several hours at least. No hurry." And with that extraordinary answer, the woman stumped up the steps, her daughter following after, and this time Viola had stolen the carriage.

Well, it might not be stealing when she had so much permission, but neither would she have taken *no* for an answer.

She batted her husband's hand away when he tried to help her into the carriage. Shoved him ahead of her, forcing him to climb inside. Then she climbed in after, the footman closed the door, and she set the empty pistol between them on the floor.

Another rocking carriage ride. Viola was no wiser than during the first one, and had less of a plan.

"Now I need to cry," she told her husband, "because I have *no* idea what just happened, and it's your job to hold me, but I *hate* you."

This great irrational lump who had once been her husband didn't turn back into the Lee she wanted immediately, but his long face showed horror and his woe in equal measures.

"I'm sorry."

"You're *sorry?*" Hunching toward him in the carriage she let her fury get the upper hand in her and she slapped him. Hard. Right across the face.

Then she fell back, horrified, while Lee looked only astonished.

This was not the wife that would keep him happy. The one she'd promised herself she wanted to be.

But right now, it was the wife that he had.

"How dare you? How *dare* you?" Each word erupted, she couldn't hold them back, nor could she stop herself from pounding a fist on his chest, even as she hated herself for the red mark rising on his face. "You can be angry, or low, or sad, or *anything* but you *do* not get to die and leave me alone!"

"I wouldn't. I wasn't." His low voice only made her angry, and now she couldn't stop the tears.

Thunder rumbled above them and soon the sound of falling rain on the carriage roof hissed and burned the rest of the world away.

"What if *I* ran around in the woods with a pistol at all hours of the night, hmm? What would *you* think? You cannot set me *free!* I am not a *hedgehog!* I can't get my own *dinner* or be *fine without you!* You're my everything, my whole *world,* and if you leave me..."

The sobs broke, conveniently masked from the world by the storm breaking outside.

"You *promised* not to abandon me. You *said* you wouldn't."

"Never."

Each thump of her fist on his chest grew lighter and lighter, each "How *dare* you," falling softer and softer as her sobs wracked her whole body and she leaned against him, letting his arms close around her finally.

"But what are you *doing?*" she managed to get out between heaving cries. "What have you *done?*"

CHAPTER 24

*L*ee didn't want to answer, but Viola had always been truthful, and he had to measure up to that.

"I get my worst ideas at the bottom of a bottle," he muttered, half-frightened he'd truly lost her, half-sullen.

"Bad ideas? *Bad ideas?* Kidnapping a husband is a bad idea. Threatening to murder a baron is worse than a bad idea!"

"I'm sorry. Of course I'm sorry." The gin had worn off long ago, he wanted more, and his head ached. It might have been from discharging his pistol, or it might have been because his wife hated him so right now.

She slapped his chest again. He barely felt the blow.

"There's no *of course* after the evening I just had. I don't even know who I married. I know this isn't the best of us. You can turn us into this but I won't just sit there and *let* you. I won't just *watch.*"

"Never." What else could he say but *never* and *of course not?*

Nothing. There was nothing else he could say. He'd put other options out of reach. He couldn't soothe her when he'd hurt her, and that pained him worse than any wound he'd got on the battlefield. "I'm so sorry."

"*That* came from a *bottle?*"

He couldn't trace the thread of how every little thing had piled up atop one another, a whole chain of wrong turns that had, admittedly, gotten out of hand.

Then he realized: this was Viola. He didn't have to.

"I got to that place where nothing makes sense yet everything is horrible at the same time," he said quietly. "It's a kind of comfortable. Or at least, familiar."

She could have thrown that back at him; she didn't. She subsided a little into the far corner of the carriage, steadying herself against its walls, hiccuping from her crying. "What kind of horrible things?" was all she said.

Ah, this was like marching toward cannon fire.

But if he couldn't give her these answers, how could he ever ask any from her?

"Your life with me isn't good enough." The words sounded clipped, felt agonizing, but he got them out. "You belong here."

He'd thought a lot of horrible things over the past few days, but those were the crux of it.

Viola just nodded, her chin crumpling and smoothing as she tried to gain control of it. "Well. I made clear during that first carriage ride that you cannot tell me what to do. Did you think I'd changed?"

"No." It was like being mortified by a schoolteacher, but far worse because this was Viola and she had his heart.

"Then why do you think I went to Hawkshope and loved you as hard as I did?"

He didn't know how to answer that. The last part he couldn't quite grasp. "You went to Hawkshope because I took you. You were ill."

"And stayed because I love you."

"You had no means to leave."

"I would *get* means to leave, as I just proved once more. I would have *walked* out of that valley had I not wished to be there. What gave you the impression I didn't wish to be there? Was it something I did? Said? Failed to do?" She swallowed, her dark eyes large. "Was it in bed?"

"No, no—"

Her outstretched hand slapped at his.

"I'd like some reassurance. But not now. We're going home. You need some sleep. I've got to think. I'll make sure Lady Dunsby's carriage goes back to her."

She looked around, apparently realizing for the first time that they had no luggage, no things at all. Neither of them even had a hat.

She sighed. "Well, this seems familiar, doesn't it?"

More miles rolled past, their silence heavy underneath the patter of the rain.

Finally Viola said, "We should go to the Faircombe townhouse. I don't suppose they'd mind if you used it once more?"

"I doubt it," said Lee heavily, scrubbing at his face with both hands. He felt dirtier than he'd ever felt at Hawkshope. "They can't really mind. I own it."

Viola didn't even bother to look surprised. "I see."

Another stretch of silence, which was not really silence, just an invisible wall between them.

Through its thickness Viola made another statement. "If they've leased it, you cannot simply loiter there."

"They're in arrears, Viola." He was so tired. The demon ideas that had chewed through his peace were quiet now, but so was everything else, as if he'd been wiped blank. The sensation was terrifyingly close to what he feared most. "The Marquess of Faircombe is nearly bankrupt."

"The Marquess of Faircombe is dead." Her blank look just watched him absorb the information. "Had you been part of the conversation, you'd have heard the news. There was a fire."

"I'm surprised I hadn't heard. I'll introduce you to my men of business." Whatever she thought about him, whatever she would ever think, she must still have all the access she wanted to his money. "You can have Hawkshope, you know. You can have anything you want."

"You're abandoning me after all?"

"Never.

"Well, I never mentioned breaking any vows."

Something worn in Lee flickered into hope. But... "You never made any vows."

"I said *I, Viola, take thee, Lee, to my wedded husband, to have and to hold from this day forward.* I remember, I was there." She rubbed her temple as if her head ached. Surely it did. "There really aren't any other vows that need to be said, are there?"

"Perhaps not."

"You have a great deal of power in your hands, Mr. Waite. A great deal. I still have to think. I said I did. But you know what this marriage can be like from the last few weeks. You can make it heaven, or you can make it hell. Just know that whatever you pick I won't leave you. I'll be here *every day.*"

He'd felt comfortable taking responsibility for her life from the moment they'd set out together. Taking responsibility for an entire marriage somehow felt weightier. "I understand."

"Do you? Because I'm still so shocked." She sighed again. "That was a horror. You can't imagine what it felt like to think I could lose you. Right there. Tonight."

"I can imagine it." He could.

She just waved a quelling hand in his direction, pulled her feet up under her skirt on the seat, and rested her head against the cushions.

He didn't think she fell asleep.

* * *

HE'D BEEN RIGHT about the gin's amount. One glass was nothing compared to what he'd drunk back in the days when he and Oliver sat round the clock at the club not talking about how to put their lives back together.

On the other hand, he'd forgotten how it put him to sleep. But didn't let him sleep.

Restlessly he woke hour after hour in the wide master bedroom, tossing in its coverlets till he was soaked with too much heat.

Every time Lee woke, Viola was curled in the chair opposite, the same one where he'd sprawled and ogled her in her transparent shift. Now, even sleeping, she looked sad. For she *did* sleep, curled into a small Viola shape, the way she had in Lady Dunsby's borrowed carriage.

Lee felt as though he'd lost the right to invite her to bed.

The last time he woke, the sun was up, and when he rolled over, he saw a tray beside her chair.

And she was awake. "I sent back Lady Dunsby's carriage last night. I asked Mrs. Winfrey to prepare breakfast. Do you remember any of that?"

"No." One glass of gin couldn't make him blind drunk. That didn't make sense.

But then it wasn't just the gin. It was the exhaustion and the lowering dark, the way they crushed his mind from the inside and twisted at his guts.

Viola was more crisp this morning. She'd changed her gown, and jealously he wondered who'd gotten to tie the tapes. Her hair was plaited again by the side of her head, and Lee had an instant's thought that he never wanted to see it any other way.

Then he silently cursed himself. Getting to see it at all might depend on what he said in the next few minutes.

"I want to talk." Well, that was his Viola, cutting to the heart of it.

"Anything you like."

"I hope you mean that." She sounded grim.

Picking up one of the pieces of toast, she threw it at his chest.

He plucked it off, only raising his questioning brows.

"Just hoping it would make me feel better. It didn't. What kinds of horrible things?"

Lee had to think back. It was like the night was a drawn-out process of slowly drowning, or surfacing. He thought he knew what she meant. "The things I told myself?"

"Yes. I didn't belong with you, I deserved to stay in London; what else?"

"Hated that Callendar bastard."

"I grasped that," she said dryly. "And I won't say it's my fault, though I never told you when I realized I didn't love him."

Those words washed over him like cool water. He felt for the first time all night, all morning, like he could take a deep breath.

Viola's eyes only narrowed. She clearly wasn't done with him. "What else?"

"Damnation." It didn't work; why did people bother swearing? "I never made you tell yours."

"I'll tell you mine. Some other day. Now, we're discussing you. What else?"

He didn't want to resist and force Viola to point out that *she'd* never aimed a pistol at anyone's heart.

He'd have hit it, too, if he'd pulled the trigger.

If he'd wanted to hit it.

"Viola, I'm not going to drink. I can promise you that." He meant it. He'd conquered that demon once before; he'd do it again. If it took walking to Scotland and back, he would, as long as his journey ended wherever she was. Clearly the drink affected him in evil ways, and even one did more harm than it could ever do good.

It wasn't just the liquor. The liquor dropped him into the same dark place she knew. That was his real problem; but she knew that.

She brushed off any promises about liquor. "I'm not interested in new vows. I've been thinking about the old ones. Was last night honoring me and keeping me? Was it comforting me in any way?"

"Most definitely not." God, he was loathsome. He wanted to bathe until he scraped himself out of his skin. He needed a new one.

"I don't think it was about me at all. I've searched my memory, every second of it. I honestly don't know anything I've said to push you into that place."

He couldn't stay still.

Lee surged out of the bed, knelt at her feet. "Of course you didn't." This close, he could see the cracks in her calm. When he touched her slippered feet, tucked under the rug on her lap, they weren't cold; but he thought he saw her shivering.

"I don't like to trouble you, but this is more difficult than I expected, so please let me finish. I should have told you more how I loved you, and I will tell you, every day." Briefly she laid a hand on his cheek; it was like water in the desert. He covered her hand with his, but she slipped hers away.

"So *then*," and she tried to sound nonchalant, "I wondered if perhaps I didn't say it enough because I was only following your lead. I know I do that, and I know you want me to ask for what I want more often. But I'm not comfortable, sir, asking for declarations you don't want to give. I think you do. Love me. And if you don't wish to say, you must have your reasons."

"No reason. I'm a fool, that's all."

"Are you? I don't think so." However difficult this was, she wasn't giving up. "I found myself wondering, in the wee hours, what, or *who*, could possibly keep you from saying what you feel. You're blunt, Lee, when you want; you're so terribly blunt. So I might have expected some blunt *I love you's*, but there's none."

"Don't do this. Viola." It was like watching a runaway carriage approaching a cliff.

"I'm truly sorry, my darling, I *don't* like to be a bother. And I know there are many empty spaces in your story I've only begun to learn. I want to hear all of them. Still I can't help but think there's something about losing your family you haven't told me."

"I told you everything. They had a fever, my wife and little girl. They died." He'd been such a fool to congratulate himself for being well up the ladder to lifelong assured adoration. A family! A war! Britain itself would admire him, thanks to the praise of his men!

He'd been a fool; he still was.

Viola sat up now, and had his hand in hers. "And you didn't feel anything."

"Nothing I should."

She had his fingers intertwined in his. "And I just cannot believe that someone with a heart as big as yours would feel nothing at that terrible loss. I don't think that happens, and certainly not to you. I'm not that bad a judge of character. You *loved* your wife, Lee, I'm sure of it. And I *know* you loved that little girl. What was her name?"

"Just Eliza. All right? Take it and be happy." Why must she press and press? He'd said he was sorry. He *was* a fool. A heartless one.

"*Just* Eliza? There was no *just* Eliza. She was all your hopes. Everything you wanted. And I think you loved her too. And after all those wounds—losing your parents, losing everyone who cared for you as I'm *sure* you loved some of them too, and too many soldiers, and too many dreams—because I don't know much about men living through war but I know enough—"

"Stop this. You're wrong." Just that quickly he turned from wanting to crawl into the chair with her to wanting to crawl away.

"—I think after all that, you just couldn't take any more losses. Maybe you were all worn away. Maybe you'd bled so much you couldn't bleed for them and live. So you just... didn't."

"What does it *matter now?*"

He realized he was shouting. And gripping her arms. He let go like she was fire, jerking his hands away.

Fragile Viola sat in the chair, shaking, and finished taking him apart.

"Because it was a *wound,* my beloved, as real as a cannonball to your chest, and I know how deep love goes now, I know how deep it must have cut. I don't think that you *failed;* you *survived.*"

He knelt at her feet, staring at her, while Viola put one hand over her mouth.

They stayed that way, removed from the passage of time, as empty as a battlefield after the shooting. After the burials. After the truce.

"That's not true." It might be.

"Are you sure?" Now Viola's voice trembled too. "Do I make you feel hollow?"

"God. No, Viola. God." Burrowing into her arms, he had to push his way into the spaces of her, hold her, let her hold him. "Never. I *love* you, Viola. I'm *full.*"

She had her arms around his shoulders, her cheek against his ear. Cradling him. Pouring her words out against his skin. "Then I think you should believe how you feel, and stop blaming yourself for when you couldn't do anything different. It doesn't mean you didn't love them. I *know* you did. You think you *failed* by surviving that wound, and you're afraid you'll fail *me,* but that was *no failure.*" She hugged his neck. "You can't have faith in yourself while you blame yourself for surviving. It won't matter how much faith *I* have in you."

When she had hold of a conviction, she never let go. He wasn't going to shake it.

What would it feel like, to see himself the way she did?

He knew it was an old scar, grieving over his parents. He still felt it every day. Wished he could have one conversation with them. Hear their voices once.

All the houses—he remembered the houses better than the people, because he hadn't blamed the houses. Couldn't one of those people, just one, have found a way to hold on to him? Had he been so unnecessary? Had they all only wanted the payments for his lodging?

And too many soldiers. His men had followed him when he knew nothing; they'd followed him when he'd gotten wiser. Still they died. The enemy ones he wasn't supposed to grieve, and the ones on his side he could.

They'd just finished digging graves. He remembered that now. He and Oliver, graves for his men, two youths just past twenty with no business on a battlefield at all.

Then that letter.

What if Viola was right? What if he'd *had* to be hollow to keep breathing, and talking, and walking, even all the way home?

Home.

"Oh God, Viola, no." No cleansing tears came with this pain. It clawed up into his heart, it took all his breath, it threatened to take his sanity.

The little house he'd bought by a farm near the stream. Gentle, uncomplicated Beatrix. Someone who would never choose to leave him. Someone who'd never have a *reason*.

And that little girl... "God, please no. *Please.*" *His* little girl. *Eliza.*

Had he been alone, the pain would have been unbearable.

As if it had been lurking right behind him all these years, it cut through him now, and Lee knew he'd felt its cut before. He'd felt it. He'd covered over the wound, and it had never healed. It festered.

Who but a man hiding that kind of cut would walk away from every place and every person they'd ever cared about, not just once, but over and over?

He didn't have to say anything to his wife. She knew. Not this kind of pain; *please,* he begged silently of anyone with the power to listen, *please never let her know this kind of pain.* But she knew what it was like to be unbearably hurt inside, and she knew what it was like to survive it, and how one might *not* survive. Not without help.

"God, Viola, *God.*" He couldn't tell if he was praying or pleading or *what* the noises meant.

Only that she was here, and so was he.

Her whisper crept through the fog of pain. Not asking for more words, but giving some. "Even if you can't forgive yourself, I'll still be here. I can't give you my faith in you, but I can keep it. I will always be here, waiting for you to find your way out. Just as you did for me."

"I won't ask that of you. I promise you." No more diving into bottles looking for demons. They were too plain a trap; he wouldn't put his foot in it again.

His deep, dark pain was real, but the wound was lanced. She didn't need him to be perfect; she understood.

Unable to give promises about when she might fall ill, she asked for none. "I won't sit by and let you abuse me. Or anyone. But I'll never abandon you. I'll never send you away because you can't control your pain. I will be what I always wished someone would be for me. What you *have* been for me. Family."

Lee pulled her close, burying his head against her soft body, letting her arms cradle his head. He felt something ease deep inside him, something that had been twisted and tightly scarred long before the war. His wife was so clever. "All the vows I need," he whispered back, voice muffled by the healing warmth of her softness and the pounding of her heart.

They both treated each other for the rest of the day as if they were wrapped in bandages.

It felt true, and Viola saw no point in pretending otherwise.

She'd thought for a few minutes that Lee might succumb to the agony inside him. Braced for the impossible, she'd simply held on. It was what he had done for her, and what he always would do. She was sure of that, right down into the center of her bones, and she wanted him with her for as long as they both should live.

She thought as long as they had each other, they could manage that.

Helping him off the floor was helping a sick man walk.

Viola found that oddly soothing. He didn't ask it, but she wanted to give him back something of the patience and care he'd given her. She couldn't understand all his pain, but she understood some, and she thought that helped a little. It felt right, it felt like they... matched.

The day wore on full of healing quiet, till she felt able to explain to Mrs. Winfrey that Mr. Waite required a mild soup. She dispatched a boy to go all the way to Leicester Square and buy her husband bread-and-butter sandwiches, as many as they would sell him.

She also personally supervised the draining of every bottle of ale and cider in the house.

"I'm terribly sorry, and I'll certainly add their cost to your wages," she said as she pulled each cork and poured them into the sewer drain in the mews behind the house, not feeling sorry at all. "You're welcome to buy and drink anything you like. Just not here."

That night she slept in Lee's arms in the master's bed, and they woke wrapped around each other like children adrift in a wide sea.

Viola hoped they'd always be that lucky, able to turn to each other and say the things that made it easier to face the day.

"I love you."

"I love you too."

"May I kiss you?"

"Please. Every day."

She wanted them to practice every morning. She'd make sure they did.

* * *

EVERY DAY WAS THEIR VOW, and a demand, and an offer of patience. Like something out of a sermon, every day it became more important, and they repeated it to each other. Apologies came out too, and confidences, and silly little secrets, and it made all the big things easier to bear. *Every day* was their reminder of all that. A love token constantly exchanged, made out of words.

By the end of a week of quiet, Viola thought Lee was different. He breathed a little easier. She told him so.

"No one breathes easier in London, Viola. Too much coal smoke. Or do you mean easier than somewhere specific?" His eyes dared her to say *Talbourne House.*

"I think I could see worry on you even while you were chopping wood up north."

"That was sweat."

"Do you think Herbert is managing without us?"

Lee leaned back from the balustrade whose polish he was replacing. There were touches all over the house that needed attention, or perhaps he simply wanted things to do with his hands. They'd discussed the journey *home*, tentatively, as if testing each other's scars. Whether by land or sea, Hawkshope was home.

"I think," Lee said thoughtfully, rubbing a thumb over the beeswax, "that Herbert is living the life of a practiced rake. I imagine he beds himself a new lady every night, scattering his illegitimate children all over the hillside, gorges himself on grubs, and sleeps through each day with the kind of fat satisfaction you see in a really immoral banker." He scratched his nose. "Perhaps a politician."

Viola ignored the snub to Parliament. "What on earth makes you think Herbert so dissolute?"

"I hate to say this, dear one, but that *is* how Herbert spends his time. Hedgehogs are depraved."

"This is just slander." At her husband's slow, serious shaking of the head, Viola put on a pitiable expression. Lee suspected it was partly real. "That can't *always* be true!"

"Not at all." He drew her down beside him, pulling her into the crook of his arm and leaning against the paneled wall, looking out through the balustrade to the grand foyer below. No one would ever catch a lord sitting in a position like this, on the floor in his own hallway; but Lee wasn't a lord, and this *was* his hallway. As long as Viola didn't care, he didn't. And she didn't. She nestled against his side, stealing his warmth. "The goshawks marry for life," he told her soothingly, "I don't know what their vows are, but they keep house together, and feed their babies."

He intertwined his fingers with hers; she laid her head on his shoulder.

"Badgers, too, though I've seen a lady badger lighten her heels when a newer, stronger badger moves in. It's scandalous."

"It *sounds* scandalous." Viola sounded very, very mildly scandalized.

"Voles, now. The voles are model citizens.Very faithful. The kinds of marriages you can rely on."

Viola nodded. "We should go back where we're surrounded by such good models of married behavior."

"Any time you like."

Someone banged the door-knocker.

Viola and Lee stayed quiet on the staircase, watching unseen from above as Mr. Darby slowly walked to the door and held it open.

He spent some minutes consulting whatever person was beyond the door.

"We haven't had visitors," whispered Lee.

"Most people don't know where we are." Viola shifted a little. "And I told Mr. Darby we're not well, and will *not* entertain visitors."

"Clever."

The pause went on so long Viola began to worry about Mr. Darby's safety. "Should we go see?"

Lee just sighed. "It's taking a risk." He looked over his wife's simple morning gown and plait of hair. "You don't mind being seen?"

"I didn't *invite* anyone here," said Viola with the perfect poise of a wife who knows nothing is expected of her that she doesn't wish to do.

Lee tucked her hand in his arm, just as if he were wearing his morning coat and not canvas trousers and suspenders over a shirt bearing streaks of beeswax.

The closer they got to the front door, the more noise they heard.

Now Viola thought better of it. "Let's just go back to bed. Or better, leave for Hawkshope now."

"You wanted to see the baby again."

"I want to see Virginia. I do hate to disappoint her."

Lee found the din worrisome enough that he made sure to open the door with Viola behind him.

"Well," said Lee loudly enough to subdue the voices. Mr. Darby's thin shoulders and bald head were nearly invisible, pressed on all sides. It was a motley crew of visitors, and Mr. Darby had held off the entire fray for quite some time. "Mr. Darby, you deserve a rise in pay, and you'll have it."

"Thank you, sir." He turned back to his employer with his customary mournful look. "Lady Dunsby has called every day for the last three days, and asked to speak with Lady Viola. Lady Rawleigh has just come with a letter. Likewise Lord Faircombe has arrived, but given the... unsettled nature of his tenancy, I told him I would make an appointment. And Lord Callendar—"

"Lord Callendar! Oh no!" Viola started forward around her husband, then slipped behind him instead, trusting him to stay right where he was.

Which he did.

He just looked down on Lord Callendar from his very great height, his position at the top of the stairs both augmenting and defensible, and asked in his calm way, "And you want?"

"I'm just here to call upon a friend. Obviously not you."

"I have no idea what's happening, but I can call again, and I will." Cass only nodded briskly, handed her letter to Mr. Darby, then lifted her practical skirts and whisked them down the pavement to the last of the carriages. A hackney.

Lee looked to make sure it seemed reputable before he let his sister-in-law out of sight.

"Lady Dunsby, do come in." Viola took possession of the elderly woman with her canes, leading her along the railing to the top of the stairs and inside.

Lee decided to take charge of his erstwhile tenant. "Lord Faircombe. I'm very sorry to hear about your father's death." He didn't actually want the man inside. He was as stiff as a stick, exactly the sort of priggish nob who lasted five minutes in the army, if they even served, and his father had been among the most pompous swines it had ever been Lee's misfortune to meet.

Until he met Viola's mother.

"Mr. Waite," acknowledged the fellow with a nod. "Naturally I don't wish to conduct our business on the steps—"

"Naturally. Mr. Darby is right, we should make an appointment. I will have my solicitor attend."

"There's no need. We are in arrears, and the debts will not soon be discharged. It is my dishonor, sir, and I only came to assure you that you will one day be paid in full."

With that one simple speech, the man drastically improved Lee's opinion of him. At least he was honest. "Come have tea, at least."

The new Lord Faircombe gave Lee a tight smile. "Another time. Your wife has a guest to entertain, and I've no reason to cast a pall over their enjoyment."

His departure down the steps left only Lord Callendar, hat in hand, turning from glove to glove.

Lee tried to remember in which county he'd left his walking stick.

But at least Lee could start by being civil. "I owe you apologies, sir."

Callendar just spread his hands, one holding his hat. "They're all accepted. I understand I offended you—I don't know all the details—but it's the least of my problems now."

He was making it hard to toss him down the stairs. "You did nothing to offend me. Well. I thought your choice of bride rather offensive, but only generally speaking. She's appalling."

"Thank you, I've been apprised. Truly, I do wish to apologize. I didn't get a chance to explain myself before all the..." He made a rolling hand motion as if to indicate all the tossing about and the loaded pistol. "As it may be. You heard me say Lady Viola didn't matter, and I shouldn't have said that, not even to appease Lady Cecily. Of course your wife matters. She's been a good friend to me. You were right to take offense."

Lee was already beginning to miss the version of himself that could sail in and out of any situation because he never intended to go back. "The magnanimous thing would be to take you in to call upon my wife, but I don't want to."

"Again, rightly so. I've been informed in no uncertain terms by many ladies, including my previously betrothed, that I should no longer be seen in company with married ladies, or unmarried ones either. My social circle must necessarily shrink. Also, I'd better start fraternizing with more men."

Lee came down a step or two. The boy looked a bit ragged. Lee had offered tea to his bankrupt tenant; he could at least do the same for someone Viola called a friend. "Come take some tea," he muttered ungraciously.

"Ah—" Callendar clearly considered it, raising up on one

foot to the next stair, then thinking twice and dropping down again. "One question. The other night; were you drunk?"

"Something like it." Lee had no intention of explaining the darker places his mind went between doses of liquor, or why he'd tried to use drink as medicine in the first place. That was between him and his wife. Maybe the pigs, once they reached home.

Maybe his children too, one day, for now he not only hoped to have them, he hoped they'd learn from his mistakes.

"Fair enough," Callendar conceded, and Lee had the feeling the lad would have confessed to murder right at that moment in exchange for a friendly word.

Then Viola appeared again at the door. She had the most fetching smile in her dark eyes, the kind that invited a man to *come find out,* and it was all for her husband.

"Lord Callendar? You're still here? I'm terribly sorry, but we must visit another day. Mr. Waite, you'll find our guest very interesting, do come in."

"Gracious every day," said Callendar with a reflexive attempt at gallantry. "I'll do just as you suggest." He offered a hopeless little tip of his hat.

Viola hadn't lost her talent for measuring people. "Is anything wrong?"

"I'm ruined. It's bleaker than you'd think. I am not received *anywhere.* Their Graces can do nothing for me. I am a despoiler of women, an instigator of duels, and in some quarters I'm being accused of smuggling opium."

"That sounds awful. Well, do as you please, I'm afraid I must take Mr. Waite for a moment. Sir, if you'll come with me?"

It was a balm on Lee's soul that he shouldn't have needed, but he enjoyed the way she took his arm and left her previously preferred gentleman standing on the steps to enter or leave, whichever took his fancy.

Viola brought him to the small ladies' parlor that didn't require climbing the stairs.

Lady Dunsby greeted him there with a smile that must have been quite flirtatious thirty years ago. "I've been making the acquaintance of your delightful wife. We've met in passing, of course, but I'd had no time for friendship till you stole my carriage."

"It's not the first one we've stolen, and I've yet to find a drawback to it," Lee said as he settled down next to his wife.

Lady Dunsby had the most delightful laugh, too, all tumbling, musical sparkle. "Lady Viola tells me you are curious if anyone in society remembers your parents."

Time seemed to slow for Lee, like it did after a cannonball fired. One heartbeat, then years later, another.

Viola placed her hand over his. "We would never wish to be a bother. It might not seem that way, after we confiscated your carriage. I only wondered."

The lady made a *pssh* noise as Lord Callendar did enter, hanging back by the door, hat still in hand. She ignored him, deeply invested in finishing her conversation. "I couldn't be more delighted! From Northumberland, weren't they? Your father had the tartan for his waistcoat; he was very proud of it. I remember that."

Lee couldn't speak. Viola just kept the lady talking. "What else do you remember?"

"Oh, many things. I went to *every* party in those days, you know, I had several suitors; it paid to notice details. Everything relies on details." Having boasted of her memory, she then struggled to produce more from it. Lee held his breath. "Tall, of course, I remember your mother was tall too, not just your father. As tall as my husband, not that he was excessive." She laughed at her own joke. "Mmm... I'm sorry to say I don't think they were popular, and I don't remember seeing them more than a few times, at Ranelagh gardens, of course. I don't remember them dancing, and I'm afraid that was my keenest passion at the time. Other than Lord Dunsby, of course. Hmm..."

Lee was waiting for her to say something about his mother's slippers. The ices they chose. Anything more than just his father's name on a list of tradable assets, without his mother's name at all.

"I think they loved each other."

Lee's wind escaped in a huff.

Whatever he'd thought she might say, it wasn't that.

And she just kept going. "I remember the way they walked the garden paths together, arm in arm, pointing at things and talking together and laughing without a care in the world. That's not too silly a memory, is it?"

"Lady Dunsby," and Lee said it with all of Viola's conviction and his own, "it's the best memory you could have had."

Then he turned to Viola. "Thank you," he said, drawing her hand to his lips and kissing its palm as if no one else were there.

"You're quite welcome," she murmured back, her own lips brushing his cheek as she stretched up to meet him with some effort. "I like to think that when I inconvenience you, I make it worth the trouble."

* * *

BY THE TIME all the guests were gone, Viola felt exhausted.

Lee looked the same.

She said what they were both thinking. "Too many guests."

He only nodded, scraping back his falling hair. "Too many guests."

"Do we *need* all these guests?"

"Have we ever?"

He sounded so much like the version of himself she still yearned to know better.

"And you're feeling so much better," she said brightly, "that you're going to stop leaving your trousers on the floor, aren't you?"

"No!" He punctuated this with a grin. "But I like how you asked for what you want."

They'd discuss clothes on the floor later. The truth was, he'd do anything for her, even stay in London. "I don't think you'll feel so ill now in London, now that you've... settled yourself a little. Will you?"

"No." His answer was instant.

She didn't think the wild look in his eye was gone forever, and that was fine. As long as he didn't leave her. As long as they loved each other. *Every day.*

"And you can hear me now, when I tell you I like Hawk-shope the best of any place I've ever lived. Can't you?"

"Yes."

He was really making the most of these short declarations.

"Then why don't we go sooner rather than later? I *do* want to visit Virginia once more, and we can always sail back here if we must, it is quicker. But there's nothing else for us in London, is there? And so much to do at Hawkshope."

"Viola, have I ever told you how much I love how you say just what I'm thinking?" Lee looked around the small parlor. Every furnishing was finer than anything they had in their tower, and Viola didn't like any of it half so much. She knew he didn't either.

So his next statement surprised her.

"If we truly plan to never come back, we need to do a great deal of purchasing. You should have a fine marble floor like this in the peel's house, and Persian carpets if you like. Some fine Chinese porcelain for eating your stew, and perhaps one of Lady Arnold's lacquered vases."

"We don't need all that. It's not like we'll be living in Talbourne House."

His attention sharpened. "Do you *like* Talbourne House?"

Viola's breath caught at the thought that if she said one word, he would build her a ducal palace on the border of Scotland. "Mr. Waite, I do not *need* a Talbourne House."

"But you want to enjoy things before it's too late. Who knows what tomorrow will bring?" He tilted back his lean body to survey all the fittings in this house, as if planning to fold them into his pocket. "Do you want to take anything from here?"

"Oh no! It's so beautifully appointed. Someone will want to lease it. Or if you don't wish to yet, you could engage a caretaker. I'd wager the new Lord Faircombe would do it for free."

His soft eyes smiled at the corners.

He tucked her hand into his arm the way she loved and started leading her up the stairs. "Do you like this bed? What about these leather armchairs? You need a dressing table, Viola. That's not a question."

"Let's burn Lady Charlotte's hairbrush." That was her only wish that was still a secret.

He laughed, an honest laugh. "Petty! I like it. Instead of choosing paintings, what if we just engaged a painter..."

Viola let his imagination go. There would be time later to revise their plan, decide on a course of action.

Besides, she didn't need anything. She had everything, and she would enjoy all of it. Every day.

* * *

Can't wait to see Lee and Viola back at Hawkshope?
Pick up your bonus epilogue for another glimpse of their
wilderness.

And stay tuned for Virginia's story in
The Lady Escape!

NEXT IN MAIDS DONE WAITING:
THE LADY ESCAPE

Virginia Díaz de la Peña is not just a pretty face.

With her money and family connections, she needn't take London society seriously.

Still, after a wearing winter and spring, she's as much in need of a holiday as anyone. She's happy to continue serving as the Duchess of Talbourne's only maid in waiting; but secretly, she hopes society will let them all have some much-needed rest.

It doesn't quite turn out that way.

Subscribe to Judith Lynne's mailing list or follow her on social media - Bookbub, Facebook, Pinterest, Instagram, or Twitter - to find out when the next society maid is done waiting!

NOTES

I hope you're glad to be back among old friends and getting new stories with *Maids Done Waiting!*

As I've shared with some of my readers, I've been dying to get lovers out of London even as *Maids Done Waiting* goes back to London society, and in *The Lord Trap* I managed to do both. We have plenty of exploration of London (and *many* old friends - I wonder if you can spot them all), but also we venture farther north than we have ever been, and I enjoyed Lee's and Viola's unique castle tremendously. I hope you did too.

The Northumberland region passed back and forth between Scottish and English hands many times, and the peels or peles were built to guard against invaders and, later, cattle raiders; so the iron cages mounted on their tops were intended for signal fires that could send word of attacks across the hill ranges as fast as the speed of light.

I loved Melody Simmons' beautiful cover, because it inspired me to write about a place in England with hills and pines. The Cheviot hills at the time did not even have villages, and they are still beautiful, still quite remote, and still have a population more scarce than anywhere else in England.

The shipping lanes that carried coal from Newcastle and London, a business so profitable they didn't even need cargo on the return trip, did indeed carry passengers on the way, and it was not always an easy sail. There were so many boats making the trip that collisions were frequent, and whether Lee's parents met their mishap sailing around the English coast or on their way to Europe's shores, based on Lady Dunsby's testimony, they were glad to be together. She was there, I wasn't, so we'll leave that up to her.

I wanted this to be a Lords and Undefeated Ladies book, without remaining part of the original series; and while Maids Done Waiting focuses on our friends in London still seeking the perfect marriage, its pairings still include some disability that is part of the story fabric, but not the basis of the drama.

I knew Lady Viola suffered from depression when she was first mentioned in *The Countess Invention* as well as when we met her in *What a Duchess Does*, and it was important to me that she get her own story. With neither medicine nor therapy available to treat depression at the time, I knew Oliver would be unable to ignore his sister's illness and unable to do anything for it either. In my experience, to a surgeon anything that can't be cut is a mystery.

And yes, I knew Mr. Waite's story in its broad outlines since Oliver suggested he come to Morland with him in *The Countess Invention,* too. There's a bit more about his history with Miss Farsworth and Lady Viola that you may yet discover in another book.

I didn't quite plan on Mr. Waite being such a perfect match, as his depression with its startling personality swings comes on fast from alcohol and his wound, which we might call PTSD. Nonetheless, there it is, and I think they suit each other right down to the hedgehog-covered ground.

I've tried to base both Viola's and Lee's experiences of depression on experiences of my own and on research, while still writing them a happy, fun love story. Any mistakes are entirely mine, and I love when readers write to me and tell me how they feel I did; I always want to do better.

Everything Mr. Waite says about the monogamous (or profligate) behavior of the native wild animals in the north of England is generally true, and I am just as shocked as you are about hedgehogs.

I look forward to seeing you in the next *Maids Done Waiting* book!

ACKNOWLEDGMENTS

Infinite thank you's and apologies for too many things to my editing and proofreading team. Anne, Holly, I love you.

And to my own beloved, for being a sounding-board, an etymology checker, a proofreader and an inspiration, you're the best husband in the world; I not only love you, I thank you.

ABOUT THE AUTHOR

Judith Lynne writes rule-breaking romances with love around every corner. Her characters tend to have deep convictions, electric pleasures, and, sometimes, weaponry.

She loves to write stories where characters are shaken by life, shaken down to their core, put out their hand…and love is there.

A history nerd with too many degrees, Judith Lynne lives in that other paradise, Ohio, with a truly adorable spouse, an apartment-sized domestic jungle, and a misgendered turtle. A past writer of SF and screenplays, she pens Regency romances of love you can believe in, with a rich sense of place and time.

If you enjoyed The Lord Trap, *help keep these books coming - share a review at your favorite bookstore, Bookbub, or Goodreads!*

Sign up for the author's newsletter, including exclusive book news and sneak peeks,
at judithlynne.com.